THE GOLDEN RULE

Elizabeth Palmer worked as a graphic designer in a publishing house when she first left school. She then worked at the *Financial Times* where she met her husband. After the birth of the first of her three children, Elizabeth started to work from home as a freelance book designer. Her first novel, *The Stainless Angel,* was published in 1993 and was followed by *Plucking the Apple, Old Money* and *Flowering Judas.* All are available in Arrow paperback.

Also by Elizabeth Palmer:

The Stainless Angel
Plucking the Apple
Old Money
Flowering Judas

THE GOLDEN RULE

Elizabeth Palmer

ARROW

Published by Arrow Books in 1998

1 3 5 7 9 10 8 6 4 2

First published in the United Kingdom in 1997 by Century

Arrow Books Limited
Random House UK Ltd
20 Vauxhall Bridge Road, London SW1V 2SA

Random House Australia (Pty) Limited
20 Alfred Street, Milsons Point, Sydney
New South Wales 2061, Australia

Random House New Zealand Limited
18 Poland Road, Glenfield, Auckland 10, New Zealand

Random House South Africa (Pty) Limited
Endulini, 5a Jubilee Road, Parktown 2193, South Africa

Random House UK Limited Reg. No. 954009

A CIP catalogue record for this book
is available from the British Library

Papers used by Random House UK Limited
are natural, recyclable products made from wood grown in
sustainable forests. The manufacturing processes conform to
the environmental regulations of the country of origin

ISBN 0 09 925702 5

Printed and bound in the Great Britain by
Mackays of Chatham PLC, Chatham, Kent

This book, which was written in Dublin, is dedicated to
Irish friends

The Golden Rule is that there are no golden rules.
George Bernard Shaw

Part 1

1

The sound of movement downstairs woke Patience up. Immediately on the alert, she opened her eyes but did not move. The illuminated dial of her small bedside alarm clock told her that it was 3 a.m. Two minutes afterwards, late and out of key as usual, the clock in the tower of the church which stood in the middle of the square verified this. Petrified, not daring to put on the light, she lay and held her breath and listened. After a brief interval there was more noise downstairs. Footsteps. Someone was walking about in the sitting room or maybe the hall. She heard the unmistakable noise of a drawer being opened and the faint musical reverberation as a brass swan neck handle tapped walnut. The sitting room. Whoever it was must be searching the desk in the sitting room. Automatically she stretched out an arm to where the panic button should have been and then remembered that there wasn't one. They had recently moved in. The alarm system was being installed later that week. Gingerly, she lifted the telephone receiver, fully aware that an acute ear, especially if the intruder was still standing by the desk, might detect a faint vibration as she dialled.

Nothing. The line was dead.

Oh heavens! This was serious. She was, or should have been, alone in a large, detached London house surrounded by an equally large garden. Who would hear her if she cried out?

Trembling, Patience slid her hand beneath the heap of soft pillows on the other side of the double bed and found what she was looking for. Her fingers closed around it.

Compactly steely, the little gun lay in the palm of her hand.

She released the safety catch.

Conscious of her own uneven heartbeat, Patience slipped out of bed and feeling her way in the dense violet darkness, crept across the room. Within a step of the door she heard rather than saw the handle begin to turn. She froze. While she hesitated, he must have been silently moving up the stairs towards her. Cat

3

and mouse. She altered her grip on the gun to something which felt altogether more businesslike. She remembered her husband saying to her, 'Do you know how to use one of these? No? It's easy, darling. Like a water pistol. You just point it and fire.'

Confronted by the dark silhouette of the intruder, Patience stepped backwards as he reached out for her and caught her foot in the Persian runner which they had thrown onto the bare floorboards until the new carpet should be fitted. Off balance, she inadvertently squeezed the trigger and the gun went off. For such a small weapon the explosion was deafening. Afterwards there was silence.

2

From a very early age Dorian Ormond had learnt that life spent within the orbit of one largely (though not, as it later turned out, universally) deemed to be perfect, could with justification be described as a bed of nails. Even when, or perhaps more especially when, that someone was your elder sister. For on top of everything else, with seniority came rank. She grew used to invidious comparisons, such as, 'Why can't you be one of those graceful girls, Dorian?' inevitably followed by, 'Like Patience.' Patience. Well at least she had done better on the name front than her impeccable sibling.

It was not until she was in her rebellious teens that Dorian finally confronted the fact that she did not actually like her sister. This recognition engendered guilt and a certain amount of confusion, for surely it was unnatural not to love and esteem one's nearest and dearest. Mulling this over, Dorian wondered aloud more than once, 'What is it about her that gets my goat?' and came to the conclusion that it was Patience's effortless appropriation of the moral high ground as if it was her right, together with an equally effortless assumption that her own inflexible, though undeniably high-minded principles were the only ones which mattered. Equally baffling was the way in which, as with certain confidence tricks, so many people were taken in.

Not all though.

At the day school the Sheridan girls both attended, where, in the fullness of time, Patience naturally became a prefect (and Dorian did not) and then, just as naturally, head girl (and Dorian did not), there was a substantial faction which regarded Patience Sheridan as perfect and another, though smaller, band of dissenters who regarded her as perfectly poisonous.

One heartening thing did, however, emerge from school and that was that Dorian was a clever girl, much cleverer in fact than her sister so that Patience took a secretarial course when she left and Dorian went to Oxford in pursuit of a degree in Politics, Philosophy and Economics. Which was gratifying but did not eradicate the sense of worthlessness ingrained by years of unfavourable comparison with the perfect one.

Money had always been a problem for the Sheridan family. In their different ways the girls reached their own solutions. Patience married a good salary and Dorian earned one. Disparate children of disparate parents, as the years passed the girls grew ever further apart from one another until they met at Christmas and that was about all.

Dorian felt herself to be a casualty of her childhood. The certainty that was Patience's, courtesy of the doting favouritism of their mother, was never to be hers. Nothing, it seemed, could replace early maternal endorsement, not even a first from Oxford. Watching the damage take place, Adrian Sheridan did his best to shore up the confidence of his younger daughter. Occasionally he remonstrated with his wife who invariably replied 'I don't know what you're talking about, Adrian!' and carried on as before. When he first met Georgina, an aspiring actress, there had been a vivacity about her which breathed life into his own cerebral existence. He fell deeply in love with her, mistaking brittleness for wit, extrovert behaviour for affection and a certain conversational sophistication for intelligence. By the time he allowed himself to recognise what a very silly woman she was it was too late, for Patience was on the way.

'Why Patience?' well-meaning acquaintances would sometimes ask. 'It's such a very . . . well . . . *unusual* name these days!'

'Because I don't know where I'd be without it! If you knew what I've had to put up with, you'd understand,' hinted Georgina darkly, casting her eyes to heaven and causing her inquisitor to look speculatively at Adrian Sheridan the next time they encountered one another. The knowledge that she was pregnant again came as a shock. By this time the acting roles, never very thick upon the ground, had all but dried up and the glittering academic career her husband hoped for had not materialised either. Each was disappointed in the other, though at this point in time neither said so.

When the second daughter was duly born, Georgina allowed Adrian to chose the name and immediately regretted it.

'*Dorian?* But that's a boy's name, surely,' objected Georgina.

'I can't see that it matters in these egalitarian times,' replied Adrian, standing his ground for once. 'I like it and that's that!'

Thereafter she regarded Patience as her child and Dorian as his. Studying the photographs years later, it seemed to Dorian that Patience appeared to be on a larger scale than herself, with a buttery bloom as though grown fat on her mother's affection, whereas she herself looked pinched, starved even and so, in an odd sort of way, did her father. She was aware that even after all these years the shortfall in her mother's love still hurt her, though no doubt the smothering histrionics lavished on Patience had not been easy to cope with either. Although Patience invariably said and did the right thing, there was, in Dorian's view, a lack of warmth about her elder sister, possibly because all through her childhood and beyond she had been under relentless maternal emotional siege. Though at least Patience had gone on to make a solid marriage, whereas her own had failed. Although it was some time since this had happened, and there had been no children so that it was more like a loss of a lover than a husband, Dorian still thought about Robert more than she cared to admit.

Robert Ormond swore under his breath, screwed up yet another sheet of paper and threw it at the overflowing waste-paper basket. He leant back in his chair.

'If I don't pull myself together, I'm never going to write this book,' said Robert aloud to the photograph of Dorian which still stood on his untidy desk. Robert often talked to her photograph like this, just as if she was still there. Gravely, she looked back at him. Devoid of conceit, the upshot of her awful mother's dismissive attitude, her face was as ever un-made-up giving it the quality of having been caught in the unflattering glare of a naked bulb. A bleach-out. And yet, and yet, there it was again, the elusive quality which had caught his attention the first time they had met. Wide light eyes stared back at him. Fine unmanageable blonde hair seemed to fly airily around her pale features and even paler lips so that the overall impression was one of light and shade rather than flesh and blood. Although, or maybe because, in a curious sort of way the photograph lacked physical definition, it managed to convey at the same time an impression of formidable intelligence.

Restlessly, Robert stood up. A tall, thin, bookish figure, he tacked for a while around the large shabby room before coming back to her photograph.

'False though she be to me and Love,
I'll ne'er pursue Revenge;
For still the Charmer I approve,
Tho' I deplore her change,' quoted Robert aloud, conscious that Congreve was here being rather kinder than was normally his wont and kinder than he, Robert, felt. He continued,

'In Hours of Bliss we oft have met,
They could not always last;
And though the present I regret,
I'm grateful for the past.'

Finally he turned her likeness in its silver frame to the wall and went back to the computer and his largely unwritten book. Both his mind and the screen were blank. After ten minutes there was still no sign of any interaction at all. With a sigh of frustration Robert took off his oval gold-rimmed reading glasses and threw them on the keyboard. Tilting back on his chair, he swung his feet up onto the desk, clasped his hands behind his head and stared up at the high, elaborately corniced ceiling. His rented flat, once *their* rented flat, was of the grandly peeling Kensington variety with an old-fashioned gas fire of the sort which exploded when lit before settling down into a sibylline hiss. Every so often pieces fell off it. Decay lurked everywhere, most especially in the inconvenient kitchen, since Dorian's departure. A supremely cautious publisher's advance on this, Robert's first attempt at biography, ensured that he was unable to afford the luxury of domestic help unless he made other stringent economies, such as giving up eating altogether. Already a dimly lit victim of the forty-watt bulb, he was not certain what else he could do. Go back to a full-time job, a real one, extend the deadline, work all day and all night as well. Maybe that was the answer. It was all very depressing.

He stared at the empty screen again. Nothing came. Finally: 'Oh, fuck it!' said Robert. Abruptly he jumped to his feet, put on his corduroy jacket whose elbows were shiny due to the amount of time spent sitting at his desk with his head on his hands either thinking of nothing or trying to think of something, and went into the bedroom. The bed was half made, Dorian's side being more or less intact and Robert's a jumble of sheets and blankets which he got out of every morning and crawled back into every night. Unable to bear his own house and the company of Alexander Pope any longer, he put on his overcoat and went out, slamming the door.

At South Kensington station, where he was in the act of hailing a cab after a long and bibulous lunch, Radley Oates passed his lover's husband in the street without realising. Peripherally he did notice a frowning, introspective passer-by but, having ascertained that the other was not about to hijack the cab he had his eye on, lost interest. London was, after all, full of embattled souls such as this one.

A late arrival back at his office in the City was not greeted with unalloyed delight. His staff of two heard the plummy tones before they actually saw him.

'Here he comes!' said Jeannie, Radley's pert Scottish secretary. 'God's Gift to the Gossip Column!'

'What colour is he?' queried Peter, lowly editorial assistant, without looking up from the copy he was subbing.

'Cranberry,' said Jeannie, managing to carry on typing and monitor her boss's appearance as Radley wove into view. 'With a slight stagger. Hardly surprising when you consider that he went to lunch at twelve and it's now four-thirty.'

'He won't be very pleased when he knows that Causton's been looking for him,' observed Peter with a certain satisfaction. Hillary Causton, the proprietor of the newspaper for which they all worked, was famously abstemious.

'No, he won't!'

By now Radley was nearly upon them. Jeannie, who knew that her boss was often lecherous after a demanding lunch, prepared to take evasive action if necessary. Although she had only been with the *Clarion* for two months, Jeannie was already secretly looking for another post.

'Has my little Scots Presbyterian got any messages for me?' enquired Radley sarcastically, pausing by her desk. His secretary's failure to respond to his overtures irked him. Droit de seigneur was the way Radley saw it, but with the social spotlight firmly on the evils of sexual harassment these days, had felt himself forced to back off.

Jeannie read out a very long list, which included several tradesmen, one of whom was her boss's wine merchant, pleading for settlement of long overdue accounts. ('It's not my fault, I'm only his secretary,' said Jeannie, fending off their complaints. 'All I can do is to pass on your message.')

'And Mrs Ormond rang, saying could you let her have time and place for tonight,' said Jeannie in conclusion. And then, as an afterthought, 'Oh, I nearly forgot, Mr Causton's been looking for you all afternoon.'

'Christ!' said Radley, visibly disconcerted. 'What did he say he wanted?'

'You,' replied Jeannie, merciless in her small triumph. 'Straight away. He first rang down at twelve-thirty.'

Radley shot Jeannie a venomous look.

'Could you get his secretary on the phone for me, please?'

It was done. Finally speaking to Causton, and apparently fielding a question as to where he had been all afternoon, 'Here and there. There's a lot going on at the moment,' said Radley, and then with Jeannie listening, 'My secretary forgot to pass on the message, I'm afraid, otherwise I would have got back to you before this. Would you like me to come up now? No. Tomorrow morning, then, 9 a.m. I'll be there.' He hung up.

On the thirteenth floor Causton also replaced the telephone receiver and turned back to his Chief Operating Officer.

'Fire him!' said Hillary Causton, referring to the eminent editor of one of the newspapers he owned. 'Get rid of him! I'm not prepared to have anybody in that job who is not in step with me.'

'But he's very highly thought of and extremely good at the job!'

'Don't be so bloody feeble, get another one,' was the tycoonish response. 'Editors are ten a penny. Everyone wants to edit a national newspaper!'

'Yes, but not everybody . . .'

Causton waved a dismissive hand. 'Just do it!' The telephone on his desk rang again. 'Ah, that will be my wife. Draw up a short list. We'll go through it tomorrow.'

Drusilla Causton entered the office, perfunctorily kissed her husband and then balanced on the broad arm of the sofa which filled the bay window of his office.

Watching him stretch out an arm for one of the telephones, she said, 'We should leave almost immediately, Hillary. It's one of those very long operas.'

'Yes, all right, Drusilla!' Causton was curt and sounded irritable. 'Am I allowed to make just one call before we leave?'

'Of course! You must do as you please. You usually do after all.'

This speech was mildly delivered with the faintest of shrugs and perfectly calculated to infuriate. They faced one another. At mental odds, they were also totally different physical types. Drusilla was tiny, pin thin and dressed scorpion-like in glistening black couture. Her pointed face was framed by a helmet of thick blonde hair. Among those who knew her well, including her husband, there was a recognition of the fact that, despite her diminutive size, it was better not to engage in gladiatorial combat with Drusilla. Hillary Causton, on the other hand, was large, larger than life in fact, with a heroic head whose thick brown hair curled onto the collar of his Jermyn Street shirt. There was an untamed untidiness about Causton which was reminiscent of certain Brontë anti-heroes in stark contrast with the severely regimented chic of his compact wife.

The phone rang and rang in an empty office. The person he was trying to ring had evidently left. Perhaps he was going to the same interminable opera.

'OK,' said Hillary, 'let's go!'

In another tycoon's eyrie Charlie Davenport, Hillary Causton's contemporary and great business rival, was also facing Drusilla. Younger but still predatory, she looked out of the confines of a silver frame into his eyes. The portrait, a black and white studio

11

one, dramatically caught the essence of the stylish sitter. Drusilla Causton eats scalpel blades for breakfast said one wag on first seeing it. Everything about it was razor sharp, from the sculpted shape of her hair to the highlit gleaming cheek bones, sharp chin and long pointed fingernails.

'Drusilla should have married me,' said Charlie. 'She's wasted on Causton.' He kissed her on the lips through the glass and then put the picture away in one of the drawers of his desk.

Because he was always being told what a perfect wife he had and how lucky he was, Hugh Allardyce found his own frustration with things the way they were hard to comprehend, let alone communicate. Theirs had never been a particularly passionate marriage. Hugh always harboured the suspicion that Patience endured their lovemaking rather than relished it. On the other hand, being a reasonable man, he conceded that he himself was not exactly highly sexed either. In the fullness of time and the competent way in which she handled everything, even the more arbitrary of life's happenings, she produced two children, one of each sex: first a daughter, Cordelia, and then a son, Christian. After which, 'Two is quite enough,' pronounced Patience and turned her attention to Good Works. These she pursued during the day while Hugh was in London being a banker, and a succession of nannies looked after the two children. It did occur to Hugh to ask himself why hired help came and went so often, but since it was Patience who dealt with replacements this question remained unanswered. Eventually, as well as being a pillar of the Church, she became a governor of one of the local schools (though she did not send her own children there) and then a magistrate. All this produced a gratifying sense of being, albeit only locally, a power in the land. Patience liked power. She liked being in charge of co-ordinating charitably inclined teams of women and most especially she liked judging the misdemeanours of others, finding the bench a perfect platform for the dissemination of her high-minded views which were not infrequently printed in the local paper.

The children went to boarding school.

'Are we quite sure we want to send them away to boarding school?' asked Hugh.

12

'Quite sure!' His wife was brisk. 'What else would we do with them?'

'They could stay at home with us and attend the local high school, the one you're on the governing board of.'

'Out of the question!' said Patience. 'In spite of my best endeavours, the education there simply isn't good enough. Did I tell you I've been thinking of standing for the Council?'

Hugh's heart sank. Insidiously, the number of his wife's commitments elsewhere had crept up to the point where she was absent more than she was present, and Hugh more and more frequently came home to a note and a cold meal he was required to heat up himself. Once the children went there was very little left. He briefly wondered if it was worth reminding his energetic partner that charity began at home and then gave up on it. Charity quietly performed within the confines of her own house was not likely to be celebrated by the world at large.

Lonelier than ever within his marriage, Hugh endured. Endured for years in fact, until he decided on a whim to take up drawing and in pursuit of this aim enrolled at an evening class.

3

The rivalry between Hillary Causton and Charlie Davenport had been going on for years and very entertaining it had been too. It was generally agreed by those who monitored its progress, namely the tabloid press and the gossip columns, that because he had a sense of humour which Hillary conspicuously did not, Charlie was probably ahead on points. Davenport was foxy whereas Causton was the heavy brigade. The Causton newspapers on the other hand, which were, among others, a quality daily, a quality Sunday and an evening, had gravitas whereas those owned by Charlie, with the exception of his financial daily for which Dorian Ormond worked, were not broadsheets and fell into the upmarket tabloid category which tended to cater for the popular and the frivolous. Because of this, Causton looked down on Charlie from a great height but by no means had the last word, since through the medium of his own irreverent titles Charlie relentlessly pulled Hillary's tail.

What was not generally known, except to Radley Oates who had unearthed the fact during the course of researching a hagiographic biography of his Chairman, was that Drusilla Causton had been the fiancée and mistress of Charlie Davenport before she married Hillary. Drusilla liked having two men fighting over her favours and had milked the situation for as long as she could before being finally obliged to make a choice. Eventually, at the end of a Causton ultimatum she found herself, in the words of Dryden, 'married past redemption' and not too happy about it. After the wedding, at Hillary's behest, she did not see Charlie alone again.

In actual fact for the first few years each was enough of a novelty to the other for the union to appear to work. Drusilla's vivacity leavens Hillary's lump, said her friends unkindly. His were equally charitable. They said, Hillary has substance and money. Drusilla is a lightweight who needs both. Whatever the truth of it, the Caustons gave powerful, rather brittle dinner parties and were a social force in the land. Asking himself the question when had it all begun to go wrong, Hillary came up with the answer that it had probably never been right in the first place. There were no children which was a huge disappointment because, above all, he would have liked a son to whom he could have bequeathed the business he had so successfully built up. Why there were no children was a mystery. Drusilla was both sexually voracious and inventive and on that level it certainly worked. Though it would probably have been true to say that on that level, where Drusilla was concerned, it would have worked with practically anybody. In fact their childlessness was a mystery to Hillary but not to Drusilla who was taking the pill when they met and carried on taking it for the duration of the marriage. I like my flat stomach and my mobility, Drusilla reasoned, and I don't like babies, so why should I have any?

After several years, boredom began to set in.

Respectability doesn't suit me, she thought, looking at her bathroom mirror reflection in the savage light of morning. My looks are going.

This was a serious situation which required swift action.

And got it.

Drusilla rang up Charlie Davenport and proposed lunch.

Dorian Ormond finished her piece for the following day's edition of Charlie Davenport's financial newspaper. She decided to have a cup of coffee from the office machine before checking her copy. The most that could be said for drinks from the dispenser was that they were wet and hot. Otherwise they tasted of nothing in particular. All the same, both hands wrapped around a steaming plastic cup provided a legitimate reason for taking a short break.

Sitting sipping, Dorian thought about the men in her life. She had not seen Robert since the day she first went to bed with Radley Oates. Dorian was aware that if they did meet again he probably would not recognise her. Meeting Radley had done a great deal for her confidence and her looks. Radley, who in the course of his job mixed with the glitterati, which included top fashion models, was fond of proclaiming with his customary gallantry and mixed metaphors that most of these svelte clotheshorses looked like ratbags when not on the cat walk. It was in this way that he was able to spot the potential of Dorian Ormond. Watching her across a crowded private view of Jack Carey's paintings at The Gallery, where she was a guest of the artist's wife Ellen, he was immediately struck by the length of her legs together with her high cheekbones and wide apart amber eyes. The hair was a complete mess, of course, and so was the awful dress she was wearing, though frock might have been a better word. She looks like a bluestocking, thought Radley, closer to the truth than he realised. Nobody else was taking any notice of Dorian at all. Relaxed and predatory, Radley sauntered across the polished floor towards her. Dorian watched him thread his way through the other guests, negotiating his way around two large potted palms as he did so, and with her customary modesty assumed he must be making towards someone standing behind her. Radley was tall and, unlike the creatively attired artistic contingent, expensively suited. A purple silk handkerchief casually tucked into his breast pocket echoed the colours of his flamboyant tie and complemented the vivid silk lining of his jacket. The whole ensemble was finished off with a dark red carnation. A City bird of paradise, was the thought which crossed Dorian's mind as she prepared to move to one side to let him pass and she was astonished when he stopped and spoke to her. He was not her type, of course, but nevertheless she accepted his invitation out to dinner.

That had been four months ago. Since then she had avoided seeing Robert. In an odd sort of way, although they were currently separated, Dorian felt like an adulteress and as though she was betraying her husband. At the same time she was aware that the affair with Radley would not prove a durable fire. Still, to be the girlfriend, or, and more likely, *one* of the girlfriends of a celebrated gossip columnist was a novel experience and one not to be wasted. Thus began a hot affair. Though not so hot on Dorian's side that she was able to turn a blind eye to Radley's less lovable characteristics. He had, for instance, a tendency to strut born out of conceit, or maybe insecurity, and was not always truthful. On one level though he had been very candid.

'I can't take you to the functions I have to attend wearing clothes like that,' said Radley.

'Why can't you take me as I am?' she feebly protested, knowing the answer perfectly well. 'Surely it's the inner self which counts.'

'Yes and no,' her lover answered cryptically, admiring her breasts as she tried on an ivory silk shirt he had just bought her. He took in hand her makeup and her hair as well and, aware of her own shortcomings, Dorian let him. There was no denying that the transformation was astonishing. She wondered what Robert would say if he could see her now. Though he probably wouldn't even have noticed the difference. He's so embattled by that bloody biography, thought Dorian crossly, that nothing else impinges. Towards the end she had felt herself to be virtually invisible, a wraith who crept about the flat trying not to disturb his train of thought, thereby provoking an outburst of rage. Alexander Pope had a lot to answer for. Radley, on the other hand, had no intellectual commitment to anything, not even to his column which was haphazardly jotted down at speed and subsequently handed to the luckless Peter to sort out while Radley went his merry way in pursuit of the next diversion.

All this Dorian observed and, as always honest with herself, recognised that in Radley's shallowness lay the eventual end of their affair. He was good for a fling but that was probably it. And, after all, why not? It's ages since I had any fun, justified Dorian to herself, hardening her heart and turning as she did so away from thoughts of Robert.

On his side, though he would have died rather than admit it, Radley was slightly abashed by Dorian. There was a refinement, dignity even, about her which set her apart from the common herd. These days, when they were out together, she attracted attention and he could see people wondering who she was. As her confidence improved along with her dress sense, it occurred to Radley that maybe his pupil would one day overtake him.

Quite often they talked about Charlie Davenport, who had been Radley's employer before he had been lured away by Hillary Causton. Poaching each other's columnists was one of the milder manifestations of the competition between the two men. Though incensed at the time by the success of this move, in the event Charlie, who knew Oates to be bone idle and had been toying with the idea of getting rid of him for some time, retaliated by enticing Julian Cazalet away from *his* current newspaper proprietor thereby ending up with a much superior gossip column. Cazalet's address book was legendary and, sensitive to the bad blood between Causton and Davenport, he took huge delight in remorselessly scooping Radley and then publicising the fact in a series of insulting footnotes.

Impressed by this, Charlie said to Cazalet: 'Any time Causton approaches you, let me know. Whatever he offers you I'll match it!'

It would have been asking a lot for Cazalet to pass up this tempting invitation and the predictable upshot was that at fairly frequent intervals, whether there had been an overture or there had not, Charlie was allowed to form the impression that there had been and Cazalet's pay cheque was duly augmented. It was beginning to look like a gravy train until, on one of the occasions when there had not been an approach, Charlie unexpectedly said, 'He does want you very badly, doesn't he? Sadly, Julian, I may have to decide to let you go. Otherwise at this rate you're shortly going to be paid more than me!' Not so gullible after all. After that Cazalet kept very quiet for at least a year.

'Which of them do you prefer working for?' asked Dorian over lunch one day. Radley stared into his asparagus soup.

'There's really nothing to choose,' he replied at last. 'All tycoons are extraordinary and newspaper proprietors seem to be more extraordinary than most. Both Causton and Davenport want everything done yesterday, have huge egos, can't abide criticism and, in spite of owning a stable of newspapers each, neither lives in the real world. They're mentally outside the stratosphere!' This was unusually eloquent and listening to him Dorian was just wondering what Radley himself classed as reality, when he suddenly said, 'And of course they're both in love with the same woman.'

'What?' Dorian was astonished.

'Yes, I found it out when I was researching my biography of Davenport.' Radley was complacent, enjoying his lover's surprise.

'I thought you were writing a biography of Causton.'

'I am now,' pointed out Radley, without a trace of shame, 'but when I worked for Davenport, I was into massaging Charlie's

18

amour propre. Now, force majeure, it has to be Hillary's instead.'

What is it about me, Dorian asked herself, that I seem doomed to surround myself with would-be biographers? Or, where Radley is concerned, hagiographers. In Robert's case she had felt her marriage gradually turning into a *ménage à trois*, with Alexander Pope as the other participant. Though she doubted, given Radley's slothful temperament, that even a combination of Davenport and Causton could cause the same amount of mental mayhem. It did, however, raise the interesting question of what else he had found out in the course of his research.

'So what's the story?'

'The story is that Charlie and Hillary were at the same university and both, through different friends, knew Drusilla, then and now regarded as a fatal lady. Don't ask me what went on in the interim, read the book, but to cut a long story short, Charlie got engaged to Drusilla. Which came as an awful slap in the eye for Hillary. Although this all happened in his pre-tycoon days, Causton, who was already beginning to display the insensitivity and single-mindedness necessary to succeed in business, did not waste time palely loitering but took advantage of the fact that Davenport was away on a trip and horned in and persuaded Drusilla that he, and not her fiancé, was the answer to a maiden's prayer. End of story and beginning of lifelong enmity.'

'So Causton was the winner!'

'Yes and no,' answered Radley cautiously. 'You haven't met her, have you? Drusilla is a primitive who takes no prisoners. She's still mentally in the era when people skinned their enemies alive.' He remembered with a shudder that time he had inadvertently lampooned one of her social acquaintances in his column and the relentless persecution which had resulted. All the same there was a certain fascination about Drusilla, a feeling that anything could happen when she was around, because she had no moral dimension that Radley had been able to discern and no scruples either. The world was a mirror for Drusilla's own desires. Whereas Hillary, on the other hand, did appear to take the moral high ground, was a regular worshipper at his local (fashionable) church and was fond of writing high-minded, ponderous articles and, occasionally, leaders in his own newspapers. In these liberal times there were many who ridiculed

Hillary's uncompromising views declaring him to be a fascist to the right of Genghis Khan. Others found them threatening. Safely insulated from criticism by virtue of his immense wealth and a generally Olympian stance, Hillary was oblivious to all of it. Even his detractors could not deny that he wielded a lot of power through his own newspapers. Sometimes Radley tried to imagine the Caustons in a domestic situation, sitting watching their favourite television programme, with suppers on trays, for instance, and could not. Visualising them in bed together was even more difficult.

'Have you ever met Causton?' asked Radley aloud.

'No,' replied Dorian, putting down her knife and fork. 'And I've only met Charlie Davenport peripherally, on one of his infrequent progresses through the lower echelons of his company. I'm quite certain he doesn't have a clue who I am.'

Possibly and possibly not, was Radley's mental reaction to that. It was his experience that Charlie knew more about what was going on than most of his staff gave him credit for. There were times when he regretted the passing of the rather more irresponsible Davenport era and found the teetotal humourless Causton oppressive, not to say irksome, especially during the course of one of his frequent dissections of Radley's expenses. He was, however, stuck with it, Radley recognised, having been employed with varying degrees of mutual disenchantment by almost everybody else already.

The second course arrived. Radley picked up his wine glass and was just about to sip when he saw Drusilla Causton and Charlie Davenport enter the restaurant. Instinctively he ducked below the table and began to fish around on the floor as though searching for something.

'What are you doing?' enquired Dorian, aware that it couldn't be his napkin he was looking for since this was lying on the table in a crumpled heap.

Cautiously Radley raised his head. Drusilla and Charlie had gone. The waiter must have taken them through to the other room.

Well, well! thought Radley. Aloud he said, 'I thought I had dropped my napkin, but I see it's here all the time! Let's tuck in, shall we?'

Watching Patience Allardyce chairing the church committee meeting in another, leafier part of outer London, Clarissa Bowen was aware of the whole process getting more and more acrimonious. Since Good Intentions were plainly abroad, to be shortly followed by Good Works, it was hard to divine exactly why this was happening. Not for the first time she studied Patience with some perplexity. What Clarissa saw was a well-groomed, carefully made-up woman in her thirties. Patience was tall and large-boned and had a stately air. She was also a good organiser and intelligent, though wasn't there something faintly stupid about her chin which was fraction too large, though only a fraction? Patience spoke quietly but with emphasis and determination and when someone else raised a point, just as May Parker, Deputy Chairperson, was raising one now, she listened pale-eyed and expressionless with forbearance until it was over, and then intoned her own opinion all over again. The problem was, Clarissa decided, that this particular Chairperson was so certain that what she was proposing was right that she was insulated from all other opinion by her own conviction and, therefore, equally impervious to discontent. Nothing wrong with knowing what you wanted, of course, but there should still be room for open-minded debate, or at least the semblance of such. It was apparent to Clarissa, though evidently not to Patience, that what was on the surface a civilised meeting was actually seething with resentment, revolution even. Not for the first time she wondered whether she shouldn't take Patience to one side and explain to her that perhaps it would be better if she was not quite so definite all the time, and that, furthermore, it might be a good idea to let somebody else have a good idea for once. Having had the thought, as usual she gave up on it. Trying to explain such a thing to someone as unselfaware and unanalytical as Patience would indubitably be a waste of everybody's time.

Patience glanced at her watch: 9.30 p.m. She began to wind up the meeting. The organisation of the summer fête had taken up most of it. Ongoing bones of contention such as the church flower rota had been left till last.

Clarissa let her eye range around the table. May was staring into the middle distance with a set expression on her face.

Margaret Harris was doodling on her pad what looked like a row of little gallows. It *was* a row of little gallows. Startled, Clarissa watched her add a row of little hanging stickpersons, or maybe chairpersons. She noticed Joan Pickering exchange some words with Laura Fitzwilliam in an undertone at the end of which they both frowned at Patience. The atmosphere was loaded. There was none of the Christian soldier-like camaraderie round the table that ideally there should have been.

Gathering up her notes, Patience stood these on end, tapped the top and then turned them sideways. Another smart tap ensured that they formed a tidy rectangle after which they were put away in a blue folder.

She stood up.

'Thank you ladies, I think that deals with everything. I'm glad we are in agreement and now I must get back to my saintly husband. Darling Hugh! He's so good.' She bestowed a collective beatific smile on the whole table. A muted murmur of good-byes surrounded her exit. There was a lull for a few moments after her departure, presumably while they all waited to make sure she had really gone, followed by a regrettable outbreak of bile. No other word for it.

May Parker said, 'I know it's an unChristian thing to say, but I'm going to say it anyway: I simply cannot *stand* Patience Allardyce!'

'Well, dear,' observed Joan Pickering, torn between a desire to join in and, in the light of May's unkind statement, an equally strong desire to capture the charitable high ground which now Patience had gone seemed to be there for the taking, 'I know you find the fact that, regardless of who's *doing* the flowers, *she* chooses them, tiresome and that this implies that we have no taste. I *do* know that. And I sympathise! Don't think I don't . . .'

'*You* got very hot under the collar the last time she did it to *you*,' reminded Laura Fitzwilliam who did not like the sanctimonious beginning of this speech.

'Yes, but it's *not* just the flowers, it's the fête as well,' said Margaret Harris, chipping in, very spiteful. 'Everything has to be done *her* way. She's very high-handed. Look at the Bring and Buy Sale. We do all the work and *she* takes all the credit! The vicar thinks she's the bee's knees.' She was aware of sounding jealous as she said this. Margaret, long separated from her husband who had been conspicuously one of the unsaintly variety, had a crush on the vicar who was unmarried and therefore available. Unfortunately he had not noticed. Too busy dancing attendance on Patience Allardyce who had a perfectly good husband of her own, was Margaret's curdled view of this.

'Ladies, ladies!' The speaker was Clarissa Bowen. 'May I remind you that we are the church committee and as such this back biting does not become us! After all, Patience does do an awful lot and who would do it if she didn't?'

Who indeed? The way that sort of busybody acquired power was usually because of the dearth of other volunteers. The rest of them, with the exceptions of Clarissa, who was seventy, and Patience herself, had full-time jobs as well as families to run. There was a short, thoughtful silence, which proved to be a regrouping exercise. After it they all joined in together. Listening to the chorus of criticism, often prefaced by the words 'Of course, I don't want to be critical but . . .' Clarissa thought wearingly, I'm seventy and quite happy to take a back seat. It really doesn't matter to me whether the church is decorated with gladioli or dahlias or even dandelions, come to that, and *au fond* it probably doesn't matter to them either. The problem is Patience's manner. It grates. And if I'm honest it grates on me too. Which is sad, because she *means* so well. Sighing, Clarissa rose to her feet. Although she had no long-suffering husband to go home to, having been widowed two years ago, and would have liked to stay on for a cup of coffee and, more importantly, some company, she decided to pass on both and take her leave too.

'Good night, ladies,' said Clarissa.

Ineptly sketching, apparently with his eyes on the model, Hugh Allardyce covertly studied the profile of Flora Munro who was working at the easel slightly in front to his left. Flora had studied at art school prior to taking a job as a graphic designer, and still spasmodically attended evening life drawing classes to keep her hand in. Painting was her first love but without the benefit of any income apart from what she earned, it was a passion which had to be pursued in her spare time. Flora's dark curly hair was

23

piled on top of her head. Small nascent curls clustered charmingly at the nape of her neck, the length of which was emphasised by her bowed head as she drew. There was an Edwardian quality about her dress which intrigued Hugh, who had never seen anything like it outside an oil painting. She wore a hunting-green smock with a small, high-waisted long-sleeved bodice whose full skirt stopped just above her ankles and over it a long, cream turn-of-the-century type pinafore which tied in a large bow at the back. On her feet were boots, which looked right for the period, but were, in fact, modern Doc Martens. Hugh knew they were because, much to Patience's disapproval, Cordelia wore them too. Her drawing was much better than his.

Reluctantly Hugh turned his attention back to the model, a slack-breasted, fat lady of uncertain age. The tutor stopped behind Flora and looked over her shoulder.

'Good, very good. Though the foreshortening of the left arm isn't quite right.' He took the pencil from her hand. 'It should be more like this, I think. But otherwise excellent!'

He passed on. Finally he came to Hugh. There was an unnerving silence. Finally, if only to break it, Hugh said, 'Perhaps I should start again?'

'Only if you think you can improve on this,' came the unreassuringly enigmatic reply. 'Otherwise I shouldn't bother.' Then, to the model, 'Take a ten-minute break now.' She got down from the small platform on which she had been sitting, put on a dressing gown and then sat down in a corner and lit a cigarette.

Flora, who had been conscious of Hugh's gaze upon her earlier, now was equally sensitive to his dejection. She came and stood beside him. 'It's not that bad at all,' said Flora kindly. Kindness, he was later to learn, was one of her main characteristics. 'You're a beginner, aren't you?'

Still mortified, he nodded assent.

'Well, there you go then. Once you learn the technique, you'll be fine. And you need to loosen up a bit. Ever thought of going to the painting classes as well?'

He stared at his drawing. She was right. It looked cramped, dwarfish even, whereas hers had an enviable fluidity of line and an even more enviable feeling for proportion.

'I attend them,' continued Flora, 'although I trained as a painter. You never stop learning, you know.' And then, unexpectedly, 'Are you a banker?'

'Yes,' said Hugh, who had taken off his tie in deference to the informal atmosphere of art school. He felt unaccountably put out. It occurred to him that maybe she and the rest of the class had been laughing at him. 'How did you know?'

'You look like one!' She smiled at him, a wide friendly smile. She radiated spontaneity and candour. He noticed that her eyes, which were rimmed with cloudy purple shadow, were such a dark blue as to appear almost black. Flora's colour was high and her cheeks rosy. But for her ringladen fingers and her *outré* clothes she might have been a country girl. Hugh wondered how old she was.

The model stubbed out her cigarette, wearily took off her dressing gown and prepared to remount the dais.

'What about going out for a meal after this?'

Hugh blinked. He wondered if he had heard right. She really was a very modern girl indeed. A vision of Patience (here he looked at his watch) still presumably bullying the church committee, though with the best of motives, of course, rose before his inner eye together with one of her cold concoctions. He dismissed it.

'Why not!' said Hugh.

4

Charlie Davenport bought himself a local radio station. Because radio was not regarded as being as glamorous as television the prospect of this purchase did not merit more than a snippet in the business pages miscellany section. In this way it slipped under the net of Hillary Causton's daily perusal of the quality papers and it was not until the consortium led by Davenport, who was also the biggest shareholder, won the franchise they were after, thereby meriting a small headline of its own, that he caught up with the news. Hillary irritably buzzed through to his secretary.

'Tell Miles Compton I want to see him straight away,' said Hillary. Miles Compton was his Chief Operating Officer. There was a servility about Miles which, while he used it, Hillary despised. Everything about the bulky Compton was oily, even down to his unctuous habit of rubbing his hands together when these were not folded Friar Tuck-like over his large stomach. Tiny eyes, like currants imbedded in a large pale bun, together with a tiny mouth were in danger of being swamped by pendulous flab which was underpinned by a cluster of escalating chins. Within the company Compton, despite his ingratiating manner, was not as popular as he liked to think and because of his effortless rise, coupled with a slippery ability to avoid taking the blame for anything, was known as Teflon Man. Having reached his present eminence by successfully undermining his predecessor and immediate boss, he was presently in the hapless situation of discovering that the position of what amounted to Grand Vizier to Causton's Sultan was not the bed of roses it had seemed to be before he achieved it, but more often than not evoked a different sort of bed, one of nails. Causton, who on that level missed very little of what was going on around him, had cynically watched Compton's manoeuvrings and now was inclined to think that, at the end of the day, he had fired the wrong person. Miles's desire to be liked caused him to have a lack of bite which rendered him less effective than the last incumbent. It's beginning to look as if Miles can't cut the mustard, was Causton's way of putting it to himself. Getting rid of him though presented a difficulty as well. To fire one Chief Operating Officer was one thing, but to dispense with two on the trot smacked of carelessness, not to mention bad judgement, and might have caused a frisson in the share price. Demotion upwards into some other grandly titled but largely pointless position was not an option either since Causton ran a tight business ship with the result that there was no slot for such a thing. On the other hand, did it really matter? *I* run this company, was Causton's view, and so long as my Chief Operating Officer cringes enough and does exactly what I tell him, what can go wrong? As yet nothing major had. Though when he was absent on one of his extended business trips somebody had to be left in charge and, as of now, that person was Compton, so on that front it was unsatisfactory.

Anticipating another wrangle on the subject of who the next editor should be and hoping that his boss had decided against firing the current one, Compton picked up the short list which they had already been through more than once and walked along the corridor. He arrived to find Causton standing behind his gargantuan desk on which what looked like all the newspapers, both broadsheet and tabloid, were spread out. Each one seemed to have a very small item ringed in red. Squinting at these, which were upside down from where he was standing, Compton was unable to decipher what they said. He was not to remain in ignorance for long.

'Radio!' exclaimed Hillary. 'Davenport's bought into a radio station!' Like a fractious bull elephant, he turned a bad-tempered eye on his manager. 'How come nobody told me about this?'

Compton, who had slipped his hand into his inside breast pocket in order to pull out the editor short list, withdrew it again. He was about to suggest that the cuttings service had let them down for once, when Causton lost interest in the answer to his own question and said, 'It'll be TV next! Expansion, that's the name of his little game! Well, I want to get there first! No tinpot little radio stations for me! I want a piece of the real action! I want you to find me a television company. Very discreetly, though, nobody must know that it's us who are interested. But I want it to be top priority.'

Compton's eyes glazed. Beside this exacting order the editor problem, up till now looming so large, paled into insignificance. The Causton empire was currently sitting on a lot of cash. There could be no objection to making it work for them through expansion and, corporately speaking, the prospect was an exciting one. What was wrong was that Causton, who clearly felt upstaged and about to be overtaken, would expect him to wave a magic wand and organise the thing in days. It puzzled Compton that Causton, an astute and level-headed business-man, should get himself into such a lather where Davenport was concerned. It was plainly time for a reminder of the role of that great steadying influence The Board before a possible impetu-ous error of judgement took place.

'Presumably you'll want to run it past . . .'

'The Board? Yes, naturally!' Causton was impatient. 'But not until you've commissioned a feasibility study. A positive one. I want to make sure they rubber-stamp it.'

The words: And if they don't, your head will be on the block, were implied rather than spoken. At this juncture Compton felt he could safely raise the editor question.

'Put it on the back burner,' was Hillary's answer. 'For now I want you to concentrate exclusively on this.'

Charlie Davenport, who knew perfectly well how irritated Hillary Causton would be by the news of his radio station suc-cess, relished the thought. Just like Causton's, his own vast desk was covered with the day's business pages. The question was: What would his rival do next? Charlie's guess was that he would want to buy his own bigger and better toy. He walked over to the window. Today was the second of April. There was a coppery bloom about the sky which possibly heralded a storm. For the moment the sun struggled through, a diffused lozenge of light. Like Causton, because he was a tycoon and it was therefore expected of him, Charlie's office suite was on the top floor of a very tall building. From it he could see far and wide. With the aid of a good telescope apiece, Charlie and Hillary could prob-ably have looked into each other's offices thereby cutting out a lot of expensive private espionage.

Suddenly feeling restless, Davenport decided to amuse himself with one of his impromptu perambulations around the editorial floor of his only upmarket paper, the financial daily. His unheralded appearance led to a flurry of concentration. Charlie started with the editor, whose presence he required on his tour. Halfway through it, 'Who's that?' he enquired.

'Dorian Ormond,' was the answer. 'Surely you've met her before. She's been with us for about five years.'

So she had. Charlie remembered noticing her by-line, after which he had read one or two of her pieces. It seemed to him that this Dorian Ormond did not look quite the same as the one he remembered. This was a beauty with long legs, a short-skirted designer suit and a bob. The other one had worn mid-calf-length dowdy dresses thereby concealing the quality of the legs (superlative) and had had lank, fine hair of indeterminate colour. The metamorphosis was astonishing. Reluctantly Charlie transferred his attention back to his editor.

'Let's move on, shall we?'

Hugh Allardyce did enrol for the painting class. He told Patience that he had done so. He did not mention his new friend, Flora Munro. 'Don't worry about feeding me on my evening class nights,' said Hugh, 'I'll get a snack at the college.' If anything this came as a relief to Patience who was still heavily embroiled in the arrangements for the summer fête and other church business, and did not feel that she was getting as much support from her committee as she felt herself entitled to expect. For reasons which were difficult to fathom, May Parker in particular was being obstructive. And so was Margaret Harris now she came to think about it. Of course poor Margaret's husband had deserted her. *So* humiliating though hardly surprising when one considered the untidy chaos of that house. Here she let a complacent eye linger on her own highly polished furniture and fresh flowers. All the same one had to make allowances. And I did, thought Patience. Only today I said to her, 'Margaret I shall put the unfortunate tone of that last remark down to unhappiness. Try not to be bitter, my dear, we all understand the strain you must be under.'

All of this she told Hugh in a tone of incomprehension one night when they did achieve dinner together.

'Perhaps you should delegate, give the others more of the action, that sort of thing,' suggested Hugh, listening to it. 'Take a back seat, let someone else have a go. After all you've been organising them for years.'

'Oh, I don't think so!' Patience was aghast. 'Hugh, they couldn't do without me.' Watching her certainty, Hugh was unconvinced. Yes they could, was Hugh's mental response. Yes they could. They'd simply bumble along inefficiently and amicably, the way in which every other parish committee except this one does.

'And anyway, apart from anything else,' continued Patience, 'I look upon my work for the Church as my duty. My own life has been so fortunate that it would be unthinkable not to put something back in for the good of the community and those less blessed than myself.' He wondered who she had in mind. Her committee perhaps. 'Besides, I'm sure the other ladies wouldn't *want* me to step down, wouldn't *let* me! We all have a very high regard for each other, you know.'

Hmm. Maybe. It occurred to Hugh not to push it, for if he did and she finally came round to his point of view they would end up sitting opposite each other every night just as they were doing now, without very much to say to one another. I gave up trying to attract my wife's attention years ago, thought Hugh, and now I'm no longer sure I want it any more. He and Flora had got into the habit of having supper together at the end of each class. Hugh looked forward to these innocent meetings. He was realistic enough to know that nothing further would ever come of them, but still he felt rejuvenated by the freshness of her company. She was constantly on his mind and once, walking along Cheapside one lunchtime, he fancied that he saw her and was inordinately disappointed, having quickened his pace and caught her up, to discover that it was not her.

Patience and Hugh sat opposite one another in silence. The sound of the grandfather clock, never normally noticeable, was suddenly loud, the vibration before it struck the hour clearly audible. Its sonorous tick measured the hours, ticking his life away. Hugh had a sudden sensation of panic, of life as it should be lived passing him by.

The phone rang.

'I'll get it. That will be Clarissa Bowen for me,' said Patience. In her absence he stacked the plates prior to taking them to the kitchen. Passing through the hall he heard his wife saying, 'But I don't understand it! I thought we agreed . . .' Agreed what? Hugh discovered that he no longer cared. Tomorrow, he remembered with a lift of the heart, he was seeing Flora Munro.

Two decorous lunches were enough to convince Charlie Davenport, as nothing else could, that he was still in love with Drusilla Causton. Sitting opposite her he longed at the very least to take her hand and at the very most to take her home to bed. In the event, because there was no hint from her that either would be welcome, neither happened and he was left wondering after each occasion what it was she really wanted. To date answer came there none. When he tried to analyse his attraction to her he found it hard to explain her magnetic pull. In the end he decided that, as was said of Byron, she was mad, bad and dangerous to know and *that* was her allure. Furthermore, the impression that she could take him or leave him also kept him in thrall, probably out of pique.

Sometime after their last lunch, he learnt through a mutual friend that in a week's time Hillary was going to Brussels on a business trip. 'No doubt Drusilla will enjoy that,' observed Charlie casually and was rewarded with the informative though unexpected response, 'Good God, no! Drusilla's not going. She can't stand Belgium.'

Can't stand Belgium? It seemed an odd country to have such pronounced feelings about. However never mind about that. Charlie rang Drusilla up.

'I gather you're going to be a grass widow for a few days,' said Charlie without preamble, 'so why don't I amuse you by taking you out to dinner?'

On the other end of the line, staring at herself in the over-mantel mirror and pleased with what she saw, 'Thank you. That would be very nice,' said Drusilla. She smiled and the reflection smiled back. It was Drusilla's opinion that just the prospect of taking a lover had already dramatically improved her looks.

'Why don't you let me cook you a meal the next time? You're always taking me out and always refuse to let me pay my share. I'd like to give you something in return.' For reasons he could not quite have put into words, Hugh hesitated. On the other hand it seemed a perfectly reasonable thing for Flora to want to do. In the end he agreed.

Flora's small flat was nothing like his own conventional mahoganied home. Hanging in one corner of the minute sitting room, for instance, was a parrot's cage within which reposed not a parrot but a luxuriant green fern. The whole room had an air of collection as though it had been assembled during the course of a dedicated trawl through a flea market. Everything, with the exception of the fern and a comatose Persian cat whose name, Hugh was later to learn, was Xerxes, was distressed. Gilt frames flaked, cloudy mirrors had lost a large proportion of their mercury, Chinese blue and white plates were cracked and candelabra were smothered in beeswax from sloping, romantically dripped candles. Neither of the two American wall clocks on either side of the fireplace seemed to be going.

'Won't you sit down?' said Flora.

He did so. The sofa was an old Chesterfield over which a threadbare though rather beautiful old Turkish rug had been thrown. The only other armchair was occupied by Xerxes, whose proprietorial air indicated that it always was.

Flora went into what he presumed must be the kitchen, calling over her shoulder as she did so, 'Can I get you something to drink?'

'Yes, please,' said Hugh absently, studying the wall opposite him with interest. On it was hung a series of large wooden gilded capital letters which spelt out Flora. Each represented a different typeface and all were highly decorative, probably orphaned survivors of various Victorian shop fronts. 'A whisky and soda would be marvellous.'

'I'm afraid I don't have anything like that.' Flora reappeared at the door. 'It's wine or wine.'

Hugh was embarrassed. No, of course she didn't. What a fool he was.

'Then I'd like wine or wine.' Getting off the subject he said, 'Where do you paint?'

'Through that door over there on the right.' She pointed

before going back into the kitchen. 'Go and have a look.'

Hugh opened the one she indicated and was embarrassed all over again to find that it led to both her studio and her bedroom. In one corner was an easel surrounded by all the predictable painter's paraphernalia. The canvas was blank. On the opposite side was a double bed behind which was an overmantel mirror. In the fireplace, whose white marble surround was a replica of the one next door, stood a tall green glass vase (chipped) which was filled with waxen creamy lilies whose expensive seductive scent pervaded the whole room. Wondering who had given them to her, Hugh experienced an unpleasant emotion he had not felt for years. Jealousy. He turned and left the room.

Later, drinking a surprisingly good Barolo red wine and eating spaghetti off battered flow blue plates, Hugh realised that he had fallen in love. Maybe it was all to do with seeing Flora in her own highly individual setting, or maybe he had been falling in love for months and had never noticed the fact. Whatever the truth of the matter Hugh saw very clearly that there was nothing to be done about it. A woman such as this would never in a million years be interested in anything more than friendship with a man like himself.

As he was finally going, Flora said, 'Doesn't your wife wonder where you are? I mean why don't you go straight home after the class?'

'My wife has her own fish to fry,' replied Hugh, 'so, no, I don't think she does. We've been married a long time.'

Feeling suddenly bereft, he kissed her on the cheek and left.

Charlie Davenport savoured the prospect of dinner with Drusilla. Lunch was one thing but dinner was definitely another.

Unaware of his wife's plans and packing to leave, Hillary Causton was at a loss as to how to account for her sunny mood. Early morning and Drusilla did not, on the whole, go together yet here she was, even offering to drive him to the airport. Though, since Hillary had a chauffeur, there was little chance of him taking her up on it.

'I may be back sooner than I thought,' he said as he kissed her goodbye.

The faintest of frowns passed across Drusilla's brow.

'How much sooner?'

'Certainly not before Friday.' Today was Monday. Drusilla watched the limousine, shiny black and sluglike, pull slowly away from the kerb and when it was out of sight went back to bed. Dinner with Charlie was scheduled for that evening.

As is the way with evening classes, an initially enthusiastic group began to dwindle until eventually it was down to four. This precipitated an announcement that, as a result, the life drawing class was to be discontinued until such a time as there should be more support for it. Painting looked as if it might be going the same way. Hugh, who was beginning to discover that he had more artistic talent than had been immediately apparent, was very disappointed and knew that this was not just because of the lessons. Since the supper in Flora's flat they had resumed their former routine of eating in a local bistro. During the course of these evenings, Hugh had learnt more about Flora's background including the fact that she was older than he had first thought. He found her captivating and wondered why she had never married. Now it looked as though along with the evening classes, their friendship which had become so precious to him might have to end as well.

Aware of his depression, in the wake of the tutor's announcement, Flora said, 'Why don't we go back to my flat instead of the restaurant this evening?'

'Yes, why not?' Hugh was conscious of an overwhelming desire to be shut away within it with her, insulated, albeit temporarily, from life as he knew it. It might after all be the last time. Driving them there he said, 'It's a shame. Just as I really felt I was beginning to get somewhere the classes grind to a halt.'

'That's evening classes, I'm afraid!' Flora was philosophical. 'Besides you can still go on drawing and painting at home, can't you?'

'Not really,' said Hugh gloomily. 'Apart from anything else, I can't see Patience offering to pose for me.' An involuntary smile crossed his face at the very idea. It was the first time he had referred to her in front of Flora as Patience rather than as 'my wife' and was aware that by doing so he had moved their friendship on to a subtly more personal level.

Patience. The very name gave Flora pause for thought. She suddenly had an idea, but did not communicate it to Hugh.

Entering her flat he had a sensation of time standing still, as though his mainly unsatisfactory life was, for the moment anyway, on hold. Xerxes monitored their arrival with a dispassionate green eye and then atypically rose, stretched, got down from the armchair and stalked out.

'Why don't you get yourself a glass of wine,' said Flora. 'There's something I have to do. I won't be long.' She disappeared into the bedroom.

Hugh did as she told him and then wandered about sipping. The heady smell of lilies pervaded the whole flat. Eventually the door opened and Flora stood before him. To his astonishment, she was wearing a floor-length black heavily embroidered kimono.

'*I* will pose for you!' said Flora.

Without a trace of self-consciousness she slipped the robe off her shoulders and let it fall to the floor where it formed a stiff circle around her bare feet. Stepping out of its confines, like Botticelli's Venus stepping out of the shell, Flora turned and walked back into the bedroom.

'There's the easel, here's a pencil. I don't mind if I sit or stand,' said Flora, very practical. 'It's entirely up to you.'

The exotic scent of the flowers seemed all at once overpowering. Taking the pencil from her Hugh felt dizzy. Not wanting her to be uncomfortable, he said feebly, 'Why don't you sit on the bed.'

'All right.' She did so. 'Like this?'

'Yes, like that.'

Tentatively at first and then with gathering confidence, he began to draw.

Charlie Davenport's evening with Drusilla Causton got off to a bad start.

'Why don't we have dinner at my flat? So much more discreet! I'll get someone in to cook it.'

'Oh, I don't think so,' her telephone voice sounded fastidious.

'You seem to forget that I am a married woman! Besides, who cares about discretion.'

Her attitude as exemplified by these two contradictory statements left him uncertain as to whether to be disappointed or not. Discretion never had been her forte. That much was certainly true. As to her being a married woman, it seemed to Charlie that whether or not he forgot it was neither here nor there. He had been hoping that *she* would.

Charlie decided to play Drusilla at her own game.

'If that's your attitude, we can be as public as you want. You choose the restaurant you want to go to and I'll book it.'

At the end of an hour, they took a five-minute break during the course of which Flora, just like the model at the art school, put the kimono on again and sat, proper as a princess, sipping her glass of wine. Eyeing Hugh narrowly over the rim she said, 'Are you shocked?'

'No,' said Hugh.

He was, of course. And knew that she knew he was.

'Just surprised,' he added, lamely.

'It's not the first time I've done this, you know,' said Flora.

Hugh could think of nothing to say. Studying him as she spoke the words, Flora thought how very attractive he was in a preppy sort of way, with his mop of fair, greying hair, his slim build and his striped banker-y shirts. There was a boyishness about him, a quality of the romantic lead which in an odd way touched her heart. She guessed he must be about forty. Flora herself was thirty and, probably because her father had died when she was only eight, had always preferred older men. She intuited that Hugh was lonely within his marriage though probably not lonely enough to consider leaving his wife. Flora knew he was attracted to her and also knew that, because Hugh was a gentleman and a married one at that, he would resist doing anything about it. At the end of the day I shall have to seduce him, thought Flora, and after that happens there will be no looking back.

'What do you mean it's not the first time?' said Hugh at last.

'I used to work as an artist's model when I was a student,' elucidated Flora, 'in order to make financial ends meet. It was a part-time job, just like any other. Others worked in

36

Woolworths. I took my clothes off. Speaking of which, shall we get back to work?'

She dropped the kimono onto a chair and resumed the pose.

'Is that about right?'

'Almost. Turn a bit more to the right,' said Hugh, trying to enter into the spirit of the thing and sound dispassionate, in reality dazzled by the sight of her very desirable body. He unclipped his first attempt and began another. Desperately wanting to kiss Flora, he sketched in her head, concentrating on her parted lips and then let the pencil run down her neck and encompass the curve of her shoulder followed by the graceful sweep of a languid arm. Heart racing he began to trace the out-line of one buoyant breast. Drawing Flora, Hugh felt as though he was touching her. It aroused him as nothing else could. His pencil moved on. It lingered on the curve of her thigh and then reluctantly moved on to where her leg tapered into a neat ankle. Through its medium Hugh made love to Flora. He went back to the torso and delicately drew the dark curls which formed the small compact triangle of her pubic hair. Instinct prompted him to stop there although so far it was only half the story. All line, no shading. He stood back. It was quite simply the best thing he had ever done.

Silently Flora watched his absorption. He did not move or look at her but continued staring at the drawing. Noiselessly she swung her feet to the floor, slipped on the kimono and on bare feet moved across the floor towards him. She was surprised at what she saw.

'It's good!' said Flora. 'In fact, it's *very* good!'

Hugh did not reply. He knew what he was going to do and that he would probably regret it later. *Don't think. Thinking inhibits action.* He was aware that there was more at stake here than just beginning a love affair. It was possible there could be a whole new life in the offing. A second chance. Hugh kissed Flora with all the frustrated, pent-up passion engendered by twenty years of sexually unscintillating marriage and then, with-out speaking, he lifted her up, still wrapped in the black robe, strode across the room and laid her on the bed.

Chic in black, Drusilla Causton, another woman who knew what

37

she wanted, sat opposite Charlie Davenport. Together they looked more of a pair than Drusilla and Hillary. There was a dandyish air about Charlie, and a deceptive aura of irresponsibility which, while it alerted, charmed as well. It had always been easy to underestimate Charlie, Drusilla remembered. She was well aware that nobody could have achieved in business terms what Charlie had without huge ambition and drive. Since the days of their former intimacy, he had grown a narrow moustache of the sort which goes with stilettos and when he was not talking and his face was in repose, this conferred an added dimension of seventeenth-century Italianate subtlety which persuaded quite a few that Charlie Davenport was not to be trusted. In physical terms he and his great rival, Hillary Causton, were as opposite as they could be.

'When did you start wearing bow ties?' enquired Drusilla, studying her menu.

'When you deserted me, darling,' said Charlie. 'I had to cheer myself up with something. Why *did* you leave me incidentally?'

'Why?' Drusilla thought for a moment. 'Do you want to hear the unvarnished truth?'

'Might as well.' Charlie braced himself.

'I thought Hillary was going to go further than you were. That's what Hillary said at the time, anyway.'

'Well, he would, wouldn't he?' Charlie was dry. 'And now?'

'I'd say it was level pegging.' Having made her choice, Drusilla closed the menu.

'*I'd* say you made a mistake! Everyone knows Hillary's heavy furniture. You could have had much more fun along the way with me.'

Drusilla, who did not like to be reminded of past possible miscalculations, made a little grimace of displeasure. 'Well, here we are now, so let's make the most of it.'

'I'd like to,' replied Charlie with irritating alacrity. 'Meanwhile, what would you like to order?'

Drusilla told him and then took a small revenge. 'Why have you never married, Charlie?'

This was a question which, at his age, Charlie was getting used to being asked and one which from time to time he asked himself. It was difficult to supply an honest answer. Of course he liked women, but was ambivalent about the idea of one around the place as a permanent fixture. Unlike Causton he did not have dynastic ambitions. *I couldn't care less if my money goes to the Battersea Dogs Home when I die*, Charlie decided. *For me the fun was making it. On that front I've been lucky for my job was also my hobby.* So why had he been so hell-bent on marrying Drusilla? Probably because although she was a woman and as such shaped like one, there was an androgynous quality about her. It was more like being with a comrade in arms than a soft, loving helpmeet.

Finally, 'If I couldn't have you, then I didn't want anybody,' said Charlie gallantly though not entirely accurately. Mollified and therefore gracious, Drusilla said, 'Then that fits in very well. I have decided that my marriage has reached a stage where it needs to be enlivened by a lover and I wondered if you would be interested.'

The hand of the waiter who was currently placing their hors d'oeuvres in front of them perceptibly shook.

'Starting when?' Charlie could hardly believe his luck. 'Tonight?'

'I thought tomorrow night.'

'But what about all that pious stuff about being a married woman?'

'I've changed my mind. We shall, however, have to be discreet.'

'I thought you didn't give a monkey's for discretion.'

'Ordinarily I don't! But the post on offer is Lover *not* Prospective Husband. I wish to go on being married to Hillary. Ergo, there has to be a modicum of circumspection because Hillary wouldn't like this arrangement.'

Too true if that was the way she wanted to play it. Charlie stared at Drusilla in admiration. She wants to have it all ways round. Two tycoons dancing attendance and all options open. Well, suits me, was Charlie's reaction. The temptation to cuckold Causton was not to be resisted.

'So what do you say?'

'I say yes!' Charlie raised his glass. 'Let's eat.'

5

His publisher rang Robert Ormond to enquire after the progress of Alexander Pope.

'He's coming along,' said Robert defensively, wishing they would ring his agent who was a mistress of the dead bat. 'Authoritative was what you said you wanted and I'm doing a great deal of research. I'm sure you'll be pleased when you see the first draft.'

There was an audible sigh of relief at the other end after the words *first draft*. Aware that he had given an erroneous impression of where the whole thing was at, Robert was at a loss as to know what to do about it. His embarrassment was compounded by congratulations on his swift progress and a thoroughly over-optimistic assessment of a possible delivery date. He dickered. Honesty said: Come clean. Tell them where it's really at. Take the pressure off. Get an extension. Prudence said: No, don't. They might cancel the whole thing if they know how much you haven't written. Come on! All you have to do is get down to it!

Prudence won. And after all, he had had a good day yesterday, hadn't he? Six pages had been completed. Never mind the fact that he had thrown five of them away at the end of a reread this morning, it just proved what could be achieved once he had the wind behind him. Pope butted in at this juncture. Pope said,

'You beat your pate, and fancy wit will come;
Knock as you please, there's nobody at home.'

'I'm trying to write your biography, you miserable bastard,' shouted Robert aloud, 'and all you do is undermine me!' *For Christ's sake, keep calm!* Panic swept over him. I need to talk to someone I can trust, thought Robert. I need advice and support. Most of all I need Dorian in my bed – *our* bed – at night.

He rang the number of the *Financial Globe* and when it answered asked for her extension. Dorian answered and the sound of her voice threw him into confusion.

'Dorian. It's Robert.'

40

'Oh. Hello.' Her voice was flat. She did not sound pleased to hear from him. In the face of what sounded like an intransigent attitude he decided not to waste time on the niceties which did not sound as though they would be warmly received anyway, and went for broke.

'I need to see you.'

Need? What about all the times I needed him and was told to get lost because I was getting in the way of bloody Alexander Pope? Old resentments surfaced. Dorian stared into the middle distance.

There was an unnerving silence at the end of which she said reluctantly, 'All right. I don't know when though.'

'What about this evening?'

'Impossible.' There was the sound of pages being turned. She must be going through her diary. 'Wednesday the twelfth, next month, is the earliest I can do.'

'Wednesday the twelfth!' Robert was thunderstruck. Economy dictated that he no longer took a newspaper and these days he usually made a practice of reading *The Times* at the local library. Since this was a paper not remotely interested in minutely chronicling the social scene as frequented by Radley Oates, he was unaware that his wife was currently being squired by a well-known gossip columnist.

'Oh, come on, Dorian! *Nobody* can possibly be booked up solidly for so many weeks!'

'Yes they can. *I* am. Anyway, look, Wednesday the twelfth. That's the earliest. Take it or leave it! What time?'

Bemused, Robert thought, I rang Dorian to beseech her to see me, to ask for a reconciliation and now we're quarrelling again.

'I'll take it.' It seemed he had no alternative. 'What time would suit *you*?' Without having intended to, he was aware of having sounded sarcastic.

'6.30 p.m. Do you want to meet somewhere in town or at your place?'

'*Our* place!'

'All right, your place then. And now if you will forgive me *I* have work to do!' In her turn, Dorian regretted the inflexion. It sounded as though he did not do any. Robert flushed. 'Goodbye, Robert.' She hung up.

'Goodbye,' said Robert into thin air. As usual, Alexander

Pope had it all summed up.

With ev'ry pleasing, ev'ry prudent part,
Say, what can Chloe want? – She wants a heart, opined Pope.

In *his* heart of hearts, Robert knew this to be unfair. Dorian had endured months of filthy temper and uneven behaviour before she finally walked out. But the greatest insult of all was that when she went, he had not tried to stop her. Or even find out where she was. He had just let her go. Owning up to the shortcomings of his own behaviour for the first time, Robert felt ashamed and was honest enough to admit that, given her hectic social life, the inescapable conclusion that she must have somebody else had put him in touch with himself and his feelings for her as nothing else could.

Sitting at her desk at the *Globe*, Dorian felt herself to be in turmoil. My problem, thought Dorian, is that although I still love Robert, at least I think I do, I don't *like* him very much at the moment. It's my view that Alexander Pope has had a distinctly deleterious effect on Robert. She wondered how the biography was going. Going nowhere was probably the answer to that. It was a pity since Robert had a fascination for the period and had long nurtured a desire to write just such a book. Maybe that was the key to it. Maybe instead of writing about the life and times of Alexander Pope he would have been better off just doing the times, at which point he could have diverted himself rather more with Dryden and Congreve et alii. As it was, just before she had finally left, he had seemed to be obsessed with his subject to the point where not only was there no sign of the dispassionate dissecting eye necessary for a successful foray into biography, but he seemed to be mesmerised into mental immobility by Pope, like a rabbit with a stoat. And probably still was. If he was, *if* he was, then she was better off without him.

The telephone rang again. Dorian eyed it warily. She hoped it wasn't Robert. Finally she picked the receiver up. To her relief it was Radley.

'You haven't forgotten we're going to the Ponsonby-Smiths' cocktail party tonight, followed by a black tie bash at Quaglino's?'

'No, of course I haven't,' answered Dorian with something of a sigh. From Pope to the Ponsonby-Smiths seemed like the sublime to the ridiculous, though Pope would probably have appreciated Quaglino's.

'And you've remembered to bring a change of clothes with you?'

'Yes.' Dorian was short. Sometimes Radley treated her like a child.

'Good, good, good! I'll pick you up from the paper at six-fifteen. Ciao!'

Click. He'd gone.

Unaccountably depressed and aware, not for the first time, that Radley's breeziness could get on her nerves, Dorian went back to her work.

Making love to Drusilla was like taking a crash course in gymnastics Charlie discovered. He didn't remember her being quite as athletic but maybe this was because when they last made love all those years ago he had been younger and, more to the point, suppler. Untouched by the rigours of childbirth her body remained much the same and despite her blonde hair she reminded him of nothing so much as the compact and apparently double-jointed Indian women illustrated within the pages of the Kama Sutra. No wonder poor old Hillary seemed to have lost his touch lately if every night was like this. But then, of course, every night was not like this. That was why he was here.

'Would you like another glass of champagne?' Charlie enquired more because he felt in need of a rest than a drink. While he poured it, she sat immodestly cross-legged on his bed, looking around the large bedroom. Looking, in fact, for signs of some sort of feminine touch. She discerned none. Opposite the four poster hung a large oil painting depicting Leda and the Swan which was flanked by mirrored sconces (Georgian?). Unaware of the masquerade, naked, Leda leant away from the predatory, magnificent bird whose powerful wings were spread. Strange subject to choose for a bedroom. There was a sexual deceit, ambivalence even, about this particular myth which was alerting. Yet why be alerted? After all here she was, cheating on Hillary. As was his habit when he was abroad without her, her husband rang each day. Replete with bad behaviour, Drusilla had sounded loving, seductive even on the telephone and claimed to be missing him. In three days' time he would be back.

Charlie returned with the champagne.

'Why are you so keen to stay married to Hillary?' enquired her lover.

'I don't know that I am. It's just that he's *there*. And now you're back in play, the balance is right again.'

Listening to her Charlie became aware that just as he did not want to share the City limelight with Causton, he did not want to share Drusilla either.

'Why don't you leave him and marry me? So much simpler.'

'Not really,' replied Drusilla patiently, 'because if I was married to you, I'd still need Hillary.'

Charlie was mystified. 'Why?'

'Each of you gives me something different without which I would be bored. *Have* been bored. Do you see what I mean? Separately you aren't enough. Together you are.'

Well, no, he didn't really see. What he did see was that, as always, Drusilla wanted to have her cake and eat it. As a successful newspaper tycoon, Charlie had a corresponding ego and did not like the suggestion that he was incomplete without backup from his arch-enemy Causton. No doubt Causton wouldn't have liked it either, but then Causton would never know. Knowing was the problem.

Drusilla put down her champagne. She lightly ran a painted sharp fingernail down Charlie's spine. His own physical response, he noticed with interest, was instantaneous.

'What shall we do next?' asked Drusilla.

The business Hillary Causton had gone to Brussels to conduct took less time than he had anticipated. Had Drusilla been with him they would probably have stayed on for a day or two in his de luxe hotel and sampled whatever was culturally and gastronomically in offer before returning home. The change in his wife's attitude had given Hillary cause for thought. Lately he had begun to feel distinctly disenchanted with his marriage to the point where her decision not to accompany him had come as something of a relief. Maybe all they had needed was some time apart. Marriage could be very claustrophobic even when conducted within the spacious Causton residence.

Hillary rang Drusilla to tell her that he would be returning a day early and got the answer phone. He looked at his watch. At eight o'clock in the morning she should have been there. Perhaps she had forgotten to turn the machine off the night before. Hillary decided not to leave a message and not to telephone again. He would surprise her instead. With this in mind he went shopping, intent on buying his wife a bauble. Drusilla liked jewellery. In the end he settled on a necklace, a choker in the form of a double row of black pearls, and looked forward to her cries of delight when he placed it around her white neck.

The following morning Causton's plane landed at Heathrow at seven o'clock. His chauffeur was there to meet him. With luck, at this comparatively early hour they would have a clear run in and he would arrive at the house around eight-fifteen. Ensconced in the back seat of the Daimler, he opened up that day's edition of his own newspaper and settled down to read it.

When he left Flora Munro's flat after making love to her not once but twice, Hugh Allardyce felt that he must *look* different, that the exaltation he felt must have transfigured him physically. Incredulously he said to himself aloud as he drove, I, boring, respectable Hugh Allardyce, have a young and beautiful mistress! The shame which he had always assumed would be endemic should he ever be unfaithful to his wife simply did not overtake him. Instead Hugh felt liberated as though a thick mist which had long obscured his view had lifted and he could now see far and wide all the way to a promised land. Contrary to what he had hitherto thought, he saw clearly that it was not too late for him.

Having parked the car, Hugh let himself into the house. Patience was in the sitting room, seated at her small walnut desk turning over the contents of a file.

'Hello, darling.' He pecked her on the cheek.

'Hello, darling.' She pecked him back.

The clock struck eleven.

'Good heavens, is that the time?' his wife said absently, her mind clearly on something else. The fête presumably. 'What held you up?'

'All the students went out for a drink,' said Hugh, amazed

that lying was so easy. 'I left them at the pub.'

'Oh, really?' replied his wife, evincing no curiosity at the end of this explanation. There was a silence, then, almost as an afterthought, she added, 'I suppose they are all much younger than you.'

'No, there are quite a few mature students,' said Hugh, as had in fact been the case. Silence fell between them once again. Some days they interacted so little that he wondered if he was really there at all.

'Have you had anything to eat?' asked Patience finally, reluctantly putting the file to one side, and was visibly relieved when Hugh said that he had. He could not help but contrast her stately lack of animation with the joyous vivacity of Flora. As he did it, he knew that it was unfair, that nothing retained its freshness for ever. Although be that as it may, it did raise the question of whether other marriages became quite as flat over the years as his had. And for that, thought Hugh, I have to take my share of the responsibility.

Aloud, he said, 'I'm tired. I think I'll go to bed.'

Without raising her head, Patience said, 'OK. I'll follow you up. I won't be long. I just want to finish this. Oh, and by the way, there's a letter for you. It's on the hall table. Looks official.'

He went and got it. Patience had not opened it. It was one of the unwritten rules of their marriage that, unless specifically asked to do so, they did not open each other's post. Standing by the front door Hugh read it. It informed him that he had been made redundant. His own reaction to something which, however you looked at it, was very bad news surprised him. It was one of shock but there was also an element of elation. It looked like all change.

'Anything interesting?' called Patience from the other room.

'No,' replied Hugh, folding the letter up and putting it in his pocket. 'Nothing interesting.'

He went slowly upstairs.

Unlike Hugh Allardyce, Hillary Causton arrived back to find nobody at home. The marital bed appeared not to have been slept in. The little red eye of the answer phone winked, indicating that there were quite a few messages. Hillary played them back. There was nothing significant and nothing to suggest where Drusilla might be. Disappointment engulfed him. Although she had not known he was coming back today, the fact that she was not here to receive his gift of love immediately displeased him. Used, courtesy of his money and his power, to having every whim gratified on demand, like a child, Causton found himself unable to rise above it. Unsure what to do next, he opened his briefcase and extracted the pearls in their presentation box. Removing the lid he lifted them out and stood, moodily irresolute, letting them run through his fingers.

The slamming of a car door outside brought him to himself.

There she was. At last! He went to the window. It *was* her. Alighting from a Mercedes. Hillary was unable to see who was driving it, but as it moved away from the kerb and she put her key in the lock, he saw the personalised number plate.

CD 1.

Causton stepped back with an exclamation and, as he did so, with a violent gesture wrenched the necklace apart. A shower of black pearls cascaded all over the floor and shot around the room. All that remained in his hands was the gold clasp on either side of which two or three of them were still attached to the thread.

He heard Drusilla enter, walk across the hall and then stop. Presumably she had just seen his case. There was an extended pause and then she opened the drawing-room door and walked in.

In common with other redundancies, Hugh Allardyce was required to leave the Bank the following Friday with a year's salary. He looked upon this as a period of grace. He did not tell Patience the true contents of the letter he had received and continued leaving the house at seven-thirty every morning as if he was still going to the office. He did this because he felt he needed time to think, to come to terms with what he felt to be a much more profound personal change than simply losing his job. To have told Patience would have released a flood of long-suffering nobility followed by a torrent of advice. So he spent his days loafing around London, passing whole mornings and afternoons in art galleries and sometimes in cinemas, trying to decide what

47

to do next and whether he should leave his wife. Courtesy of the mild weather, he ate sandwich lunches in one or other of the parks. It was a strange, footloose sort of existence bizarrely conducted wearing a pin-striped suit, as though he was existing simultaneously in the new life and the old. Sometimes Hugh wondered whether he was having a nervous breakdown but having no previous experience of such a thing, did not know.

He did not tell Flora, whom he now saw twice a week at her flat in place of painting and life drawing, what had happened to him either. Flora intuited that something was amiss but could not begin to guess what it was. Too tactful to ask, she watched Hugh with sympathy and concern. He struck her as curiously detached. Adrift almost. Flora knew that she loved Hugh, was *in* love with Hugh, and that he said he loved her but that was as far as it went and as far as it was likely to go. On the whole, married men did not leave their wives. They did discard their mistresses.

It was Patience who unwittingly brought the whole thing to a head. Patience did something she never normally did. She rang Hugh at the Bank.

'I'm afraid Mr Allardyce is no longer here.'

No longer here?

Patience looked at her watch. Puzzled she said, 'Surely he can't have left for home already. It's only four o'clock!'

'May I ask who would like to speak to him?'

'Mrs Allardyce.' Patience was crisp and totally unprepared for what came next.

An astounded silence greeted this last. Eventually regrouping, the secretary said, 'But Mrs Allardyce, surely you know . . .'

'Know what?'

'Mr Allardyce isn't with the Bank any more. He no longer works here,' she added, underlining it so that there could be no possibility of further confusion. 'He left two weeks ago to be precise.'

Two weeks ago!

In a daze Patience replaced the telephone receiver. Never mind the job, though that was serious enough, what had Hugh been *doing* all day for the last fortnight? And what did he *think* he had been doing? Until he arrived home there was no answer to that. It was Thursday which meant no art class. He would be home at the usual time of 7 p.m. Patience dialled the number of Clarissa Bowen. When it answered she said, 'Clarissa, it's Patience here. I'm afraid I'll be unable to attend the meeting this evening. It's just that something has come up. No, no, nothing serious. Please apologise to the rest of the committee for me would you?'

Afterwards she went to the kitchen to check that there were enough of the cold cuts she had been about to leave out for Hugh for his evening meal to feed both of them. They did not look very appetising, she suddenly noticed, but there were, just, enough.

As a result of the disturbing news she had just been told, Patience found herself unable to concentrate on anything else. She sat down on a chair by the kitchen table and prepared to wait for her husband to return.

'Hillary! Darling! You're back early! How lovely!' Drusilla did not miss a beat as she advanced across the large drawing room. Causton neither moved towards her nor greeted her. So hostile was his aspect that Drusilla stopped in her tracks. As she did so she was aware of crunching something underfoot. She looked down. The carpet appeared to be strewn with small, round beads of unusual hue. How very strange! It was, however, not the time to investigate this phenomenon now.

'Don't I get a kiss?'

'No,' replied Hillary, 'you don't! Where have you been?' There was an even menace about the way he spoke. He looked and sounded dangerous. Aware that she probably had a salvage operation of heroic proportions on her hands, hampered by the fact that she did not know whether or not he had seen Charlie's Mercedes and hoping against hope that he had not, Drusilla decided to sidestep and play for time.

'Darling, I don't understand why you're so cross!'

'Don't you? I'm cross, as you put it, because I've caught you out two-timing me. And since you apparently don't want to answer my question, I'll answer it for you and I'll tell *you* where you've been. You've been with Charlie Davenport.'

This was a disaster. He had seen her getting out of the car.

In the face of this reversal, Drusilla kept her composure though only just.

'Yes, I know how it must look but it's not really what you think at all, Hillary. Not at all! It was all perfectly innocent, I swear! I can explain everything. You must believe me, you really must!' Drusilla was aware of protesting too much. If he asked what the perfectly innocent explanation was she would be in even more trouble for what explanation could there be? Better not to push it. It was, as the saying goes, a fair cop. Unsure what to do next, she stared at him. He did not look convinced. Finally, in desperation, 'Don't you *trust* me?' Hurt, misunderstood bewilderment. The last throw. Try to achieve some sort of physical contact too. She put a hand on her husband's arm.

Causton was brutally dismissive. He brushed it off.

'No I don't and while we're on the subject, Drusilla, *nothing* you do is innocent.' Coldly, he turned away from her. Furious and baffled by his controlled aggression, Drusilla was aware that had he shouted and lost his temper the confrontation would probably have deteriorated into a very physical fight at the end of which they might well have ended up in bed together. At which point, thought Drusilla, I could have, no *would* have, won the day.

Hauteur was the only possible reaction in the face of such a comprehensive vote of no confidence. Very *grande dame*, Drusilla said, 'I regret to tell you, Hillary, that I find your attitude both unchivalrous and insulting.'

'No more chivalry from me,' said Hillary. 'I've shot my bolt on that one where you're concerned. I suggest you get on with feeling insulted and then go and pack!'

'Go and . . .?'

'Pack! I'm going into the office now and when I return I want to find you gone. Is that clear?'

It was very clear. Astounded, and reflecting that he never had had a sense of proportion where Charlie was concerned, Drusilla said, 'Are you saying that our marriage is over? That thirty minutes ends it? Just like that?'

'Just like that! Goodbye, Drusilla.'

He went. Disbelieving, she heard the front door slam. Rage

and humiliation swept over her. The urge to destroy predominated.

Drusilla picked up a substantial Meissen parrot and flung it at the overmantel mirror. Flying through the air for the first and last time in its life it exploded on impact into a hundred pieces. The mirror dramatically cracked. More Meissen was not hard to find. Hillary collected it. It was one of his passions.

'Just as *I* used to be one of his passions.' Drusilla, who was beginning to enjoy herself, spoke aloud. 'So let's go together.'

She threw all of it, varying her targets and in the process scored a very satisfactory hit with a shepherdess on a ponderous oil portrait of Hillary.

'Time to call a halt, I think,' said Drusilla. She pushed back her hair and as she did so caught sight of herself in the fragmented overmantel. Flushed and exhilarated with the exertion she looked better than she had for years.

The car, a Jaguar, was parked in front of the house. Drusilla piled her clothes still on their hangers in the back of it, together with her jewellery and then went back into the house once more. I need something to keep me in my old age, she thought. I married Hillary for richer or for poorer and this is definitely poorer. The obvious choice was the unmatched pair of Claude Lorrain paintings. Picking her way through the remains of the Meissen, towards where they hung to the right and left of the marble fireplace, once again Drusilla trod on something small and round and hard. Reminded of the beads she had noticed all over the floor just before the beginning of the end of her marriage, she stooped and picked one up. Lustrous and cloudy it lay in the palm of her hand. It was, unless she was much mistaken, a black pearl. Without hesitation, Drusilla, who was as grasping of jewellery as of life, dropped to her silken knees and began a trawl of the floor. By the time she had finished she was confident that she had, if not all, nearly all of them. Hillary had either bought her one long string or a two-strand choker. Since she never wore long dangling strings of anything, deeming such things an unchic nuisance, forever getting in the way of whatever it was you were trying to do, the latter seemed more likely. Drusilla laid the pearls out in two equal rows on the coffee table. The mystery of where the clasp had got to was solved when she found it in an ash

51

tray where Hillary had thrown it. Drusilla dropped the whole lot in an envelope which she sealed and tucked into her handbag. She glanced at her watch. A quick getaway was of the essence. She turned her attention to the paintings and decided that probably the most irritating thing she could do would be to take one and leave the other. A single Claude would see anybody's old age out. This raised the question, which? Both were exquisite. One depicted a bevy of nymphs in a pastoral landscape with the winged horse, Pegasus, who was tied to a palm. In the background was the graceful ruin of a classical temple. The canvas radiated the limpid light of early morning. The other depicted Psyche and Cupid in front of Cupid's imposing palace which stood on a hillside overlooking a calm and shining sea in whose waters the orb of an ethereal sun was mirrored.

It was very hard to choose.

In the end, probably because flight was in the forefront of her mind, Drusilla chose Pegasus. With difficulty she lifted the painting down. It was surprisingly heavy. Well aware of its value, she wondered how to pack it. In the end she wrapped the painting up in one of her fur coats and put it in the boot of the Jaguar. Leaving what had been her own front door wide open, she switched on the ignition, dialled Charlie Davenport's number and drove away.

Hugh Allardyce arrived back at seven o'clock precisely, briefcase in hand, just as though he had come from the Bank. The sight of Patience, whom he had not expected to find at home, sitting in the kitchen alerted him.

One look at her face was enough.

'You know,' said Hugh. It was a statement, not a question.

Her reaction was one of reproach followed by incomprehension.

'Why didn't you tell me? I gather it happened two weeks ago. What happened? Why you?' Without waiting for his reply she stood up and led the way into the sitting room.

Following her, Hugh shrugged. 'Everybody knew there were redundancies in the offing. I just never dreamt that one of them would be me. I can only suppose that my performance must have been rather more lacklustre than I realised.'

Patience was affronted. 'But I thought you were one of their high fliers!'

'Apparently not.' Hugh was dry. Actually, he thought, at the beginning I *was* but as my marriage atrophied so, I suspect, did my approach to my job. Meeting Flora has made me realise that I have been bored stiff for years. With an effort he refocused his attention on what his wife was saying. As he had feared it was nobility in the face of adversity to the platitudinous fore.

'We shall overcome,' Patience intoned. 'It will be a difficult time but you can rely on my support. After all we are a team!' She decided to overlook the curious fact that half the team had not been told what had happened when it happened. They could discuss that later when he had been re-established. The disquieting spectre of a triumphant gloating Margaret Harris rose before her inner eye. 'And I think you're quite right to have kept the whole thing quiet. When you've got another job, we'll announce the fact. No need for anybody to know how and why it came about.'

'I'm not sure I want another job in banking,' said Hugh. 'Or in the City, come to that.'

Patience was astounded.

'What else would you do? Besides we need the income. Oh no, you must find another job as soon as possible. There can be no question about it.'

Her irritating certainty that she knew what was best for him settled it. Doubt evaporated and the way forward was suddenly obvious.

'What for? The children's school fees are being paid courtesy of my mother's estate. You could get a job!'

'A job?' Patience was aghast. 'But I have a job. I am a wife and mother.'

'Well, why not?' Hugh decided to get it all off his chest. 'Other wives and mothers work. You've got a brain. Instead of terrorising those miserable women on the church committee you could be cutting a swathe through the upper echelons of the Civil Service. Bossing them around *and* getting paid for it. In any case it's my view that it's time we went our separate ways. You won't miss me. We haven't communicated in any meaningful sense for years.'

The ominous implications of the words *it's time we went our separate ways* followed by *you won't miss me* began to sink in.

'What do you mean, I won't miss you?'

'I mean, I'm leaving! We'll sell the house, and divide the proceeds. You'll have to move into something smaller.' Listening to the sound of his own unemotional voice speaking the words, Hugh thought: It's the only way to do this. If I don't break away now I never will. It is no coincidence that with the advent of Flora has come the loss of my job. A few months ago I would have regarded the latter as catastrophic. Now I see it as a release.

The light was beginning to fail. Hugh rose and put on one of the table lamps. Abruptly Patience stood up and turned away from him. She probably did not want him to see her face.

'I implore you to reconsider. Not to do this!'

Her hands convulsively twisted and untwisted the rope of pearls he had given her following the birth of one of the children. Cordelia. It was symptomatic of their very unphysical marriage that while beseeching him not to leave she did not attempt to touch him. Hugh did not directly answer her, but only said, 'I'd better go and pack.'

'But where will you . . .?' Then, as the key to it all dawned on her, 'You've got somebody else! You have, haven't you? How *could* you do such a thing to your children!' In anguished outrage Patience jerked the pearls which broke and another necklace showered all over the polished floor boards with a brittle reverberation like rain striking glass.

Pearls are for tears.

Neither of them took any notice.

The children. Of course Hugh had thought about the children. Had thought about them endlessly in fact. But Cordelia and Christian were about to leave home. To all intents and purposes *had* left home, had left home in fact the day Patience had packed them both off to boarding school.

Hugh was uncharacteristically firm. 'The children are almost grown up. They have their own lives ahead of them. I must consider mine, what's left of it.'

'And what about *my* life?'

'*You* must consider your life. What you do with it next is down to you. Look I think I'd better go.'

'*Please* don't!'

'I think I better had.'

Patience heard him moving about upstairs. Half an hour later the front door quietly closed behind him. He had gone. Shaking, she went into the kitchen. She threw the cold cuts away and then went and sat down again at the table in the chair she had been occupying when he came home. The telephone rang and was ignored. Hot tears began to fall.

'I don't understand it!' sobbed Patience. 'I've been the perfect wife and mother and done my best for the community. I just don't understand where I went wrong.' It was one o'clock in the morning before she finally went to bed.

Hugh left the car for Patience. Carrying his large suitcase he trudged off in the direction of the nearest taxi rank and was relieved when, halfway there, he succeeded in flagging one down. The back of the cab was dark and quiet. Mercifully the cabby was not one of the garrulous variety. It was a relief to be out of the line of fire. Hugh could hardly believe what he had just done. He supposed that he and Patience had had a row. Though like the rest of an anodyne marriage it had been bloodless. He wondered what the children's attitude would be. Perhaps they would side with their mother to the point where they would not want to see him again. Hugh felt suddenly exhausted. There would be a great deal to disentangle and of course he would have to look for another job. Patience had been quite right about that.

The cab drew to a halt. Hugh got out, heaved his suitcase on to the pavement and paid the driver. Flora's semi-basement flat fronted onto a small square. The air smelt of newly mown grass and a scented shrub that he could not identify. Hugh and Xerxes arrived on Flora's doorstep together. A light was on. She must be in. He rang the bell.

Charlie, who was spending the day working from home, discovered himself to be less than ecstatic to find Drusilla on *his* doorstep. She was carrying something large and rectangular wrapped up in what looked like mink. He took it from her, examining the contents as he did so.

'Good God!' exclaimed Davenport. 'Is this yours?'

'It is,' replied Drusilla, 'by which I mean it used to be mine and Hillary's. *With half my worldly goods I thee endow*. This is half of a pair of Claude Lorrain paintings. Aren't you going to ask me in?'

Charlie blinked. What would have happened to Leda and the Swan in similar circumstances? Presumably she would have cut it in two. It occurred to him that getting what he had always thought he wanted might not prove to be unalloyed delight.

6

In spite of the fact that she spent most nights at Radley Oates'
Knightsbridge flat, Dorian Ormond had retained her own and
usually went by there once or twice a week to pick up her post.
It was during the course of one of these visits that she discovered
a letter from her sister. The writing was unmistakable. Patience
wrote in biro, which Dorian disliked, in a round, upright hand
of great clarity. Ts were immaculately crossed and Is punctil-
iously dotted. Reading one of her letters was like being told
something very loudly and very slowly as though one was at best
a benighted foreigner or at worst a bear of small brain. It was
totally different from Dorian's own which rushed across the
page in a harum scarum fashion and frequently ran up the side
and along the top when space threatened to run out. Warily
Dorian looked at it and then, with something of a sigh, slit the
envelope open. She felt it boded no good. After a momentary
hesitation she extracted the sheet of paper, opened it up and
began to read.

My dear Dorian, wrote Patience,
  *We have not always seen eye to eye so no doubt you will be
surprised to receive this letter. I am writing to you because I
feel I have no one else to turn to. In spite of our differences we
are sisters and as such perhaps it is time to put past pettiness
aside.* (She must want something very badly indeed to
write like this, reflected Dorian. Intrigued she let her eye
run on down the page.) *What has happened is that Hugh has
left me!* (Good God!) *I can hardly tell you what a shock this
was.* (It's a shock to me as well. I never would have thought
nice, boring old Hugh had it in him. She went back to the
letter.) *This all happened two weeks ago and coincided with
the loss of his job.* (!) *Since then I have learnt that he is living
with a woman called Flora Munro who is an artist.* (What!
Hugh has a mistress! An *artist* moreover. How on earth

57

had Hugh managed to stray into the land of Bohemia? How had Patience managed to let him? Well, well!) *Dorian, I honestly think Hugh has gone mad. He is refusing to come home and I am beside myself with worry. I do not know what to do for the best. I am putting off telling the children in the hope that he will come to his senses and our life will go back to being what it was.* (Some hope, reflected Dorian, reading this. Hugh's been oppressed for years. I should have thought that the chances of him going back, now he's out from under, would be zero.) *Dorian, Hugh has always had a very high regard for you.* (Has he?) *Would you* . . . (Oh no! Oh heavens, here it came!) *. . .go and see him for me? I know he will listen to you. You are the only person who might be able to break the hold That Woman has on him and make him see sense.* There was more in the same frantic uncomprehending vein plus Hugh's new address. It ended, *Please ring me as soon as you receive this letter. Your loving sister Patience.*

That was a step forward at any rate. Up until now *your disapproving sister Patience* would have been more like it. Mulling the whole thing over, Dorian stood and looked out of the window. There was no telephone number with Hugh's address. Perhaps, because he did not want long harangues punctuated with martyred tears, he had thought better of giving one to Patience. It meant that she would have to go and visit Hugh on the off chance that he was in. On the other hand, given the fact that he apparently no longer had a job, presumably her brother-in-law was in these days more than he was out. She got out her diary and leafed through it. I'll go on Thursday, at lunchtime, decided Dorian, and if he isn't in I'll leave a note asking him to make contact via the office. But I should definitely see Hugh first and spy out the lie of the land and not just for my sister's benefit either. If the marriage is irrevocably over and I'm going to have to tell Patience and then stick her together again, like Humpty Dumpty, I'd rather know.

Thursday came and Dorian went.

He was in. And so was That Woman. She it was who answered the door.

'I hope I've got the right house,' said Dorian. 'I'm looking for

58

Hugh Allardyce. I'm his sister-in-law.'

Startled, Flora stepped back a pace.

'It's all right! I'm not here to make a scene.'

From inside the flat she could hear Hugh calling, 'Who is it, Flora?'

'Your sister-in-law.' Flora looked questioningly at Dorian. I'm afraid I don't know your . . .'

'Dorian Ormond,' said Dorian.

'Dorian Ormond,' called back Flora.

Hugh appeared by her side. He said, 'Do you mind if Dorian comes in?'

'No, of course not.' Flora stood aside to let her pass. 'I'll make a cup of tea, shall I?' Tactfully she went into the kitchen, leaving the two of them alone.

Hugh and Dorian looked at one another.

At last she said, 'So you've really left.'

'Yes. Are you shocked?'

'Why would I be shocked? As you know the state of my own marriage is hardly an example to the rest of the world.' Dorian was wry. 'I've been deputed to come here to appeal to your better nature, to find out if there is any chance of you changing your mind.'

'None whatever!' said Hugh. There was not a trace of hesitation. Which in one sense was a relief. An hour of indecision on the one hand, on the other hand would have been trying. It seemed there were no pros and cons to weigh up. 'Why don't you sit down?' He gestured towards the armchair and as he did so picked up a comatose Xerxes who registered his objection to the move by turning himself into a dead weight like a protester at a peace rally.

Dorian sat down. 'Then that's that!' The Persian got on her knee and, making a point, sat on Dorian sitting on his chair.

'Push him off if you don't want him,' said Hugh.

'No, I like cats,' replied Dorian, stroking Xerxes's bushy head. 'Look I'm not here to persuade you one way or the other. I'm here because Patience asked me to come to find out if there was any hope. Frankly I feel how you conduct your marriage is none of my business.'

Hugh remembered how Patience had interfered or tried to

when Dorian and Robert had split up and how, in the middle of the resulting mayhem, he wished she had had the common sense to pursue a similarly non-interventionist policy.

'There is no hope!' said Hugh.

'What are you going to do?' She looked around. 'This room is charming, by the way.'

'Isn't it?' Hugh's face lit up, his delight in accepting a compliment on behalf of his mistress evident. Hugh is in love, thought Dorian, probably for the first time in his life and that being the case all Patience's tenacity isn't going to get him back. Flora entered with a tray. She proceeded to pour tea out of a distressed Minton teapot into distressed Minton cups. Afterwards she sat down beside Hugh on the Chesterfield. Looking at the two of them together, Dorian mentally wished them luck. She estimated Flora to be in her late twenties, early thirties maybe. The telephone rang in the room next door and Hugh got up to answer it.

When he had gone, Flora said, 'I hope you don't think I was the direct cause of the breakup of your sister's marriage.'

'But you were having an affair with him,' observed Dorian, 'which presumably didn't help.'

'Lots of married men have affairs. They just don't tell their wives. I didn't ask Hugh to leave and I didn't expect him to. I thought he was just another one of those. Until he turned up on my doorstep, that was. I didn't know he'd lost his job either. He wasn't very happy, you know.'

No, Dorian dared say he wasn't. There had been the look of someone enduring rather than living about Hugh for years. There was an artlessness, naivety even, about Flora which was attractive. Flora was not the hardbitten gold digger which Patience no doubt supposed her to be. If Dorian was right she would make Hugh feel good about himself and who, except for Patience, was to say that that was a bad thing? She smiled at Flora. 'I know,' said Dorian. 'But be that as it may, I'm not here on a mission to judge. I'm on a mission to find out and report back. It's something I'm not looking forward to doing.' Changing the subject and noting some canvases stacked against the wall, she said, 'I gather you're a painter. I'd love to see some of your work.'

Flora rose. She lifted up the canvases and propped them up

60

around the room. Three, which were still lifes, were obviously by the same hand. The fourth was not. It was an unfinished nude of Flora herself.

Dorian smiled at her. 'This is you!'

'Yes. Painted by Hugh.'

By *Hugh*!

It was nothing like as accomplished as the other three and yet, as Dorian examined it, she was aware of something latent, something there.

'I didn't know Hugh could draw,' said Dorian.

'Neither did Hugh!' riposted Flora. 'There's a lot we don't know about ourselves unless we look for it. When I met him, Hugh was ossified.'

Ossified. What a very good word. That's exactly what Hugh had been. He wasn't ossified now though.

The subject of their conversation entered the room. Dorian looked at her watch.

'I have to be going.'

Escorting her to the door, Hugh said, 'How is Robert?'

'Still wrestling with Alexander Pope. As somebody else famously said, there were three of us in that marriage.' On the threshold she paused and turned.

'Do you know,' observed Hugh, noticing it for the first time, 'you look completely different.' He kissed her on the cheek.

'So,' said Dorian, 'do you.'

With a wave she was gone.

The following morning, Dorian told Radley that he would have to get through the evening without her company. Typically Radley complained first and asked why afterwards. Radley said, 'Oh, fuck. Are you sure? I *hate* going to that sort of function on my own!' He did not, Dorian noticed, say 'without *you*.'

'Well, just for once you'll have to!' Dorian was brisk. 'After all, the night we met you didn't have anyone else in tow.'

He was gloomy. 'No, and look what happened. I met you and now you're about to leave me on my own again. It's not fair. This date's been in our joint diaries for weeks!'

Dorian felt exasperated. This was like dealing with a five-year-old.

'Don't you want to know *why* I'm not coming?'

'I suppose so.' Radley was grudging. 'All right, *why* aren't you coming?'

His lack of interest in anybody's problems but his own appeared to be total. Dorian was aware of the existing cracks in their relationship widening.

'My sister wrote to me to tell me that her husband has just left her. I'm going to go and see her.'

'Oh, is that all!' The social world observed by Radley was strewn with the wreckage of shattered marriages. Surely one more couldn't make any difference. It suddenly occurred to him that he had not, in fact, known that his lover *had* a sister.

'I didn't know you had a . . .'

'Sister? That's because I never see her. We fell out ages ago.'

'Then why bother?' It was hard to believe anyone could be so predictable.

'Because,' intoned Dorian patiently, 'it was a conciliatory letter and she is bereft.'

'Which means *I* shall be bereft instead.'

Christ, his mother had a lot to answer for. Dorian discovered herself to be out of patience with it. Via her memory Alexander Pope inserted his own view into her mental assessment of Radley. *A brain of feathers and a heart of lead*, Pope opined cruelly.

'Look, Radley, I'm going and that is that.' There was an awful inflexibility about the way she delivered it which caused Radley, who had opened his mouth with the aim of registering another protest, to close it again. Perhaps taking an interest would be advisable. Instead he said, 'What does she do? Your sister I mean?'

'Oh, she lives in a well-heeled suburb of London where she performs good works, and has two children plus a husband called Hugh who's a banker. You know the sort of thing.'

Radley did, though he would have preferred not to. He rolled his eyes. *Worthy* was the unfortunate word which came to mind. It occurred to him that some women would have expected him to accompany them on what sounded like a stupefyingly dull errand of mercy. All in all maybe he had had a lucky escape. On balance, he decided to cheer up.

Dorian looked at her watch. Eight o'clock.

'I'd better be going.' She drank her coffee at a swallow. 'Aren't you deigning to go into the office today?'

Still sitting at the breakfast table clad in monogrammed towelling, her lover said, 'I thought I'd do some work at home this morning.' They both knew he would not. Do any work, that was. Passing through the front door, Dorian thought: We really are an odd couple. With every day that passes we get more and more like a caricature of the fable of the grasshopper and the ant. I'm surprised Hillary Causton puts up with it. Or maybe all gossip columnists were like that. Maybe Radley's indolence was simply par for the course.

She let herself out into the street and rejoined the stream of other ants all making their way to the teeming heap that was the City. Everybody was walking in the same direction, making for Knightsbridge station. At six o'clock they would all be walking back again. There was an invigorating blue freshness about the air. The leaves on the trees were emerald and very still and the grey London flagstones at this hour were cool. As she stepped out, Dorian reflected on the chequered family history of her sister and herself. I am not looking forward to seeing Patience, thought Dorian, but I must do it. I owe it to both of us. Even to herself she did not sound convincing. On the principle that sufficient unto this evening is the sticky interview thereof, she decided to face it when she had to and not before. Instead she let her mind dwell on the subject of Robert, also estranged. What to do about Robert was the next question. Here Pope butted in again. Not surprising when one considered that he had been an integral part of their marriage for its final year.

Men, some to Bus'ness, some to Pleasure take;
But ev'ry Woman is at heart a Rake;
Men, some to Quiet, some to public Strife;
But ev'ry Lady would be Queen for life, sniffed Pope.

Oh, shut up! was Dorian's internal response to that. It's *your* fault that we're currently separated.

Mentally shrugging him off, she descended the steps into the Underground.

Dorian's first sight of her sister for months quite shocked her.

Normally svelte and well-groomed without a hair out of place, today Patience looked as if she had not combed hers for a week. With an effort she managed, or hoped she managed, not to let her dismay show. Warily they embraced. As she followed her sister into the drawing room, Dorian noticed that she was wearing *carpet slippers*. The rest of the world of course wore them to rest their aching feet at the end of a long day pounding city pavements or the like, but never Patience. Patience despised, or used to despise, carpet slippers deeming them sloppy.

'Would you like a drink, Dorian?'

'Yes, please. A gin and tonic would do it.'

Narrowly she watched Patience as she made it. Patience was moving very slowly like a somnambulist. Presumably there had been a lot of sleepless nights. Stretching out her hand to take the proffered glass, Dorian saw that her sister was not wearing any makeup and looked colourless as though life as she was currently living it had drained her. There was no sign of her famous certainty. Pity and concern struggled for supremacy within Dorian. Not love though. Too much had happened between them for that to re-emerge quite so soon. Perhaps it never would.

Silence fell between them. Dorian had the feeling that, reluctant to hear the worst (and it was the worst), Patience dreaded asking her about her meeting with Hugh. Equally I dread telling her, thought Dorian. It had to be done though. She braced herself. She could think of no tactful means of reporting what had happened. Trying to marshal her thoughts she stared into her drink giving it a little shake so that the translucent slice of lemon spun and the ice cubes struck the Waterford crystal causing a faint musical reverberation. In the end, 'As you requested I did go and see Hugh . . .' she started off. She hesitated.

Patience leant forward. 'And?'

This was awful.

'. . . and he was adamant that the marriage is over. I'm so sorry, Patience.'

With a resurgence of her old positive attitude, Patience said, 'It's early days. I'm sure he'll change his mind. Over the years Hugh and I between us have built an edifice on the survival of which two other lives depend. He would be mad to throw all that away.'

64

Listening to it, Dorian was unconvinced. The word edifice was unfortunate. It made her marriage sound like a mausoleum rather than a joint endeavour of flesh and blood. Patience was continuing. 'And I'm sure, Dorian, when you put it to him like that, he will see sense.' *When I . . . ?* Dorian was aghast. 'Hugh is a very honourable man who has been well looked after all his married life. Love in a garret will not suit him.'

It was, Dorian noted, the first time love had received a mention. Patience had explored her marital predicament from every practical and material angle but it was only with an oblique reference to Flora, otherwise known as That Woman, that love had entered the equation. And that was why, if he did have any sense, Hugh would cut loose now, while he had the choice.

Dorian said, 'Patience, please don't misunderstand me when I say that I cannot be responsible for brokering a reconciliation between you and Hugh. Only the two of you can do that, if he wants to.'

'Are you saying you won't help me?' The old accusatory Patience was momentarily back.

'No. I'm saying I can't, which is quite different. Apart from anything else you'll both have to meet if only to decide what to say to the children. Isn't it half term quite soon?'

'Yes. Next week, I think.'

Next *week* she *thought*! Normally Patience was right on top of that sort of thing. Dorian made a mental note to remind Hugh, whose telephone number she now had, and point out that it was essential that he and Patience thrashed out what was going to happen next before then.

Trying to reiterate and instil the idea that perhaps he would not return, so that when it happened it would not come as quite such a shock, Dorian said, 'What are you going to do if it turns out that the whole thing has irretrievably broken down?'

'Let me get you another drink.' Patience took Dorian's empty glass from her and bore it away. Over her shoulder she said, 'I thought I'd try counselling!'

This was so unexpected that Dorian gaped. It was, in fact, her opinion that there was too much counselling around these days. People had got out of the habit of falling back on their own resources and went for counselling instead at the drop of a hat.

65

On the other hand this did seem like one of those occasions where a little self-knowledge might be very useful and pave the way for a more satisfactory future.

'I think that's a brilliant idea,' enthused Dorian. 'It will help you come to terms with what has happened and rebuild your . . .' (the temptation to say edifice was almost irresistible) '. . . life.'

Patience looked at her sister as if she were mad.

'I meant train to do it *myself*, not receive it. Why should I need counselling? No, no! I feel myself to be in a unique position to advise others, to dispense it. What about some food?'

Over supper they talked over certain aspects of their joint past. Dorian was constantly struck how two perceptions of the same incident could vary so fundamentally. There was no point in having a fight about it now, however. Between them they drank a bottle of wine and by the end of the meal Patience's spirits had lifted considerably. As she was finally leaving, Dorian said, 'What about your friends and colleagues at the church? I expect they've been very supportive?'

'After a fashion,' came the enigmatic answer. 'They seem to think that with the domestic crisis it was all too much for me to cope with and insisted that I stepped down, temporarily of course, as chairperson. They were trying to be helpful, though I'm quite certain I could have coped.' She did not add that she had told Laura Fitzwilliam in strictest confidence what had happened and that two days later the whole committee seemed to know all about it. After which, with the best possible humanitarian motives of the sort with which Patience herself was all too familiar, they had voted her out.

It did not sound like a very helpful move to Dorian. She wondered if Patience was telling her the whole story. Usually people who had a crisis to cope with, domestic or otherwise, benefited from having something to do rather than sitting on their own within four walls all day. It seemed odd that eight female pillars of the church, in the form of the committee, all presumably dedicated to the pursuit of faith, hope and charity, especially charity, had not discerned this. Perhaps, on the other hand, they had not wanted to.

On the doorstep the two sisters embraced.

Watching Dorian walk away and briefly distracted from her obsession with herself and her own woes as she did so, Patience suddenly noticed that her sister looked completely different. Gone was the unflattering Virginia Woolf get-up with the inevitable droopy cardigan. In its place Dorian was wearing a short black shift dress and matching coat. Even her hair, generally agreed to be unmanageable, had been reinvented as a burnished, svelte bob. Unable to stop herself, Patience called after her, 'You've changed!'

At the gate, Dorian stopped and turned. All she said was, 'I know!' and then, with a smile, she was gone.

7

At the behest of his wife, Hugh Allardyce went back to the house he had lived in for the past twenty years, so that the two of them could tell the children what was about to happen. Walking up the path to what had until lately been his own front door, Hugh was struck by his sense of detachment. It could have been anybody's house. Although he still possessed a key, he rang the bell. After a short interval Patience opened it. She had lost weight, he noticed, but otherwise looked the same as usual and had, in fact, taken a lot of trouble with her appearance prior to his arrival. Without a greeting she stood aside to let him pass.

It was difficult to know what to do. Normally Hugh would have kissed her, probably on the cheek. However, in the present circumstances it occurred to him that even this innocuous gesture might be misunderstood. In the end he did not do anything. They both began to speak and both stopped. Then, 'After you!' 'No, after you!' Left with the initiative after this small ritual of good manners in a situation where otherwise they had broken down completely, Patience bit her lip. After a moment's hesitation she said in a low, urgent voice, 'Are you quite sure you want to go through with this? There's still time to change your mind.' She fixed her eyes on Hugh's face. He could feel the power of her ferocious will. In the face of this onslaught he recoiled.

'I'm sure,' replied Hugh, avoiding her intense gaze and feeling shifty as he did so. 'Quite sure. Whatever we had,' (very little in actual fact) 'it's gone. I'm sorry!'

Sorry.

The sheer inadequacy of the word filled him with a mixture of guilt and shame, but what else was there to say? Another baffled pause ensued. He sensed the depth of her chagrin.

'Where are the children? And why are we whispering?' whispered Hugh.

Patience put one finger to her lips and said, 'Ssssh!' in a very irritated way. 'Keep your voice down! In the drawing room.

Obviously we don't want them to hear this conversation!' No, he supposed they didn't, although if he stood his ground they were shortly going to hear another one very like it.

'But never mind *where* are the children,' she resumed, vehemently, 'what *about* the children? Don't you *care* about your own children?' By now practically hissing, Patience verged suddenly and unexpectedly on the melodramatic. The phrase *milking the situation for all it was worth* crossed his mind and was dismissed as unfair. Until her next action, that was. In certain works of literature it was quite common for women to wring their hands, though it was something Hugh had never encountered in real life. He was fascinated to see Patience wring hers now and was reminded of her noisy, attention-seeking, attitude-striking mother. Watching it, he experienced a sudden mental click. It was as though a glass wall had dropped between his former persona and his new one, sealing him off from the old Hugh, Hugh the henpecked husband, whose finer feelings urged him to bow before this assault on his better nature. Behind it was the new liberated Hugh, whose mantra these days, intoned over and over to himself, was: What about *me*?

He suddenly became aware that Patience, furious and *sotto voce*, was asking, 'Are you listening, Hugh?' Hugh jumped and refocused on his wife.

In an indignant whisper, 'Yes, I am,' he lied, finding achieving a full and frank exchange in an undertone exhausting. It was like trying to have a row in a very strict library.

'What have you told them?'

'*I? I've* told them nothing! Except the fact that you've managed to lose your job!' The way this was said made Hugh sound careless. 'They don't know what is about to happen. I simply said we both needed to talk to them.'

'What!' Hugh was aghast. 'You haven't prepared them in any way!'

'It isn't me who wants to leave,' said Patience, 'it's you.' She unexpectedly changed tack and became placatory. It was as though accusatory Patience had stepped aside for the moment in order to let tractable Patience in. 'I've been hoping against hope that you would change your mind. Why don't you? We need never refer to this again.'

He had forgotten how very tenacious she could be. He thought of Flora with love and desire. The word Love, he noticed, had never crossed Patience's lips. In this context they might as well have been speaking a foreign language. It appalled him to think that this was the one they had employed throughout twenty years of marriage.

'It's out of the question.' Still whispering but somehow managing to sound firm, authoritative even, he was aware that on the other side of the glass even-tempered, anything-to-avoid-an-argument alter ego Hugh was growing fainter, fading in fact to the point of extinction.

'But I thought maybe once we were all together again . . . Oh, Hugh *please*.' Frightened by his inflexibility and desperate to change his mind, Patience found herself forced into physical contact. She took his hand. '*Please!*' she reiterated. Reflecting that there is nothing worse than a loving overture, even one as minimal as this, bestowed by someone with whom one is no longer in love and, as in his case, actively trying to escape from, Hugh resisted the unkind impulse to withdraw it. His hand lay inert and unresponsive within hers.

This is awful, thought Hugh, just awful.

Receiving no encouragement she eventually released him. Hugh hardened his heart against her stricken look. Neither of them could find anything to say. *I must get this over with.* Finally, in normal tones he said, 'Let's go and tell the children, shall we?' *Oh, God, now I sound almost jocular!* To forestall further debate, he turned and led the way.

While this pianissimo dialogue had been taking place in the hall, Christian and Cordelia who were sitting beside each other in the drawing room were having a discussion of their own. Christian, a tall, lanky youth with Hugh's *Salad Days* good looks, though these were marred by a weak mouth, sprawled in one of the armchairs.

'What on earth do you think they're doing?' said Cordelia, who was biting her fingernails, a habit Patience abhorred.

'If you really want to know what I think, *I* think they're about to tell us that they're getting divorced,' said Christian sounding bored. 'Why else would there be all this secrecy? And anyway if everything's hunky dory, then where was Dad last night?'

The same thought had crossed his sister's mind. Cordelia said, 'Mummy doesn't believe in divorce.'

'Mum's only half the equation. Everyone does it,' said Christian, two-thirds of whose form mates at the school they both went to were the product of broken marriages. 'If you still have two parents living together people think you're odd these days.'

'I do hate it when you try to sound blasé.' His sister flushed and looked away. Cordelia knew that she looked like her mother, albeit on a more willowy scale, and now was conscious of sounding like her as well. Christian opened his mouth to jeer, 'You read too much romantic fiction,' when the door opened and the subjects of their discussion entered the room. It was the first time Cordelia had seen her parents together since she and her brother had arrived the previous evening and the moment she set eyes on them she knew that Christian was right. There was an aura of martyrdom, of chaste, irreproachable womanhood spurned about her mother's folded hands and dignified sorrowful mien. Whereas her father had an air of sombre, solitary resolution. The emotional distance between the two of them was so pronounced as to be almost tangible. Christian shot a triumphant look at Cordelia. See what I mean? said the look.

Embracing first his daughter and then his son, Hugh thought: Christ, I hope they can find it in their hearts to forgive me. Aloud he, he said, 'Why don't we all sit down?' Then, without preamble, clearly and concisely, he told them. He omitted any mention of Flora. At the end of what was a comparatively short speech there was a profound lull, probably born out of intense embarrassment. This was a family which was unaccustomed to talking out its feelings and nobody knew quite what to do next. Patience twisted her wedding ring round and round her finger. Eventually Hugh spoke again.

'Everything will go on as before,' said Hugh, more to break the silence than anything, 'except that I shall be living elsewhere.'

Cordelia spoke for the first time. 'But won't this house have to be sold?'

'It's my intention to try and avoid that at least until you've both left home. I repeat, everything will go on as before except that I shall be living somewhere else.'

71

'With another woman!' Patience was able to contain herself no longer. Her voice was high-pitched. Everyone looked away. Unsuccessful supplication had metamorphosed into ire. Hugh, who had intended to leave the sensitive subject of Flora until a more propitious moment, found himself flushed out. Warily he eyed his wife, conscious of the fact that she might be about to indulge herself in a display of the sort of histrionics to which her stagey mother had been prone. To his relief she appeared to regain control and, just as suddenly as she had spoken, she subsided again.

'Daddy . . .?' Cordelia turned a shocked, blue gaze on her parent.

'It's true.' Hugh did not elaborate and hoped he would not be required to. No doubt he could safely leave Patience to do that when he had gone.

Christian whistled under his breath, revising his opinion of his father upwards as he did so, for who would have thought the old man still had it in him? Cordelia rose to her feet and went and sat beside Patience. She put her arm around her mother's shoulders. As a result of her action Hugh's family were now all in a row facing him, or, rather, ranged against him.

Patience said unexpectedly, 'Hugh, if you insist on pursuing this course of action and abandoning us, *I* shall insist on putting this house on the market and moving to London.' The spectre of a gloating Margaret Harris telling all mutual friends and committee members how very sorry she was for *poor* Patience was not to be borne. The emotive use of the word abandon caused Cordelia to begin to cry which in turn caused Hugh to feel even more of a bastard than he felt already. At the mention of the capital, Christian, who had said nothing at all up to now but just listened slumped in his chair, became interested. Currently incarcerated in a very traditional boarding school whence he came home to the suburbs in the holidays, Christian was fascinated by the bright lights of the city.

'I think moving to London is a brilliant idea,' said Christian.

'And I think you're heartless,' sobbed Cordelia. 'You don't care that the family is breaking up, you just care what's in it for you!'

'Oh, don't be such a drip,' said Christian. 'If Dad is determined to leave, like Mum I don't see any point in going on mouldering here.'

More heartrending weeping followed the use of the word leave.

'I don't understand it,' cried Cordelia. 'I simply don't understand it!' Speaking to Hugh, she continued, 'You've told us the fact but not the reason. I don't understand *why* you're doing this. Mummy doesn't want it, I know she doesn't!'

Christian cast his eyes to heaven. Watching his son, Hugh thought: Notwithstanding his age, there are times when Christian would benefit from a bloody good hiding. Now, however, was not the moment. He addressed himself carefully to Cordelia instead.

'Mummy and I have been together a long time. We still love each other but we are no longer *in* love . . .'

Intent on sabotaging the last and at the same time gaining the moral high ground, Patience said, '*I* still in love with *you*!'

This provoked fresh torrents of tears. Cordelia appeared inconsolable. 'There you are! There you are!'

'No, Cordelia, there you aren't.' Speaking as to an idiot, Christian was scathing. 'Because Dad doesn't love Mum any more. He loves somebody else.'

Hugh winced. As statements of fact go, this was particularly bald and afforded Patience the Niobe-like opportunity to dab her eyes with a small lace handkerchief of the sort Hugh had never seen her use before. Perhaps she had bought it specially. Largely because it was impossible to go on lamenting quite so energetically for very long, Cordelia began to show signs of calming down. Encouraged by this Hugh was moved to try and achieve the end of his sentence.

'. . . because over the years we have grown apart. Our marriage has,' here he groped for the word and eventually came up with, 'calcified.'

Both women dissolved into tears again. Christian said, with something of a smirk, 'Dad, I don't know what you mean.'

It was at this point that Hugh surprised himself and everybody else by losing his temper.

'I mean,' shouted Hugh, 'that it's all of ten years since your mother and I last had a fuck! Understand? And now I think I'd better go.'

73

He went. In the wake of his departure there was dead silence.

When Hugh arrived back at the flat it was ten o'clock. Flora was painting and listening to Vivaldi. The subject was a blue and white soup tureen (cracked) which was filled with oranges and lemons. Behind it stood a jug, also blue and white and also cracked, filled with large creamy daisies whose centres echoed the vibrant yellow of the lemons. Xerxes, who was sitting among the tubes of paint washing his face with one paw, monitored the arrival of his mistress's lover with a jealous green eye. Hugh's gaze lingered on the fruit. The density of its colour caused it almost to appear illuminated from within. A small everyday miracle, it glowed. It was the sort of thing he would never have noticed before. The arrival of Flora in his life had altered the way Hugh looked at even the most ordinary objects. She had taught him how to see.

Flora put down her paintbrush. She smiled at him. He took her in his arms and kissed her. Huffed, Xerxes leapt off the table and stalked out.

'How was it?'

'It was excruciating.' Hugh moved away from her, sat down in Xerxes' armchair and put his head in his hands. Resuming her painting, Flora said, 'How did your children take it?'

Hugh raised his head. He looked strained and very tired.

'At first it was almost as though they were expecting it.' The memory of Cordelia's accusing blue gaze meeting his own before she rose and put a protective arm around her mother shamed him. 'Then Cordelia had hysterics.' Hugh did not tell Flora that the revelation of her own existence had precipitated this. 'I made an awful hash of telling them. Patience didn't make it any easier, but then why should she? As she rightly pointed out, the one causing all the mayhem is me.'

'You shouldn't be too hard on yourself,' observed Flora, who was currently concentrating on reproducing the willow pattern on the side of the tureen. 'There is no blueprint for passing on that sort of bad news. The main thing is to be sure that you are doing the right thing.' She shot him a bright sidelong look. 'After all it's a big step you're taking.'

'I *know* I'm doing the right thing but all the same I hate

74

myself.'

'Well try not to,' said Flora. 'In a year or so the children will have left home, and then what will there be left for you? From what you've told me, Patience has all the hallmarks of a survivor. She'll marry again. Take your chance while you've got it. After all, regardless of what they all want, you've got a life too and a responsibility to yourself to do something constructive with it.'

'I know,' said Hugh. 'I know.'

Flora wiped her brush on some rag and then proceeded to clean it. When she had finished she turned back to Hugh.

'Let's go to bed, shall we?'

She held out her hand.

8

Hillary Causton found being a tycoon without a wife inconvenient. Being a tycoon without a wife like Drusilla, on the other hand, did have its advantages though. Swings and roundabouts. In particular the insurance on the Meissen was proving a problem since, because his collection had not been removed by a burglar but comprehensively and deliberately shattered by Mrs Causton, the company was unwilling to pay up. Why should we have to foot the bill for the fallout from a marital row, albeit a spectacular one, was the stance. This unhelpful attitude extended itself to the oil portrait of himself which had sustained a large hole in the region of his heart. All this and his companies to run with no domestic back-up except one daily and a benighted Filipino, who had been programmed to do nothing without her mistress's say so and who was frankly terrified that her volatile employer would return and catch her out using her initiative.

Dinner parties were a struggle as well. As part of his business life it was politic for Causton to do a fair degree of entertaining. All this could be achieved by means of the deployment of caterers and flower arrangers, but that was as far as it went. After that, keeping these gatherings on the effervescent conversational boil so that guests departed saying what a stimulating time they had had, rather than what a struggle it had all been, was a talent all of its own and not, unfortunately, one that he possessed. So on that level he did miss his estranged wife and, if he was honest with himself, he missed her in bed as well. Her day-to-day exacting presence was less of a deprivation. Most of all, sitting in his vandalised drawing room, currently being refurbished, Hillary missed his Claude. Tentative attempts to negotiate its return to its rightful place on his wall had got him nowhere. It was beginning to look as if he would have to sue his own wife in the courts for its return. The undignified prospect of doing such a thing was dreadful to contemplate. The orphan depicting Cupid and Psyche on the other side of the mantelpiece was a constant reproachful reminder.

The breakup of the Causton marriage was causing problems in other areas too. For different reasons neither of London's principal gossip columnists felt themselves able to write about it. Julian Cazalet waited for the word from Davenport and did not get it. Which was odd because wasn't Davenport the winner? In the past he had never resisted the opportunity to crow. In fact Charlie was discovering, like Hillary before him, that despite her many social attributes, Drusilla was a less than perfect house guest, and within the oyster that was his orderly bachelor flat she operated as a piece of grit which showed no signs of becoming a pearl. To cap it all, she was also very musical, which Charlie was not, and he found himself subjected to evenings of interminable opera of the Benjamin Britten, Janáček variety. After these happenings they usually went out for a large, and for him, indigestible, meal (in spite of being thin, Drusilla had a voracious appetite) and then went home to bed at which point a voracious appetite of a different sort came into play. All in all it was like being part of an ongoing Roman orgy, albeit a mini one since only two of them were involved. As a way of life, restful it was not and because of his growing ambivalence concerning the whole arrangement, Charlie was unwilling to go public, at which point he and Drusilla would have been regarded as what the likes of Cazalet and the idle Oates termed 'an item'. If it could be achieved, Davenport would have liked everything to have gone back to the previous status quo with Drusilla once again Hillary's wife and his own regular though clandestine mistress. Since she had purloined half of Hillary's pride and joy, namely the left hand Claude Lorrain and, in spite of repeated stern legal requests, showed no sign of giving it back, there was, he recognised, scant chance of that.

Radley Oates was also not publishing for the simple reason that Hillary Causton had told him not to.

'There's a chance that we might get back together again,' said Hillary, his mind more on himself and the Claude than on himself and Drusilla, 'and I don't want to upset a delicate balance. So no publicity.'

It was Radley's view that there was nothing delicate about

anything to do with Drusilla Causton, but an order was an order and as an employee he was forced to comply. He sulked about this to Dorian who had her own troubles and was less than sympathetic.

'It's hardly surprising that he doesn't want his own gossip column to dissect his private life,' pointed out Dorian. 'I mean, would you? Besides, if you feel that strongly about it, you could always print it anyway. Publish and be damned, that sort of thing. Then you would have your scoop. Though I wouldn't like to be in your shoes if you did do that.'

No, quite. Radley briefly contemplated the likely upshot of such an action and swiftly looked away. Certain it was that in the wake of it his shoes would no longer be in their habitual position on his desk but standing in the dole queue instead. The only consolation was that, probably for similar reasons, Cazalet had not published either. Due to the fact that a lot of the sort of people Radley wrote about had left the country for different watering holes, there was a significant lack of anything much to write about. Even his proprietor, embattled as he was by a fragmented Meissen collection and the looted Claude Lorrain, noticed.

'Your column's become lacklustre,' complained Hillary. 'Perhaps you need a change. A move to features or news perhaps.'

Radley froze. A move to either would cause his social life to wither on the vine. He would have to work for his living.

'It is a bit quiet at the moment,' reassured Radley, thereby implementing the first rule when dealing with tycoons which was to agree with them, 'but I've got some good stuff coming along . . . interesting . . . titillating,' he added in desperation, noting a sceptical look. *Though*, he could have added further, *not half as titillating as the news that your wife has left you, or been thrown out (probably more likely) and is currently shacked up with your arch-enemy and rival newspaper tycoon, Charlie Davenport!*

'Let's hope so for your sake.' Hillary was plainly unconvinced. 'We'll see. It may just be that you're stale. It happens to us all from time to time, you know. Maybe the moment has come to give young Peter his head and let you explore pastures new . . .' *Peter?* Radley gaped, wondering if he had heard aright.

Causton sounded like someone ruminating aloud. All the same this was serious. It would depend on whether something else, such as a new acquisition, came along and distracted his attention. Meanwhile he, Radley, would have to put his nose to the grindstone and pray that it did. For Radley consignment to the News Desk could only be likened to consignment to outer Siberia. Not for the first time he wondered irritably why Causton paid good money for an editor and still felt compelled to put his own finger in an otherwise perfect pie.

Causton stood up. The interview was at an end. Hopefully he would forget all about it.

The other interview of note due to take place that week was the one between Robert and Dorian Ormond. Robert's flat, once their old flat, was in Cranley Gardens. Dorian could vividly remember walking away from it after their last cataclysmic row, two weeks before Christmas. As often happens in the wake of an unexpected and therefore unrehearsed dramatic gesture she found herself out in the street wearing all the wrong clothes and with nowhere to go. A thin, freakishly early covering of snow which was not to translate itself into a white Christmas was slippery and this made the going hazardous. It was a dark, winter Sunday afternoon in the city. The wind was biting. Dorian had neither gloves, nor scarf nor hat. Going back for any of it would have been unthinkable. Drawing her shoulders together against the cold, she turned up her coat collar and, sliding slightly on the glassy pavement, set off slowly and carefully in the direction of the Old Brompton Road. In her heart of hearts she had hoped, no, *expected*, that Robert would come after her.

He did not.

Frozen in spirit as well as in body, Dorian crossed the street and set off up Gloucester Road towards Kensington Gardens. By now it was four o'clock, perhaps the most dismal time of day in winter to be outside and alone. Inside toasting crumpets and drinking tea would have been a different matter. The light was imperceptibly beginning to fade. Soon the pale fluorescence of street lights would illuminate the darkening park. It was not the best time to be out walking and alone, but such was Dorian's inner turmoil that she decided to press on. Walking did not inhibit thought, and all of Dorian's thoughts were painful, but it did give an illusion of positive action. At the Round Pond she stopped and, with a leaden heart, stood for several minutes staring into the black water.

'I'll never forgive Robert for this! Never!' said Dorian aloud. 'Or bloody Alexander Pope!'

She started walking again. Few people were about now. It looked as if she was almost one of the last. A string of white lights ahead, fitfully visible through the tossing bare branches of the trees, indicated that she was nearly at Queensway. Time to bring this odyssey to an end, but what to do next was the question. Eventually, chilled to the marrow, Dorian found a wine bar. Once inside it she ordered herself a large brandy and asked if there was a phone that she could use. It was lucky that the one thing she never went anywhere without was her shoulder bag.

The number she dialled rang several times in a house in the country. Dorian was just about to give up on it when Ellen Carey picked the receiver up.

'Dorian!' exclaimed Ellen. 'What a pleasure. Where are you?'

'I'm in a bar in Bayswater.' A combination of the brandy and a sympathetic voice caused tears to well. 'I'm frozen stiff and I've just left Robert!'

There was a pause at the other end, followed by a beeping noise. Dorian put some more money in the slot. With the connection re-established, Ellen could be heard saying, 'Don't tell me. Let me guess. You walked out with just the clothes you're currently standing up in and nowhere to go. Am I right?'

'Absolutely! How did you . . .'

'And even though you've walked miles and had a good fume, you're too proud to go back so you've still got nowhere to go!'

'Yes, that's right.' Dorian felt shaky.

'If I had a thousand pounds for each time I've been through that same scenario with Jack I'd be a rich woman,' said Ellen. Dorian was silent. She remembered a certain Carey exhibition private view at The Gallery which had ended in mayhem and Ellen herself stalking out. It had been all over the newspapers. Dorian had always held the opinion that, despite the riches they were presumably accruing now he was famous, co-existing with

80

the unreliable Jack Carey must be a living nightmare.

'Yes, it *is* a nightmare,' said Ellen, surprisingly. *Good heavens, she must be psychic!* '. . . and before you ask me how I knew what you were thinking, it's what every woman who knows him thinks when Jack's name comes up. Except the one he's currently sleeping with, and I don't mean me. Anyway, on the subject of my erratic husband, Jack is currently in Texas being supervised by Victoria Harting while he, in his turn, supervises the hanging of a retrospective of his work at the Maybrick Gallery. I'm due to fly out there the day after tomorrow so that Victoria can pass me the baton and I can take over the chaperoning. What this means is that the studio is empty, so you *do* have somewhere to go. You can go there. We're away for a month which should give you enough time to find somewhere to live. Unless Robert comes to his senses first, that is.'

With a resurgence of her old spirit, Dorian said, 'I don't want Robert back, whether he comes to his senses or not!'

'Quite so,' was Ellen's response to this. 'I should just let him stew. And it goes without saying it will be a lot easier to do that with the studio at your disposal.'

'Oh, Ellen . . .' In the face of her friend's generosity, Dorian felt emotional. 'I really don't know what to say.'

'My dear Dorian, there's no need to say anything. A drinking crony of Jack's who lives in the same building has a key. Only problem is you might have to wait until he gets back from the pub before you can get in, but I'll ring him anyway.'

'Ellen, you must let me . . .'

'All you have to do in exchange is to water the plant which Jack regularly neglects. Have you got the address?'

'Yes . . .'

'Fine! I'll ring you tomorrow and tell you how everything works.'

The beeping began again. Dorian upturned her purse. No more change. Never mind. For the moment everything that needed saying had been said. She went back into the bar, which was beginning to fill up, resumed her seat and continued sipping her brandy. And that was how a new phase of her life had begun and how, ultimately, she had met Radley Oates.

Now she was about to meet Robert for the first time since the day she moved out. With a flutter of the heart, Dorian rang the bell.

Robert came down. Because it was so long since she had seen him and she herself had grown used to her own new plumage, she was unprepared for her husband's stupefaction when he first saw her.

'Aren't you going to ask me in?' queried Dorian.

'Yes. Yes, of course!' Robert pulled himself together. 'It's just that you look completely different!' He did not enlarge on whether the change was for the better or the worse.

The flat looked the way it always had. The one concession to her visit was a jug of fresh flowers. A memorial to a previous incarnation was there too, on the mantelpiece, in the shape of a collection of brown sticks and fossilised papery blooms which were standing in half an inch of brackish water and probably had been since they died round about the time of her departure. Their presence indicated that while he might or might not have been celibate since she left, there almost certainly had not been a live-in lover.

'Would you like a drink?' said Robert, who seemed hardly able to take his eyes off Dorian. 'I don't have any spirits I'm afraid.'

She was amused. 'Robert, you know I never drink them. Next you'll be asking me if I take sugar in my tea.'

In the face of this gentle mockery he forbore to point out that her appearance had changed so radically that for all he knew so had her diet.

'What about a glass of champagne?' As he purchased it, a huge extravagance in his current penurious state, Robert had reflected that it would have to be bread and cheese for the rest of the week.

'I'd love one!' Before he could stop her, she had followed him into the kitchen. For a moment it was as if she had never gone away. 'Is there anything we could nibble with it?' She opened the fridge door. Apart from the bottle itself, it was practically empty. There was one egg, half a loaf of suspect bread and a very small carton of milk. Dorian was startled. 'Good heavens! What do you live on?'

'Very little!' Robert was dry.

82

So it seemed. While he was easing the cork, she went back into the sitting room. Disquieting evidence of writer's block was all over the desk in the shape of endless screwed-up sheets of computer paper. The wastepaper basket had overflowed onto the floor with more of the same. On the floor were open tomes bristling with markers and piled one on top of the other. A thin wad of typescript to the right of the computer was the most likely indication of how far Robert had not got. Dorian examined the last page. Sixty-one. She wondered if he had alerted the publisher. At the back of the desk, presiding over all the chaos, stood an old photograph of herself. Propped up against it was a postcard on which Robert had written, presumably *pour encourager*, *What is written without effort is in general read without pleasure*. The quote was attributed to Samuel Johnson and was very much in the bracing *say not the struggle naught availeth* mode. Well, yes but there must be a happy medium, was Dorian's attitude to this, surveying the chaos all around. It seemed to her that Robert had passed beyond mere effort and had tipped over into being a modern Sisyphus trying to push a large biographical stone up a mountain of research. It was difficult to believe that anything pleasurable could possibly come out of such a hard grind. All the same he had probably been wise to look to the good Doctor for encouragement rather than Pope.

Robert entered the room with two full glasses, one of which he handed to Dorian. As he stood in the kitchen he had wondered how to broach the subject of her return. Better, perhaps, simply to go for broke.

'There's something I want to ask you,' said Robert.

He paused.

She waited.

'Dorian, I love you! I miss you! I want to ask you to come back!' He rushed on. 'Oh, I know I've been an absolute bastard . . .'

Dorian held up one hand. 'It isn't you that's the problem. It's him!'

Did she mean her current lover? For she must, Robert suddenly saw with great clarity, have a lover. Nobody changed as much as she had done without one. Which only served to drive home what a comprehensive mess he, Robert, had made of their marriage. It also made it imperative that he got her back before it was too late.

'Who?'

'Pope! I won't even entertain the idea while he's still in situ.'

'*Pope*? Do you mean *Alexander* Pope?'

'Yes!'

He stared at her. 'But Dorian, Alexander Pope can't possibly be a threat to you. He's *dead* for God's sake!'

'I know that.' Dorian was tart. 'But he's still capable of causing a lot of trouble. If I come back, *if* I do, I want it to be with a real chance of success. I've invested too much in creating a new life for myself to throw it away lightly.'

In the face of this declaration of no confidence, if not in himself, certainly in the subject of his biography, Robert's face fell. He felt defeated.

'So you want me to give up writing this biography?'

'No, I don't. But, equally, I don't want to be around while the creative process is going on. It may be problematical for you but it's hell on earth for me.'

'What do you suggest we do?'

The initiative, it seemed, was all his wife's. Dorian shrugged. 'Nothing to do. Except leave it until you've finished and then, when you have, address the whole question again.'

Until he had finished. Robert's heart sank. Heaven knew when that would be. At his current rate he looked like being a biographical version of the *Flying Dutchman*, endlessly travelling never arriving. Until the publisher blew the whistle that was. Maybe it would be better if that happened.

Dorian interrupted all this rumination by standing up.

Alarmed, Robert said, 'You're not going?'

'I have to.'

'At least have one more glass of champagne . . .'

'I can't. I'm expected somewhere else.' She bent down to pick up her sling bag from the floor and as she did so her hair swung forward in a shining curtain and veiled her face. Like a lance, jealousy of the person she was presumably going to meet, got to the heart of the matter. His pain was intense.

'How do I know you'll still be there when I've finished this?' He gestured hopelessly towards his unproductive, untidy desk.

By now they were at the door. She turned back towards him. Unable to resist it, Robert drew her towards him and kissed her. It was a chaste kiss. Her restraint made it plain that nothing more was on offer. All the same he felt the fact that it had taken place at all betokened a promise of sorts. At the end of it she opened her strange, light eyes and looked into his. *La belle dame sans merci.*

'You have my word,' said Dorian.

When she had gone, Robert went back into the kitchen. The champagne would not keep so he might as well cane the bottle. Eventually he fell asleep in the armchair, freed for a few hours at least from his own unhappiness and the tyranny of Alexander Pope.

9

Flora was quite right in her assessment concerning what Patience Allardyce did next. As soon as she was quite certain, or as certain as anyone could be, that Hugh was not coming back, Patience threw herself into survival mode. Nobody was able to gloat over her discomfiture due to Hugh's defection because nobody saw her. She stepped down from all her committees, resigned from the Bench and gave up her post on the governing body of the local school. Thus unencumbered, as she had said she would, she put the house on the market at a very competitive asking price and busied herself, with her customary efficiency, trying to find another one in central London. A combination of an improvement in the housing market and a desire on the part of both her house agents to get the demanding Mrs Allardyce out of their hair produced a quick sale followed in due course by a convenient purchase.

Patience wrote and told the children all about it. As was her habit she duplicated the same letter, personalising each top and bottom.

Darling Cordelia/Christian, wrote Patience.
   You will be glad to know that I have just exchanged contracts on a London house. It is in Holland Park, the unfashionable part I'm afraid, but it is within walking distance of the tube.

'Great!' said Christian. 'What do you think she means by the unfashionable part?'
'I don't really know. Shepherd's Bush end, probably,' answered Cordelia after a moment's hesitation.
'So, Holland Bush is where Mum's new house is then.'
They both laughed. 'That's right. Holland Bush!'

   The couple I bought it from are going abroad and wanted a

quick sale, so as a cash buyer I got it at a competitive price, continued Patience. *It has three bedrooms, one of which is tiny and a very small garden at the back, largely paved. Fortunately it is in good decorative order so I shall simply be able to move in without having to commence huge building works. The other good news is that there is a very active, evangelical church in the locality where no doubt they will be glad of another pair of hands and I shall be able to go on doing my little bit for the community.*

Reading this last caused Christian to grimace.

'Christ! I do wish Mum would give it a rest.'

'Yes, I know what you mean,' said Cordelia. 'She's so occupied keeping everyone else on the straight and narrow that she tends to forget about us.'

'You *don't* know what I mean,' stated Christian. 'I *want* her to forget about me. I'm *glad* she isn't a hands-on mother. Haven't you noticed the haunted looks on the faces of those she insists on helping. I don't think *they* always want it either. And look at the name I got saddled with as a result of all the religious fervour that was flying around the last time. When I'm old enough I think I might change it by deed poll. I also think that if Mum had paid more attention to Dad *he'd* still be around.'

This remark caused Cordelia to blush. Not her mother's child for nothing there was a fastidiousness about her, a morally prudish thin skin. As a result she shied away from the memory of her father's last shouted remark before his dramatic exit. Although she knew that her parents presumably had had some sort of sexual relationship, Cordelia did not want it, or, in this case the lack of it, spelt out the way it had been the last time they had all met. Since then Hugh had written to both his children but only Christian had written back. Consumed with embarrassment, Cordelia had been unable to think of anything to say to him. Anxious to get off the subject of their father, she went back to the letter, 'Mummy's talking here about moving in late June. That's quite soon.' Cordelia, a child who had never wanted to go to boarding school in the first place, pictured her bedroom being dismantled and her few possessions being transported to Holland Bush and felt troubled.

'I wish things could just go on as they are,' she said abruptly. 'I hate the idea of a divorce.'

'Well, better get used to it.' Christian did not say this unkindly but in a matter-of-fact way. His sister had a very soft heart and it was his view that the sooner she braced herself to face this particular unpalatable fact, the better. Knowing perfectly well he had not, he added casually, 'Did I tell you that Dad's asked me to go and meet The Other Woman?' This last was delivered dramatically, the way Patience might have declaimed it. 'You're invited too, if you want to go.'

In turmoil, Cordelia turned away. 'I *don't* want to go.'

'Why not? Aren't you curious?'

'No, I'm not!' She was, of course. 'And I honestly don't think you should go either. It's disloyal.' She began to tear at the remains of her fingernails. Christian gave up on it. He ran his eye down the rest of the letter. Right at the end, Patience wrote:

It looks, by the way, as though your father may have found himself a job. No doubt he will write to you himself and tell you all about it. In the light of what has happened I shall have to do the same.

The sniff with which this was written was practically audible. *Your father*. It was interesting, reflected Christian reading this, that Dad, once everybody's, had now been passed over to the two of them. Patience closed with the words,

Naturally I shall be interviewing various removal firms and obtaining quotes. Here Christian stole a look at his sister. He hoped she was not about to cry again. *In the light of this I should be grateful if you could let me know whether you wish to pack up your own belongings or whether you wish to have them packed up for you.*

The two of them spoke aloud together and each answered the question perfectly in character.

'Pack up my own,' said Cordelia, stifling a sob.

'Have them packed up,' said Christian. 'Why should I bother when there's somebody on offer to do it for me?'

Unaware that in the greater scheme of things Fate was taking a hand and that she and its proprietor were destined to meet, Patience, as was her habit, read Hillary Causton's quality daily while she ate her breakfast. She liked its stern moral stance, its Conservative politics and (especially now) its emphasis on family values.

In his dining room Hillary also perused his own paper. On the whole he approved of what he found except for the Social Diary, the *Clarion*'s highfalutin title for its gossip column. Boring, was Hillary's dissatisfied verdict on what confronted him. Same tired old society faces doing the same old society things. There was much self-congratulation around one so-called scoop which Causton had seen two or three days prior to this in the Cazalet column. Otherwise there was no inside track information of any sort.

'It's just one long dreary bloody list,' said Causton aloud, throwing the newspaper down on the breakfast table in disgust. Feeling thoroughly out of sorts, he picked up his coffee cup and went into the drawing room. Perhaps he was missing his daily muted breakfast row with Drusilla. It was difficult to decide which was worse: breakfast in silence or breakfast conducted as a sparring match so that Drusilla could get herself up to speed for the rest of the day. His eye rested with disfavour on the space where the Claude should have hung. Meissen sized spaces abounded too. The fact that the room had been redecorated highlighted these significant gaps. The Meissen could be replaced with other Meissen once the wrangle with the insurance company was resolved, but in the case of the Claude there was stalemate. It was beginning to look as though in order to retrieve his own painting he was going to have to have his wife back as well. Over my dead body, was Hillary's reaction to this. Maybe the way to settle the whole thing was to have dinner with Davenport, preferably at his club which did not admit women. In that way a relatively civilised discussion could take place which would not happen if Drusilla was present. As a means to an end this was not ideal and on one level Causton found the idea of a whole evening spent in the company of his detested arch-rival abhorrent. Maybe a discussion over a pre-dinner drink would be better. Short and sweet. Drinks or dinner, something had to be done. The recovery of a painting by Claude Lorrain was high stakes whichever way you looked at it.

He looked at his watch recalling as he did so that his first appointment was a meeting with Miles Compton who was due to present the first draft of the TV feasibility study. It occurred to Hillary that one way of getting round solitary early mornings and keeping his own executives on the ball would be to introduce into his own company the American habit of the 7.30 a.m. business breakfast meeting. This would not be popular especially among those who lived out of London in places such as Sevenoaks. But, thought Causton, I am the boss. What I say goes. They'll just have to get used to it. In the light of that day's lacklustre column he decided to commence this bracing new regime the following day, with Radley Oates.

When he arrived at his head office, Compton was already waiting for him.

Unaware of his boss's reservations concerning his suitability for the job he now held, in the interests of his own survival Compton had studied the way his Chairman operated. It was impossible to escape the conclusion that the day there was a major mistake, even if the decision to do it had been Causton's and his alone, there was no way Hillary's head was going to end up on the block. Were a scapegoat to be needed this would be a privilege reserved solely for Compton himself, so the incursion into the new, and for them uncharted, medium of television could be a risky one.

Accordingly, when a few minor preliminaries had been dealt with and feeling that this was the right moment, he said tentatively, 'Are we sure about expanding into television?'

It was not the right moment. Causton's eyebrows drew together.

'We? Who is *we*?'

'Well, we the Company,' Compton had the presence of mind to stammer.

'Allow me to remind you since you appear to have forgotten, Miles, there is no we. *I* am the Company.' This statement was followed by a brooding, displeased silence. Causton rose and went and stood looking out of the window with his back to Compton. It seemed that a perfectly reasonable question was being treated as *lèse-majesté*.

Worse was to come.

Compton opened his mouth to try and salvage the situation. Causton, who was still standing in front of the window and appeared to have eyes in the back of his head, raised one imperious hand. Compton subsided. It would be all too easy to say the wrong thing again, thereby compounding his error.

'Television,' pronounced Causton, who had not considered moving into such a thing until Davenport trumped him, as he saw it, with the radio station, 'television is the medium of the future. If you are uneasy with such a prospect, Miles,' (here the use of his Christian name sounded more like a threat than a friendly intimacy) 'then perhaps you are in the wrong slot in this company!'

'Oh, no, no, no!' emphasised Compton. 'No, no, I was just . . .'

The commanding hand went up again. There was an unnerving, Kafka-esque sensation about conducting an exchange like this with somebody who refused to turn round. As though he had not heard, Causton carried on speaking. 'Maybe,' he mused aloud, 'the culture at one of our subsidiaries would suit you better. Of course, it would mean moving to Watford . . .'

Inwardly Compton panicked. To be syphoned off in such a fashion was the equivalent of being sent to the Salt Mines. This was corporate terrorism. Grovelling flattery was the only way out. He laid it on with the proverbial trowel. Outwardly relenting, inwardly unsympathetic, Causton was not impressed. As far as he was concerned the jury was out where Miles was concerned.

He held out his hand.

'Right, let's have a look at the feasibility study.'

The feasibility study. Oh, God! Compton flinched. The feasibility study was full of *ifs* and *buts* and *perhapses* culminating in a cluster of *inadvisables* and *probably nots*. In short it was the sort of lacklustre cautious document which, given the present climate, in the short term was more likely to precipitate his own redundancy than a disastrous foray into television.

'Ah, yes, the feasibility study! I'm afraid that's had an accident!'

A mental picture of his shattered Meissen rose before Causton's inner eye.

'Go on,' he said.

'A computer accident,' elaborated Compton. 'The temp I was using at the time because Rosa was ill, managed to lock it somewhere in the system and until we find it again, we can't print it up.'

'Can't you get somebody from the electrical department to help you? And anyway I thought the research firm we normally use were doing it.'

'They were.' Compton fervently wished the whole interrogation was at an end. 'They supplied the information and figures and I collated and presented it all so that it would have the best possible chance of approval by the board. Which is what you said you wanted.' Into a sceptical silence he added, 'And you did say you wanted the whole thing to be kept absolutely confidential.'

Causton opened his mouth to say, 'In that case what was a tempo rather than a personal secretary doing sorting it out in the first place?' and then gave up on it. He stood up, thereby bringing a very unsatisfactory meeting to a close.

'No ifs or buts or maybes,' said Causton, unwittingly echoing the feasibility study in its present incarnation, 'I want it on my desk by tomorrow morning. If necessary one of my own secretaries can give you a hand.'

'No need for that,' answered Compton hastily. 'I'm sure I'll manage to crack the code.'

'I certainly hope so for your sake,' was Hillary's pleasant parting shot.

Finally outside in the corridor Compton opened his briefcase with trembling hands and took out the report. Back in his office he went through it from first to last with a blue pencil, giving the same information an optimistic slant in the opposite direction so that all conclusions were positive, after which he put the corrections into the computer himself. When the whole thing was printed up again, on the principle that one could not be too careful, he shredded the original version.

It was now almost the end of June. A promising May had been the forerunner of a disappointingly uneven summer although the temperature remained warm. There was a lot of cloud. On better days this took the form of an opaline haze which filtered the sun like gauze and on less clement days it was denser, high and buff coloured, every so often silently disgorging heavy, shining showers of tepid rain.

The day on which Christian had arranged to see his father and to meet Flora Munro was one of the second sort. The weekend was an exeat. Christian told Cordelia where he was going but did not inform his mother. The house move was imminent and he left both women packing up Cordelia's room. His sister was subdued and lachrymose, his mother at her most domineering. The prospect of getting out of the house was a great relief.

'Where are you going?' Patience wanted to know, managing to sound caring and not very interested all at the same time.

'Off to see a friend,' replied Christian, lying with the practised ease of one who had been doing it almost since he could talk. He sent Cordelia, who said nothing, a loaded look. She avoided his eye. 'I don't know whether I'll be back for supper.'

'That's all right. So long as you let me know.'

His mother, who had been depositing books in a crate, went back to doing it. As he let himself out, he heard her say to Cordelia, 'Are you sure you want to take *all* this?' followed by his sister's dignified and poignant reply, 'Quite sure. It's all I've got to remind me of my life here.'

Christian caught a train and then took the tube. When he emerged at his destination it was to find that there had been another heavy shower of rain. The paving stones were glassy with water and his sneakers sucked slightly on the wet surface. Crossing the garden of the square in which Flora and now his father lived he was aware of the sweet heady smell of wet flower beds. Trees, lush and dripping as a result of the deluge, leant over him towards each other, forming an arched green tunnel along which he walked. Water made a light pattering as it slid from leaf to leaf before finally falling to earth and the air was humid, steamy almost. The clammy atmosphere reminded Christian of the palmhouse at Kew Gardens.

Eventually he passed through a black-painted iron gate of which there were four, one on each side of the square. To the left was number 45, whose basement tenant was Flora Munro. It occurred to Christian that he had no concept of what his father's mistress might be like. Although he had lost his virginity six months ago during the course of a fumbling, inexpert grapple with his then girlfriend, he had no point of reference for the sort of mature liaison that his father had embarked upon. He had a vague vision in his mind of Flora as either a peroxide blonde or a vampish version of his own mother. He hesitated on the edge of the kerb and then crossed the road.

In common with the rest of the square, 45 was half a gracious Victorian villa which had seen better days. Sturdy stuccoed pillars of the flat-topped variety stood on either side of the front garden entrance and on one of these sat a large Persian cat. At Christian's approach it rose and put its tail in the air. In the centre of a flaring aureole of long hair its face was snub-nosed, cross and tiny, like a screwed-up ball of paper. Christian, who did not like cats, ignored it and, in the manner of cats everywhere, it therefore ran after him along the path and down the steps to the basement where it stood calling rather than mewing and rubbing itself against his legs.

Christian rang the bell.

It was his father who answered the door. Emotionally Hugh embraced his son looking over his shoulder as he did so.

'Cordelia didn't come?' He was clearly very disappointed.

'No, Dad,' said Christian, adding by way of further explanation. 'She felt she couldn't handle it. She's very much on Mum's side.'

'Yes. Yes, of course.' Hugh turned and led the way into the sitting room. 'Come and meet Flora.'

At the first sight of his father's inamorata Christian was astonished and frankly envious. All preconceptions vanished. This was a very pretty girl indeed. She stood up and as she came towards him and passed as she did so into the light from the window, he saw that she was older than he had first thought. Older than he was, certainly. All the same he was dazzled. Flora's dress was three-quarter length and flowing, with tight elbow-length sleeves. Although this was made of summery tee shirt material, its colour which was black, together with the simplicity of its shape, gave it a dimension of formality, importance even, which it otherwise would not have had. Above the dip of a moderately low-cut bodice her neck rose plump and peachy, unadorned

94

except for a massive pair of barbaric silver earrings which exactly complemented the concave curve between jaw and shoulder. But it was the face he could not take his eyes off. Those eyes. When he grasped the hand she held out to him which was heavily ringed it felt surprisingly firm, a resolute hand.

'You look just like Hugh,' said Flora. '*Just* like Hugh!'

She smiled at him and Christian smiled back.

'So what's she like?' The speaker was Cordelia.

'I thought you didn't want to know.'

Christian, who did not want his sister to guess his inner confusion, was ultra casual though in fact there was nothing he would have liked more than to celebrate his first meeting with Flora Munro by talking about her to someone. Unfortunately Cordelia was not that person. For the time being he would have to keep his dazzlement to himself.

'In a way I don't and in another way . . .'

'You do. She's all right. Sort of unusual-looking,' was the closest Christian felt he could safely get to it. 'Quite nice, really,' he added.

'What's the matter with you?' Cordelia looked sharply at her brother, who did not sound his usual lofty, dismissive self. 'You'll be saying you're in love with her next!'

Christian did not deign to reply to this flippant remark but all the same it touched a nerve.

10

Charlie Davenport, who had been waiting for Causton's next move, looked forward to having a drink with his old adversary, confident that between them they were about to negotiate the repatriation of Drusilla to the marital home. After which life could go back to normal. It's not, reasoned Charlie to himself, that I no longer love Drusilla, it's just that I find her too much for me on a daily basis. He did not tell her about the meeting.

He arrived at the club to find his protagonist sitting ascetically in front of a glass of mineral water.

'What would you like?' enquired Hillary.

'A vodka and tonic,' said Charlie. 'Is that what you usually drink these days?' He gestured at the Perrier.

'Mainly, yes,' said Hillary. 'Alcohol rots the brain cells you know.'

'So we're told,' said Charlie, blithely taking a deep swig of his own drink when it arrived. 'Now,' (knowing perfectly well) 'what can I do for you?'

Hillary stared into the middle distance, frowning while he marshalled his thoughts. Eventually he said, 'You've got something of mine that I want back.'

Charlie was startled. *Odd way to refer to his wife!* In spite of his desire to hand Drusilla back, the temptation to make Causton sweat was too much to be resisted.

'It's not as simple as that,' said Charlie.

'I can't see why. My property is my property. There can't be any debate about that.'

Good Heavens, thought Charlie listening to this. I had no idea Hillary was such an unreconstructed male chauvinist. No wonder Drusilla was so restless.

Aloud he observed mildly, 'What about personal inclination? You can't dictate somebody else's feelings for them.'

'I can't see where feelings come into it!' Hillary was terse. He signalled to the waiter. 'Another Perrier for me, please, and . . .?'

'Another brain cell decimator for me,' said Charlie.

'Are you saying you won't help me? What's happened is a criminal offence, you know!'

Leaning back in his chair, Charlie decided that Hillary had finally lost his marbles. It often seemed to happen to newspaper proprietors. He himself would have to be careful. Maybe he should cut down his alcohol intake. After all look what was happening to Causton on a liquid diet of mineral water. Heaven only knew what vodka was capable of doing.

Patiently he said, 'It isn't a question of not being helpful. Look, whatever my feelings on the matter are, nobody can persuade Drusilla to return to you if she doesn't want to. Though personally I think she should. You and Drusilla belong together, in my view.'

Suddenly and unaccountably, Hillary was amused. As one on whom light dawns he said, 'Ah, *now* I *see*! You're fed up with her! Well, so am I. I don't want Drusilla back. I wouldn't take her back if she *begged* me. She's your problem now. No, what I want back is my Claude Lorrain!'

Charlie was thunderstruck. Another tycoon with his own spectacular paintings, he had forgotten all about it.

Feebly he said, 'I really can't help you there'.

'What do you mean? I assumed it must be hanging in your flat!'

'I haven't seen it since the day Drusilla turned up with it. I drew the line because of the insurance. I also told her to give it back.'

'What did she say?'

'She told me to mind my own business and that she'd do as she bloody well pleased and she'd thank me not to interfere!'

'Quite so,' observed Hillary. 'That sounds like Drusilla. And this loving exchange took place at the beginning of the idyll? No wonder you've had enough by now.' He chortled. 'Anyway, back to business. The Claude Lorrain. Where is it?'

In spite of his own discomfiture, Davenport was glad to see his next remark wipe the smile off Causton's face.

'It's in the bank vault. And don't ask me which bank or where because I don't know. She took it away wrapped in a mink. If you want to get it back you're going to have to deal directly with

Drusilla.' He stood up. 'I have to go. I have another appointment. Thanks for the drinks. Good luck. Strikes me you're going to need it!' They did not shake hands. He went.

'And so are you!' said Causton to Charlie's retreating back, determined to have the last word.

He signalled for the bill.

House moves should be simple. The pantechnicon arrives, everything is packed up, taken to the new residence and, if required, unpacked again. In the event, life rarely runs as smoothly and Patience's relocation to Holland Bush was no exception. The removal men swarmed all over the house. No-one admitted to the post of foreman. Upstairs, downstairs, in my lady's chamber they went, packing as they moved along to the music of a ghetto blaster. It was impossible to be everywhere. Nevertheless, Patience, who treasured her belongings and her mahogany furniture, tried. Wherever she was not, there were alarming crashes and even more unnerving cries of 'Whoops!' and even once a shout of 'Nearly Lost That One!' followed by coarse laughter. Heaven only knew what was happening in the further reaches of her large house. When lunchtime came they all streamed out, along the garden path, up the ramp and into the back of their van where they remained closeted for one hour exactly. This seemed to be the moment to do an inspection in an attempt to discover exactly what they had been doing. On the surface it all looked fine though whether the sealed dining-room crates, for example, were filled with all the pieces of her twelve-setting dinner service or her twelve-setting dinner service in pieces was hard to determine. The first two firms Patience had tried, both recommended, had been booked up. This one was straight out of the Yellow Pages and appeared to have no booking problem whatever. Now she knew why.

The sound of marching feet accompanied by the ghetto blaster signalled the return of the mechanicals some of whom bore more than a passing resemblance to less dynamic members of the seven dwarfs. There was, it seemed, nothing to do but get on with it. Before this happened, Patience determined to give them all a pep talk. As they prepared to disperse, she clapped her hands.

'Gather round please everybody! I have something to say to you!'

They all shuffled forward.

'Now,' said Patience, deciding to have one more shot at it, 'who is in charge?'

They all pointed at each other. Thinking: How very juvenile, she waited. Finally a reluctant hand went up.

'Ah!' exclaimed Patience. 'And you are?'

'Seamus O'Byrne.'

'Well, Mr O'Byrne, I should like you to know that I have some very valuable furniture and objets d'art . . .'

'Objets de what?' asked an uncouth voice from the back amid sniggers.

'. . . in this house,' continued Patience, ignoring it, 'and I shall hold you personally responsible for ensuring that there are no breakages . . .'

Hitherto reluctant, Mr O'Byrne put up his hand again with an air of triumph and eagerly opened his mouth.

'One minute, please, Mr O'Byrne!' To forestall the inevitable offering *we are fully insured, Mrs Allardyce*, which gave them carte blanche to break as much as they wanted because someone else would end up paying for it, Patience finished her sentence by saying, '. . . because much of it is irreplaceable. Ir-re-place-able! Do you understand me?'

In the manner of a Gilbert and Sullivan chorus they all sang together.

'Yes-we-do.'

Smirks all round.

A strong sense of getting nowhere made her decide to round the whole thing off. 'Good. Thank you for listening. You may now all go back to your work.'

The moment she finished speaking the ghetto blaster was switched back on and they all fanned out. Minutes later she heard what sounded like a collision upstairs which was succeeded by raucous laughter and then a tinkly expensive-sounding crash from the direction of the dining room.

When they had finally gone, Patience and the echo walked around the shell of what had once been a family house. The great adventure of the move to inner London no longer seemed like that but more like a leap into a rather bleak unknown. Loneliness swept over Patience. On impulse she picked up the telephone receiver and dialled her sister's number. Dorian was not there. Only the answer phone requesting her to leave a message. Patience did not bother. The moment for communication was now, not in a week's time or whenever Dorian picked up her messages.

Patience checked her handbag for the collection of house keys which she was due to drop off with the estate agent. It only remained to read the meters and go. She was in the process of doing this when the door bell rang. Surprised, she went to answer it and found Clarissa Bowen on the door step.

'My dear,' said Clarissa, 'I found out quite by accident that today was the day of the move. I've come to ask you back for a reviving cup of tea. You must be absolutely exhausted.'

Gratefully, Patience said, 'I am.' The need to talk to someone was overwhelming, the further need to sit down for half an hour or so before commencing the next leg of her new life odyssey, imperative. Lucky that Clarissa was the caller and not Joan Pickering or worse Margaret Harris. Clarissa would not sympathetically gloat nor would she ask intrusive questions. Clarissa was that old-fashioned thing, a lady, with all the delicacy and perfect manners this implied. But there was more to her than that, Patience suddenly saw. There was an unshockable quality, an unjudgemental acceptance of human frailty which indicated that during the course of her long life Clarissa had come up against more than just the thinnest of bone china tea cups.

Because she did not ask, Patience told Clarissa more than she otherwise might have. She did not, however, mention Flora Munro. Pride forbade it.

'So what will you do next?' wondered Clarissa aloud. 'It will take you a while to get to know people. It's a new area for you after all.'

Cradling her cup of China tea, Patience replied, 'Well, tomorrow I'll have to spend all day taking in the crates and trying to get the kitchen up and running, but on Sunday I thought I'd go to church.' It was hard for Clarissa to understand why listening to this innocent intention filled her with foreboding. She found herself having to suppress a sudden urge to say, 'Well, watch out!' Don't be absurd! Clarissa chided herself. What could possibly go wrong in *church*? The answer to this sensible question turned out to be: More than one would think.

Unaware of Clarissa's misgivings which probably would not have made much difference anyway, Patience did go to her new local church but because she ran out of time she went to even-song rather than the Sunday morning service. St Cuthbert's was a relatively old church but not a particularly beautiful one. What set it aside from other churches was that it was absolutely packed. There were even people standing in the aisles. Wondering about the fire regulations, Patience, who had arrived early and who therefore had secured a seat in one of the front pews, scrutinised the flowers. These were artfully arranged but in clashing colours. Clearly there was scope for improvement here. She turned her attention to the brass and was forced to concede that this had been properly and assiduously polished. The small band, standing to the left of the altar, caused Patience to raise her eyebrows and so did the first hymn which swung, no other word for it, and was accompanied by rhythmic clapping supplied by an enthusiastic audience. Congregation was hardly the word, she decided. The vicar was interesting too, being of the fire and brimstone variety rather than the self-effacing saintly sort to which Patience was more used. He was tall and thin to the point of concavity, with a head of thick black hair which was greying at the temples and brushed his collar. Piercing eyes, deepset under jutting eyebrows scanned the pews, momentarily resting on Patience. Gripping the pulpit, he began to berate his listeners. The sermon was delivered with great energy and a certain amount of accusation. The theme of it was from the gospel according to St Matthew, chapter 19, namely that it is easier for a camel to go through the eye of a needle, than for a rich man to enter into the kingdom of God. It even occurred to Patience, not herself the most tactful of women, that given his conspicuously well-heeled flock this was not necessarily the most appropriate of texts. Although on the other hand maybe he had his eye on a full collection plate and when this eventually came round during the course of its jour-ney from person to person it did overflow.

At the end of the service the participants began to disperse. Patience waited in her pew until she was almost the last and then started for the door. She emerged from the dim church interior into the honeyed warmth of the July evening. In the west a fiery sun was sinking behind the pollarded lime trees which encircled the church yard. The sky was shot with scarlet. The vicar was standing on the step surrounded by the sort of coterie of middle-aged ladies whom Patience recognised. In the ambience of this particular church groupies might have been a more apposite description. All were vying for his attention and all were therefore put out when he turned this towards Patience.

'I believe you are new here,' he said.

'I am,' replied Patience, shaking his hand.

'Then allow me to introduce myself. I am Cedric Renfrew.' Once again his eyes appraised her.

'And I,' said Patience, 'am Patience Allardyce. I hope to be a regular worshipper here. I should also be delighted to help in the running of the church. The flowers. That sort of thing.' She wondered if St Cuthbert's held a summer fête. Probably not. Too urban. No room. 'Perhaps we could have a meeting some-time to discuss it?'

This last caused a disapproving rustle among the groupies who probably did not want an interloper on their patch and especially not one as focused as this person appeared to be.

Impervious to this, 'I should be delighted,' said the Reverend Cedric Renfrew. 'Another pair of hands is always welcome.' If the row of dismal faces behind him was anything to go by, no, not always. After more pleasantries, Patience took her leave and turned to go. All in all it had been an interesting interlude. Her last impression was of his angular figure, like that of a very big black crow, standing outside the porch, a dark shadow amid the mellow brilliance of the evening light. In a curious way that she could not immediately define although, like the rest of the group within which he stood, he appeared to be *in* the light, he was not *of* it. Cedric Renfrew was a man apart. Intrigued and still think-ing about him, she walked off along the road.

Hillary Causton, who had been at the service too, walked along the same road but in the opposite direction. Mainly because Drusilla had never attended church with him this was one of the few occasions when he did not feel lonely. And even when he did feel lonely it was not the company of Drusilla that he missed but just the company of someone. Most of all he missed the Claude. It would be true to say that Hillary pined for that painting.

He reached his car mulling over the sermon. It was hard to escape the uncomfortable feeling that it had been directed at him. As a result a twenty-pound note had joined the tenners and fivers in the tray. On the other hand others had probably squirmed as well. Causton, who had spent a large part of his childhood in Scotland, liked a fierce priest. It seemed to him that whereas godly humility probably never changed anything, a good rant might well do the trick. It was, after all, how he ran his newspapers. All the same there was something about Renfrew that was unsettling. It was as though he was a throwback to another era, a John Knox for the nineties, if you like. There were certain other aspects that Hillary was uncertain about as well. There had been one occasion when a Canadian apostle of the so-called Toronto Blessing persuasion had been invited to conduct a service, the upshot of which had been that large numbers of a normally upright congregation, though not Hillary himself, had fallen to the floor in droves. A sudden outbreak of speaking in tongues had caused a certain amount of publicity too, as well as some derision in the press, Charlie Davenport's tabloid rag being one of the first to poke fun. However, be that as it may, St Cuthbert's was full and how many other churches could one say that about these days? Hardly any was the answer. All the same, he was aware that there was a maverick quality about Renfrew which, together with the man's arrogance, might make him a huge force for good or its opposite. There would be nothing much in between.

By now he had reached his car. In two days' time what Causton privately called his dynamic breakfasts were due to commence and would be conducted within the civilised portals of the Savoy. His guest for the first of these was to be Radley Oates. In advance of this happening, courtesy demanded that he appear to confer with Oates's editor after which ritual dance he, Hillary, would issue his orders and that would be that. The fate of the editor himself had yet to be decided.

The end of the school term arrived. Cordelia went off on a French exchange and Christian came home to Holland Bush for a week prior to setting off to stay with a friend and his family in Dorset. In terms of getting the house sorted out this was very useful to Patience who had reached the stage where a hod-carrier was a necessity but could not afford to employ one. Grumbling all the way Christian did as he was asked. On Thursday he decided to go and see his father. He told his mother so.

Her face expressionless, she said, 'I suppose that means you'll have to meet That Woman!'

Christian did not inform her that he already had but simply said, 'Maybe'. Then getting off that side of it, 'Did Dad get that job he was after?'

'No. No, he didn't.' Patience was short. She herself had advertised in the local press with a view to taking in typing. It occurred to her to wonder whether the Reverend Cedric Renfrew who had no wife and who therefore presumably did his own letters would be able to put some work her way. It might be worth asking. Meanwhile she had managed to get herself on the church committee where she liked to think she was cutting a swathe through existing inefficiency. By those with whom she came most in contact in this capacity, Patience was variously described as a pain in the neck and, when charity was abroad, 'effective' by which bossy was really meant. Oblivious to discontent and certain that all was going well, she pressed on. No one could deny that the improvement in the flower arrangements was anything short of spectacular. In September the election for chairperson was due to take place.

Thursday came and because he did not want to have to endure his mother's wounded sighs, Christian forced himself to get out of bed and left early with the intention of buying himself a large greasy breakfast in a cafe.

The brief golden flare of real summer had gone out for the time being. Today warm, silky rain fell from a high light sky. Once again what he thought of as Flora's square glistened with its soft sheen. Halfway across, because he was early, he sat down on a dripping slatted bench. The shower petered out and a ray of sunshine filtered through taupe-coloured cloud, causing the massed leaves to become a translucent, almost luminous green. Christian sat for several minutes enjoying it until, as unexpectedly as it had arrived, the sun withdrew. Damply he got to his feet as the rain began again.

It was Flora who answered the door. This time, probably because of the weather, there was no sign of Xerxes. She was wearing what looked like a long black robe and her hair was wrapped in a towel. Perhaps she had been washing it. Whatever the reason she looked astounded to see him.

'Christian! We weren't expecting you until tomorrow! I'm afraid your father isn't here.' She stepped back to let him pass.

Tomorrow! How on earth had that happened? It had probably happened because he, Christian, was not organised enough to have a diary and attempted to keep all his arrangements in his head instead.

'Well, look, never mind. At least come in and have a cup of coffee now you're here.'

Standing in the kitchen watching her make it, Christian admired Flora's profile as she reached up for the jar of coffee. The towel which was wrapped into a peak with a fall behind, together with the graceful sweep of the wrap had a medieval look. It reminded him of the way the wife of a crusader might have looked welcoming her husband home from the war. Fascinated he watched as she bent down to extract the milk from the fridge. For a few seconds her breasts were tantalisingly visible. The kettle boiled. Christian was suddenly aware of the scent of some sort of exotic flower. Where this was coming from he had no idea. Its sinful sophistication caused him to feel almost faint. As if from a great distance away, he heard Flora say, 'Would you like sugar?'

Without replying he spun her round, slid his hands inside her robe and pushed it off her shoulders so that her bare breasts, hitherto only tantalisingly seen for a second, were revealed. Then he took her in his arms and clumsily kissed her. The cup and saucer, both already cracked, fell on the floor and smashed.

11

Although the idea of Radley Oates's transfer to Features had already been floated across his horizon, the actual happening still came as a horrid shock. With the sole exception of Peter, nobody was happy about it. Faced with the choice between an unsatisfactory Features man and an unsatisfactory gossip columnist his editor would infinitely have preferred the latter. As it was, once Causton had dropped his bombshell in the name of discussion, it swiftly became obvious that discussion was the very last thing on the agenda. I'd like to consult you meant I'm going to tell you. The knock-on effect would, of course, be a headache too, a journalistic version of musical chairs.

Radley complained to Dorian at length. Bored by the whole subject, Dorian said, 'Why tell *me*? I can't help you. Why not go and see your editor?'

So he did. It was not a satisfactory interview. The editor said, elliptically, 'Look, Radley, I don't want you in Features either. Journalistically speaking it's much too important a job. But the old man has decided and that's it! Nothing I can do.' In order to underline this unpalatable fact, he spread his hands and then, for good measure, shrugged his shoulders.

'And *Peter*!' said Radley reproachfully. '*Peter*, of all people! He doesn't *know* anyone. How can you have a social diarist' (Radley's own pompous description of his occupation) 'who doesn't *know* anyone?'

'Once again, Peter was Causton's idea, not mine,' said the editor, who was privately of the opinion that practically anybody could cover the London social scene and that the transition from Radley to Peter would be virtually seamless. Apart from the byline, nobody would notice the difference. He wished the same could be said vis-à-vis the Oates move to Features. 'Try to look upon it as a challenge.' Listening to him, Radley was well aware that this was a phrase which was generally trotted out when something dire and unavoidable was in the offing.

The news got around.

Watching her boss sitting disconsolately at his desk, Jeannie was overtly sympathetic and secretly exultant.

'Is there anything I can do to help?' asked Jeannie for the third time.

'No,' replied Radley. 'Or, rather, yes. Stop asking me if there is anything you can do to help. There is nothing anybody can do to help.'

Hovering, Peter said, 'What about your address book? You won't be needing that in . . .'

Radley did not hesitate.

'It's *my* address book and I'm hanging on to it,' said Radley. 'You're on your own now.'

'Why don't you look at it as a challenge?' suggested Dorian when he told her the upshot of the interview.

'Why does everybody keep saying that? What's so wonderful about a challenge?' Radley was peevish.

'It's the half full, half empty syndrome. Since it looks as though you're stuck with this job, you might as well take a positive attitude.'

'You realise what this is going to do to our social life, don't you?'

Well, yes, Dorian did. The prospect of coping with Radley without two or three parties each night to leaven the lump was an alerting one and probably ranked with trying to live with Robert, Alexander Pope and writer's block. These days when Dorian thought about her husband it was with affection rather than exasperation. It was as though meeting him again in their old flat, so touchingly and transparently glad to see her with the champagne and flowers which he probably couldn't afford, had overlaid all the hurt and misunderstanding of the past. In one sense honour was satisfied but the problem still remained. And, thought Dorian, I could not bear to go back and have it all collapse on me again for the very same reason. And then there had been that last kiss . . . a formal kiss, but all the same . . .

You must remember this . . .

The sound of Radley's voice saying competitively, 'What are you thinking about?' brought her out of this particular reverie.

. . . a kiss is still a kiss . . .

'I was thinking about you,' fibbed Dorian. 'Look, you've got another month before the new incarnation so let's make the most of it! You never know, Causton might change his mind. Tycoons are notoriously unpredictable.'

Without voicing the fact aloud, each thought that this convenient volte-face would not take place.

'I blame Drusilla for all this.' Radley was morose. 'If she hadn't left Hillary none of this would have happened. He hasn't got anybody to have breakfast with, that's his problem. People can be very destructive over breakfast.'

'You mean that's *your* problem!'

Clutching her robe around her as she struggled to free herself from Christian's embrace, Flora stepped backwards and trod on Xerxes. Xerxes screamed, jumped in the air and attacked the interloper rather than his own mistress. With all four paws wrapped around one jeaned leg, claws painfully imbedded, he was very difficult to dislodge. 'Fucking cat!' shouted Christian, shaking the leg and aware of looking ridiculous in front of the one person in the world he would have liked to impress. To his horror the animal began to climb. The prospect of what might happen next if this threatening advance continued made immediate action a necessity. Xerxes' bushy tail thrashed. There was a look of aggressive devilment about him. Christian briefly entertained the idea of trying to peel the cat off his leg like ivy off a wall, and wary of sustaining another flesh wound, dismissed it. He sent an imploring look to Flora.

Who laughed.

'Serves you bloody well right!' said Flora.

The sound of her voice appeared to calm the cat who lost interest in the leg, carefully extracted claws and sauntered off. With a gesture of supreme contempt Xerxes sat down with his back to Christian and began to wash his face. In the face of such a comprehensively undignified rout it was hard to know what to do next. Flora saved him the trouble of working it out.

'I think you'd better go!' said Flora. 'Now.'

Her icy dignity was such as to admit of no appeal. Humiliated and feeling like weeping, Christian ran out of the flat, slamming the door as he went. The rain, which had held off for the duration of his disastrous visit, fell straight and heavy like a silver blind, temporarily blotting out the square and the houses around it.

After his tempestuous exit, Flora gathered up the remains of the cup and saucer and threw them in the bin. Then she went into the sitting room, looked at her own reflection in the over-mantel mirror and began to sob.

'What on earth made him do that?' wept Flora aloud. She scrutinised herself. Tears which were charming at twenty were disastrous at thirty. Her face had a nude, peeled look. These days without makeup it was a face undressed. She was thirteen years older than Christian. The idea that he had done it because she was his father's mistress and he had thought of her as easy was unpalatable but probably true and it hurt. Feeling violated and suddenly vulnerable she picked up Xerxes for comfort and went over to the window, where she stood, holding him tightly and stroking him and staring out at the sheeting rain. Of one thing she was quite sure. There could be no question of telling Hugh what had happened. She loved him too much to do that.

It transpired that the Reverend Cedric Renfrew did need secretarial help and was prepared to pay for it, though not very much. It had not escaped his noticed the Patience was a forceful addition to an otherwise, dithery, twittery church committee. It did not escape his notice either that this did not make her popular. While regretting this, Renfrew took the Jesuitical view that the end justified the means. Church affairs were being galvanised, that was what mattered. They would all have to like it or lump it.

Cedric Renfrew was unmarried because, as he put it to him-self, it will have to be someone very stalwart to marry *me*. One or two who nearly had would probably have concurred with this view, though not for his own reasons. All the same, in the Church of England a wife was an asset and Cedric was very ambitious. It was his opinion that Patience Allardyce would make a very good vicar's wife. It was a pity then about the divorce, for surely it must eventually come to that. In the nor-mal course of events every so often Renfrew would have thun-dered from the pulpit about the iniquity of divorce, already *had* thundered from the pulpit of St Cuthbert's about the iniquity of divorce. No longer. Circumspect probing, under the guise of pastoral care, elicited the information that she and her husband were separated, that he was living with somebody else and that Patience herself was the innocent and wronged party in all of this. He also learnt that she had two children.

'Are they practising Christians?' enquired Cedric in severely clerical mode.

Well, no, honesty made Patience admit, they were not. But the conditioning was all there and she was sure they would come round in the end. And if they did not, thought Renfrew listening to it, he would be there for them. He would guide them. They would be brands plucked from the burning.

Further judicious questioning elicited the fact that Patience did not want a divorce.

'I believe in the sanctity of marriage,' declared Patience.

'Yes, of course, and rightly so!' replied Cedric preparing carefully to balance the teaching of the Church against what he himself might want out of this. 'But if your errant husband is quite determined to have one, eventually he will get it. Sadly that is the way of the world. The secular world that is,' he added. 'And you, my dear Patience, have so much to offer. Perhaps, in the fullness of time, somebody else will be the benefactor.' It was the nearest he could get towards saying: Like me. It occurred to him to wonder if she had any money of her own. The Church did not remunerate her servants as well as perhaps she might have done and a little extra was always welcome. During the course of brief visits to Patience's house to collect immaculately typed letters he noticed some fine furniture and at least two pleasing paintings. Upstairs, where he had never been, no doubt there was more. On the other hand, sadly, it had to be said that at the end of a divorce more often than not one affluent couple demerged into two penurious individuals. The other thing he noticed was that Patience was house proud. There were fresh flowers and the distinctive smell of beeswax pervaded all, though these days the polisher was Patience herself rather than a daily. In comparison with this comfortable haven, the vicarage was a desert of battered filing cabinets, 1950s furniture and a kitchen which called to mind state of the ark rather than state of the art. To have a graceful home such as hers was would add to his prestige and make entertaining possible.

Not infrequently, while Patience's head was bent over her notebook during the course of one of their weekly secretarial sessions in his study at the vicarage, Renfrew allowed his gaze to linger on her. The Song of Solomon came to mind. *O thou fairest among women,*' said the Song of Solomon usefully elaborating, further on, *Thy neck is as a tower of ivory; thine eyes like the fishpools in Heshbon, by the gate of Bath-rabbin: thy nose is as the tower of Lebanon which looketh toward Damascus.* Whether Patience would have appreciated her nose being compared with a tower, even one which looked towards Damascus, was a moot point. As it was Renfrew's mental preoccupation caused a prolonged silence. Sitting, pencil poised, waiting for the vicar to utter, Patience raised her head enquiringly. For a brief few seconds their eyes met. Mindful of her current (presumably) celibate state the Song of Solomon threw up another apposite quote, namely, *A garden inclosed is my sister . . . a spring shut up, a fountain sealed . . .* In its wake Renfrew found himself thinking, *I should like to penetrate that garden . . .*

Unaware of all this, 'Is that all?' asked Patience, very business-like.

'No,' said Renfrew, pulling himself together. He added another couple of sentences and then pushed his chair back. 'Right, that is it. Yours sincerely etc. And now I think we should turn our attention to the parish newsletter. And then, when we have finished that, there is something else I should like to sound you out about.'

The something else turned out to be very unexpected.

When he finally told her what it was, 'But why me?' asked Patience, astonished. 'Why not you?'

'Because they want a woman. This will be a television debate concerning the ordination of women priests and will take place on Sunday fortnight during the course of what is known as, lamentably, the God slot. I was asked to recommend one of my parishioners to take part and you, Patience, were my first choice. Most especially because I believe your views on the subject to be sound, that is to say they agree with mine.'

'I am most definitely against it!'

'Quite so! So what do you say?'

'Well, of course the last time I did anything like this was as a member of the school debating team and, as I'm sure I don't have to tell you' (here she sent him a glance which just might have been faintly flirtatious) 'that was quite a few years ago.'

'Not that many, I'm sure,' murmured Renfrew gallantly, his eyes fixed on her face. (*Thy lips are like a thread of scarlet, and thy speech is comely: thy temples are like a piece of pomegranate within thy locks . . .*)

'But I'm sure I could still do it. And I do have very pronounced views on the subject. *Very* pronounced views.'

Patience stared into the middle distance. Television. What a platform! It certainly eclipsed the Bench on that score. If she made a success of it, who knew what might follow. The old certainty which had been at a comparatively low ebb since Hugh's defection, rushed back and with it came the old optimism, the conviction that she, Patience Allardyce, was destined to make a mark on the world for the greater good. The banner was still there to be carried. All she had to do was pick it up.

Renfrew leant forward. His bony hands were clasped together on his breast as though he was praying. Hunched in his chair he had the look of a bird of prey, a hawk not a dove.

'So you will do it!'

'I will do it!'

'In that case, maybe you and I should get together before then to decide exactly what it is you are going to say.'

Patience frowned. 'Do you really think that's necessary? Of course I shall be delighted to listen to your opinions but I do have plenty of my own and shall be more than happy to expound them.'

Renfrew was momentarily non-plussed. The veneration, hero worship even and desire for his wise counsel as expressed by certain other ladies of his parish seemed to be conspicuously lacking here. Attempting to retrieve the situation, he said, 'I think it would be just as well! After all, we don't want to get it wrong, do we?'

'We? However, if you really feel it would be a good idea, then of course!' Patience was gracious. He had the feeling that the newest member of the church committee was deigning to do it as opposed to dashing to do it. He was also uncomfortably aware that no matter what might be decided in the privacy of his study or her drawing room once she was in the studio and on air he would have absolutely no control over what she said. But it would have been true to say that *whatever* she did or did not say troubled him less than her lack of deference. He had an uncomfortable feeling of having let a genie out of the bottle.

By now both Patience's children were away. She sat down and wrote the customary round robin to them topping and tailing each separately.

Darling Cordelia / Christian, you'll never guess, wrote Patience, *I'm going to be on TV! Isn't it exciting?* She went on to relate how this had all come about. Predictably their reactions to her news were quite different. Cordelia, when she finally received her letter in France, was pleased for her mother. She hoped it would be the beginning of a new era for her. Christian, on the other hand, though not against the idea of a new era in principle, dreaded the thought of her becoming some sort of TV pundit on religion and (even worse) morals generally. Nor did he very much like the sound of the Reverend Cedric Renfrew (. . . *the Reverend Cedric Renfrew is wonderful and* so *encouraging* . . .) *Who knows, maybe I shall become a media personality,* speculated his mother further on. Who indeed? was Christian's reaction reading this. He let his eye wander on down the page. There was nothing much else of interest. She did not mention his father at all.

He put the letter to one side. In one sense it was the least of his problems. After the *débâcle* of his encounter with Flora he had not gone back there the following day as had been originally arranged, but had rung to say that he was ill. Dad on the telephone regretting the fact that he was not going to see his son before he went away sounded exactly the same as usual in the circumstances. There was no hint of reproach or accusation that Christian could discern, which probably meant that Flora had not told him.

Flora.

Christian supposed he must be in love. He dreamt about her, thought about her constantly and even wrote mawkish letters to her which he never sent. He was obsessed with her. Even her homicidal cat featured in his dreams. Sometimes he fantasised that he and she ran away together in young Lochinvar fashion which in the circumstances was possibly the only solution. Worst of all, when he thought about the ridiculous figure he had cut at the end of their last meeting, he burnt with shame. For the time being there was nothing to be done. He was in Dorset and she was in her flat in London. With Dad. Christian groaned aloud. Each day of the holiday he had been looking forward to passed more slowly than the one before and desperation began to set in.

For Flora, after her initial dismay, the passing of the same days brought greater peace of mind rather than its opposite. As the incident receded, she was more and more inclined to dismiss it as the impulsive act of a hotheaded adolescent. Obviously she and Christian would meet again and when we do, thought Flora, I shall simply behave as if nothing has happened and, if Christian has any sense at all, so will he.

She and Hugh settled into their life together. Hugh got himself another job. It was not as high-powered as the one he had had taken away from him but this was a different life with different expectations. He asked Flora to marry him.

'But, darling, you're married already,' she pointed out.

'Yes, I know. It's my intention to get un-married as soon as I can.'

'Let's talk about it when you have succeeded. After all we're quite happy as we are aren't we?'

Well, yes they were, but Hugh Allardyce was a conventional man and, though he did not say so, was afraid of losing Flora. As evidence of his honourable intent, he said, 'I'm going to try and see Patience later this week. I want to get the show on the road as soon as possible.'

When Patience received Hugh's telephone call suggesting that they meet, she knew that it could only herald one of two things: either he wanted to come back (unlikely) or he wanted a divorce as soon as possible (likely). I will make one more appeal to Hugh's better nature, decided Patience, and if he remains obdurate then he'd better have one.

On the appointed evening, Hugh arrived at Patience's front door step together with a fearsome-looking cleric. While waiting

114

for the front door to open, they introduced themselves.

'Cedric Renfrew,' said the cleric. 'Vicar of this parish.'

'Hugh Allardyce,' said Hugh, resisting the temptation to add, in similar vein, Husband of Patience Allardyce of this parish.

They shook hands after which neither could think of anything to say. Like two dogs waiting to be let in, they both turned expectantly towards the front door. As they stood there, it occurred to Hugh that maybe the Reverend Renfrew had been asked by Patience to mediate between them and, if that's the case, if it is, then I'm simply going to walk out, decided Hugh.

It was not the case. If anything he received the impression that she was not pleased to see the other caller either.

'Hello, Hugh,' said Patience. 'Oh. And Cedric. I thought we agreed tomorrow.'

'We did,' came the reply, 'but I was passing and just thought I would call by on the off chance that you had done it.'

Done what? wondered Hugh, mystified.

'As a matter of fact I have,' said Patience. 'If you wouldn't mind showing Hugh into the sitting room, I'll get it.'

While she went off in search of whatever it was, Hugh followed in the wake of the Reverend Cedric Renfrew who was wearing a flared jacket together with very narrow trousers which gave him a gaitered look. Apart from his dog collar, all was in inky black producing a Trollopian effect. In what Hugh found a repellent, rather lupine way, he was a good-looking man and, Hugh sensed, probably a vain one.

They both sat down.

'Am I to understand that you are Mrs Allardyce's husband?' enquired Renfrew.

'Estranged husband,' answered Hugh, laying it on the line and resenting the question as he did so.

'Ah, yes,' said Renfrew settling back in his chair and crossing one insecty leg over the other, 'Mrs Allardyce, Patience, I should say, has talked a little to me about her marital difficulties.'

Thinking *this really is intolerable*, Hugh said shortly, 'There are no difficulties. We are separated and about to get divorced. It is all very straightforward.'

'Nothing in this life is ever straightforward, I fear,' observed Renfrew, intent on pursuing the subject and apparently impervious to the frosty atmosphere. 'The consequences of our actions can have far-reaching and damaging effects where others are concerned. We should not be dismissive of this fact as we pursue our own gratification.' Abruptly he got to his feet, strode across the room and stood with his back to the fireplace.

'Romans 8, verse 5, *They that are after the flesh do mind the things of the flesh; but they that are after the Spirit the things of the Spirit. For to be carnally minded is death,*' declaimed the Reverend Cedric Renfrew sternly.

The man was a walking sermon. Astonished and affronted at the same time Hugh was just opening his mouth to try and frame a suitably crushing riposte when to his inestimable relief the door opened and Patience entered.

'Here they are,' said Patience, handing Renfrew a sheaf of what looked like letters and envelopes. Immediately the hectoring stance subsided. The vicar became, comparatively speaking, a normal person again.

'Thank you, thank you!' said Renfrew, taking the bundle from her. 'You must let me know how much I owe you.' He leafed through the correspondence. 'Very good, very good! When is our next little session?'

'Friday,' replied Patience.

There was a pause. Nobody said anything. 'Well, I'd better be going,' said Renfrew, without much conviction. Another pause. Evaluating this little scene, Hugh's view was: he's waiting to be asked to stay and have a sherry so that he can carry on interfering. Patience's response to this was to lead the way to the front door.

'Goodbye,' said Renfrew to Hugh. 'It has been a pleasure meeting you.' The glittery-eyed look which accompanied this made a pleasantry sound more like a rebuke. Unable to reply to this in similar vein even just on a superficial social level, Hugh merely nodded. Renfrew passed out of the room, there was a brief exchange on the door step and then he was gone.

'Seems a very uncompromising sort of a fellow,' observed Hugh mildly as Patience re-entered the room. 'And not over-endowed with a sense of humour either.'

Patience looked surprised and then replied obscurely, 'A sense of humour? Cedric does not need a sense of humour. *He*

116

is a vicar!' Listening to this, it occurred to Hugh that since Patience did not have one either, it was not something she was likely to miss much. 'Anyway, enough of that. You wanted to see me.'

'Yes,' said Hugh. 'I've come to ask you to give me a divorce!'

She was pretty certain her next words were a formality but she spoke them anyway. 'You're quite sure you want one?'

'Quite sure.'

They stared at each other across the impasse of complete breakdown. It was hard for Hugh to believe that for twenty years he had shared a bed with the woman in front of him, so complete was his indifference. Only the entrancing present existed. The past was dead.

Patience, the stranger who was bizarrely still his wife, moved the wedding band he had given her in another life up and down her finger. 'Then, if that is really the case,' she said at last, 'I suppose you must have one.'

Part 2

12

Time passed. Although not very much appeared to alter, there was in fact a great deal of change taking place below the surface. Old allegiances and perceptions were dissolving and re-forming thereby making certain lives ripe for upheaval particularly those of Drusilla, Charlie and Hillary. Charlie remained in thrall to Drusilla by night and frankly disenchanted by her demands by day when he needed all the energy he could muster in order to run his complex business affairs. In the short term he could see no prospect of dislodging Drusilla from his flat that it might become the peaceful bachelor haven of the old days, the more especially since Hillary had vetoed any question of her return to him. It was scant comfort that Hillary's Claude Lorrain still reposed in a bank vault to which the only person who retained a key, apart from the bank itself, presumably, was Drusilla.

Most irritating of all, Miles Compton's rosily re-adjusted TV feasibility study had been put before Causton's board, ummed and aahed over and finally in principle approved. By this time in anticipation of their approval, Causton had shopped around and found himself a consortium to join which already had a TV company in its sights. When the news of the bid appeared in the business press, on top of all his other troubles it was Charlie Davenport's turn to feel trumped.

'What does your husband want a TV company for?' grumbled Charlie. 'It's a ridiculous acquisition!' The use of the words 'your husband' suggested that in some way Drusilla was to blame for it.

'No more ridiculous than you suddenly upping and buying a radio station,' riposted Drusilla without looking up from the pages of *Vogue*.

'I have a strategy. I intend to expand further into radio,' said Davenport loftily. 'I intend eventually to get right out of newspapers. In media terms newspapers are old hat.'

'How do you know that he isn't intending to do the same?'

Drusilla stopped leafing through the pages of her magazine, her attention caught by a photograph of a vampish violet Versace evening dress. She handed the magazine across the breakfast table to Charlie, tapping the picture as she did so. 'What do you think of this?' Well aware that what this really meant was: Will you buy it for me? and that Drusilla's dress bills were something else he would like to hand back to Hillary, Charlie was noncommittal, damning with faint praise.

'Quite nice,' said Charlie.

'*Quite nice?*' Drusilla was aghast. 'That won't do at all. Very sinful is what I want!' Clearly put out, she looked across the toast at Charlie who seemed distracted. 'Look, if you're so upset about Hillary's television company, which, by the way, he may have bid for but he hasn't got yet, why don't you get one of your own? Or better still,' here Drusilla became animated at the mayhem the next suggestion could be relied upon to cause, 'muscle in and take his!' Charlie briefly entertained the idea and then dismissed it. It was a tempting scenario but probably it was too late for that. He looked at his watch. Time to go. He looked forward to some peace and quiet in his office. It was the only place he got any these days.

Someone else who decided peace and quiet was at a premium was Dorian. Radley in his new incarnation as a member of the Features team alternately moped and railed. Stoicism was a foreign concept to Radley. The invitations to first nights and parties and openings began to dwindle, hijacked by the useless over-promoted Peter. Thrown increasingly into each other's company with no diversions, the cracks in the relationship between them perceptibly widened. Trying, without success, to read a book one evening while Radley fretted and paced, Dorian recognised that she would like to extract herself from an affair which was no longer doing anything for either of them. Even the sexual side was flagging, commensurate perhaps with the fact that it had always been based on lust rather than love. It was as though Radley's libido had wilted in sympathy with his social life.

Watching her lover narrowly Dorian thought: But I can't leave now. Not while he's so down. It just wouldn't be fair. It would look as if I had been using him. And, of course, said conscience ever uncomfortable, you have. Facing this fact and ashamed of it, she also faced the fact that she was still in love with Robert. At night Dorian dreamt about him. Quite often in these dreams, which had begun after their last meeting, they were both dressed in the elaborate fashion of the eighteenth century. The emotional atmosphere was highly charged although, significantly, they did not touch one another and when it appeared that they might be about to do so, Dorian woke up bereft and exhausted, afraid that Radley had heard her speak her husband's name aloud in the course of her restless sleep. A common participant in most but not all of these dreams was the cynical and, as Dorian perceived it, destructive shade of Alexander Pope. Since their last meeting she had not heard from Robert and in the light of what she had had to say on the subject could not reasonably expect to until the book was either dropped or finished.

In another part of London, the said biography was inching forward at a snail's pace but at least it was inching forward. Robert had days when he thought it was good and days when he thought it was hopeless. This ebb and flow of confidence was unnerving. He wished Dorian, by whose opinion he set great store, was there to advise him, but Dorian had said that she would not see him again until this particular agony was over. It seemed there was nothing to do but battle on alone. And while Dorian dreamt of Robert, Robert also dreamt of Dorian but in far more physical terms. In Robert's dreams he undressed his wife, kissing and caressing her as he did so until finally he entered her. After it was all over they fell asleep in each other's arms and when he finally awoke and opened his eyes it was to find her looking at him, her strange light cat's eyes dispassionate, searching even, as though all the time they had been making love she had not been really engaged at all. It was almost as though she did not know who he was. So vivid was this disconcerting image that in the morning, still half asleep at the end of a fitful, disturbed night he believed that she was still there and stretched out his hand to where she should have been. All these dreams were essentially the same until one night there was a change. At the end of their lovemaking Dorian rose and slowly

123

and silently dressed, after which, without a backward glance, she left him *together with someone else who must have been there all the time, whose face he could not see.*

The message would seem to be clear. He had lost her. Even in dreams sexual jealousy had to be the worst kind. His pain was acute. He became aware that his face was wet with tears.

'I've been such a fool,' said Robert aloud. '*Such* a fool!'

Christian also felt he had made a fool of himself. All his pale loitering as he agonised as to what to do about Flora was brought to an abrupt end by the letter she sent him. Because he did not recognise the hand, he went to the end of it first and the sight of her signature caused his heart to lift. Not for long though.

> *Dear Christian,*
>
> *I shall make no bones about the fact that I was shocked and upset by your extraordinary conduct the last time we met,* wrote Flora, very severe. *However, despite the fact that I am unable to comprehend why you behaved as you did, for your father's sake, I should like to clear the air between us. Eventually we shall have to meet again and when we do I do not wish there to be any residual tension or indeed misunderstanding between us. With this in view, I have decided to put your actions down to overwhelming though, it must be said, misguided impulse. Impulse, I have learnt to my cost, can cause havoc, but only if we let it. What I should like to do is to wipe this particular slate clean on your behalf since you may be too embarrassed to do so yourself and say that, as far as I am concerned anyway, the whole episode never took place. And because it never took place we need never refer to it ever again.*

This missive was simply signed *Flora*.

Full of conflicting emotions, Christian stared at the letter. It was the first time he had seen her handwriting. Flora wrote in slanting script which marched across the page. Unusually in this the era of the biro, she used a fountain pen whose broad nib emphasised the strong black symmetry of the letters, giving the whole an elegant, calligraphic look. Christian who, prior to the arrival of her note, would have given a great deal for a letter from

Flora, now found himself in the position of deciding he would have given a great deal for any letter but this one.

He read it again.

It was cool. It was dignified. It was the letter of someone seeking to defuse a situation. There was no indication that she felt anything for him whatsoever except insofar as he was his father's son and because of this she was prepared to overlook his precipitate pass. In her eyes he had made an ass of himself. Contrary to the desired effect, the brief physical contact of his clumsy embrace had put him at arm's length as nothing else could. Desperately he read the letter again, searching for some sign that what she wrote was not what she meant, that all the time it was a coded message of love and was forced to conclude that it was not. In the light of this humiliating fact, infatuation curdled and turned into dislike. That night Christian slipped out of school. Well aware that this was a sacking offence should he be caught, he went to one of the local pubs where he got very drunk indeed.

For Patience life was not running as smoothly as it might either. The divorce was in its final throes. Shortly she and Hugh would be uncoupled at which point, no doubt, he would marry The Other Woman. Disconcertingly, the glamorous career she had envisaged for herself, kickstarted by the television debate, did not materialise for the very simple reason that the programme itself had been put on the back burner for the time being by the channel concerned. In the light of this disappointing fact, the generous offer of an uncontested divorce so that she would be free to get on with an exciting new life, now looked like misplaced magnanimity. A compensatory factor, on the other hand, was the Reverend Cedric Renfrew's obvious interest. Eyes modestly cast down over her spiral bound notebook (Cedric did not possess a dictaphone), Patience was aware of his gaze upon her. Although she did not find Cedric particularly attractive, it was gratifying to have cornered the interest of one whose attention was so eagerly sought by the other ladies of the parish and it was certainly better to have an unsatisfactory admirer than no admirer at all. Had she been aware of his exact thoughts as he stared at her, she might have been less flattered.

'*Thy neck is like the tower of David builded for an armoury, whereon there hang a thousand bucklers, all shields of mighty men,*' mused Renfrew, eyeing it, innocent of the pearls which she had not got round to having restrung and picturing himself kissing its soft flesh. Because she was still married (just) there could be no question of him Speaking, a fact which suited Patience who did not know what she would have done with such a declaration had he made it.

She did, however, introduce him to her children who for once agreed on something, namely that they both disliked him.

'Creepy!' was Christian's verdict.

'*Very!*' was Cordelia's.

At the school they both attended Cordelia was sensitive to the fact that her brother appeared to be suffering but had no idea why. When she asked Christian about it, he was snappy.

'Is it Mummy's friendship with the Rev?' Cordelia wanted to know.

'No, it isn't! Why don't you leave me alone?' was the ungrateful response.

'You're my brother,' said Cordelia simply. 'I don't like to see you unhappy.'

'I know,' said Christian, ashamed in spite of himself, 'but it's something I can't talk about.' Then noting her clouded brow and hurt expression, added, 'Not even to you.'

He wondered whether this was the moment to tell her that he had just had a letter from Dad suggesting that he and she might like to go and have dinner with himself and Flora. *Because I have something to tell you*, said the letter without elaborating. It probably wasn't the moment but then it probably never would be so he decided to pass on the information anyway.

To his surprise, Cordelia said, 'I know. I've had the same letter. I've been wondering what to do about it!'

She was not the only one. For different reasons Christian had been wondering what to do about it too. It occurred to him that this was a meeting which would be easier if his sister was present rather than if it was just the three of them.

'I think you should come,' said Christian. 'After all you can't go on ostracising Dad for ever. It isn't going to change anything.

They're getting divorced and that's that.'

Cordelia bit her lip. The intervening months had softened her resolve to have nothing to do with her father's new ménage. Always closer to him than to her mother, Cordelia missed her father. Despite her silence, Hugh still wrote to his daughter regularly. To date, Cordelia had read his letters, wept over them more often than not and then put them away unanswered. She had kept every one. Oddly enough the prospect of him starting a new life and a new marriage (possibly) had seemed easier to accept once the house they had all lived in as a family had been sold. Here in even entertaining the idea of a second marriage, Cordelia was ahead of Christian who shied away from the very thought of such a thing.

At last, Cordelia said, 'All right. I will go. It couldn't be any worse than meeting the Reverend Cedric Renfrew.'

No, it couldn't. Just thinking about that particular encounter set the teeth on edge. Watching the hungry, no other word for it, way Renfrew's eyes followed their mother round the room, both had been dismayed. Not that she had responded in kind. Mother had been her old impervious self. Worse if anything had been his jocular insidious bullying concerning her children's religious proclivities. *I'd like to punch him!* was Christian's less than godly mental reaction to one sally. *It's none of his business.* Finally, after dinner, Renfrew had stood in front of the fireplace and held forth on the subject of the morals of the nation and those of the young in particular. He was plainly not interested in debate. At eleven o'clock precisely, as though a switch had been flicked he stopped talking and prepared to depart saying that he had a sermon to write.

'I would say he's already written it,' observed Christian *sotto voce* to Cordelia as he was leaving.

'What do you think?' enquired Patience brightly, when he had finally taken himself off.

'I think he likes his Port,' replied Christian, deliberately missing the point. 'He had three glasses and never passed it to me once.'

'Or me,' said Cordelia.

'No, no,' said Patience hastily getting off the unsatisfactory subject of Renfrew's drinking habits. 'I meant what did you think of *him*?' She looked directly at Cordelia who blushed and said, uncertainly, 'He seems very, well . . . *definite* . . .' Here her voice trailed away. She looked towards Christian for help.

'He *has* to appear definite, as you put it,' said Patience. 'He is a man of God! Faith is what it's all about.'

'Yes, but I don't want *his* faith pushed onto *me*.' Christian had been definite as well. 'What he does with it on his own behalf is his affair. The problem is that he seems incapable of conceding that someone else might have a different point of view. He does-n't have an open mind.'

'I'm not certain you can have faith and an open mind,' ventured Cordelia. 'Doesn't one cancel out the other?'

'Probably,' conceded Christian, 'but it shouldn't prevent tolerance coming in.'

Reflecting that her brother was probably one of the least tolerant people she had ever met, in the interests of family harmony Cordelia decided not to voice this opinion. Patience, who had also noticed Renfrew's incapacity to listen and re-evaluate, nevertheless felt pained. Why is it, Patience asked herself, not for the first time, that other people's children always seem more biddable than mine? I have brought them up in the Christian tradition and all they ever seem to want to do is question it. Why can they not simply accept it? It did not occur to her that possibly a forced march along the road of Christianity from babyhood had stimulated resistance to it to the point where trench warfare was the order of the day.

'You should come to church with me one morning,' encouraged Patience. 'Hear him preach! He's a very powerful speaker, you know.'

Hear him harangue you mean, was Christian's reaction listening to this. Aware from her son's blank look that her suggestion had fallen on stony ground as far as he was concerned, Patience turned her attention to her daughter.

'You'll come, won't you, darling?'

Kindhearted Cordelia, who did not want to go either but was sensitive to her mother's single and probably lonely existence, said, 'Yes, of course I will. I'll come with you on Sunday.' The prospect was not an alluring one and meant there would be no Sunday lie-in reading the latest romantic novel. Imperceptibly,

Cordelia sighed.

The event itself turned out to be unexpectedly interesting. Like her mother before her, Cordelia noticed how very full the church was with worshippers practically hanging from bell ropes and belfry. The music impressed her as well. All too often she had found church services dolorous. This one was positively cheerful, hip even. She wouldn't have thought it was up Mummy's alley at all. Until the advent of the Reverend Cedric Renfrew and his sermon that was. As the priest climbed the steps to the pulpit a respectful silence fell. Cordelia and Patience were sitting three pews back from the front. Under craggy brow the baleful eye of Cedric swept the church before briefly coming to rest on Patience and her daughter. Then, like a bird of prey, he hunched over the pulpit and let his congregation have it. Christian had been right. It was almost word for word the diatribe to which they had both been subjected on Friday night. He must have taken the opportunity for a dry run. Looking covertly to right and left, Cordelia saw that he had the rapt attention of the whole church.

'*Save me,*' said Renfrew, quoting in conclusion the Prayer Book of 1662, '*and deliver me from the hand of strange children: whose mouth talketh of vanity, and their right hand is a right hand of iniquity.*

'*That our sons may grow up as the young plants: and that our daughters may be as the polished corners of the temple.*'

Declaiming these words he looked piercingly and directly at Cordelia for quite a long time, so that those in front turned round to see whom he was addressing and those behind craned in order to do the same. Cordelia, who had no desire to be a polished corner of his temple or anyone else's for that matter, flushed scarlet to the roots of her hair. She fervently wished the floor would swallow her up. Hillary Causton who was also in the congregation but further back felt not for the first time that Renfrew had gone over the top and wondered why he had singled out for special rebuke the pretty dark-haired girl who, judging by the resemblance, was sitting beside her handsome mother. At the end of the service, though one or two people came up and spoke to Patience, nobody addressed Cordelia who was, however, the target of a barrage of curious looks. Maybe they thought her right hand was a right hand of iniquity. Whatever the reason, she felt she could endure no more.

'I'm not feeling well,' said Cordelia to her mother. 'I think I'd like to go home.'

'What?' Unaware of the depths of her daughter's humiliation, Patience was put out. 'You seemed perfectly all right this morning. Don't you want to come and congratulate Cedric on his stirring sermon?'

Without directly answering this, Cordelia said, 'I think I'm going to be sick. I'll go on ahead. I need some fresh air.'

She went.

At home she found Christian in a dressing gown reading the sports pages of the *Daily Mail*.

Without looking up he said, 'Hello. Where's Mum!'

'I left her behind.' Cordelia was short. So short that even Christian noticed. He put down his paper and eyed her curiously.

'What was it like?'

Cordelia's pallor was startling. There was a spot of colour on each cheek.

'The service was fine. Happy clappy, that sort of thing. I quite enjoyed it.' All this was delivered in a normal tone of voice which made the vehemence of her next words all the more surprising, 'But that fucking priest is odious! ODIOUS! I was mortified! MORTIFIED!' She ran from the room, slamming the door as she went. Minutes later he heard stormy weeping.

By the time Patience arrived back this had subsided.

'Where is Cordelia,' she enquired of Christian who was sitting in the same place still trying to read the same article, 'and isn't it time you were dressed?'

'Upstairs,' answered her son, deciding to reply to the first question and ignore the second. After a moment's reflection he added, 'She seems upset.'

'Yes. Your father has a lot to answer for.'

13

Hillary decided that he wanted a divorce and quickly. He wanted to be shot of Drusilla, and even more than that he wanted his Claude Lorrain back. He was well aware that the painting was being held to ransom and expected to have to pay through the nose for the privilege of having his own property returned to him. Accordingly he rang Gervase Hanson, the solicitor he used to deal with all his corporate affairs.

'What I need is a rough, tough divorce expert,' said Hillary to Gervase.

'You need someone,' said Gervase, without hesitation, 'who as well as knowing how to play hard ball, is very civilised so that he doesn't put the opposition's back up right from the start, unlike some I could name. Whoever you select will be very expensive, of course.'

'Money's no object,' said Hillary dismissively. 'However pricey a hot-shot divorce lawyer is he still might be able to save me a packet.' Suddenly wistful, he added, 'She took my Claude Lorrain you know.'

Leaning languidly back in his chair with the telephone receiver tucked under his chin, Hanson raised his eyebrows. 'What, she walked out with it under her arm?'

'More or less. She drove off with it in the Jaguar and it's now mouldering in a bank vault somewhere. Naturally I want it back!'

'But you don't want Drusilla back?' This was a statement more than a question. The rumours that the Caustons had split up had, of course, been circulating London society for months. Unusually, especially for Drusilla, nobody appeared to have confirmed or denied this officially and nothing had so far appeared in the gossip columns, though there was speculation that she was in fact living with Hillary's arch-rival, Charlie Davenport. Thank heavens she's not living with me, thought Gervase, who knew Drusilla of old. Aware that the unmatched

Claude Lorrains were, apart from his Meissen collection of course, Causton's pride and joy, he observed aloud, 'She's got herself a very good bargaining chip there, Hillary. It looks as though you could have quite a fight on your hands. Might be cheaper to get back together again.'

'Over my dead body!' Hillary was short. Listening to him and mindful of the way Drusilla operated it was Hanson's private opinion that it might very well come to that.

'When did you last see Drusilla?'

'The day I told her to leave.'

'Don't you think it might be worth trying to defuse the situation by meeting her for lunch? Try to get the whole situation on to a more civilised level. Explore the possibilities, that sort of thing.'

The same thought occurred to each simultaneously, namely that civilisation and Drusilla had very little to do with each other. All the same, quite a lot of time had gone by and tempers had cooled. Maybe it *was* worth a try.

'I might just do that,' said Hillary at last, though without very much conviction.

'Alternatively, you could, of course, sue your wife in the courts for the return of the painting but you probably wouldn't want to do that.'

'I wouldn't!' Hillary was quite decided. 'The publicity and ensuing scandal would be very damaging.' He might have added: and Charlie Davenport would have a field day at my expense, but did not. Hanson, who knew both men, intuited the unspoken remark without having to hear it.

'No, discretion must the name of the game!'

Once again the same thought crossed both their minds at the same time: Drusilla doesn't know what discretion is. 'Insofar as that is possible,' added Hillary in the wake of it.

Reflecting that whichever way you looked at it, Causton was in one hell of a jam, Gervase said, 'In that case I strongly urge you to try to reach some sort of amicable arrangement between the two of you.' (As one, they both thought, Drusilla doesn't know what amicable means.) 'Meanwhile, as we have been talking I've had some ideas as to whom you might use should the worst come to the worst. The names are as follows . . .'

Because she was currently ensconced in his rival's flat, Hillary did not telephone his wife to suggest lunch, he wrote instead. The letter was a short one. It said,

> Dear Drusilla,
> I think it advisable that we should meet. Would you please telephone me either at home or at the office to arrange time and venue. I suggest lunch one day next week.
> Yours, Hillary.

Some might have been wounded by this cold communication but Drusilla, who had been waiting for just such an advance on her husband's part, was pleased with it. At last things were beginning to move. In anticipation of just such an approach she had already made enquiries as to the value of the Claude. Since Hillary always dealt with such mundane matters as the insurance of their valuables, she had never known its exact worth. The sum mentioned was astronomical. It was certainly enough to keep her in couture.

Since Hillary had indicated that he wanted a lunchtime discussion, Drusilla determined that it should be dinner instead. I'm at my best in the evenings, reasoned Drusilla to herself, and besides it gives me a chance to dress up. I shall wear scarlet and the black pearl choker. The real reason, of course, was that it would both annoy Hillary and show him who was in charge of this particular negotiation. The point was not lost on him. He grumbled but acquiesced. They agreed to meet on neutral territory the following week.

February was very cold that year. The weather retained a steely cutting edge indicating that, despite spasmodic sallies of high light skies and pale sun, winter was by no means on the retreat. The day on which Christian and Cordelia traversed Flora's square on their way to have lunch with their father and his mistress was one such. The sunshine was fitful and under the trees where it did not penetrate at all, grass and ground cover were still laced with frost. A broad, spurred band of cloud arched white as a fish bone across a sky of watery blue. Cordelia turned up her coat collar against the chill. This was not, in fact, an exeat weekend as such but, in response to a letter to the school from Hugh, a special dispensation had been granted. For different reasons both Cordelia and Christian felt apprehensive.

It was Hugh who opened the door.

'Hello, Dad,' said Christian before moving aside to make way for his sister who had followed him down the steps.

'Hello, Daddy,' said Cordelia unsteadily. She sounded on the verge of tears. 'I've missed you so much.' Without a word and plainly deeply moved, Hugh drew his daughter towards him and embraced her. Watching them because he was unwilling to confront Flora by himself, even Christian, who professed cynicism on occasions such as this, found his own eyes were moist. Eventually they all went in.

The first thing Cordelia noticed in Flora's sitting room was the exotic scent of flowers which was probably heightened by the heat from a coal fire. A large vase of creamy, waxen lilies stood on a low table to one side of the mantelpiece. The second was the rest of the room. Accustomed to her mother's more conventional approach to interiors, Cordelia had never seen one like this. It was almost impossible to imagine her father living in this small outpost of Bohemia. Flora Munro, who must have been in the kitchen, entered the room carrying an enormous cross cat of the long-haired variety which she put down on one of the chairs.

'Flora,' said Hugh. 'Christian you know already, of course, and this is my daughter, Cordelia.'

Flora and Christian exchanged opaque smiles. Perhaps it was not so easy to pretend that nothing had happened between them after all. Flora turned her attention to Cordelia. They shook hands. What a lovely girl, was Flora's first reaction to Hugh's daughter. A beauty in the making. But damaged, was her second. A walking wounded casualty of all this. The aura of disillusion and hurt was practically tangible. Poor Cordelia! Her eyes took in the other's thinness which was emphasised rather than concealed by a loose purple dress and Doc Marten boots. There was a sweet-natured gravity about her oval face of the sort that is found in certain portraits of the eighteenth century and a vulnerability that touched Flora's heart.

'Shall I pour us all a drink?' Asking the question, Hugh looked at Flora in a way in which he had never looked at her mother, not since Cordelia could remember anyway. It was a proud, proprietorial look which said to the world: I am in love with this woman, and it went hand in hand with a lightness of being such as she had never associated with her father before. He looked ten years younger. Confused, Cordelia looked away. She felt happy for him and desperately sad for herself.

'Yes, why don't you. Lunch will be at least twenty minutes.'

These were not, as it turned out, prophetic words for lunch was destined not to take place.

While rummaging through one of the drawers of her desk on one of her ever more frequent forays to her own flat, Dorian Ormond came across the keys to the front door of the flat she had shared with Robert and Alexander Pope. Turning them over in her hand she experienced a sensation of being part of that life again. And in a way she was. Keys were very symbolic. There was no need to have studied Jung to know that. These two, a Yale and a mortice, had opened the door to their life together time and time again. On impulse Dorian dropped them into her current shoulder bag, probably a foolish thing to do because from here on out they would endlessly get muddled up with the keys to Radley's flat, also a Yale and a mortice. Turning away from the vexed subject of life with Robert she went through her post. There was quite a lot of it, all mundane, mostly bills and circulars. There was only one message on the answer phone which turned out to be from someone who had changed his or her mind about leaving one. Maddening. Restlessly Dorian wandered from one room to another. The flat smelt faintly musty and was distinctly chilly. Because it was currently uninhabited it was without a point, a furnished shell, the bloom and vibrance which occupation gives to interiors all gone for now. Pensively she wrote her name in the film of dust on top of a small mahogany table. Underneath it she wrote Robert and drew a heart with an arrow through it. Shortly it would be St Valentine's Day. There would be red roses from Radley. Red roses on Valentine's Day were a knee jerk reaction for Radley. Not for Robert. Robert had a problem remembering birthdays and anniversaries, let alone frivolities such as Valentine's Day. Dorian looked for the last time at what she had written and then blew the dust away. Dorian, Robert, heart and arrow were almost obliterated as if they had never existed. But not quite. The faintest impression remained of a past which might yet, once again, become a present.

Double locking the door on her way out with yet another Yale and mortice, Dorian thought: I own the keys to three properties and yet I don't feel as though I belong anywhere. What *am* I doing with my life? It was a salutary question to which there was presently no answer.

She turned away and walked down the stairs, through the front door of the block and out into the street.

'Can I give you any help in the kitchen?' The asker of this atypical question was Christian.

'No thank you, Christian,' said Flora, levelly, 'though it's very kind of you to offer.'

She left the room, firmly shutting the door behind her as she did so leaving the three of them alone together. Sipping the glass of Sauvignon that Hugh had poured for each of them including Flora who had taken hers with her, Cordelia said, 'What was the important thing you wanted us to know, Daddy?'

Hugh had meant to tell them over lunch when Flora was there but now the question had been put could see no point in waiting until then. Insensitive because he felt so happy, he said, 'I have asked Flora to marry me and she has accepted.' He was aware of sounding very old-fashioned and it occurred to him to wonder whether the heady excitement of co-habiting would evaporate once they were both locked into the respectable institution known as marriage. But I can't do it any other way was Hugh's verdict on himself. I *am* old-fashioned.

Cordelia, who had been half expecting it, was just opening her mouth to frame lacklustre congratulations when Christian, who had not allowed himself to contemplate such a thing and for whom the shock had therefore been immense, jumped to his feet. Trembling violently he shouted, 'You can't marry her!'

Amazed by his extreme reaction, Hugh and Cordelia turned to look at him.

'Why not?' both said as one.

'She tried to seduce me! She's a whore!'

136

Aghast and speechless his father and sister stared at him. Part of Christian was aghast at himself but it was too late, he'd said it now. *Why* he had said it was another matter.

It was at this point that the door to the kitchen opened allowing the music of Vivaldi to filter through.

'Lunch is ready,' said Flora.

When his door bell rang, for one wildly optimistic, hopeful moment Robert thought it might be Dorian, that she had at last come back to him. It was not. Initial disappointment was eclipsed by astonishment at the sight of his niece Cordelia on the step instead. He had not seen either of the Allardyce children since Dorian had left him and had imagined that this was because Patience was promoting him as an unsuitable influence.

'Cordelia!'

'May I come in? I've nowhere else to go.' She was very distressed indeed and because of this he had difficulty in understanding what she was saying. 'I tried Aunt Dorian's flat but there was no one there.' No there wasn't. Robert had also tried ringing her at the flat. Pulling himself together and thinking as he did so that Cordelia looked as though she might be about to faint, Robert said, 'Yes, of course!' He led the way into the drawing room where, in the interests of economy, there was no fire. Robert lit one.

'I'm afraid I've very little to offer you.'

'I'm not hungry,' answered Cordelia, who felt at the moment as though she could never be tempted by food again and especially not by lunch, 'but I'd love some tea.'

While he was making it in the kitchen, she stared at the gas fire which burnt a brilliant blue and would do until heated up. Shivering and at the same time soothed by its muted roar, Cordelia stretched out her hands towards it. She felt very tired. Robert came back with the tea and a blanket.

'Here, wrap this round you.' He gave it to her. 'Look shouldn't you phone your mother? Tell her where you are?'

'Mummy doesn't even know I'm in London,' said Cordelia. 'It was Daddy we came up to see. I suppose we should phone the school. They're expecting me back tonight.' She was suddenly fearful. 'You won't make me go back tonight will you?'

'No, of course not if you don't want to. But what about Christian? Where is he?'

'I don't know.' *And I don't care* was implicit in the way this was uttered.

'Would you like me to phone the school now?'

'Would you mind? Otherwise there might be hue and cry.'

He went off and did it, wondering what could have traumatised Cordelia to this extent. Although it was true to say that Cordelia had always been more emotionally fragile than, say, Christian. When he came back she seemed altogether calmer.

'I'd like to tell you what happened,' said Cordelia, 'because I don't understand it but maybe you will and maybe talking about it will help.' She hesitated. 'You know that Mummy and Daddy have just got divorced?'

'I know the fact but not the detail,' answered Robert, who had been too wrapped up in his own problems to listen very carefully when Dorian had told him about the breakdown of the Allardyce marriage and who had never had much time for Patience anyway. Though Hugh was a good sort.

'Daddy went off with an artist,' said Cordelia.

'An artist!' Robert was agog. He had expected a nurse or a teacher maybe. One of the more dependable worthy professions. But an *artist*! He wondered how, tucked away in leafy suburbia, Hugh had managed to meet such a person, especially with Patience standing guard over him. His sister-in-law must have let her concentration lapse.

'And Mummy has a dreadful vicar in tow. But this isn't really about her. Daddy wrote to Christian and me asking us to go round to meet himself and Flora, that's his . . .' here she hesitated, finally saying, '. . . friend. It was the first time I'd seen him since he left us. Christian kept in touch but I didn't feel I could handle it. He'd been there before so he'd met Flora already. I thought he liked her. He told me he did. That's why I couldn't believe what happened.' Remembering it she fell silent for a few moments, frowning and biting her fingernails.

'What *did* happen?'

Faintly, Cordelia said, 'Daddy announced that he was going to marry Flora.'

'What's your view of that?'

138

With an air of resignation, Cordelia shrugged. 'I don't want him to be married to anyone but Mummy but it's no longer what he wants and I think she's given up on it too. But what I think is immaterial because I don't think it's going to happen now anyway.'

'Why not?' asked Robert patiently.

Cordelia took a deep breath. 'Christian . . . Christian took it very badly. I was amazed. As I said he told me he liked her. I kidded him about it. I said he sounded as though he was in love with her.'

'What did he do?'

'He began to rave and shout. He shouted that Daddy couldn't marry Flora because she was a whore. That she'd tried to seduce him.'

'Good God,' ejaculated Robert, mesmerised by her tale and unable to imagine Hugh Allardyce in the middle of this sexual maelstrom. By now Cordelia was weeping again. Between convulsive sobs she said, 'Christian is destructive. He can't stop himself. He looks like an angel but he's not, he's a devil. Lucifer, not Christian.' Listening to her Robert thought that she had over-promoted her brother. Nothing to do with devils, was Robert's view. A combination of over-indulgence and neglect have turned Christian into an immature, spoilt brat. In terms of other people's sensibilities he's an unguided missile.

'And then what happened?'

'Daddy hit Christian . . .'

Well, good for Hugh! It had long been Robert's view that Christian needed a punch on the nose from somebody.

'. . . and then Flora, who'd been in the kitchen, walked in and said lunch was ready . . .'

This was a prime example, Robert recognised, of mayhem and the mundane coming together.

'. . . and Christian ran out of the flat! When he'd gone Daddy, I've never seen him so angry . . .' (Robert had never seen Hugh angry at all) '. . . Daddy confronted Flora with what Christian had said but she didn't deny it, she just stood there looking at him. Finally she said, "And you believed him?" at which point Daddy said, "Yes, I did. He's my son. Why would he lie?"'

Robert, who could think of plenty of reasons and who also

thought he could see a pattern emerging from all of this, was silent. He waited to see what she was going to say next.

'So then Flora said very quietly, "You've asked me to be your wife but you don't believe *me*," and Daddy said, "Well, you haven't denied it," and Flora said, "I shouldn't need to!" I said, "Look, I think I'd better go!" and they both turned towards me in surprise. It was as if they had forgotten I was there . . .'

They probably had. It was Robert's own experience that during highly concentrated rows such as this one the main participants tended to look neither to right nor left but concentrated on destroying one another.

'. . . Flora said, "I'm so very sorry, Cordelia." I left them facing one another. As I said I've no idea where Christian went.'

At the end of Cordelia's narrative they were both silent. The only sound in the room was the humming of the gas fire which now burnt hot orange. The room felt stuffy and airless. Outside the light was beginning to fade. It was on a winter's afternoon such as this one that Dorian had left him, Robert remembered. *And he had let her*. There was no point in dwelling on it. Robert had gone over the scene in his mind a hundred times and still could not explain his own behaviour. Now it was probably too late. He looked across at Cordelia. She was sitting with her hands folded and her head tilted back, gazing at nothing in particular. Her exhausted immobility suggested someone who had shot their emotional bolt and for the time being anyway had no reserves left to draw upon.

Gently, Robert said, 'Cordelia, are you sure you don't want me to telephone your mother?'

'Quite sure!' her reply was so faint that he had to strain to hear it. 'I haven't got the resilience to cope with another emotional scene. Mummy can be quite draining you know. Besides Christian may have gone there and I just don't feel I can cope with him either. Not right now anyway. Actually, I'd quite like to go to sleep.'

'No problem so long as you don't mind using my bed.'

Embarrassed, Cordelia said, 'I'd be quite happy with the sofa.'

'Better if we do it the other way round,' said Robert, 'since while you crash out, I intend to go back to my work.'

Without further debate Cordelia went. Much later on he knocked on her door, and receiving no reply looked in to make sure that she was all right. He found her lying on her back still wearing the purple dress with her hair spread around her on the pillow. He noticed with a pang that she was on Dorian's side of the bed. Her hands were clasped on her breast like those of an effigy of a princess on a tomb. All that was missing was a little dog at her feet. The relaxation of sleep had erased the shock and strain of the previous few hours and for the first time since her arrival Cordelia looked at peace. Robert covered her up with a quilt and went back to do battle with his biography.

The following morning she was up before he was and materialised at the end of his sofa wrapped in the quilt. Bare shoulders indicated that Cordelia must have woken up in the night and put herself to bed properly.

'I thought I'd make us both some breakfast,' said Cordelia. 'I feel I have to do something to earn my keep.'

Still half asleep after a very uncomfortable night, Robert said, 'You don't, of course, but if you're offering I'll accept. The challenge will consist of finding some food in the house.'

'I already have! Two eggs or one?'

Lying listening to the clatter in the kitchen accompanied by the radio, he suddenly realised how lonely he had become. Ironically it was company which drove this depressing point home. Even though it was only his niece Cordelia, the very air seemed invigorated by her presence. Fuck Alexander Pope! Even if I have to go down on my knees I will get Dorian back, vowed Robert to himself.

Ye gods! Annihilate but space and time,
And make two lovers happy.

Having lived with Robert and Pope as long as she had, Dorian had almost as many quotes at her fingertips as he did. It was Sunday morning. Radley, who had never been north of Watford, was away in Liverpool working on a story. Complaining bitterly of the unfairness of his lot, he had had to look it up on the map to find out where it was. It was a relief when he finally went. No good relying on the gods. There was just one way to annihilate space and time and make two lovers happy. On impulse Dorian decided to go to Kensington and surprise Robert. Just taking the decision filled her with elation and a sense of going home at last. Light of heart, she checked that she had the right keys and set off.

The faltering sun of yesterday had been replaced by low ochrous cloud. It was still and cold. The Sunday London streets were empty. On the assumption that Robert no longer took a newspaper, Dorian stopped at a newsvendor's stall and bought several. When she arrived outside the flat, *their* flat, she parked and before getting out of the car sat for a while savouring the moment, looking up at the windows. Then with an anticipatory lift of the heart she crossed the road and let herself into the block.

Mounting first one flight of stairs and then the next, Dorian noticed that the stairwell had been repainted and that one set of the neighbours who had been resident when she was there had been replaced by another. Max Pointing, a homosexual antique dealer who had been on friendly terms with the Ormonds in less traumatic days was apparently still there as his name remained beneath his bell. She ran up the last flight and waited for one breathless moment before inserting her key in the lock.

Inside, despite the hour, the entrance hall which had no window of its own was dark. Moving quietly along it, as had always been her habit Dorian opened the door to their bedroom in order to let in a wedge of light. As she did so she noticed something purple lying across the unmade bed. Pretty colour! Curiously, she picked it up. It was a dress. She was standing holding it when she heard the voices in the sitting room.

One belonged to a woman, the other was Robert's.

Dorian dropped the dress and leant against the door. Her head swam. She felt as though she might collapse. The knowledge that, as well as Alexander Pope she apparently had a flesh and blood female rival, caused her to feel physically sick. There was no doubt which was worse. Getting out before they discovered she was there was a priority. Noiselessly Dorian retraced her steps. Once outside the door she raced for the stairs, very nearly falling down them in her agitation. Tears streaming she passed out into the street, threw herself into the car and blindly drove away.

Max Pointing, who happened to be looking out of his window

142

at the time, saw her leave and remarked on the fact to his current live-in companion. At that distance he was too far away to notice her distress. Max had liked the Ormonds and wondered if this sighting meant that there had been a *rapprochement*. Because he liked them both, he hoped so. Since Dorian's departure he had not seen much of Robert and when they had passed one another on the stairs, he had seemed morose and preoccupied. Tactfully Max had kept his distance even to the extent of no longer asking Robert to feed his cat, Rastas, when he was obliged to go away on one of his buying expeditions. Since the situation was clearly a sensitive one, he wondered whether to mention the fact that he had seen Dorian the next time he and Robert ran into one another and, in the end with typical delicacy, decided to play it by ear.

Blissfully ignorant of all this, Robert said to Cordelia, 'You don't have to leave so early, you know.'

'Oh, I think I should get back. I'll go and get dressed and leave you in peace.'

Much as he enjoyed the unaccustomed company and fond as he was of his niece, Robert admitted to himself that he was relieved. Very little had been achieved yesterday and it therefore behoved him to get down to it today.

As she was leaving, Cordelia flung her arms around his neck.

'Dear, dear Robert. I'm so grateful. Thank you.' She kissed him on the cheek.

Afraid that she was going to cry again, he said, '*Courage*, and if you want to talk, you know where I am. It will all work itself out, you know.'

They walked out into the hall. Suddenly she said, 'I do hope you and Dorian get back together again. You should, you're right for one another.'

'I know,' replied Robert simply. He sighed. 'I know. I've been the most monumental fool.'

She was just turning to go, when he unexpectedly said, 'What scent do you wear?'

Surprised, Cordelia said, 'I don't wear any. Well, that is hardly ever. If I'm going out I usually borrow some of Mummy's. Why?'

'And she uses?'

'Chanel Number 5,' was the unsurprising answer. 'Why?' said Cordelia again.

'Then it can't be that!' said Robert almost to himself and disregarding the question. And then becoming aware of her puzzled look, 'It's just that I can smell Armani. Dorian used to wear it. Can't you? It's all around.'

'I can't,' said Cordelia, 'but I do have a slight cold so I probably wouldn't be able to. Are you sure you're not imagining it?'

'No,' said Robert.

When she had finally gone he wandered back down the hall. Haunting and evocative, the perfume lingered on. It seemed to be particularly noticeable by the bedroom door. He *must* be imagining it. Either that or he was living with an olfactory ghost. Perhaps living on my own is causing me to go quietly mad, thought Robert. Feeling himself in imminent danger of getting seriously depressed he decided that doing something was the way to stave this off. Accordingly he went and sat down in front of the computer and turned it on, after which he sat for a long time staring at the words Chapter Three at the top of an otherwise blank screen.

14

In the fickle way in which certain companies work, the television channel suddenly decided that it did want to resurrect the God slot debate Women Priests: Yes or No and contacted Patience Allardyce. Patience experienced a sudden surge of destiny re-establishing itself in her life. She was very excited and rang Cedric to tell him so.

Renfrew was altogether less enthusiastic. The participation of Patience had been his idea and yet they had contacted her without informing him. He did a certain amount of self-interested praying on the subject of how to bring the thing under control but received no heavenly guidance worth speaking of and found himself thrown back on his own resources. The divine silence also raised the question as to whether God himself was perhaps in favour of female vicars. Impossible! Renfrew dismissed the very idea. He decided to go and see Patience and then, with rare subtlety, decided to wait and tackle her on the subject over a sherry after their next dictating session.

Elsewhere, the disarray was absolute. Cordelia arrived back at school to find that Christian had got there before her. In spite of repeated attempts on her part to talk to him, he avoided her and even appeared to be working. He seemed very subdued. She would dearly have loved to know if he had heard from their father, though the presumption had to be that if she hadn't, then he hadn't. She thought a lot about her father and worried about him so much that there were times when Cordelia felt as though she was the parent and he was the child. The weekly letter did arrive from their mother but not from their father and from it each learnt that her television debut appeared to be back on track.

I am thrilled, absolutely thrilled, gushed Patience. *It is scheduled to be broadcast on Sunday March 3rd at 5 p.m. and promises to be a spirited discussion. I am, of course, nervous but nevertheless convinced of the rightness of what I have to say. It is a pity that such an important discussion is not to take place during what in television parlance is referred to as prime time,* she continued, *however we must look on the bright side and I suppose it would be true to say that at that hour on a Sunday there will be less competition from the more popular channels. I look forward to hearing what you think of my performance!*

'Christ, anyone would think she was Sarah Bernhardt,' said Christian aloud to himself, reading the last. He was also well aware that this particular sentence was Mum-speak for *I shall be mortally offended if you do not watch my performance*. He fervently hoped her appearance on the box would be a one-off. To his relief there was no mention of the previous weekend's fracas so she mustn't know about it. Like his sister, Christian also wondered what had happened between his father and Flora after he left but could think of no way of finding out without phoning Flora's flat. Worst of all was the sensation of not knowing where he himself was at. He experienced days when he felt deeply ashamed of his own behaviour and other days when he felt positively exultant at the extent of his own destructive power over events. Which was the real Christian remained to be seen.

After the *débâcle* of her visit to Kensington, feeling that she had had enough of men for the present, Dorian moved all her belongings out of Radley Oates's flat and into her own. He was not due back in London until Tuesday, which gave her ample time to do it. If nothing else, at least this particular decision had simplified the key problem, she reflected, as she posted Radley's set back through his letterbox.

Back in her own domain, she first hung up all her clothes and then, notwithstanding the cold, she threw open the windows. It was while she was opening the one behind her desk that she noticed that the red light on the answer phone was flashing. Because she had been living elsewhere for so long it had not occurred to her to check it immediately she arrived. The message was from Robert.

'Dorian, darling,' said the voice of Robert, 'it's 12 noon on Sunday 4th.' (Good God, he must have made the call while the other woman was still there. Or maybe she had just left.) There

146

was a pause while he presumably marshalled his thoughts and then he continued, 'What I've rung to say . . .' Here he appeared lost for words again, then apparently losing patience with his own halting start, decided to go for broke. 'Oh, what the hell! Look, what I'm trying to say is: Fuck Alexander Pope, it's you I want!' ('Oh, yes?' Frowning furiously at the machine purveying the message, Dorian spoke aloud, scathing in her disbelief.) 'Please, please ring me when you get this message, darling. I love you . . . I can't go on living without you . . .' In the light of what had happened this was outrageous. Unable to stomach listening to any more of it, she flicked the switch and then erased the message after which she took the receiver off the hook.

'Now,' said Dorian aloud and implacable, resolutely looking away from the wreckage of her romantic life, 'apart from cleaning this place up, I need to buy fresh flowers and food, so let's get on with it!'

As he sat, head in hands, in a frankly sordid hotel bedroom, Hugh Allardyce wondered what he had done to deserve the mess his life appeared to be in. Perhaps, conjectured Hugh, he had made a comprehensive cock-up of things in a previous incarnation and that was why this was happening. On the other hand he did not seem to be making a much better fist of things this time around. He put the pros and cons to himself endlessly. For years, thought Hugh, I tried to live by the Golden Rule with Patience alongside me doing the same and look where it's got me, us rather. If virtue was its own reward why had he been so unhappy latterly? Perhaps some people were cut out for saint-hood, Patience for instance, and others, no matter how good their intentions, were not. All the same, after striking out for freedom, what had he ended up with? The answer to this was depressing. No wife, two disturbed children both currently farmed out to a mediocre boarding school, no home as of the moment, just this awful room (here Hugh's eyes dwelt with disfavour on two large gloomy daguerreotypes which were not enhanced by the maroon and cream flocked wallpaper with which the room was decorated) and, worst of all, no Flora. At the end of it all he had even alienated the one he loved.

Hugh was ashamed of his treatment of Flora but possibly not

quite ready to acknowledge the fact to himself. He had made it plain that he doubted her word and when, with haughty dignity, she had refused to confirm or deny Christian's allegations, he had lost his temper. All this had been witnessed by Cordelia, already in a fragile state as a result of the divorce. Hugh groaned. Worst of all, he knew that Christian did lie when it suited him because down the years he had been caught out doing it. So why had he taken his son's part instead of going into the thing properly? The answer was probably a combination of being knocked off balance by the suddenness of Christian's verbal onslaught, coupled with a guilty conscience where his children were concerned which in turn produced a need to ally himself with them against all comers, even Flora. And now that he had calmed down, he could see that Flora's refusal to defend herself against Christian's accusations could as well have been born out of disdain for his lack of faith in her as out of guilt.

All this introspection did not solve anything but it did raise the question of what to do next. At this moment in time he had no idea what had happened to either Cordelia or Christian. The presumption had to be that they had made their way back to school, but presumption was all it was. Without divulging the fact that he was no longer at Flora's address he rang the school to find out. To his inestimable relief both were there. The next thing to do was to let somebody know where he was so that if any crisis blew up he was not incommunicado, although heaven knew with the one he had on his hands at the moment any more would have been gratuitous. Both confident in and humbled by his daughter's capacity to forgive, Hugh decided to write to Cordelia.

My darling Cordelia, wrote Hugh,

I do not know how to express my unhappiness over what took place last weekend and I hope you believe me when I say that in the wake of everything else that has happened the very last thing I wanted to do was to distress you further. Please forgive me. I am currently staying in (here he named the hotel) *in Bayswater. I feel that I have a great deal to sort out in my own mind but one thing that has never been in doubt and never will be is my love for you, my daughter. For the time being I should prefer that my whereabouts is known only to you and me. God bless you darling, Daddy.*

Hugh was not the only one to put pen to paper.

In the wake of unmitigated social disaster, with the sole exceptions of Patience who was busy wrestling with her thesis for the television debate and Drusilla and Hillary, who were shortly to engage in a fight to the marital death over dinner in an effort to thrash out their problems, everybody wrote to everybody else. The universal perception, albeit separately reached, was that, whether one was justifying, dismissing, defending or attacking, doing it face to face had proved calamitous, and discretion as the better part of valour in the shape of a letter was a safer way of passing on sensitive information. For the statements in a letter were all there in black and white. They could not be misinterpreted or interrupted or shouted down. The only hazard might have been a refusal on the part of the recipient to read anything at all but how many people have the strength of will to do that? The answer in this particular case was that none of them did.

In the aftermath of his outburst, Christian was surprised to receive a communication from Flora whose handwriting on the envelope he recognised. Warily he held it in his hand for a while before finally turning it over and slitting it open. It said:

Dear Christian,

I am writing to appeal to your better nature (that is assuming you have one) and to implore you to contact your father and tell him that all the accusations you made against me on Saturday were false. Why do you do these things? (It was a good point. Why did he? Unable to think of a smart answer, Christian read on.) *Anyway, given the fact that you do, a great injustice has taken place. I have not seen your father since it happened and do not even know where he is, but I assume you do. The ball is in your court now.*

This bereft little missive was simply signed *Flora Munro*.

Like the last letter she had sent him, this one left Christian with mixed emotions. Reading it, he pictured her candid gaze and before this felt sheepish. But then she had spurned him in favour of his own father, hadn't she? Christian's self-esteem, never very high in spite of his swagger, required bolstering. He needed to win that round. If she preferred the old man that was her choice but he, Christian, wasn't going to help her. He checked his watch, realised he was late for English again.

'Oh, bugger!' said Christian.

He dropped her note on his desk, gathered up the requisite books and went out.

During his absence, desperate to speak to her brother, Cordelia arrived at his study door. She knocked. No answer. She entered. As usual his room looked like a tip. There was a strange, sweetish smell in the air which Cordelia was unable to place. Odd. Anticipating that he might not be there, she had brought a note. Since this was of a private nature it occurred to her that it might be a good idea to put it in an envelope, assuming Christian possessed such a thing. She opened a couple of drawers, one of which was empty and the other contained only a packet of what looked like cigarette papers. It appeared that her brother preferred to strew his possessions all over the floor. Cordelia's eyes wandered over his desk. On the left hand side was the inconclusive beginning of what looked like an essay on Andrew Marvell. Christian was currently complaining his way through the metaphysical poets. Beside this was a biro. Giving up on envelopes since he did not seem to possess any, Cordelia was just about to fold her note in two and write his name on it when she caught sight of something else. It was the name of Flora Munro. With a furtive glance over her shoulder before she did so, Cordelia picked up the letter and read it. When she had done so, she replaced it, put her own note, which was now redundant, back in her pocket and swiftly left the room.

Cordelia's answer to her father's letter was brief but heartfelt.

Dearest Daddy,
   I was so relieved to get your letter and will, of course, do as you ask. Poignantly, she went on, *While I love you and Mummy, I understand that you no longer want to be married to one another and that I have to come to terms with this. I am*

doing my best. I want you both to be happy. You would have to ask Christian what he wants. At present he is avoiding me so I have not spoken to him since Saturday. Daddy, there is something I must tell you but please, please don't ask me how I know. I think you may have been very unjust to Flora, in fact I am sure of it. Having passed on this information, Cordelia was uncertain what to do next and finally decided to leave it as it was. What happened next was down to him. Changing tack she resumed, *Did you know that Mummy is going to be on television in the near future?* She gave him the date. *It's some sort of debate about women priests.* Cordelia chewed the end of her pen, wrote down some odds and ends of news about school and then rounded the whole thing off with *Very best love, Cordelia.*

A different series of misunderstandings, this time between Dorian and Robert, were compounded rather than clarified by another exchange of letters.

Robert's was heartfelt.

Darling Dorian,
  I have left copious messages on your answer phone yet not a word from you. I know you are not away because when I tried your office number (in desperation), I was told you were unavailable, not once but several times. What is going on? Surely you could at least return my calls? I need you Dorian! As things stand I can't work and I can't sleep either. All I do is think of you. Please, please get in touch.
  Robert.

It was amazing to Dorian that a man she had been married to and thought she knew, could be as perfidious as Robert had turned out to be. A man who was betraying not one woman but two. Maybe more than that for all she knew. It raised the question of what he thought he was doing. Well, whatever he was doing, she wanted no part of it. Clearly a letter was called for if only to stem the flood of calls. The following day, while she was still pondering what to put in it exactly, another letter arrived containing more frantic outpourings of undying devotion, this

151

time from Radley Oates. His arrival back from Liverpool to find an empty flat with Dorian and the belongings she kept there gone, confirmed his worst fears. His pupil had outgrown him and departed. The upshot of this uncompromising statement was that, by dint of her absence, Radley discovered, or thought he did, that Dorian Ormond was the love of his life. He wrote as much, his prose becoming more florid as his agitation increased.

Darling, darling Dorian,
   How could you be so cruel? Radley wanted to know. *So cold? I adore you. Adore you! My life, especially now that I am forced to work in the hell-hole that is Features, has no point without you. You are my muse . . .* ('Poppycock!' said Dorian reading this) . . . *my goddess . . .* On and on it went, page after page of escalating anguish, culminating in poetry inspired by somebody else's muse.
   I cried for madder music and for stronger wine,
   But when the feast is finished and the lamps expire,
   Then falls thy shadow, Dorian! The night is thine:
   And I am desolate and sick of an old passion,
   Yea, hungry for the lips of my desire:
   I have been faithful to thee, Dorian! In my fashion.

Radley had evidently had no qualms about making free with Ernest Dowson's verse but this could be looked upon as simply an extension of his attitude to other people's work generally. On the other hand there had never previously been a hint of the fact that he read poetry. On the whole Dorian was inclined to think that in spite of the fact that Dowson and Radley in terms of style were a perfect fit, rather than being born out of an old familiarity, this was an acquaintance which had come about as a result of a dedicated trawl through the Oxford Dictionary of Quotations.
   It now seemed two letters were called for.
   Feeling all at once very tired, she decided to do both together.

Dear Robert, wrote Dorian,
   After much heart-searching I have come to the conclusion that there is simply no future for us as a couple. I'm sorry to put

*it as bluntly as that but can think of no other way. I shall
always treasure the memory of the good times we had. Good
luck with the biography. Don't give up. You can do it!*

And to Radley, Dorian wrote:

Dear Radley,
   *After much heart-searching I have come to the conclusion
that there is simply no future for us as a couple. I'm sorry to put
it as bluntly as that but can think of no other way. I shall
always treasure the memory of the good times we had. Good
luck with the new job. Don't give up on it. You might even
come to enjoy it!*

This done, she stamped and addressed two envelopes,
inserted the letters, double-checking as she did so that the right
letter went in the right envelope, and then she went out and
posted them. Afterwards she sat solitary and thoughtful in her
small sitting room until the gathering dusk caused her to light
the lamps. Rather like someone who has commenced a fast, she
felt both light-headed and physically released by the decision to
lay down the burdens of her unsatisfactory marriage and her
equally unsatisfactory love affair.
   Alone again, Dorian contemplated her future.

Hugh read Cordelia's letter and immediately telephoned Flora.
As he dialled the number he braced himself. It was entirely
likely, Hugh recognised, that Flora would refuse to have anything further to do with him. He wondered what to do if she was
not in.
   She was in.
   Without preamble, Hugh said, 'Flora, it's Hugh!' and then,
when there was no response, 'Flora, I've been a complete
bastard. I've behaved despicably . . .'
   'Just as long as you know!' said Flora, speaking for the first
time.
   Hugh felt elation at the sound of her voice and terror that she
would dismiss him. Humbly, he said, 'Can you ever forgive me?'
   'Down the years I've learnt that I can forgive anybody just

about anything. Even what you did to me, Hugh,' replied Flora with an odd combination of magnanimity and censure. 'So, yes, I suppose I can.' She sounded flat, as though every word was an effort.

Full of contrition, Hugh hesitated. He dreaded the answer to his next question.

'Flora, will you take me back?'

There was another loaded silence.

More to break it than anything else, he added, 'I shall quite understand if you say no.' Listening to himself speaking the words, he thought, *What will I do if she does?*

'I don't know why you want me to!' Her voice was choked with tears. 'You said such awful things.'

'I know!' Then, quoting Cordelia and, unwittingly, Flora herself, 'I've done you a great injustice and I despise myself for it. You would be perfectly justified if you said you never wanted to see or speak to me again.'

There was an extended pause at the end of this speech and Hugh was preparing himself for the worst when Flora said at last, 'Very well. Come home. But *now*. Not tomorrow, or the day after, *now*!' She sounded exhausted.

Sitting as he was in his horrible hotel room, her use of the word *home* touched his heart. He could have wept with relief.

'Oh, Flora! Darling Flora! I'll be there in forty-five minutes.'

Later, as they faced one another across her kitchen table, Flora said, 'What caused you to have such a change of heart?' There was a gravity, regality even, about her which was daunting. Hugh would have liked to make love to her there and then, but did not dare suggest such a thing.

'The rage subsided. Purely and simply I calmed down and began thinking straight. Then I received some information . . . after that I just had to speak to you.'

He leant across and took her hand but did not elaborate.

'Information? What information? Who from?' Flora was agog.

'I promised I wouldn't divulge that to anybody,' said Hugh. 'It didn't say anything specific just underlined what I already knew about you. What I still don't know about Christian is why he did what he did.'

Flora was silent. Her letter to Christian must have shamed him into exonerating her. She had been about to tell Hugh exactly what had taken place between her and his son and now decided not to. Better to let a repentant Christian off the hook rather than distress Hugh even further and cause even more trouble all round. Eventually she merely said mysteriously, 'Maybe he was jealous.'

'Jealous?' Hugh was startled. 'Of me? But I'm his father!'

Dear honourable Hugh. For the first time, Flora smiled.

'Let's put it this way, Christian's very complicated. Hormones in uproar, plus I suspect he doesn't like himself a lot of the time. He's going to need a lot of support from you. So does Cordelia but in a different sort of way. It's easy to support Cordelia. But Christian . . . I suppose I'm asking can you forgive *him*?'

Hugh raised Flora's hand to his lips and kissed it.

'If you can forgive *me*, then I can forgive *him*.'

That night they did make love. Afterwards, when Flora was asleep, Hugh lay on his back listening to her quiet breathing. Above him the ceiling rose was a graceful circular twist of acanthus leaves from which was suspended a huge round Japanese paper lantern. Where it reached that far, the light from numerous beeswax candles had given the white walls of the bedroom a golden bloom and when the flames flickered, shooting left and right like lizards' tongues, the profound darkness just outside their orbit was momentarily illuminated. In this way the easel in the corner of the room took a brief bow and so did the green glass vase full of lilies which Hugh had bought for Flora as a token of his contrition and his love. The sweet, sophisticated scent mingled with the smell of oil paint and infused the bedroom so that even while he could not see her favourite flowers, he was still aware of their exotic presence.

Two of the candles brightly flared and then, with the faintest of hisses, guttered. Hugh got up and went to the kitchen where he poured himself a glass of wine. Sipping it he went back into the bedroom and as he crossed the floor caught sight of his own naked reflection in the pier glass to the right of the fireplace. Pale as a ghost and strangely youthful it stared back at him, an insubstantial flickering imprint of his presence there. And in an odd sort of way, Hugh recognised, Flora *had* given him back his youth.

Another candle guttered. He moved to put them all out.

On his way, he went over to her side of the bed. Flora lay with one arm flung wide, her hair spread around like that of an underwater swimmer, a naiad. Darkness shadowed the sockets of her closed eyes, and gathered in the hollows beneath her cheek bones and around the curve of her jaw, so that the planes of her face were thrown into relief. Before her unconscious beauty Hugh felt humbled. On impulse he lifted back the sheet which barely covered the swell of one of her breasts and kissed its rosy nipple.

Flora stirred but did not wake.

The narrowness of his escape made him feel all at once breathless. For what if she had not agreed to take him back? What would he have done then? Hugh doused the remaining candles one by one and then slipped back into the bed, *their* bed. Needing the feel of her body for reassurance, he curled himself around his sleeping lover. I have come home, Hugh thought, and I shall never leave again.

Some time after this scene took place, Christian received a letter. It was from Flora Munro and consisted of two words: Thank you. Baffled, he stared at it. What could she mean? Finally, deciding that no amount of conjecture was going to solve the mystery, he dropped this, her third and, as it turned out, last letter to him on top of his untidy desk, where it joined the other two.

15

Hillary Causton arrived at the restaurant early and Drusilla late. He wanted to go straight to their table, she wanted to have a drink at the bar. When they finally did get to their table, he ordered meat, she ordered fish thereby making the wine difficult. It was a microcosm of their married life. When they at last had the wine waiter sorted out, swallowing his irritation at her behaviour so far and mindful of his lawyer's advice not to alienate his wife more than she was already, Hillary said, 'You're looking very glamorous tonight, Drusilla.' Even to his own ears he sounded insincere. Not because she did not, but because at present it was not his inclination to pay his wife a compliment of any sort. He noticed that she was wearing the black pearl choker he had bought her in Belgium. The last time he had seen it, it had been scattered all over their drawing-room floor. Drusilla must have crawled around on hands and knees and picked every single pearl up. Grasping was the word which came to mind. Which always *had* been the word to come to mind where she was concerned. It did not bode well for the negotiation on which they were about to embark.

Although they both knew what they were there to talk about, to begin with neither made any move to bring the subject up. Instead they engaged in a ritual dance around the arts, comparing notes on what each had been to see. As usual his wife's comments were well-informed, acerbic and witty, all qualities which had made her an accomplished hostess. Since her departure social occasions had become stilted, Hillary recognised. At the end of the day if Drusilla had not had such a capacity for destruction, there would probably have been no reason for the marriage not to have been perfectly satisfactory.

The first course arrived, thereby providing the perfect interruption for a change of conversational tack.

'Well, now!' said Hillary.

'Yes?' said Drusilla. She slipped off the black, sequined jacket

157

she was wearing, which was piped with purple. At the last minute she had decided that the scarlet dress she had originally had in mind was too brazen and would put Hillary immediately on the alert. Where her décolletage was concerned she had had no such inhibitions. Hillary's mesmerised eyes travelled from the black pearls, down Drusilla's pale throat to her breasts which were barely concealed by what, even by her standards, was a very revealing neckline. Oddly enough, the effect of long sleeves, normally a force for modesty, in this case had the opposite effect by providing no distraction from a spectacular creamy cleavage. Hillary felt a treacherous twinge of desire which he immediately repressed by sternly reminding himself that Drusilla in bed was only half the story. This was business. In the course of conducting it, he did not want to end up with Drusilla back at home again. Remembering the Meissen, he hardened his heart.

'Do you like this frock?' asked Drusilla, more to get her husband going than anything else. 'Charlie chose it for me.'

'Really!' said Hillary. 'I congratulate him on having the financial liquidity to be able to afford your dress bills.'

'Charlie is *very* generous,' was her riposte to this. *Unlike you* was insinuated though not stated. If she was trying to irritate him, she was certainly succeeding. Hillary could feel his blood pressure rising. All right, then. If that was the way she wanted to play it, gloves off.

'Divorce!' said Hillary portentously.

'Yes?' said Drusilla again.

'We both want one!'

'Wrong!' She was triumphant. 'I don't!'

'Well, I do!' By now Hillary was thoroughly out of sorts. The only thing which stopped him from losing his temper with her was a vision of his lawyer saying, at their last appointment, 'Whatever you do, don't let Mrs Causton get under your skin,' which as anybody who knew Drusilla could testify was easier said than done. He was just opening his mouth to elaborate when she continued, 'And because I don't, unless I receive what I consider adequate, no! *generous*, remuneration I'm going to obstruct you in every way I can. Which will cost you a small fortune or maybe just a fortune in legal fees.'

Hillary glared at her. Once again, in his mind's eye, the lawyer wagged a long, thin legal finger at him. With an effort, he controlled himself. He took a swig of his wine. Normally teetotal, Hillary had come to the conclusion years ago that, when duelling with Drusilla, something more than bottled water was required.

'All right! How much?'

She named a sum. A heroic sum.

Hillary choked over his tournedos Rossini.

'After all it's not as if you can't afford it,' observed Drusilla reasonably. Delicately she extracted the flesh from one of her lobster claws with one of the sharp, shining tools provided and just as delicately she ate it.

'It's outrageous! Outrageous!'

'I am outrageous. It's one of the reasons you married me.'

Yes, and what a mistake that had been. No longer feeling very hungry, Hillary refocused on his plate. He had been desperate to tie the knot at the time. If only he had known then what he knew now.

'And then there's custody.'

'Custody?'

'Of the Claude Lorrain, of course. Don't say you'd forgotten about that!'

'That does not belong to you!'

'If possession is nine-tenths of the law, it sure as hell does at the moment.' She was serene. 'I had it valued, you know. It's my view we've been under-insured all these years.'

'Fuck the insurance, I want my painting back!'

'And I'm quite happy to give it back!'

'When?'

'When we have agreed terms. Failing that you can sue me for it!'

They both knew he would never do that. At this useful moment the waiter reappeared. Sensitive as all good waiters are to the fact that this couple appeared to be having a row, or rather one half of the couple appeared to be having a row and that the starched white square dividing them was more like a battlefield than a tablecloth, it seemed politic to try and advance the meal course by course during lulls in the hostilities. In response to his inquiry vis-à-vis pudding, Drusilla said, 'A marquise au chocolat for me, please. What about you, darling?'

'Nothing. Just the bill. And don't call me darling!' snarled Hillary.

Feeling superfluous the waiter departed.

'So what about it?' Drusilla sat back in her chair. 'You give me the money and I give you the Claude! Nothing could be simpler!'

He had, of course, been expecting it, nevertheless the sheer cheek – never mind magnitude – of her demand shocked him.

'You're asking me to . . .!' Words failed him. By now Hillary was volcanic. 'It's my own property for God's sake!' Another mental vision presented itself, this time the lawyer had his head in his hands.

'We've been through that!' Drusilla shrugged.

Puce in the face, with difficulty Hillary got a grip. Breathing hard, he said, 'OK. Let's have a negotiation about the money.'

She reiterated the sum mentioned earlier. He offered a much lower one. She lopped a couple of thousand off her original demand. ('After all, I don't want to appear greedy,' said Drusilla. 'No, of course you don't,' said Hillary, upping his own offer but not much.) Hovering at a distance with the bill and watching them haggle, though not knowing what over, the waiter was relieved that at last they had apparently found something on which they could agree. At one point, he reflected, it had looked as though a knock-down, drag-out fight might have been on the cards. Eventually when they were a few thousand pounds apart, 'Let's split the difference,' said Hillary.

'Done!' said Drusilla, who had added on a huge contingency sum in the first place and had now wound up more or less where she had hoped to be and with Hillary in a much better mood.

'Wait a minute,' said Hillary. 'Just before you jubilate, this is dependent on two things. The first is that you do nothing to impede a speedy divorce by consent. If you do, the deal's off! And second that the exchange of painting and money takes place in my lawyer's office.'

'You almost sound as though you don't trust me,' observed Drusilla equably, well aware that he did not.

'How could you possibly think that?' asked Hillary through gritted teeth as he signed the bill.

In spite of all Patience's lamentations concerning the hour on Sunday at which the debate was to be televised, for one reason or another, almost all of the people who knew her saw it. Because she loved and admired her energetic mother, Cordelia watched and so did Christian, who knew it would be more than his life was worth if he did not. Hugh and Flora watched because Cordelia had told Hugh about it. Hillary Causton watched because Cedric Renfrew had alerted him to the programme and furthermore had hinted that Mrs Allardyce was a protégée of his and would be holding forth as coached by himself. Neither Dorian nor Robert saw it, because neither knew it was on. One other person who did see it, though more by accident than design, was Radley Oates. Radley, who had spent most of that particular Sunday brooding on his unsatisfactory lot, had been slumped in an armchair watching a very old film and had been too idle to turn off the television at the end of it. In that way, he found himself a captive audience of the God slot.

Lantern-jawed, prissy woman was his first reaction to Patience Allardyce. Earnest too. Never having met her, he did not know that he was watching Dorian's sister, although Patience was an unusual name and, that being the case, oddly enough he dimly recollected having come across it in some other context recently. Dismissing the matter he settled down to watch and gradually became aware that on the screen in front of him, in the shape of Mrs Allardyce, was a natural media personality. Not the prepossessing sort but the wilful, powerful variety. Mrs Allardyce might not be a bundle of laughs, was the way Radley put it to himself, but she was compelling. On this occasion he and she were on the same side. A male chauvinist to the marrow of his bones, Radley was dubious about women having the vote, let alone prancing around being priests. Watching Patience Allardyce cogently arguing her politically incorrect point of view, he found her both ludicrous and impressive and had no doubt that she would be asked to pontificate again on other subjects. He pictured her on a Victorian Values soapbox and it occurred to him that this sort of well-meaning, humourless crusader might be good for a mocking feature or even two.

The following morning Radley took the trouble to scan the

reviews, aware that this particular programme would probably have passed unnoticed. To his surprise the critics of at least two influential newspapers, including one of Causton's, had tuned in. Maybe this was because the debate was a highly topical, not to mention thorny one. Or maybe they had been toasting crumpets after a healthy walk at that moment in time and, like Radley himself, had seen it by accident. Of the two newspapers, one agreed with Mrs Allardyce's views (Causton's) and one did not. Both had been impressed by her confident performance and both stated that they expected to see the newcomer on the screen again.

Christian, when he read that last, groaned. Like Radley he could see the way it might go and did not like the prospect.

'Why does she do it?' he complained to Cordelia, who he was no longer avoiding. 'Why can't she be like other mothers? *They* don't spout on the box and embarrass their families!'

'Some of them do,' said his sister. 'Anyway, why can't you just be glad for Mummy?'

The reply to this was inaudible.

'I expect they'll ask her to do it again,' she added.

'Yes, I expect they will,' assented Christian gloomily. Then he said, 'By the way, I received this. I haven't a clue what she's on about, have you?'

He handed Cordelia Flora's last note. Cordelia looked at it in silence. She saw immediately what had happened and why Flora had jumped to the wrong conclusion.

'No. No, I don't,' fibbed Cordelia. 'I wonder what she means.' Always a guilty liar to the point where, unlike Christian, she almost never did it, she could feel herself beginning to blush. Luckily her brother, who was leafing through a magazine which he had just picked up, did not observe her heightened colour. 'I'm glad they're back together again though.'

'Dad's making a big mistake there,' opined Christian. 'She's not worth it!'

'You told me you liked Flora!'

'Did I?' Christian was elaborately casual, pretending to forget that he had said anything. 'Well, I don't now!' He was suddenly venomous.

'Do you know what *I* think?'

'No. Tell me what *you* think,' said Christian without much interest and preparing to patronise. Here he should not have let down his guard, for Cordelia, not normally famous for the rapier-like thrust, unexpectedly got to the heart of the matter. 'I think you're jealous!' she replied.

Brother and sister stared at one another for a few seconds.

Then, 'Balls!' parried Christian, pulling himself together. 'Absolute crap!' He was aware of overdoing the denial, thereby sounding unconvincing. Anxious not to prolong the conversation, which had taken a turn he wasn't expecting and didn't like very much, he said, 'Anyway, look, I've got to finish this essay on Andrew Marvell, so if you wouldn't mind . . .'

'I thought you already had,' observed his sister, preparing to take her leave. 'Wasn't that supposed to be handed in at least a fortnight ago?'

'Yes,' said Christian. It was with a feeling of relief that he shut the door behind her.

Hugh and Flora watched Patience's performance together. It interested Hugh that looking at his ex-wife's image on the screen, he felt nothing at all. His detachment was total. Not so Flora. Flora had not even seen a photograph of her and was therefore inordinately curious. What she saw was not what she was expecting. When she asked herself what that was, the answer was: a battleaxe. Whatever else she was, Patience Allardyce was not that. She did have some of the qualities though, one of which was that she was domineering. Not domineering in a fierce and noisy fashion but just relentlessly pushing her own convictions all the time. Flora had the impression of ferocious will and an inherent distrust of debate, although that was what she was currently nominally engaged in. Or maybe Patience regarded discussion as simply a waste of time. She knew she was right. Her appearance was unexpected too. Here was no dowdy middle-aged matron of the sort, if Flora was perfectly honest with herself, she would like to have been confronted by. This woman, though large-boned, was not fat. Her dress, which was classic, became her and she was perfectly groomed and very self-possessed. Patience's profile put her in mind of certain particularly formidable Roman empresses.

Flora ventured, 'She's very . . .' here she searched for the word and finally came up with '. . . *powerful*, isn't she?'

'Yes,' said Hugh, with something of a sigh, watching the credits roll up the screen, 'she is.'

He switched off.

After her first television appearance, Patience was flushed with triumph. Cedric's congratulations, it was true, had been muted but those of everybody else had been so fulsome that this hardly mattered. In the wake of it had come invitations to do other things, as well as a commitment from the company that they would use her again. All of which was very gratifying. Even more gratifying was an approach from a newspaper in the person of a journalist called Radley Oates who said he would like to do a feature on her and would she be interested? As he had forecast, she said she would. All in all life was looking up.

The following Sunday, Hillary Causton looked out for Patience in church. At first he could not find her and then saw her enter alone, walk down the nave of St Cuthbert's and make her way along a pew near the front. She was taller than he would have expected and had a dignified air about her. Intrigued, Causton leant forward to see better. Pretty, he decided, was certainly not the word to describe Patience Allardyce, but handsome most certainly was. When she finally sat down he lost sight of her.

The service began. No female priests here and a good thing too. I have enough emancipation on my plate already in the shape of Drusilla, thought Hillary, and I certainly don't want another manifestation of it coming between me and my God. He wondered what the theme of Renfrew's sermon was going to be today and did not have to wait long to find out: *Vanity thy name is woman*. Was it his imagination or did some of it appear to be being directed at Mrs Allardyce, who, however, sat with her head bowed as if in prayer and seemed not to notice?

It was a longer service than usual and at the end of it all, because he was late for an appointment to do with his forthcoming divorce and therefore in a hurry, Hillary slipped out before the other worshippers. All thoughts of the intriguing Mrs Allardyce went out of his head as he marshalled his thoughts in advance of the meeting. Despite the fact that, as a result of their dinner together ('The most expensive meal I ever bought anybody!' he was to say wryly in weeks to come) all appeared to be set fair, Hillary knew too much about Drusilla and the way she operated to take his eye off this particular ball.

As she shook his hand on the church steps at the end of the service, Patience was surprised when Cedric suggested that she wait behind because he had something he wanted to sound her out about.

'Very well,' said Patience. There was, after all, not a great deal to rush home for these days. Waiting for him inside the church she wondered what it was he wanted. It had not escaped her noticed that since her debating success Cedric's attitude towards her had been perceptibly cooler. She hoped that she was not going to be forced to endure a reproof of some kind. Although the words *sound you out* did not, in her view, herald that. They had more the ring of a project about them. Or maybe it was just that he wanted something.

As always the groupies took a very long time to go. Like limpets they clung to Renfrew in spite of all his attempts to dislodge them. Sitting in one of the back pews, Patience could hear the competition for his attention. In the end after repeated efforts to extract, he became brusque, at which point Patience heard the twittering voices begin to recede along the path. As they retreated, she was aware that Cedric had become benevolent once again. It was an interesting exercise in approval followed by disapproval followed by approval again and put her very much in mind of Pavlov's dog.

Cedric reappeared.

'My dear Patience, forgive the delay.' He exuded affability yet Patience knew that affability and this particular vicar did not go together. 'Are you warm enough here or shall we repair to the vestry?'

'I'm perfectly all right where I am,' replied Patience, wishing he would get on with it. She raised her eyebrows enquiringly. Renfrew frowned into the middle distance and then cracked his knuckles. In the deserted church the noise was disconcertingly loud, rather like a series of pistol shots.

'I have been asked to preside over a Commission,' announced

Renfrew at last. 'A high-profile Commission which will examine and report on the morals of the nation!'

The words *high profile* caught Patience's attention.

'Who is going to be on the Commission, besides you?'

'We will be a diverse collection. There will be a social worker, a Mr Jonathan Larch, a philosopher, a doctor, a psychologist and a lawyer, all yet to be chosen, and you, my dear Patience, if you consent, representing the average housewife. We shall also require another, elderly lady to represent the older generation. So, what do you say?'

Although unkeen on the pedestrian title *Average Housewife* which she determined to do something about, it was Patience's opinion that here was her chance to put herself firmly on the map.

'I should be honoured to serve,' said Patience. 'You may definitely count on me. And I have a friend called Clarissa Bowen who would be a perfect representative of the older generation.'

16

When Robert received Dorian's letter he read it and then stood, immobile, holding it. The shock was immense. His first impulse was to try yet again to telephone her but days of doing this had yielded nothing and now he knew why. As he had feared, he had conclusively driven her away. Demoralised, his morning cup of coffee forgotten, he went and sat down in the armchair by the fire, which was not on, and remained there staring into space for upwards of an hour. His suffering was acute to the point where he felt he could hardly bear it. In the end, chilled and despairing, he went back to bed where he fell into the sort of dreamless, heavy sleep which drugs but does not refresh. When he awoke it was late afternoon. Wintry, parchment-coloured light filtered through the curtains. Robert checked his watch. For a moment he could not recollect what he was doing there and then came remembrance and with it leaden depression. Worst of all was the knowledge that what had happened was all his own fault. Robert turned over and closed his eyes again. Anything to shut out the unpalatable present.

The next week was spent mainly sleeping. It was the only way he felt he could cope. Sometimes he stood in the hall hoping to recapture the elusive, evocative smell of Dorian's scent but, like her, it had gone. Occasionally the phone rang and there were letters. Robert could not bring himself to deal with any of it. All interruptions by the outside world felt like intrusions into private grief. In the way in which animals cope with illness, so Robert coped with this and simply shut himself away until the awful sense of loss should start to abate. Perhaps it never would.

On the morning of the seventh day, he woke up feeling different, almost imperceptibly lighter of heart. There was nothing to which he could attribute this marginal improvement. Perhaps the depth of his distress had been such that in an odd sort of way he had exhausted his own capacity for misery. The sight of his face in the bathroom mirror came as an unwelcome surprise.

Haggard and unshaven, his own image stared back at him. He looked more like an old tramp of the sort to be found sleeping rough in shop doorways than the literary and (he hoped) urbane Robert Ormond. A shave and a bath went a long way to correcting this. Performing these mundane tasks, he was interested to observe that the piercing heartache of the past week had metamorphosed into something altogether duller, so that although it was still there it was as though the edge had been taken off it. Living with it was now possible.

In the drawing room, Robert confronted his desk. The light on the answer phone flashed furiously. There were messages from his agent who sounded exercised and messages from his publisher who also sounded exercised. The mess on his desk was exactly as he had left it though covered in a thin film of dust. He began to tidy it up, stacking books and research in neat piles and putting the caps back on dried-up pens. Finally he gathered up the typescript he had written to date and placed it in the centre of the desk, in front of the computer. Satisfied that order prevailed at last, he considered the photograph of his wife and discovered that, in spite of the anguish she had caused him, he could not bring himself to throw this away. Instead, after one last, long look at it he placed it face down in the drawer of what had been her bedside table when she still lived there.

Back at the desk and sitting behind it, Robert discovered that a week of eating very little, sleeping a great deal and for once worrying about something other than Alexander Pope had done more for him than he would ever have expected. With resolution and concentrating hard, he read through all he had written to date. At the end of doing this, he dropped the whole lot in the wastepaper basket.

'Useless!' said Robert. 'Fucking useless!'

This assessment of his own work did not produce the dejection it once had, however, for now he saw with great clarity how the thing should be approached and structured, and knew that he could do it. The research was all there and simply needed classifying. All he had to do was write it. As proof of his new-found belief in himself and resolve, he rang his agent with a frank disclosure concerning the non-progression of the biography.

'So what do you think I should do?' asked Robert in conclusion. 'I suppose I had better alert the publisher hadn't I?'

His agent, who had been bracing herself for something of the sort, was less taken aback by the stage Alexander Pope was at than might have been supposed. Her ear was also acute enough to divine that, at last, Robert appeared to know where he was going.

'Leave it with me. I'll sort the publisher out! You write the book!'

'I'll need an extension on the delivery date.'

'Well, obviously! Just get on with it. I'll get back to you.'

The relief in the aftermath of this confession was life enhancing. It occurred to Robert that having been a force for destruction, Alexander Pope now looked like salvation instead, a means of burying his anguish. Light of spirit though not of heart and properly focused for the first time in months, he switched on the computer and began to write.

Patience rang Clarissa Bowen and told her all about the Commission.

'It's a very exciting opportunity . . .' enthused Patience (Who for? wondered Clarissa listening to this), '. . . and you and I do work very well together. Do say you'll do it.'

Clarissa sensed that Patience had decided that she *would* do it. It was true to say that they had worked well together, though this was probably mainly due to the fact that she was not a contemporary of Patience's and therefore did not feel herself to be in direct competition. It was also true to say that when Patience had been chairperson of their own small parish committee, life had been more interesting due in part to constant internecine warfare, all of which had been cloaked in godliness. Now she had gone they were still all disagreeing, but this time with one another rather than ganging up on Patience and the result to date had been organised chaos. Nothing got done until the last minute and the fête had narrowly missed being a shambles. Clarissa was aware that many such church committees lurched along in similar fashion but this did not stop the whole thing becoming very wearing. All the same, she was cautious. Clarissa had a keen sense of the ridiculous and had a strong intuition that this project, which apparently was being organised by a priest she had never heard of called the Reverend Cedric Renfrew, could end up being just that. But, be that as it may, thought Clarissa, it would give me something else to do. As things are I spend a lot of time on my own doing nothing in particular. I may be old but life's not over yet. I know I've got a brain and here's somebody actually asking me to use it for the first time in ten years. She was dimly conscious of Patience's voice expanding, elucidating and persuading.

'No need to say any more,' said Clarissa crisply, 'I'll do it! Who's going to serve on the Commission with us?'

'Apart from you, myself, Cedric and a social worker called Larch we don't yet know. Other members are being recruited as we speak.'

'And when do you expect the whole exercise to get under way?' enquired Clarissa.

'Not much before the end of May, beginning of June, I shouldn't have thought,' said Patience. 'I'm looking forward to it. It should be very stimulating!'

'Oh, *very*!' echoed Clarissa with just the faintest trace of irony. Doubt as to whether this was such a good idea surfaced again and was brusquely dismissed. There was no point in doing anything without a positive attitude. Otherwise one might as well not bother.

In May, Cedric Renfrew, who had the rest of his team in place, approached Hillary Causton and asked him if he would like to sit on the Commission as a representative of the world of business.

Hillary declined.

'I'm much too tied up at the moment what with one thing and another, I'm afraid,' apologised Hillary, 'but I'll monitor your progress with interest.'

With that Renfrew was forced to be content. And, in truth, Hillary did have a lot to field at that moment in time. The divorce had been moving at a snail's pace. It would have been out of character for anything Drusilla was involved in to proceed smoothly. Because of Hillary's warning concerning spoiling tactics and what would happen if she indulged in them, Drusilla

170

had been obliged to be troublesome in a covert manner. Wrangling therefore was muted and when it took place did so between their respective solicitors. It was hard for Hillary to pin down the exact source of it. What he found galling was that in spite of the agreement they had made, it was all starting to cost a lot of money. Finally they were almost there. Between the nisi and the absolute. After the absolute, painting and money were finally exchanged, as Hillary had stipulated, in his lawyer's office.

The day he became a free man, he was surprised by his own ambivalence. Where there should have been relief, there was a sensation of rootlessness and loss, sadness even. Hillary was unable to comprehend it. I *wanted* this divorce, he reminded himself. It was my idea. Perhaps the feeling of loneliness was exacerbated by the finality of it. All Hillary knew for certain was that he did not feel jubilant, as one liberated from a thoroughly unsatisfaction union, but mopey and unable, for the moment anyway, to say, along with Dryden that *"Twas well an old age was out, And time to begin a new.* Even the sight of his Claude Lorrain back in its rightful place on the wall opposite the other one did not raise his morale, for the beauty of its classical, poetic landscape was clouded by its more recent history.

He was not the only one to feel ambivalent. Charlie Davenport discovered, as have many before him, that now he had the freehold of the thing that he thought he most wanted, it seemed a lot less alluring than the former setup of a flexible lease. He also would not have put it past Drusilla, now that he was cast in the worthy role of partner and protector, to recast Hillary in the more exciting and glamorous one of lover. In their different ways both men felt they had a great deal to come to terms with.

Radley Oates also felt that he had a great deal to come to terms with in the wake of his new Features incarnation and the defection of Dorian, whom even Ernest Dowson's poetry had been unable to move. When it became obvious that she was not going to change her mind, or not in the short term anyway, Radley stopped languishing and took her advice vis-à-vis getting on with his new job. Unaware that the new God slot media success, Patience Allardyce, attended the same evangelical church as his chairman did, he set up an interview with her. It was during the course of this that he learnt of the proposed Morals of the Nation report. Listening to her talking about its aims in an exalted, high-minded way and describing the probable composition of the Commission, it was immediately obvious to Radley that this would be a sitting duck and that the first interview should be a sweetener, a means of lulling Mrs Allardyce into a false sense of security where he, Radley Oates, was concerned and not the demolition job that he had formerly had in mind.

Accordingly, he said, 'I think the first interview should be an introductory piece. As a follow-up, with your agreement of course, I should like to do an in-depth piece, maybe sit in on one or two of your meetings, that sort of thing, make sure you get the sort of publicity you deserve!'

Make sure you get the sort of publicity you deserve. Patience, who craved the limelight and therefore had a long memory for that sort of phrase, was to recall this slippery double entendre in days to come. For the moment there was no reason to take it at anything other than face value.

She beamed, thinking as she did so it was a pity that, notionally anyhow, this was Cedric's project and she would have to clear it with him first.

'How very kind of you,' said Patience. 'I should have to run the idea past our chairman, of course,' and then, underlining the extent of her influence, 'but I'm quite sure that, if it is something I recommend, he will agree.'

'Oh, I'm sure he will,' soaped Radley.

'I hope I may take it that you are a practising Christian, Mr Oates?' enquired Patience, 'for I should not like to entrust this task to anyone who was not!'

'Yes, oh yes!' lied Radley.

'May I ask which church you attend?'

This caught Radley totally unprepared. In desperation he plucked a name out of the air. 'St Trinian's,' said Radley, aware as he said it that it somehow did not sound quite right, more like a girls' school than a church. Apparently it did not sound quite right to Mrs Allardyce either, for she said, 'St Trinian's? Really? I have to say it's not one I've heard of. Where exactly is it?'

With a strong sensation of exposure getting nearer, Radley opened his mouth in order to compound his lie, when the telephone rang.

'Would you please excuse me,' said Patience. She was away for five minutes and when she returned, apologising, Radley seized the opportunity to make his escape.

'I'm afraid I have to get back to the office. I have another appointment.'

'I quite understand.' Patience was gracious.

'I'll make sure you see a copy of the interview before we run it,' promised Radley, reflecting as he did so that this would be the first and last time that such a thing happened.

'Thank you. Goodbye, Mr Oates!'

'Goodbye, Mrs Allardyce!'

When Radley first presented his project to the Features Editor, who also had no idea of their Chairman's evangelical connection with Mrs Allardyce, the response was cautiously enthusiastic though cynical.

'You really think you can hang them out to dry!'

'I'm certain of it!' Radley was breezily confident. 'It's all shaping up to be a laugh a minute.'

Relieved, among other things, because, at last, Oates was not only initiating an idea but even sounding enthusiastic about doing some work on it, his editor said, 'OK, if you're sure, go for it, but keep the laudatory enticement exercise as short as possible'.

'Don't worry, I will,' said Radley.

Cedric Renfrew was both pleased and irritated by Patience's suggestion concerning Radley Oates. Pleased because it looked like being positive publicity for the project but, more importantly, for himself if he handled it correctly, and irritated because it was her idea not his. At the same time he still lusted after her and, now that she was safely and blamelessly divorced, wondered whether to reveal his hand. He and she would make a formidable team. Preferment would surely not take long with her by his side. In the end, mindful of the fact that it was possibly too soon after the demise of her marriage, he decided to delay matters until his Commission should have made its report.

Meanwhile Renfrew fantasised about Patience at night and thanked Heaven that he was not a member of the Roman Catholic priesthood and therefore committed to celibacy.

Interest without action suited Patience, who had no idea of the depth of his interest. She was unable to decide whether she found Cedric attractive or not. In his own domain he was powerful, there was no doubt about that and Patience liked power. He was also looked up to and flattered by a large proportion of the other ladies of the parish, who hung upon his every word. There was also no doubt he had what the Americans call charisma and in a forbidding, craggy sort of way she supposed him to be handsome, though she herself did not feel drawn to him physically. On the other hand she had not felt drawn to Hugh physically either, but, thought Patience, that didn't stop me marrying him. Hugh had been a relatively uncomplicated man though, until he had suddenly bolted with an artist, when he had suddenly become more interesting, desirable even. This one she sensed to be of altogether darker hue. In an odd sort of way Renfrew put her in mind of the unlovable Mr Brocklehurst in *Jane Eyre*. He was a priest, a devout man of God, who followed the light believing in and upholding the same uncompromising values as she did and yet she was conscious of something unChristian about Cedric. Almost a feeling that he had entered the Church as a means to an end. Not having access to those women who had known Cedric well and who had seen a different sort of light where he was concerned, she found it surprising that he had never married. Next week the first meeting of the Morals Commission was scheduled to take place. Patience looked forward to it, recognising that she and Cedric were about to work closely together and that, by the end of such a collaboration, she would have got to know him much better.

One evening on impulse she rang Dorian who, of course, would not be there because she never was. Since their *rapprochement* when her marriage had run into trouble they had been spasmodically in touch but that was all. Patience did not ask too many questions concerning her sister's private life because she instinctively knew she would disapprove of it.

Dorian did answer.

'Good heavens! You're in!' exclaimed Patience.

'Well, I do live here after all!' replied Dorian mildly, who had spent so many solitary evenings in recently, watching television, that she almost found herself missing Radley. Not quite though. Patience was disappointed to learn that Dorian had not seen her own television début.

'But I have it on tape,' said Patience, 'and I'll send you a copy.'

'Do!' answered Dorian and then, meaning it, 'I'd be very interested to see it.'

She wondered what her sister wanted. It would be very out of character for her to telephone without a reason. Clearly very excited, Patience told her about the projected report.

'Ah!' said Dorian, understanding. *The morals of the nation?* The whole thing sounded fraught with peril to Dorian's ear.

'Are you sure this is a good idea?' she asked cautiously.

'A good idea? Of course it's a good idea,' said Patience, sounding very huffed. 'What could possibly be the matter with it?'

'On the surface, nothing, nothing at all,' conceded Dorian. 'It's just that certain sections of the press can distort even the best intentions and from what you say this sounds as though this is going to be quite a high-profile exercise.'

'I hope it is!' was Patience's answer to this. 'I already have a journalist lined up, not one of your tabloid variety by the way, and hope that where he leads more will follow.'

'Well, just be careful!'

'I can't see what can possibly go wrong!' It seemed Patience wanted to learn the hard way. Dorian shuddered as she imagined the hacks all treating themselves to a field day at the expense of those high-mindedly pursuing this particular morality chase. It would be open season on Patience and her luckless fellow Commission members. Verbal ritual slaughter. She was just about to make one more fervent plea for caution when, changing the subject, Patience suddenly asked, 'By the way, have you ever come across a church called St Trinian's?'

'No,' said Dorian, 'but then I never go, so I wouldn't. Why do you want to know?'

'Oh, it's just that I met someone the other day who said he attended it and I just wondered where it was,' replied Patience vaguely. 'No other reason.'

When she had rung off, Dorian sat for several minutes mulling over what her sister had told her. It sounded as though Patience had set her heart on taking part in this survey and Dorian knew from past experience that deflecting her in such circumstances, once she had made her mind up, was practically impossible. Mentally she braced herself for what was beginning to look like the inevitable.

17

Radley Oates's deferential interview duly appeared. The Features Editor found it unelectrifying but hoped for more acerbic observation on the same subject from Radley's pen in the not too distant future. Hillary Causton, who knew some of those mentioned in it, approved, feeling that the article struck the right serious note and admitted to himself that he wouldn't have thought Oates had it in him. He also found himself intrigued by Patience Allardyce. Her image stared out of his own newspaper at him. Finding Mrs Allardyce a strong character and not altogether enchanted by her, the photographer had underlined this through the medium of his camera. Artily grainy, with strongly contrasting black and white, the photograph was more a bleachout than a half-tone. No grey areas here was the message. Patience was unsmiling, grave even, and the unkind lighting emphasised her chin. The overall impression was one of inflexibility and, at the same time, moral conviction. I know what's best for *you* said this portrait, blazing with certainty. All of this appealed to Hillary, who did not have the lightest touch himself. He was about to leave on one of his foreign business trips but made a mental note to ask Cedric Renfrew to introduce him to Mrs Allardyce on his return.

Dorian also saw both article and picture and immediately divined what had happened between Patience and the photographer. And this is just the beginning, was Dorian's reaction. This is before the Commission has even had its first meeting.

The first encounter of all the participants was a wine and cheese affair convened at Patience's house so that they could all meet each other in informal circumstances. It was the first time Clarissa Bowen had met the Reverend Cedric Renfrew and she was distinctly taken aback when she did. That man is rapacious, was Clarissa's first reaction. And patronising too. Just because I'm over seventy he treats me as though my brain is addled. She watched Renfrew's eyes following the social progress of

Patience round the room and found herself observing a sub-plot in the making. Her first impressions of the rest of the Commission were hardly less reassuring. The doctor and the lawyer seemed relatively normal but the social worker, the psychologist and the philosopher bordered on the eccentric. And why a philosopher anyway? Clarissa wondered.

She suddenly noticed that Patience was beckoning.

'Clarissa,' she said when Clarissa arrived at her side, 'allow me to introduce you to Jonathan Larch.'

Larch and Clarissa shook hands. His felt limp and small-boned, like a little dead animal. She looked at his wispy ponytail with disfavour. But I mustn't be so narrow-minded, Clarissa chided herself. This is the way young people dress these days. Although Larch wasn't that young, she decided, looking at him more closely, nor did he seem about to initiate sparkling conversation. Clarissa was relieved when they were joined by the psychologist, but not for long. To her older-generation eye, while Jonathan Larch looked as though he came from a foreign country, this one, whose name was Godfrey Ballard, spoke as though he did. Clarissa dimly remembered reading about psycho-babble and, though she had never encountered it before, assumed this must be what she was listening to. On and on it went, each sentence more convoluted and more meaningless, to her ear anyway, than the last. It occurred to Clarissa to wonder whether they intended to carry on at meetings like this after which, no doubt, their incomprehensible pontifications on the moral mores of the world at large would be duly recorded for posterity in the minutes. She looked around the room for a means of escape. For once appearing to be listening, Cedric Renfrew was standing beside the philosopher, whose name was Heinrich Muller. Muller was huge and hugely untidy. Iron-grey hair resembling the mane of a lion rushed back from the high forehead of a large head and surged over his collar. Clearly his mind had been on higher things that morning, since he appeared to have shaved only one side of his face. Perhaps the telephone had rung in the middle of what he was doing. There couldn't possibly be a Mrs Muller, Clarissa decided, taking in his frayed shirt collar whose tomato-coloured points shot upwards and in opposite directions like the wings of a large

178

butterfly, and his lamentable whiskery jacket, which was too short and box-shaped and made out of the thickest ginger tweed she had ever seen. Baggy grey trousers, several inches too long with turnups, drooped around surprisingly small feet which were shod in pussyish, furry suede. Although she could not see them, Clarissa would have been prepared to put money on the fact that he was wearing odd socks or maybe, and more anarchically, no socks at all. A missing ear piece had caused his round, steel-rimmed spectacles to have a pronounced list. Larch and Ballard were currently discussing Chaos Theory but in Clarissa's view might as well have been discussing Heinrich Muller. Her eye lit upon the doctor and the lawyer whose wine glasses were empty.

'Would you excuse me?' said Clarissa to Larch and Ballard, neither of whom appeared to hear her. She moved off in the direction of Patience.

'Would you like me to top up the glasses?' asked Clarissa.

'Yes, that's a good idea,' said Patience. 'I'll look after the white if you do the red.'

In this way, Clarissa joined the lawyer and the doctor, both of whom turned out to be members of the congregation of St Cuthbert's church. Pouring each a tot of red wine, 'Is the sum total of the Commission here tonight, do you know?' she enquired.

'There's one more still to be chosen,' said John Hardcastle, the doctor.

'Oh really?' Clarissa was intrigued.

'Yes, someone to represent the business community. I believe Cedric approached Hillary Causton who was unable to help due to all his other business commitments, so the hunt is on for somebody else.'

The lawyer, whose name was Mark Ashworth, observed, 'That's probably a good thing. Causton is so rich and powerful that in my view his inclusion could have upset the balance of the Commission. We need another team member, not somebody who's used to being an overlord.'

This struck Clarissa as a sensible comment although, on the other hand, like most other people she had heard of Causton and would have liked to have met him. But what we really need, thought Clarissa, mindful of Larch and Ballard and then turning her attention to Muller who was still in full flow on the other side of the room, is someone with both feet on the ground. Someone sensible, who is prepared to listen as well as expound their own theories. In short, someone with an open mind.

At this point, Patience clapped her hands. Everybody, even Heinrich Muller, stopped speaking and turned towards her.

'And now,' said Patience, 'Cedric is going to say a few words to you all.' She turned towards him. 'Cedric.'

Although he had his Claude back, this did not solve the problem of lonely early mornings and solitary meals. Accordingly, Hillary instigated a new round of Savoy breakfasts, beginning with Miles Compton and it was while he watched Compton eating Eggs Benedict that Causton had a good idea.

He decided to implement this immediately. 'I've suddenly had a good idea. I'm going to second you on to a commission which is going to write a report on the morals of the nation,' announced Hillary. 'They need a representative from the world of business and you can be it!'

The morals of the nation? Compton's jaw dropped. He wondered if he could have heard right. In consternation he put down his knife and fork.

'Oh, I really don't think . . .'

'I'm not asking you, Miles,' said Causton, breaking in, 'I'm telling you. They wanted me to do it and because of the time involved, I felt I had to turn it down.'

They? Who were they? Deciding to disregard this for the moment, 'Exactly!' said Miles, seizing at this straw, 'and my problem would be the same!'

It transpired that this was not the right thing to say.

'Nonsense!' said Hillary. 'There can be no comparison between your work load and my own and I shall expect you to fit in both. It's just a question of getting organised.'

Miles felt quite faint. Getting organised was easy when you had a fleet of secretaries and a host of serfs and toadies at your disposal as Causton did. He stared disconsolately at his plate. Eggs Benedict would never taste the same again.

'What about the whole television project? That's going to

need careful nursing.' Without much hope in his heart, Compton decided to have one more go at getting out of it.

'Oh, I thought your deputy could take that on for the time being. Challenging for him to have some added responsibility. Good experience,' came the unreassuring answer.

Well aware that being seconded away from the centre of power, albeit temporarily, was akin to being thrown into an oubliette, especially with a thrusting deputy ready to step in, Compton wondered if this could get any worse. 'I don't think there'll be any need for that,' he said hastily. 'I'm sure I can cope with both.'

'Didn't sound so sure just now!' observed Hillary.

'On further reflection I'm certain I can.'

'I have to say I expect my managers to think faster than that!'

Haplessly, Compton attempted another mouthful of Eggs Benedict. It was cold. Being terrorised over breakfast, usually a tranquil, unthreatening meal, was a new and dreadful experience. After a no doubt uncomfortable spell on the beach, his predecessor had gone on to more lucrative employment which did not include reporting to an unpredictable, irascible tycoon such as this one. Not for the first time, Compton wondered whether in achieving the job which had been his heart's desire he hadn't made a mistake and whether, at the end of the day, the man he'd shafted hadn't had the last laugh.

Causton paid the bill and they both stood up to leave. With another disconcerting mood shift, he clapped Compton on the back as they reached the door.

'Good man! I'm glad you're so enthusiastic about the survey. It's very important that as well as taking what we need out of the community, we all put something back and here's your chance! If I had the time I'd do it myself.'

Undeceived by this Miles tried to look grateful. He felt exhausted, as though he had been up all night. Stealing a look at his watch he discovered that it was still only nine o'clock.

Christian said to Cordelia, 'Have I told you that I'm going to form a band?'

'No,' answered his sister. 'What are you going to call it?'

Her brother was smug. 'Christ and the Archangels.'

Cordelia was aghast. 'Oh, Christian, *don't*! You know that will upset Mummy. Can't you call it something else?'

'Why should I? Besides, it's time Mum became more tolerant.'

'She's never going to change now, as you perfectly well know. Why do you have to make trouble all the time?'

'I don't make trouble *all* the time.'

'Pretty nearly!'

'Look, Mum doesn't have a monopoly on God, you know, regardless of what she may think!'

'That's not the point. The point is her feelings. Why do you have to be such a pain?'

Christian, who had sometimes asked himself the same question but had yet to come up with an answer, was stuck for one now. In self-defence he decided to close the discussion with maximum aggression. 'Little Miss Perfect! Why don't you fuck off, Cordelia!'

Before he had reached the end of what was after all a very offensive sentence, she had gone, banging the door behind her.

Hugh and Flora got married. Only Cordelia and Dorian were there, Christian having declined to attend. It was one of those dashing, hopeful May days, airy and invigorating. Small white clouds shot around the blue sky and a glancing sun entered into the spirit of the thing, fitfully illuminating the brilliant green, tossing leaves of the trees. All was movement, light and shade.

Watching them exchange vows, Dorian felt suddenly sad. She was not envious of their happiness but mourned the loss of her own. For one who had told herself that she no longer cared about her husband, the unhappiness was surprisingly acute. She remembered her own registry office wedding and the party afterwards. They had all danced late into the night, even Patience who had disapproved of the secular nature of the ceremony and had felt free to say as much. At the end of it all she and Robert had gone to Paris for a long weekend, which was all they had been able to afford at the time. In fact, strictly speaking, they had not been able to afford even that but had gone ahead and done it anyway. As they left their own party, sitting in the back of the taxi, Robert had kissed her. 'I'll never stop loving you, Dorian,' Robert said. And now he had. The sheer finality of it caused Dorian to draw in her breath. Tears started to her eyes. She felt as though she might be about to faint. But they had been in love, hadn't they? They had been happy. Hadn't they? These days Dorian was no longer sure. Perhaps they never had. What she was sure about was that somewhere along the way happiness had got lost, but so imperceptibly had it ebbed away from them that by the time she had noticed the slippage it was all too late.

The ceremony was over. They were married. Hugh kissed Flora.

Smiling, Cordelia turned to Dorian and was astonished to see that her aunt's eyes were full of tears. Concerned she said timidly, 'Dorian?'

'It's all right.' Dorian fished about in her small sling bag for a handkerchief and failed to find one. She brushed her hands across her eyes. 'I always cry at weddings. I don't know why I do, but I do. I'm fine, really I am!'

Aware that some sort of gesture of support was needed and unaware that she herself was the unwitting cause of the estrangement between the Ormonds, sensitive, sympathetic Cordelia took Dorian's hand and held it for a brief moment, before the two of them followed Hugh and Flora out into the May sunshine.

Patience tried to tell herself that she did not care about Hugh's remarriage and in one sense she did not. Sexually she did not miss him although on the other hand it had to be admitted that the fact that another, younger woman found him attractive was alerting. In moments of introspection it occurred to Patience to wonder whether perhaps she had not brought out the best in Hugh. She certainly felt bereft. And lonely. The absence of someone to come home to and to go out escorted by, made her realise how much she had taken for granted. Worst of all was the feeling of failure, of still not understanding how and why it had all gone wrong, which opened up the unnerving possibility that the same thing could happen again. Time and time again, Patience went over the history of her marriage, usually in the small hours of the morning when she could not sleep, and time

and time again confessed herself baffled. Other similar partner-
ships appeared to endure, why not hers? In the end, whatever
the reason, she was forced to say to herself that it had gone and
nothing she could do or say was going to bring it back. In a rare
burst of confiding in her daughter, she said as much to Cordelia.
Cordelia, who had had to grow up fast in the light of all that had
happened, to the point where she often felt herself to be more
mature than either of her parents, dickered watching her
mother's puzzlement. Was there anything to be gained by a
frank opinion concerning what had happened and why? On the
whole she thought there was not. Daddy was happily remarried
and not about to change his mind and at her age Mummy was
not about to change, full stop. In the event, she simply said, 'I
don't understand it either,' (which was partially true) 'but
people do change and I suppose that when you're married to
someone it's hard to detect gradual change because you're so
close to it on a day-to-day basis especially when you were so
busy . . .' Cordelia's voice trailed away. She felt she had come
perilously close to the real heart of the matter, to saying that her
mother had not taken enough notice of her father. Patience was
oblivious. Patience said, 'Oh, there I can't agree with you. Your
father and I were always very close! And *that's* what makes the
whole thing so inexplicable!' Here it occurred to Cordelia to
wonder if Mummy knew what *very close* meant. Certain it was
that her definition was not the same as that of the majority of
other people. 'No,' continued Patience, 'he was lured away.
Lured! By That Woman!' Her voice rose.

Better to change the subject.

Hastily, Cordelia said the first thing that came into her head
and immediately regretted it as she did so.

'Has Christian told you that he's formed a pop group?'

'Yes, I believe he did mention it,' said Patience. 'Do you
know what he's going to call it?'

'No,' fibbed Cordelia, thinking as she said it that there was no
point in stirring up a hornets' nest with that one at this stage.
Maybe Christian would think better of his initial blasphemous
idea, though frankly she doubted it. Causing controversy had
become something of a way of life for Christian lately. Whatever
he decided let *him* break the news to Mummy.

'He tells me that he will be the lead singer,' said Patience pursuing it. 'And rightly so! He had the most wonderful soprano voice as a boy. Perfect pitch. Do you remember how angelic he looked singing in the church choir with that white frilled collar and scarlet surplice? I was so sorry when he gave that up.'

'It gave him up,' reminded Cordelia, 'when his voice broke.'

'He could have joined an adult choir,' Patience pointed out.

It was another example of a change she had not registered. Cordelia sighed and then doggedly resumed trying to bring the thing up to date.

'I don't think he enjoys singing that sort of music any more.'

'What? With a marvellous voice like his?' exclaimed Patience, ignoring the fact that a superlative soprano had matured into a thoroughly mediocre baritone. 'All the same, I'd like to hear him singing with his band.'

Cordelia flinched. Time to change the subject again.

'I meant to ask you, how's the report going?'

Patience beamed. '*Very* well. The planning stage is over. We go public and start work in earnest on Monday.'

18

June dazzled. One peerless day followed another. With heat came sloth and probably because of that it was what the newspapers call a slow news period. Maybe this was one of the reasons for a larger than expected attendance at Cedric Renfrew's modest press conference which had been convened in a local church hall.

Cedric made his introductory speech with the rest of the Commission sitting behind him to the right of an old upright piano on a dusty platform. When he invited questions, the first one, from a broadsheet journalist, was: 'Is there any particular strata of society on which you intend to concentrate or are you going to address all of them?'

'We intend to begin with the deprived and spiritually darkened,' replied the Reverend Cedric Renfrew portentously and without missing a beat. Listening to it, Clarissa hoped he was not going to embark upon his impersonation of John Knox.

'Meaning?' came a baffled response.

'Meaning that we shall commence our survey by penetrating the low life of the capital before exploring other areas, right up to the establishment itself in order to present a comprehensive picture of the sexual mores and morals of the nation.'

The words sexual mores caught the attention of his cynical, wilting audience.

'Are you saying that you and your Commission intend to visit brothels and strip joints in your quest for information?' The questioner this time was one of the tabloid variety. His eye lingered with interest on the line of tweedy ladies, intellectuals and do-gooders perched on bentwood chairs behind the vicar. In a corner and infinitely preferring his own judgemental euphemism *low life of the capital*, Cedric was forced into saying, 'If you must put it like that, yes'. There was a stirring in the audience. Although it was hot and stuffy and too soon after lunch, there was a distinct heightening of interest among the

186

hacks. Sitting in the front row Radley Oates, the man on the inside track, was smug. He eyed Miles Compton, who was sitting at the piano end of the row and looked as though he wished he was behind the instrument rather than beside it. Radley, who did not like Compton, possibly because he recognised in the other man some of his own deficiencies, relished the sight. As the pack moved in and the questions went on, verging on the ribald, all humourlessly fielded by Cedric Renfrew, Compton grew evidently more and more uncomfortable, shifting in his seat and glassily staring into the middle distance. Clarissa Bowen also watched the spectacle with dismay. At one point she looked sideways at Patience wondering if one of the other Commission members should perhaps intervene but Patience appeared oblivious, serene even, and displayed no inclination whatever to help Cedric out. In the end, after the third furtive look at his watch, it was Miles Compton who suggested that they drew the whole thing to a close. He did this with a sense of relief which was tempered by the knowledge that the next item on his agenda, or more accurately the next item ten minutes ago, was a meeting with his chairman to discuss various unsatisfactory matters, including this one.

Afterwards, Radley cornered Patience Allardyce.

'Congratulations on a very successful introductory meeting,' Radley lied suavely.

'Thank you,' answered Patience regally; she had her own reservations about the way the afternoon had gone, but was not about to air these in front of Radley Oates.

'I hope you haven't forgotten our agreement concerning my own participation,' said Radley. 'Provided you let me know the programme in advance, I can provide a cameraman and as much coverage as you want.'

'I had not forgotten,' said Patience. She opened a file she was carrying and handed him two A4 sheets stapled together. 'Here you are. This is it.' Radley ran his eye over it, trying to conceal his delight. It was better than he had dared hope. It began with a trawl through Soho.

Another journalist who had been watching this little transaction and had observed Radley's gloat, but could not hear what was being said, sidled over.

187

'Have I missed out on something? Are you handing out information sheets,' he asked Patience hopefully.

'Yes, but only one and not to you,' she answered, very crisp, recognising him as one of those who had been baiting Cedric. Turning to Radley she said, 'I must be on my way. Perhaps when you have had time to read it you could find the time to give me a ring and let me know what you do and don't intend to cover.'

Making a mental resolution to try and do it all, Radley said he would. Even if half his copy got spiked he would get a good laugh out of it. And I need cheering up, thought Radley.

Miles apologised for being late and then took a seat opposite his chairman. As always behind his gargantuan desk, Hillary looked far away and at the same time very important. A bit like God, thought Compton, sourly. The office was stifling. The air conditioning must be switched off. No cooling breeze came in through the open window and the late afternoon sunlight suffused the atmosphere, giving the still air a golden density which was soporific. More relaxed than usual, Causton, who was uncharacteristically informal in shirt-sleeves with loosened tie, seemed to be affected by this enervating influence too and when he began to speak even his habitual aggression seemed to have been neutralised. Buzzing through for coffee, he enquired mildly, 'What did you think of Cedric Renfrew's Commission now you've finally met them?'

Had he given an honest answer to this seemingly innocuous question Compton would have said, 'I think they are a mixed bunch of do-gooders, pseuds and nutters and furthermore I think the whole thing is going to end in a welter of ridicule and tears!' What he actually said was, 'Impressive.'

'And was there anybody who struck you as particularly impressive?'

Compton hesitated, wondering what Causton was getting at.

'Mrs Allardyce, for instance. What did you think of Mrs Allardyce?'

Mrs Allardyce? It was the first time he had met them all and this was not a question he had anticipated. Compton racked his brains. Oh, yes! Hadn't she been the unamused one? The one who had been speaking to Radley Oates as he himself took his leave, a large-boned handsome woman with an autocratic manner and a level stare which caused even Cedric Renfrew to subside from time to time. Compton had initially put her down as one of the do-gooders but then decided that there was more to her than that, in the shape of a ferocious will.

'*Very* impressive,' said Compton. It was evidently the right thing to say. Causton became expansive. 'That's my opinion too! Did you see her television début? *Extraordinarily* good!' His enthusiasm was as sudden as it was unexpected.

'When did you meet her?' asked Compton, anxious to prolong this sudden benevolence.

'I haven't,' came the surprising answer, 'but I intend to make it my business to do so.'

Good God, thought Compton, watching his boss closely, *I think the Old Man's in love!*

Perhaps because he had said more than he intended, Causton switched tack again and with a surge of the old irascibility, as if it had been Compton who had been holding matters up rather than himself, said, 'Well come on! Let's get on with it! We've got a lot to get through, you know. Let's start with the question of a new editor. Where have you got to on *that*?'

At last Causton did meet Patience Allardyce. Talking about her to Miles Compton cemented resolution and, rejuvenated by an hour spent bullying his luckless Chief Operating Officer, he decided on impulse to go to evensong at St Cuthbert's. Quite apart from anything else it was better than sitting in his palatial house by himself. He hoped Mrs Allardyce would be there. She was, for very much the same reason. Patience was still surprised at how much she missed Hugh, or maybe it was just the reassuring presence of *someone* rather than Hugh in particular. An empty evening house left one confronting oneself in an unnerving way at a particularly vulnerable time of day. With fading light came fading self-confidence.

At the end of the service, Causton took Cedric Renfrew to one side and told him that he required an introduction to Mrs Allardyce. Renfrew was taken by surprise by this and not pleased about it, though he was not altogether sure why he was not.

Whatever he felt, there was no way of getting out of it so he complied. Watching them shake hands, he knew that he had made a mistake. The mistake was not the introduction itself but the fact that he should have pressed his suit long ago where Patience was concerned. Had he done so she would by now be committed to him (Renfrew did not even entertain the idea that she might have refused him) and an encounter such as the one he was witnessing now would have been of no significance. As it was, two things struck him. First, no sooner were the reluctant words, 'Patience Allardyce, Hillary Causton. Hillary Causton, Patience Allardyce,' out of his mouth than he felt himself to be redundant and, secondly, even on such short acquaintance, these two looked like a couple. With a social ruthlessness that echoed its business equivalent, having got what he wanted out of Renfrew and, therefore having no further immediate use for him, Hillary partially turned his back on the vicar and addressed himself exclusively to Patience. Feeling more than a little put out, Cedric was left with no alternative but to step out of their orbit and, as he did so, was engulfed by adoring groupies, each of whom had been waiting for an opportunity to get the vicar to herself. Feeling himself taken for granted, their adulation was, for once, balm to a soul whose *amour propre* had suffered a setback.

Hillary and Patience appraised one another. Each thought the other handsome, but because neither could be described as vivacious and neither possessed charm, this immediate attraction was all each of them had to work with. *Hillary Causton*. The name was familiar to Patience, who read at least one of his newspapers but who had never taken much interest in who the publisher was. Frowning, she tried to place him. After initial stilted pleasantries, as he cast around for something with which to leaven this conversational lump, it occurred to Hillary to mention her performance on Women Priests: Yes or No.

Tactically speaking this was an astute move. His praise was not only fulsome but sincere and in the face of phrases such as *cogent arguments*, *highly professional performance* and, best of all, *natural television presence*, Patience relaxed considerably. After Cedric's curmudgeonly restraint concerning her broadcasting début, Causton's unstinting admiration was heartening and disarming all at once.

'No doubt you'll be asked to do more,' said Hillary.

'I certainly hope so. There has been talk, but so far nothing has happened.'

Patience smiled at Hillary and Hillary smiled back. He felt himself to be in the company of an open, uncomplicated *moral* person with none of Drusilla's scorpion sting.

'I'm about to own a piece of the action in a television company!' said Hillary.

He did not amplify this statement.

Tantalised, as she was meant to be, 'Are you,' said Patience, 'are you really? When you say *about to* does that mean that you aren't already in the television business?'

Chastened by the fact that she had apparently never heard of him, Hillary said, 'I'm a newspaper proprietor. I publish the *Clarion* among other things.'

Ah! Of course! That's who he was! Now she had made the connection, Patience's response was gratifying. 'Of which I am a regular reader. I thoroughly approve of its editorial right-wing stance!'

Remembering all the times Drusilla had made fun of the very same thing, Causton felt that here indeed was a kindred spirit. Maybe, he thought with a burst of benevolence as he listened to this, he would not sack his editor after all. Conscious that he had not only her undivided attention but also her approval, Hillary said, 'Would you accept if I asked you out to dinner tonight?'

'Yes, I would,' deigned Patience, secretly delighted. 'Thank you!' The spectre of another solitary evening receded. Then she remembered that it was not in fact scheduled to be an altogether solitary evening after all. Watching her brow momentarily cloud, Causton said, 'Is there a problem? We can always do it another night, if so.'

'Nothing that I can't sort out. Would you please excuse me for a moment?' Ruthlessness, it transpired, was not just the prerogative of tycoons. Patience cornered Cedric Renfrew and stood him up.

'I'm sure you'll understand. After all we can indulge in a glass of sherry and a chat about parish business any day of the week.'

And you don't get asked out to dinner every day of the week by a millionaire businessman, thought Cedric, vastly put out, the more especially since he had decided that tonight he would declare his feelings for her. (*Set me as a seal upon thine heart: as a seal upon thine arm: for love is strong as death. . .*)

'Also we don't want to offend someone as rich and influential as Hillary Causton, do we? He could be very useful in our current joint endeavour, for instance.'

Renfrew's mouth turned down. Hitherto he had seen it as his brief to nurture the sensitivities of such important members of his congregation and keep them sweet. Now, as with the glory accruing from Women Priests: Yes or No?, Patience was on his patch again, taking over what he considered to be his privileges. If anybody was about to have strategic meetings with Hillary Causton over an expensive dinner, it should be himself. God damn and blast the woman! (. . . *jealousy is cruel as the grave* . . .) He ground his teeth as he watched them leave together.

19

Max Pointing and Robert Ormond ran into each other on the stairs of the block of flats in which they both lived. This had, of course, happened before but both had been in too much of a hurry to stop and talk. Today Max was carrying what looked like a large oil painting swathed in a bubble wrap under his arm and was accompanied by a doe-eyed beauty who was introduced as Nigel. Max, who had not seen Dorian since that day in February when he had seen her walking away along the street, and had assumed that there had been a reconciliation between the Ormonds, wondered where she was.

'How's the book going?' he asked Robert.

'Fine,' answered Robert. 'I'm about halfway through, which is a great relief to everybody.'

By everybody Max assumed he meant Dorian, his agent and his publisher, in that order.

'Especially Dorian, I should have thought,' observed Max, who knew some of the history of the biography of Alexander Pope. At the mention of his wife's name, Robert's face closed.

'I haven't seen Dorian for months. As you know, we're separated.' Speaking the words, he reflected that it was unlike the tactful Max to make that sort of insensitive mistake, even if they had not properly met for a long time.

Max was puzzled. He handed the painting to Nigel.

'Be a love and take that to the car would you?' He handed over the keys. 'I'll be down in a minute.'

When the youth had gone, he turned to Robert.

'But I saw her! Not to speak to. I saw her from the window. She let herself out of the front door of the building and walked off down the road. I naturally assumed there had been a *rapprochement*. If that isn't the case I'm very sorry.'

'No *rapprochement*. In fact, quite the reverse. It looks as though it's all over.'

Robert looked and sounded bleak. With sudden curiosity he said, 'When do you think you saw her?'

'Not *think*!' Max was emphatic. 'It was definitely her. It was sometime in February.' He cast his mind back. 'I know! It was a Sunday. I think it was the Sunday before I was due to go on a buying trip to France, so it must have been around the beginning of the month.'

A Sunday! Robert was thunderstruck.

'Impossible! Dorian hasn't been here on a Sunday for at least a year, maybe longer.'

Max shrugged. 'I can only tell you what I saw. Does she still have the keys to the flat?' The car horn sounded. 'That's Nigel getting impatient. He's a naughty boy. All the same, I'd better go. Why don't you drop down and have a drink with us sometime next week?' With a wave, he went. In turmoil, Robert stood thinking over what he had just been told and then turned and followed Max downstairs.

When he returned half an hour later with a meagre bag of groceries he was still mulling the whole thing over. It had been sometime in February that his niece Cordelia had turned up unexpectedly on his doorstep, he remembered. On a Saturday night. But Max couldn't possibly have mixed up the two women, who were completely different physical types. Besides there had been no uncertainty about Max's memory of the event, even in the face of Robert's scepticism. With a pang, he recalled the odd business of the smell of the scent Dorian always wore, which he had noticed while showing Cordelia out and which had pervaded the hall of the flat like a sweet ghost. 'What's that perfume you're wearing?' he had said to Cordelia. Not Armani but Chanel Number 5 had been the answer. In the absence of any other explanation, Robert had been forced to put it down to imagination. All the same, it had been odd.

But what if Dorian really had been there that morning? *Does she still have the keys to the flat? Max had asked.* The answer to that was that Robert had no idea, but supposed that she probably did. And if she had indeed turned up at the flat that morning and had let herself in, she could, no *would*, have heard Cordelia's voice without knowing who it was. After which the possibilities for misunderstanding were Mozartian. Which would follow, for hadn't it been after that that she had dismissed him and told him she no longer wanted him in her life at all.

The question now was what to do about it. Contacting somebody who sent back letters and refused to take telephone calls was virtually impossible, and a row in the street if he succeeded in waylaying Dorian there was not going to help matters either. Suddenly Robert saw very clearly what he must do. He rang Cordelia at school and left a message for her. When she finally returned his call, he said, 'Cordelia, I want to ask you to do me a great favour.'

'Anything!' answered Cordelia, surprised and mindful of Robert's kindness the night she had materialised bereft on his doorstep. 'What is it?'

'When you next have an exeat, I want you to go and see Dorian for me and explain what happened and why the night you stayed at this flat.'

'Nothing did happen!' Cordelia sounded mystified. 'Look I'm more than happy to do it, but won't she think it a bit odd? I mean why don't you tell her yourself?'

'Because,' said Robert, 'with things as they are, she wouldn't believe me but she *would* believe you.'

Cordelia was silent. She remembered Dorian's tears at her father's wedding, secret, hopeless tears. At the time she had wondered about them and had not been deceived by her aunt's explanation.

'What do you want me to do when I've told her?' Cordelia was keen not to make an already sensitive situation worse.

'Nothing!' said Robert. 'No need to elaborate. What happens next is down to her.'

As soon as she put the receiver down, conscientious Cordelia picked it up again and rang Dorian.

'I know the next exeat is two weeks away, but I do want to see you,' said Cordelia, 'so I wondered if I might come round for tea?'

'Yes. Of course.'

They confirmed date and time. Cordelia was struck by the fact that Aunt Dorian's voice sounded faint and very very far away but in the end put this down to a bad line.

Ye gods! Annihilate but space and time,
And make two lovers happy.

As the first heady enthusiasm for a firm stand and an independent life wore off, unhappiness crept up insidiously on Dorian. Like someone who is being stalked, she was aware of her own desperation without exactly acknowledging the fact to herself. The breakdown when it came therefore was horrifying in its sudden completeness. A mental ambush. One day she was holding down a job, going through the motions of everyday living and just about handling it and the next she found herself unable to get out of bed. Luckily, or maybe because of the fact, this coincided with a week's holiday. The crying was exhausting. Wracking, endless sobs brought no relief of any kind and at night there were dreadful dreams of deprivation and loss. It felt like a savage assault by a deeply unhappy subconscious on an apparently well-ordered façade. As one day followed another Dorian became frightened and yet too debilitated to do anything about it. Am I going mad? was a frequent rhetorical question which remained unanswered. Sometimes, when the weeping briefly subsided, she sat dully in front of a television screen purveying the sort of old films which had been screened hundreds of times before but were still apparently considered suitable fare for weekday afternoon viewing. Cary Grant, Gloria Swanson, William Holden, Lauren Bacall et alii, even on one occasion Louise Brooks, all in old-fashioned black and white, flickered before Dorian's mesmerised eye and were company of a sort.

On Friday, even though she was eating scarcely anything, what little food there was ran out. With a huge effort of will, like a somnambulist, Dorian assembled keys and money and went out. Moving along the London pavement she felt dizzy and light-headed and as though she might be about to faint. It was late afternoon and still warm. Indigo shadows were long and the traffic was heavy. London going home. Locked into an inner world of despair and bitter regret, Dorian briefly paused out of habit at the junction of her own street and the main road and then looking neither to right nor left and still sleep walking, stepped out. The car which shot around the corner at the same time tried to avoid hitting her and failed. She was conscious of stunning impact and a cerebral jolt, not unlike an electric shock, after which the mental and the physical seemed to separate. With a curious sense of detachment, as though watching somebody else, she saw her body rise into the air before it fell, slithered over the hard shiny bonnet of the car and tumbled into the gutter where it lay like a broken doll.

When she finally regained consciousness in hospital, Dorian remained very still with her eyes open. She remembered everything that had happened, including the eerie sensation of being outside her own body. The curtains were drawn, tentlike, around the bed. Cloistered within their small enclosure, Dorian felt very peaceful. It was as though the shock of the accident, like a session of ECT, had dissipated depression. She supposed she was lucky to be alive but more importantly, Dorian *felt* she was lucky to be alive.

The curtains parted and someone came in.

'Ah, good! Awake at last!' said Sister. She shot the curtains back and then proceeded to shake a thermometer with vigour. 'We've been very worried about you. Can you remember what happened?'

'All of it, until I blacked out.'

'And you remember who you are?'

Dorian was astonished. 'Yes, of course I do!'

'Well,' said Sister sounding quite accusatory, '*we* have no idea. You arrived here with no identification of any sort. Just a small purse and some keys which someone who witnessed the accident found on the pavement. The driver of the car came with you to the hospital. He was quite beside himself. He kept saying, "There was nothing I could do to avoid it. She just walked straight out."'

'He's right,' said Dorian, 'he couldn't have done anything to avoid it. I did walk straight out. I was in a daze at the time. I owe him an apology. Did I hurt myself very badly?'

It was a roundabout way of asking a question to which she dreaded the answer.

'You're bruised all over and when you start to move about again you'll know all about it. And you've fractured your left arm in quite a complicated way. No, the real question mark was over when you came round and in what state. You also received quite a severe blow to the head.'

'I can't feel anything,' said Dorian.

'You wouldn't,' said Sister, 'because you're sedated and also full of painkillers, but, as I say, when you start to resume normal life you'll feel it. Now, before you drift off again, who are you and is there anyone we should contact?' Her bracing manner reminded Dorian of Patience.

'I'm Dorian Ormond. Look, I *must* make some telephone calls. What day is it today?' Panicking, Dorian tried to sit up. The pain, as predicted, was excruciating. She fell back.

'No telephoning!' decreed Sister, very controlling. 'I'll make any calls that are necessary. Who would you like me to notify, Mrs Ormond?'

Who indeed. The thought of being marooned in a hospital bed with Patience, for instance, running rampant all around as God's answer to Florence Nightingale, was not to be borne. Certainly not yet, anyway, though she would no doubt have to be told at some point. Dorian thought of Robert, wavered and then hardened her heart. Robert on his own would have been fine, but Robert with bloody Alexander Pope in tow was why she was here in the first place. And Radley, who fell into decline when anybody but himself had the temerity to be ill, she regarded as part of her past. Which raised the interesting question as to why her husband, whom she had also relegated to the past, perversely continued to feel so much part of the present. In the end, Dorian settled for Cordelia, who was due to come and see her anyway, and the Paper, where by now colleagues must be wondering what had happened to her.

Sister hesitated and then, eyeing the patient's gold wedding ring, felt officiously duty bound to say what was on her mind.

'But what about your husband, Mrs Ormond? Don't you want . . . ?'

'No,' said Dorian, who was beginning to feel very drowsy again. 'I don't!'

Sliding into sleep, she muttered something else and leaning close to her in order to hear what this was, Sister was scandalised to hear, or thought she heard, though it wasn't the sort of thing one usually made a mistake about, 'Fuck my husband,' followed by, incomprehensibly, 'and fuck Alexander Pope too.'

The moment she heard the news, Cordelia tried to phone Robert and got no reply. He had evidently gone on one of his minuscule shopping expeditions and had neglected to switch on his answer phone. One hour later, she tried again. There was still no reply. One of Robert's defences against the outside world when he was attempting to work was to turn off the bell of the telephone, leaving the machine to take the messages. Today, she guessed, he had forgotten that it was still switched off. There was nothing to do but keep trying, which Cordelia intermittently did all day with no luck at all. Tomorrow, having obtained compassionate Saturday leave in advance of the usual exeat, she was due to visit Dorian at the hospital. I'll ring Robert after that, decided Cordelia.

'One of our writers is in hospital,' said Charlie Davenport to Drusilla. 'Dorian Ormond.'

'Really!' was Drusilla's acknowledgement of this piece of news. The inflexion made it sound like *so what?* She continued turning the pages of *Vogue*.

'Yes,' said Charlie, persevering. 'She was knocked down by a car.' He waited for some expression of shock and sympathy and was destined to receive neither.

'Really!' said Drusilla again.

'Yes,' said Charlie again. 'I thought I'd go and visit her.'

Drusilla was astounded. This time, eyebrows arching, she did look up.

'Whatever for? After all it's only a member of staff! That sort of person will have plenty of visitors. No need for you to bother, surely.'

Not for the first time Charlie was brought face to face with the true nature of the woman he was living with. He rued the day she had left Hillary Causton. Suddenly losing his temper he shouted, 'You don't care about anyone but yourself, do you? You're a selfish bitch, Drusilla, a hard, selfish BITCH!' Such abuse was a comparatively mild verbal example of the violence that was becoming more and more frequent during the course of their lovemaking, which she appeared to enjoy.

199

Drusilla stood up and stalked out, no doubt going to the bedroom where she hoped he would follow her. He did not. Whatever she thought about it, Charlie decided to make his hospital visit anyway.

Cordelia was shocked when she first saw Dorian who looked diminished, frail even. Knowing nothing of the mental trauma which had preceded her accident, Cordelia put this down to fall-out from that. With tears in her eyes, she kissed her aunt.

'How are you?'

'Much better than I was.' Dorian was not in fact referring to her physical injuries but to her mental state, though Cordelia did not know this.

'Sister says you don't want anyone else to know you're here.' It was on the tip of her tongue to add, 'not even Robert?' when Dorian said it for her.

'Not Robert and especially not my sister, your mother. It's not that I don't love her dearly,' said Dorian insincerely, 'I just don't feel up to it at the moment.' Cordelia knew exactly what she meant. Mummy had a habit of coming on very strong when somebody else in the vicinity was *hors de combat*. It was as though her strength burgeoned as theirs waned. It was odd because she meant so well. Cordelia had had this debate with herself before and had been unable to come up with an answer as to why her parent's good works were quite so draining. Loyalty forbade that she should say any of this and Aunt Dorian knew it anyway, so in the event she just smiled and said, 'No, of course you don't, though she'll have to be told sometime and when she is I think it's better if she doesn't know I was told first.' Damn, thought Cordelia as she said the words, without at all wanting to be I'm now part of a conspiracy, albeit a small one. She decided to give up on being fair to her mother and concentrate on Robert instead.

'There's something important I have to tell you,' said Cordelia.

When she had finished, Dorian was silent for a minute or two. Then she said, 'Is that the dress you were wearing that day?'

Surprised, Cordelia, who had two favourite dresses one of which was crimson and one of which was purple and happened to be wearing the purple today, looked down at it and answered, 'Yes, I believe it was.'

'Such a pretty colour. Lean forward. Let me feel the material. Yes, that's it. I saw it lying on the bed and thought Robert had another woman with him. Which in a manner of speaking he did. You. Oh, Cordelia . . .' With a gesture of resignation Dorian sighed and lay back on the pillows. 'Did Robert say that he wanted to see me after you told me?'

'The smell of your perfume was all over the hall,' said Cordelia, dreamily irrelevant. 'He couldn't understand it.' And then, pulling herself together, 'He said the next move was up to you.'

'He's quite right. I have a lot of fences to mend. It may be too late. Does he know what has happened?'

'No,' said Cordelia. She elected to draw a veil over the fact that in spite of having been specifically asked not to, she had tried to tell Robert. 'Do you want me to tell him?'

'Yes, please.' Dorian's voice was very low. 'And tell him I'm so very sorry.'

'I will!' Cordelia looked at her watch. 'Look, I'd better go. I'll ring up and see how you are tomorrow.'

'Close the curtains as you go, would you? I'm going to try and get some sleep. I feel tired all the time at present.'

As Charlie Davenport was about to enter the hospital ward, a slim girl in a purple dress drifted past him, evidently on her way out. In spite of the fact that he was wrestling with a large basket of fruit and a substantial pot plant, he was struck by the sweet gravity of her oval face. There was a fragility about her unself-conscious beauty which touched Charlie's heart. For there was nothing fragile about Drusilla, he reflected, turning to watch his nymph until at the end of the corridor she turned the corner and was lost to sight. Living with Drusilla was very like living with one of those terrifying Roman women. Messalina in particular came to mind.

Charlie resumed his quest for Dorian Ormond and halfway down the ward was intercepted by starched, officious Sister. Still awake, but only just, Dorian heard some sort of muted altercation followed by Sister reluctantly saying, 'Well, five minutes then, but that's all. Rules are rules, you know! This is the end of the visiting hour and Mrs Ormond needs rest!'

Who on earth could it be? Her heart leapt at the thought that it might be Robert. A figure appeared at the end of her bed almost hidden by a mountain of fruit and what looked like a large bush. Feeling herself at a distinct disadvantage, Dorian recognised not Robert but Charlie Davenport.

Cordelia rang Robert's number on her way back to school. This time he was there. Pausing only to put more money in the slot, she recounted the whole story.

'She wants to see you,' said Cordelia. 'Oh, Robert, I don't know what has gone wrong between you, but she regrets it so much.'

'I'll go now!'

'No point in going now. It's one of those old-fashioned hospitals with specific visiting hours and Sister's a dragon who won't let you in outside them. Go tomorrow morning.'

'God bless you, Cordelia!'

20

There was one last planning meeting before the Commission's investigation into the morality of the nation got underway in earnest. The doubters concerning the manner in which they were going about it, of whom one was Clarissa, were silenced early on by Renfrew. 'How can we properly and effectively spread the Word,' he reasonably asked, 'unless we know what we are up against? The Church needs to understand the moral climate of today.'

'Yes, I understand that,' said Clarissa, 'but are we quite sure that the publicity is a good thing? Would it not be better to keep a low profile until all our findings are complete and reserve the high-profile publicity for the published report rather than the participants?'

Listening to Mrs Bowen, Miles Compton privately agreed but was not prepared to put his own head above the parapet and openly support her. The dissembling habit of a business life-time, which was to appear all things to all men, applied equally here in Compton's view. Better to seem to be on everyone's side until absolutely forced to do otherwise. This moment was closer than he knew, for Mrs Bowen's next suggestion was that they should put it to the vote.

Vote?

This was all getting a little too close to democracy for Renfrew's liking. He stared disapprovingly at Clarissa who was emerging as that most undesirable thing, a woman with a mind of her own. It now seemed that he had two of them on his hands. They did vote. It was interesting to Clarissa that Miles Compton, who had indicated to her more than once that he shared her feelings on this matter, voted for the other side. He did not look in her direction as he did so. More interesting, though, was the composition of the two sectors. The vainglorious and self-important voted unanimously for as much high-voltage press coverage as they could garner from the beginning.

Because there was a preponderance of that sort of person on the Commission, in the shape of the likes of Muller, Larch and Renfrew himself as well as the treacherous Compton, vanity won the day. All the same it was close.

'The motion is defeated by only one vote,' announced Renfrew. 'Nevertheless it *is* defeated. And now, after Mrs Bowen's little diversion, perhaps we can get on with more important agenda!' Clad in his habitual black and hunched over a spiralled notebook, Cedric looked more than usually spidery today. Accepting her rebuke in silence, Clarissa thought: He really is awful. Staring straight ahead thereby avoiding her eye, Compton thought that since he intended to duck out of as many of the Commission's activities as he could get away with without his chairman noticing, the outcome of the vote did not matter much one way or the other. The main thing for Miles, whatever his own thoughts were, was to be on the winning side whenever possible.

Patience consulted her notes.

'So, we kick off on Wednesday night with a visit to a Soho cinema of the doubtful sort.' (It was the nearest Patience felt she could get to the words pornographic sort.) 'Then on Thursday we shall be interviewing some ladies of easy virtue in the same part of the world, followed on Friday by a visit to a nightclub where there will be dancing . . . .'

'Dancing!' said Muller. 'Jolly good.'

'*On-stage* dancing, I mean.' Patience gave him a long look. 'This, of course, is just the beginning! All these activities will be chronicled by the estimable Mr Radley Oates who has promised us maximum coverage in his newspaper.'

Radley Oates! Compton's blood ran cold. He had had no idea of Oates's follow-up negotiation with Patience Allardyce though he had known, of course, about the first innocuous article. So innocuous that he had rather wondered at the time why it hadn't been spiked on the grounds of sheer dullness. Now he thought he knew. It had been bait. There would be no holds barred when it came to chronicling, as Mrs Allardyce had quaintly put it, the visits of a Commission composed of church worthies, do-gooders and intellectuals, not to mention businessmen like himself, to a pornographic cinema, a brothel and a strip club in that order. *They would be followed around by Radley Oates and a photographer.* Oh God! He would be pilloried in one of the company's own newspapers, never mind about the rest. And *he*, Miles Compton, had voted for it! He resolved to have a word with Oates at the first possible opportunity. The other possibility of salvation was to get the Old Man to veto the whole enterprise, but Hillary was currently in America whence he had travelled by Concorde yesterday and would not be back for a week, by which time it would be too late. It looked as though an appeal to Radley Oates's better nature was his only hope.

In the days that followed it, Patience thought a lot about the dinner with Hillary Causton and also about the man himself. She found the aura of omnipotence and money on display attractive. At the very expensive restaurant to which he took her, he appeared to have his own table, and as they sat down they were surrounded by attentive waiters who flapped napkins, waved menus and wine lists and commented politely on the weather.

When they had ordered their food and the flurry of waiters had retreated, Causton leant back in his chair and said to Patience, 'Now, tell me all about yourself.' She did and then, repaying the compliment, asked him the same question. It turned out that they were both recently divorced and that, broadly speaking, they both shared the same aims and ideals. At the end of it, Hillary said, 'I'm off to America tomorrow and I'll be away for about a week.' And then, very courtly, 'But perhaps we could have dinner together again on my return?'

'I'd like that very much!' Patience was quite decided. When he dropped her off outside the Holland Bush house, he would have liked to kiss her but, receiving no encouragement either by look or body language that this would be welcome, did not. Nor did she ask him in. Hillary could not help but reflect that had this been Drusilla the niceties would have been over ages ago and they would have been in bed by now. Which was how she had taken him by storm in the first place. Advisable, perhaps, to take it more slowly this time. All the same, Causton was not a patient man. Over dinner he had made up his mind that he was going to marry Patience Allardyce and having reached that decision, all his instincts told him to get on with it. On the other hand, this was a woman of the old-fashioned sort who would no doubt prefer to be courted first and it was probably better not to rush his fences. With this in mind just before he turned to go he took her hand in his and, bowing over it, kissed it. Then, gazing into her eyes Hillary said, 'I'll ring you the day I return,' after which, like a hero in a Victorian novel and feeling faintly ridiculous, he resolutely strode in the direction of his car and without a backward glance drove away.

Once more inside her own house, Patience was conscious of a feeling of excitement and, more than that, a heady sensation of destiny taking a hand. Hillary Causton had power and influence and because of this was attractive to her. She was single and so was he. Long and earnest discussion over dinner revealed the fact that they held the same values and believed in the same things. In every way they complemented one another.

'I should like to marry Hillary Causton!' said Patience aloud to her empty drawing room, 'And I *will*!'

Miles Compton decided to eat humble pie and ask Radley Oates out for a drink. As they saw awkwardly opposite one another in The Nag's Head, which was the newspaper's local, he wondered how to bring the subject up. Radley lounged. Miles noticed that he had given up the brilliant plumage of the editor of a gossip column and had reinvented himself sartorially for Features. Part of this disguise was a long, belted stone-coloured mac with big shoulders, turned up collar and a vent at the back, of the sort Hollywood actors used to wear when playing journalists or seedy detectives. All it needed was a fedora and no doubt that would be produced as well when the weather got colder.

'So! How can I help you?' enquired Radley, who had never been under any illusion that this was just a social event.

Ill at ease and trying to cover it, Miles smiled so that the boot button eyes almost disappeared into his fleshy face. He hesitated while trying to decide what was the best way of putting what he had to say.

'Looking forward to your stint on the Morals Jamboree, are you?' Radley had a grin on his face as he said this, which confirmed all Compton's fears.

'It was about that that I wanted to talk to you,' said Miles. 'I gather from Mrs Allardyce that you are going to take a keen interest in it.'

'I am,' said Radley with relish. 'As opportunities go, this one's too good to miss. Saving yourself, of course, I've never seen such a naive collection. Lambs to the Fleet Street slaughter!' It suddenly felt very hot in the pub. Compton mopped his brow and had a sip of his bitter. 'Of course,' resumed Radley, 'I never wanted to be seconded to Features, but since nobody lifted a finger to stop it,' (the inference here could have been *especially you*) 'I'm bloody well going to make the best of it and this little lot are God's gift, to coin a phrase!'

'Nobody asked me what I thought of you going to Features,' protested Compton, tripped into answering a question which had never been specifically asked.

Radley was not deceived by this.

'No, but if they had, by which I mean if *Causton* had, you would have said "you're right" whether you thought he was or not! Don't deny it! You're in that job because of your ability to say "yes, Hillary" a hundred times a day. The reason your predecessor went was because he was his own man.'

Feeling spineless, as he was no doubt meant to, and deciding that there was no point in being offended, Compton resolved to have one more go at it.

'Look, if you'll back off on Renfrew's Commission, I'll try to get you the social diary back. Is that a deal?'

'No,' said Radley.

Miles was disconcerted. '*No?* Why not? It's what you want, isn't it?'

'Yes, but the one comes before the other, by which I mean that, if I back off now, by the time Causton gets back from the Big Apple the strip clubs and brothels, never mind the blue films, will be in the past and they'll all, no *you'll* all, be interviewing tweedy ladies in the shires whose views nobody wants to read about. At which point you'll be in the clear with no need to do anything for me. You'll say, "Sorry old boy, I did my best with the Old Man but no dice".'

The accuracy of his cynicism quite took Compton's breath away. It seemed his reputation had preceded him.

'Are you saying,' asked Compton pompously, 'that if I gave

207

you my word of honour you still wouldn't believe I'd do it?'

'Yes,' said Radley.

It was a rout. There as nothing for Miles to do but swallow the remainder of his beer and go.

'You'll be sorry,' he said to Radley, sounding unconvincing even to himself.

'You'll be sorry first,' was the answer to this.

Compton's last hope was Hillary Causton. He put a call through to New York. As usual his boss was in a meeting, to be followed by another meeting and then another meeting and then a business lunch. He finally caught up with Hillary in the latter's hotel room where he was putting the finishing touches to a speech to be delivered at a dinner that evening.

'Well, what is it? All going smoothly, I hope?' Causton, who was running his eye down the typescript as he spoke, sounded distracted.

'Yes, very smoothly,' reassured Compton. 'There is, however, just one thing I want to sound you out about.' He hesitated.

'Come on, man, get on with it,' barked Hillary. 'I'm in the middle of writing my speech for tonight.'

'It's about the Commission. As things are at present, Radley Oates is standing by to write up everything we do as we do it, with a photographer in harness.'

'And?'

A subtle change in the intonation of this indicated to Miles that, for whatever reason, he suddenly had Hillary's whole attention. In fact, Hillary was seeing the alluring, crusading Patience Allardyce in his mind's eye.

'And I think we're going about it the wrong way, that it would be better if the publicity centred on the publication of the report itself rather than the participants themselves . . . on the *message* if you like, rather than the medium.'

Hillary's eyebrows drew together in a displeased frown.

'Why can't it centre on both?' By now interest had given way to irascibility.

'Yes, that's a good idea!' Compton tried to salvage the situation.

'That was *always* the idea. Besides which I have promised Mrs Allardyce maximum coverage and I intend to honour that commitment!'

Miles blinked. Mrs Allardyce again! That woman was *everywhere*!

'Of course, Hillary, put like that you're right! Though with you away in the States, much as I would like to, I fear I shall be unable to devote as much time as I would have wished to the initial activities of the Commission . . .'

Listening to the fellow wittering on, Causton stared in frustration at his unfinished speech and then looked at his watch.

'Look, Miles, let me spell it out for you. I asked you to take my place on Renfrew's Commission and that's what I want you to do! I don't want to be told you can't do it. You've got a deputy. Let him cope while we're both away. Let's see what he's made of!'

The line went dead. Had they been cut off or had his Chairman hung up on him? Miles had no way of knowing. What he did know was that this was the perfect example of Morton's Fork. If I don't do it, I'm stuffed, thought Miles, and if I do do it I'm also stuffed.

The short-term answer, insofar as there was one, seemed to be a stiff drink.

21

Radley was as good as his word. The Commission were photographed wherever they went and, caught in the glare of the flashbulb, looked furtive. Compton lurked on the fringe, and tried to stay out of the frame every time a photograph looked imminent. They were pictured en masse entering the pornographic film club, and afterwards talking earnestly with those who worked there and with other surprised members of the audience, most of whom would have preferred to remain anonymous. They were also immortalised on film sitting in a row in Striparama Girls! Girls!! Girls!!! watching an odd tableau which featured whips and boots and then interviewing more of the punters and one of the girls whose speciality, apart from taking her clothes off to music, appeared to be the bizarre ability to swing tassels suspended from her nipples in circles.

Radley wrote it all down. With the visit to the brothel yet to come, and armed with the photographs, he went to see his editor who knew a good story when he saw one. He grinned at Radley.

'You'll write it tongue in cheek?'

'You bet!' said Radley.

'I think it's one for the colour mag. You could have a field day! When could you file copy by?'

'As soon as you like,' said the born-again, enthusiastic Radley. 'Apart from more photographs, I hardly need to go on the next little junket in order to write about it.'

'Good man. Crack on with it!'

Hugh Allardyce was very happy. So happy that he could no longer understand how he had tolerated the aridity of his first marriage as long as he had. But then he had had no yardstick to judge it by in those days. Fondly he looked across the room at his wife. Flora was sitting reading with the aid of halfmoon spectacles which gave her a charmingly serious, bookish air. Xerxes sat on the rug between the two of them, washing his face with one fastidious paw. Hugh experienced a surge of love accompanied by an unnerving undercurrent of fear. What if he should lose her? For me, he thought, life without Flora would have no point. Sensitive to his intense gaze, she looked up.

'What is it, darling? Is something wrong?'

'No, nothing. I just can't believe how lucky I am!'

Flora frowned. Then she closed her novel with a sigh and took off her glasses. She was silent for a moment before she spoke. 'Hugh, there is something I have to tell you. I've been putting it off and putting it off because I didn't know how you'd react, but now I've just got to talk about it.'

Hugh felt his heart contract. He had noticed that Flora had been preoccupied lately, as if turning something over and over in her mind. At one point he had even asked her about this and had received a denial that anything was the matter. Now she was going to tell that she had decided he was too old for her after all and probably too staid as well. He should have known that it was all too good to last.

Anticipating the worst, he braced himself.

She hesitated and then said, in a rush, 'Hugh, I'm almost sure I'm pregnant. I'm going to see the doctor tomorrow. I hadn't intended to say anything about it until it was officially confirmed but I just can't keep it to myself any longer.' Flora's voice was unsteady. She suddenly began to weep. Through her sobs he heard her say, 'You have a grown-up family already. You probably don't want another child. Not everyone cares to start again. I thought you might be angry! I even thought you might leave me. *Please* don't leave me!'

Angry? Leave her?

Hugh was thunderstruck. Protective tenderness coupled with relief flooded through him. He fell on his knees beside Flora's chair and took her face in his hands.

'Darling, darling Flora, of course I'm not angry, I'm ecstatic.'

'Are you? Are you really?' Eyes brimming, she faced him uncertainly through her tears. 'It will make a huge change to our life together.'

'I know we didn't plan it, but that doesn't matter.' He kissed her. 'Sweetheart, it's *wonderful* news! What else can I say to convince you?'

Laughing and crying all at the same time and then kissing him back, Flora whispered, 'Oh, Hugh, I love you *so* much. The day I met you was the best day of my life.'

As he had promised, the day he returned from New York Hillary rang Patience up and arranged to take her out to dinner the following evening. Sitting opposite her he was more than ever convinced that this was the woman for him. Patience was dressed in black. Her hair was up and she wore the restrung pearls which were lustrous against her throat. With her dignified air, there was something of the high priestess about her which probably appealed to Hillary's Godlike view of himself.

It was while he was selecting his first course that a voice at his elbow made him sit up.

'Hello, darling!' said the voice.

It was Drusilla. Drusilla wafer-thin in purple, a colour he knew from experience she often chose to wear when in a dangerous mood. She was also wearing pearls, the black ones. Hillary looked around for help in the shape of Charlie Davenport and could not see him.

'Charlie's not here yet,' said Drusilla, interpreting the look correctly. 'Aren't you going to introduce me?'

'Not unless I have to,' said Hillary.

'Then I shall have to do it myself. I am Drusilla Causton, Hillary's wife.'

'Ex-wife, thank God,' said Hillary.

She held out her hand. Patience did not take it.

'And *I* am Patience Allardyce.'

'Hillary's mistress, I presume! Hillary used to bring me here, you know. It was quite our favourite restaurant, wasn't it, darling?'

'Drusilla!' Causton was outraged. 'Look, are you waiting for Davenport or are you just passing the time of day, because if so . . . Ah, here he is!' The note of relief in his voice was unmistakable.

Minimally acknowledging Davenport, Drusilla addressed herself directly to Patience.

'This is Charlie, who is my current lover.'

'How do you do,' said Patience, prune-faced.

'Aren't you going to tut?' asked Drusilla, noting her expression.

Charlie was also prune-faced. The word current had been calculated to offend. It made him sound at best ephemeral and at worst disposable. Not very gently he took Drusilla's elbow and spun her round.

'Time to go, dearest Dru. Say goodbye nicely.' Firmly he steered her off in the direction of what Patience assumed must be their table. Hillary beckoned to the head waiter, Ronald.

'Could you make sure that the couple who have just left us sit as far away as possible? Preferably where we can't see them.'

'It has already been organised, Mr Causton,' said Ronald, who knew the ex-Mrs Causton and who was not head waiter of one of London's top restaurants for nothing. 'And now perhaps *I* can take your order for you.' He flourished his pencil. 'May I recommend the *foie gras* this evening?'

When Ronald had gone, Hillary said to Patience, 'I can't apologise enough for that. Would you prefer to go somewhere else?'

'Not at all,' she answered, 'for that would leave Drusilla in possession of the field, wouldn't it?' She sent him a complicitous look together with a smile that might almost have been flirtatious.

Her attitude delighted him. 'That's the spirit!' said Hillary, ever original. 'Now tell me how the Commission got on. I gather Radley Oates is writing you up.'

'He is,' said Patience, 'and I'm sure that, as a committed Christian, he will be sensitive to what it is we are trying to achieve.'

Hillary was startled. Oates had never struck him as committed to anything very much. Maybe getting away from the frivolity of the gossip column had brought about a sea-change. Whatever the cause, it was long overdue, that much was certain.

'Yes,' Patience continued. 'I spoke to Mr Oates today and he tells me that there is going to be a substantial article in the weekend colour magazine. It's all very exciting!' Flushed and sparkling, she was almost girlish in her enthusiasm.

And to think, thought Hillary, that if I had listened to that idiot, Compton, I would not have been witness to all this innocent pleasure. He leant across the table and took Patience's hand. Her wedding ring, he noticed, was a plain gold band with one diamond. He, Hillary, would do better than that when the time came.

'My dear Patience . . .'

'Well, this *is* love's young dream. Or maybe we should say love's *old* dream! But don't let *me* disturb you.' Drusilla passing, presumably on her way to the loo. Nothing Ronald could have done about that.

'You *have* disturbed us!' By now Hillary, whose nerves were thoroughly jangled, verged on apoplectic. 'Go AWAY!'

He wondered how he could ever have believed himself to be in love with Drusilla to the point where he had actually married her. For better or for worse said the wedding service. It had all been worse, all of it. Now he was beginning to wonder whether, despite a hugely expensive divorce, he would ever be shot of her.

'You'll never find anybody else who's as good as I am in bed,' remarked Drusilla conversationally, preparing to move on and without lowering her voice. 'Certainly not Mrs Goody Two Shoes here. Don't say I didn't warn you!'

She went.

Aghast, Patience said into the profound silence that enveloped four adjacent tables following her departure, 'How long did you say you were married to her?'

'*Too* long. It was like serving a life sentence by the end,' said Hillary, gloomily. Probably Patience Allardyce would not want to see him again after being subjected to Drusilla's appalling behaviour. On the whole romance and gratuitous insults did not go together. His surprise then, when the opposite appeared to be the case, was total. This time Patience took *his* hand.

'You poor, *poor* thing. Oh, Hillary, how I *feel* for you!' Her compassion caused him to feel sorry for himself in a way he never had throughout the marriage. Embattled, yes, but self-pitying, no. This must be what it was like to be cherished rather than in a permanent state of war. To Hillary's disappointment the main course arrived and she was forced to release his hand. With trepidation they both watched Drusilla re-emerge from the ladies' loo. This time, to his huge relief, she did not make an approach but simply bestowed on them a smile and a wave like

214

a normal person and was gone. Breathing freely at least for the present and trying to recover the situation insofar as that was possible, Hillary went further than he had intended and said to Patience, 'I think you and I could form a very good partnership.'

Not sure exactly what he had in mind, she stared at him questioningly.

Aware that the way he had phrased this made it sound more like a business statement than a romantic one, he added, 'On a personal level, I mean.'

A woman who knew what she wanted and saw no point in beating about the bush, Patience said, 'Are you asking me to marry you?'

It was what he had had in mind but not at this precise moment in time. The idea had been to move the ritual dance of courtship forward, a step or two beyond the first formal bow and curtsy, rather than bring it to a conclusion. For one brief, uneasy moment Hillary entertained the idea that he was again in the grip of a strong woman, before dismissing it. On the other hand, living with Drusilla had taught him that these were egalitarian days. Patience had a perfect right to ask just as he had a perfect right to say no.

In the event, because he was a man who was used to taking business decisions the moment they presented themselves, he did not do this. Faced with the question his instinctive response was positive. 'Yes, I am!' said Hillary. At the same time he was slightly uncomfortable with the speed with which this had happened. It was faintly reminiscent of the last time. Although, of course, Patience was quite different from Drusilla. All the same, as a consummate and wily businessman, the habit of hedging his bets was endemic. *Marry in haste and repent at leisure*. There was no getting away from the fact that that was what had happened before. 'Though I think we should enjoy getting to know each other better, spend a little more time together before finally tying the knot, don't you?'

In an odd sort of way, it all felt back to front.

'I do!' Patience did not hesitate. There was no point in pushing it any further. Tonight, by dint of seizing the initiative and aided rather than the opposite by the intervention of the truly awful ex-Mrs Causton, she had got closer to what she wanted than she had ever dared hope. 'After all we have both been married before and neither of us wants to make a mistake.' Besides which, she might have added but did not, I've got my hands full at the moment and immediate marriage would only make them fuller.

She smiled at him.

A slightly awkward silence fell. Neither knew quite what to do in the wake of the commitment they had just made to one another underpinned as it was by so little real intimacy. Nor, it transpired, was any intimacy likely in the physical sense until after they were married, for although Hillary kissed Patience on the lips for the first time at the end of the evening, that was as far as it went and not only did her kiss lack the abandonment of (say) Drusilla's, but it was disappointingly well bred, prim almost. No doubt, thought Hillary driving himself home alone, that would change as their intimacy increased. However, because Patience, unlike Drusilla, was a virtuous woman (as he kept reminding himself) it was perfectly possible that sex before marriage might well be out and the Getting To Know Each Other Better process about to take place on a purely platonic level. Since it was impossible to quarrel with such high-minded principles, if he wanted Patience in his bed, and Hillary was in no doubt that he did, this argued for marriage sooner rather than later. That way they could do it all at the same time.

Hillary and Patience told nobody of their pact and the upshot of this was that prior to one of his evening visits to collect typing, talk about parish business and the progress of the Commission in particular, Cedric Renfrew resolved to Speak. One minute he was sipping his third sherry and talking about the newsletter and the next he was striding about being biblical and declaiming inappropriate excerpts from the Song of Solomon. Patience had, of course, seen him do this sort of thing before though not with the Song of Solomon, but nevertheless was unprepared for what came next. Half listening because she had been devoting more thought to the forthcoming *Clarion* article about their joint Commission endeavours than to what she assumed must be Cedric practising for Sunday, she suddenly heard him say:

'*Thy breasts are like two young roes that are twins, which feed among the lilies.'*

When he followed this up with: '*Thy navel is like a round goblet, which wanteth not liquor: thy belly is like a heap of wheat set about with lilies,*' she felt bound to protest. Never mind about the stylistic *faux pas* of two lots of lilies so close together, the text he had chosen did not seem to Patience suitable for a family service.

She said so.

Renfrew was thunderstruck.

'My dear Patience, this is not my sermon,' explained Cedric, as he grasped the depth of the misunderstanding, 'I am *proposing* to you!' Before she could say a word, he pressed on:

'*Who is she that looketh forth as the morning, fair as the moon, clear as the sun, and terrible as an army with banners?*'

He fell on one knee.

'*Thou art all fair, my love, there is no spot in thee.*'

The fact that he appeared to have temporarily run out of breath gave Patience the opportunity to stop him. *Terrible as an army with banners* seemed to be the right note to strike.

'Stand up, Cedric,' said Patience, very severe. He did so and then, impervious to her freezing displeasure, swooped and caught her to him. Never keen on physical contact at the best of times, Patience was nauseated by his embrace. He smelt musty as though he had been packed in mothballs. When, to her horror, he slid his hands over her breasts she thought she might actually be sick. It was all getting out of hand. Pushing him away she shouted, 'Cedric, DON'T!'

To her relief this caused him to step back a pace, after which, not at all upset, he said, 'Of course! You are overwhelmed! Perhaps my passion has caused me to be too precipitate! But Patience, my love, when you think it over you will see where your duty lies!'

Her *duty*?

Patience had always been very hot on duty where other people were concerned but now she found it being proposed to herself in a less than congenial form, recoiled.

'I don't know what you mean!' said Patience.

'Your duty to God,' elucidated Renfrew. 'Between us we can move mountains in His service! I am sure my dear Patience that when you think it over you will see the light!' To her horror he began to quote again. '*A garden enclosed is my sister, my spouse; a spring shut up a fountain sealed.* Open yourself up to Me and to God! I shall leave you now. Tomorrow I am confident that your answer will be Yes.'

He turned and went. With unutterable relief she heard the door slam behind him. That was not the end of the story though. The thought of another confrontation tomorrow was not to be borne without the whole thing being sorted out first. Since Cedric was one of those people who transmitted but did not listen, probably the only way to achieve this was to write to him *now* and then hand deliver the result. She glanced at her watch. It was still only eight o'clock. Patience poured herself another drink, a whisky this time and set about it. After some thought, she wrote,

My dear Cedric and then, on the grounds that he did not need any encouragement and might go over the top again if he felt he was getting it, changed this to the more formal,

Dear Cedric. At this point she paused and put down her pen. In spite of her revulsion, it seemed important that she should not make an enemy of him while at the same time making him see that a marriage between the two of them was out of the question. Equally out of the question was telling him about her understanding with Hillary Causton. Quite apart from anything else, it was none of Renfrew's business. After all, I didn't ask him to come and propose to me and am not aware of having given him any encouragement either, thought Patience. In the end, she continued,

I was honoured by your proposal of marriage, as any woman would be. Unfortunately I am unable to accept it.

This sounded bald, but her recent encounter with Renfrew convinced Patience that this letter had to be couched in the plainest of terms so that there could be no misunderstanding. *As you know, I am a devout Christian and would like nothing more than to move mountains in His service. Alas, I fear this cannot be with you, for I am not in love with you. I value your support and . . .* here, after a short hesitation occasioned by the fact that she frequently found his advice irksome, she put *guidance* and went on in conciliatory vein, *and hope, despite what has happened, that our friendship will continue.* They would have to meet again and that

218

being the case there was, she decided, no point in alienating Cedric more than she had to. *This is my final decision,* underlined Patience, just in case he still had not got the message, *and as such I feel there is no need for us to refer to what passed between us this evening ever again.* She ended the letter *Yours sincerely, Patience Allardyce* and, having read it through once more, put it in an envelope on which she wrote his name and the words By Hand. It only remained to deliver it which she did. The vicarage appeared to be in darkness as she parked her car. Perhaps he was working at the back of the house. Whatever he was doing it was no concern of hers.

She put the envelope through the letterbox and drove home.

As he told Cordelia he would, Robert Ormond went to see his wife on the Monday. When he got there he discovered that there was no official visiting hour that particular morning. There was no sign of the tyrant who was Sister as described by Cordelia so Robert just walked in. When he found Dorian, although the curtains around the bed were open, she was asleep. Robert stood for a moment looking down at her. He felt a mixture of emotions including contrition and concern, but the dominating one was love.

Very quietly he pulled the curtains and then he sat on the side of the bed and took her in his arms.

22

Patience received a sudden urgent summons to the school with a view, they said, to discussing her son's future there. She rang Christian who did not return her calls and she finally spoke to Cordelia.

'Do you have any idea what this is all about, darling?' asked Patience. 'They wouldn't discuss it on the telephone.'

'I don't, Mummy,' said Cordelia truthfully, 'but I'll go and ask Christian myself if you want me to.'

'Why don't you? Tell him I'm coming down to the school tomorrow.'

Cordelia found her brother in his room. The blind was down. Christian was lying on his bed in the dark listening to very loud music.

'I've just had a call from Mummy,' said Cordelia.

'Oh yes?' Christian sounded wary.

'She's coming here tomorrow for a meeting with the Head. They want to see her, not the other way around. Apparently it's about you. Would you mind turning the music down a bit?'

He did so, without making a fuss about it which was unusual, and then let up the blind. For a few moments he stood with his back to her looking out of the window. Finally he turned around and said, 'Well, you might as well know'.

Cordelia felt trepidation.

'Know what?'

'I've been sacked!'

His sister gasped. It was the last thing she expected. 'Oh, Christian! What for?'

'Drugs.'

Cordelia drew in her breath. They both knew there was no appeal against that. The school's policy on that particular offence was tough and non-negotiable.

'What sort of drugs?' Cordelia dreaded the answer to this.

'Hash.' Christian was laconic. 'It's not just me,' he added, 'it's the band as well,' and then, with a trace of his old swagger, 'I don't care, I'm fed up with school anyway. I'm fed up with being treated like a child and I'm fed up with having nothing to do and nowhere to go. I want to live in London.'

It crossed Cordelia's mind to say, 'Maybe if you behaved more like an adult, you'd get treated like one,' but she decided not to on the grounds that at this stage it wouldn't help. Instead, she said, 'It's going to be the most awful shock for Mummy. Don't you think you owe it to her to ring her tonight and tell her?'

'Mum needs to make it into the twentieth century,' said Christian. 'Everyone does drugs these days. It's not a big deal.'

'No they don't and yes it is!' She was not prepared to let him get away with this. 'Look if you don't tell her, I'm going to have to.'

'OK. I'll do it.'

He turned the music up to full decibel again. Cordelia knew this was her cue to leave and with a heavy heart did so. Walking back to her own room it occurred to her to wonder whether their father had been contacted as well. Probably he had which meant for the first time in a very long while her parents would travel down to the school together.

That evening Hugh rang Patience. By this time she had talked to Christian and sounded shell-shocked.

'Do you think there's any hope of them keeping him there?' asked Patience.

'In a word,' said Hugh, 'no. That college takes a very hard line on drugs and rightly so!'

It was impossible not to agree with this. 'And totally rightly so!' Patience found herself forced to concur. 'Do you know, I just don't understand it. Christian had a very moral upbringing . . .'

Hugh did not feel like listening to her crossing the Ts and dotting the Is on the mysteries surrounding bringing up children. 'He'll have to go to a crammer in London unless we can shoehorn him into another boarding school. Anyway, look, we can discuss all that on the way down. I'll pick you up at ten, shall I?'

It was an index of their growing closeness that that evening, over dinner, Patience told Hillary all about her problem with her son. Anticipating censure, she was amazed at his relaxed attitude.

'Obviously we don't want him making a habit of it but try not to worry so much, my love.' Hillary was used to the indulged, wayward children of equally rich friends. 'I have contacts. We'll get him into another school. What you don't want is Christian on the loose in London. And the other thing you don't want is the Press to get a whiff of this.'

'I'm sure the school will want to hush the whole thing up, although according to Christian the rest of his band were caught doing it as well. It looks as if four of them are probably going to be asked to leave.'

'That might be slightly less easy to keep quiet,' said Hillary. 'What's the name of the band?'

'I don't know,' answered Patience. 'I asked Cordelia but she didn't know either.'

'I'm looking forward to meeting your children,' said Hillary, 'and, darling, what do you say about setting the date for our wedding?' His eye travelled appreciatively over his wife-to-be. This evening she was wearing a well-cut dark green dress which set off her voluptuous figure to advantage. Its neckline was low, though not immodestly so and tantalised with a hint, though only a hint, of cleavage. Celibacy does not suit me, thought Hillary. The sooner we get on with it the better.

Patience wondered whether to tell him about Cedric Renfrew's extraordinary proposal as well and decided against it. After all, she, Patience, had not encouraged Cedric who nevertheless had managed to get the wrong end of the stick at some point in their dealings. On the whole she decided that it was better to let sleeping dogs lie. She had told him No and that was that.

She smiled across the table. 'Let's look at our diaries, shall we? What date did you have in mind?'

Patience was destined to find out the name of Christian's band sooner than she knew. At the end of what proved to be a short visit to the school Hugh and Patience took their son and all his belongings back to London with them.

'While the search is on for another boarding school, you will

222

study at home, supervised by me!' said Patience over her shoulder. A second country incarceration was the last thing their son wanted.

'Why can't I go to a London crammer?' Christian wanted to know.

'Because,' said Patience, very firm and quoting Hillary, 'I don't want you on the loose in London.'

Piloting the car, Hugh privately supported this view, although he recognised that finding another establishment would not be easy. 'Or you can live with Flora and myself,' offered Hugh, 'and *I'll* supervise the work until we're all sorted out. Whichever you prefer.'

There could be no question of him living with his father and Flora for reasons Hugh did not know about. Sulkily, citing the practical, Christian said, 'Dad, you haven't thought it through. You don't have a spare room so I'd have to sleep on the sofa or in the bath. I think I'm probably better off with Mum. And what about money? Do I get an allowance? I'll need some money to spend.'

'This isn't a holiday you are embarking on, Christian!' Patience was tart. 'You will get the same amount of pocket money as you did at the school and since I will be providing your board and keep that should suffice.'

Put like that it sounded like prison with Mum as the warder. 'Dad?' appealed Christian.

'I support your mother on this,' said Hugh. 'Frankly you've let us down and now is not the moment to be asking for favours!'

It was as he sat in glowering silence in the back of the car for the remainder of the journey that Christian had an idea.

In the event, by the middle of the first week of his stay it became evident that it was not possible for Patience to supervise her son as closely as she would have liked for she had her own commitments, not the least of which was the Commission. On the Wednesday after his arrival while she was out of the house, he rang up a tabloid newspaper, related a spiced-up version of why he, the lead singer, and three other members of his band had been expelled from a well-known public school and negotiated himself a fee for doing so.

CHRIST AND THE ARCHANGELS BUSTED FOR DRUGS was the headline chosen and was seen by Hillary Causton who took all the newspapers and spotted it during the course of his habitual trawl through them. The piece featured Christian's name, which fact had earned him more money, though not the names of the others. Even he had stopped short of divulging those. Ye Gods! Hillary decided not to tell Patience over the telephone what had happened, rightly surmising that she would be distraught, but over lunch when he could calm her down. Unfortunately, because she was out and so apparently was the disgraceful Christian, he was unable to catch up with her. So it was that Cedric Renfrew, who had had the piece pointed out to him by a gleeful church groupie, got there first.

Without speaking, he handed the newspaper to Patience and watched her as she read it. Since her letter the atmosphere between them had been cool. Cedric felt himself spurned and had not forgiven it. *Vengeance is mine saith the Lord.* Well, yes, but, that being said, He had certainly dropped it right in His vicar's lap. There could have been two ways of looking at this, the first being that he was being tempted to take matters which were normally the prerogative of a much higher power into his own hands and was expected to resist. The second possibility was that he was being pointed in the direction of righteousness. Delegation was taking place and he, Cedric, should act accordingly. Hell-bent on revenge, he elected to believe the second.

'Perhaps we should have a quiet word in the vestry,' suggested Cedric, gimlet-eyed. He led the way.

As she sat down opposite him, Patience's thoughts were not to do with Renfrew at all, but centred on Christian.

Why had he done it? What had gone wrong? How could it be that someone brought up to live by the highest principles could behave like this? And not just drugs but highly publicised blasphemy as well. I am mortified, thought Patience. *Mortified!*

With an effort, she focused her attention on Cedric who was leaning back in his bentwood chair with one black eyebrow raised and a quizzical expression on his face. He must have asked her a question.

'I'm sorry,' said Patience, pulling herself together. 'Did you ask me something? You must forgive me. I'm very worried and upset . . .'

'*I'm* very upset too,' interrupted Renfrew. The competitive way in which this was delivered indicated to Patience that while she might be the parent of the errant Christian, her upsetness was as nothing compared to his.

'I appreciate your concern,' said Patience doubtfully, not exactly sure what he was getting at.

'My concern,' pronounced Cedric, clearing the matter up, 'is not for you but for the Commission. Such dire publicity concerning the child of one of its leading lights can do nothing but harm. It is my opinion that those of us in the public eye, working for the public good, must be above reproach!'

'It is my view that I *am* above reproach!' Patience was nettled.

His eyes bored into her. He showed no sign of having heard her response.

'In short, I think you should consider your position!'

'Consider my . . .?'

'Resign! Step down! Do the honourable thing! Do you understand me?'

It would have been hard not to. Astounded but regrouping, Patience said, 'I have no intention of resigning! I haven't done anything wrong. Why should I resign? And may I ask whether the private lives of the rest of the Commission are going to be put under scrutiny? And whether, if found wanting, they are going to be asked to resign too?'

Employing the age-old tactic of continuing to intone what he had to say and ignoring all awkward questions, Renfrew bypassed this one. 'You must resign for the Greater Good! The Commission is more important than one of its members.'

Cedric stood up and began to pace up and down. She recognised it as the prelude to a biblical harangue.

'*Pride goeth before destruction*,' warned Renfrew, '*and an haughty spirit before a fall*. If you persist in this headstrong attitude, having invited you to serve on the Commission in the first place, I shall be forced to disinvite you. It will be seen as my decision rather than your own. I shall refuse to throw light on why I have done this. On top of everything else, there will be Speculation.' He decided to end on a note of triumphant admonition. 'And remember Proverbs! *A continual dropping in a very rainy day and a contentious woman are alike.*'

Outraged, Patience stood up and smartly went over his head by addressing the Diety direct. '*Oh Lord, thou has seen my wrong: judge thou my cause.*' She rounded on Cedric. 'Lamentations!' She swept from the room.

Left sitting by himself in the darkening vestry, it occurred to Renfrew that she was unreasonably very irritated and not at all contrite. It also occurred to him in the face of her intransigent attitude that maybe he had won the battle but not the war.

Radley Oates's article appeared and the world laughed. Or, rather, that part of the world that had a sense of humour and was not personally involved, laughed. Dorian Ormond read it in silence and then, without a word, handed it to her husband across the breakfast table. It was worse than she had feared. Photographically petrified in trendy black and white, the Commission sat in a solemn row under the headline: *MORAL VIGILANTES STORM SOHO*. Writing about something as opposed to nothing in particular had tightened up Radley's prose style no end, Dorian noticed, or maybe it was just that going for the jugular concentrated the mind. Her sister, a vicar called Renfrew, Miles Compton, whom Dorian had met once, and a social worker called Larch, together with a philosopher called Muller had been singled out for special mention. A smirking photograph of Radley accompanied his by-line. Dorian stared at it. It was hard to believe that he and she had ever been lovers. Now she was back with Robert, the whole episode seemed like a dream.

'Good God!' ejaculated Robert, reading on with relish and guffawing from time to time as he did so, 'what on earth did they think they were doing? I'm surprised even Patience didn't see this one coming!' He turned the page and found himself confronted by a collection of colour photographs. One depicted an earnest Heinrich Muller apparently in scholarly conversation with a statuesque stripper who was wearing nothing apart from a G-string and feathers on her head. In another a fugitive-looking queue straggling along the side of a pornographic cinema waiting for the doors to open was being quizzed by a combination of Jonathan Larch and the vicar, and in yet another Patience herself, chin jutting, was to be seen sitting on red plush in a pink draped interior vaguely reminiscent of a harem earnestly talking to three women. *Sadie, Marlene and Cherry explain the finer points of prostitution to Mrs Patience Allardyce* elucidated the caption. In almost every picture a sheepish Miles Compton could be seen lurking on the periphery until the photographer had finally caught him full frontal, so to speak, standing beside a saucy placard advertising Girls! Girls!! Girls!!!

With tears of merriment in his eyes, Robert eventually handed the magazine back to Dorian. 'What are you going to do? She's bound to see it!'

'I know,' said Dorian, 'and the answer to your question is, nothing at all. I'm going to keep right out of it.' She decided not to tell Robert that the mysterious lover whose existence he had guessed at was in fact Radley Oates. And the other person who must never, never know was Patience. 'Hopefully my upright sister will have the common sense to keep quiet and the whole episode will be a nine-day wonder and swiftly forgotten.'

'I wouldn't bank on it.'

The next meeting of the Commission was a fraught one. All the participants turned up with a copy of the *Clarion* colour magazine under one arm. Aware that because the offensive article had been run by one of the newspapers in the Causton stable he would be the target of particular censure, Miles Compton pleaded illness and did not attend. Because Cedric had fired her, Patience was not there either. In the light of the unfortunate Oates article, he wondered whether perhaps he had been too precipitate. As things stood it looked as if he was going to have to take most of the flak by himself.

His entry was greeted with expectant but stony silence which proved to be the lull before the storm. When he stood up and began to speak, commencing with the words, 'I'm sure you will all have been dismayed by the deplorably flippant approach of the article in the Saturday *Clarion*, of which we all had such high hopes . . .' there was a surge of indignation followed by uproar. Everybody talked at once.

'Whose idea was it to allow Oates to tag along anyway?' a disgruntled Jonathan Larch wanted to know. Larch, who was secretly sexually ambivalent and who had been caught by the camera in front of a club for gays, felt he had been 'outed' and, in the process, made to look particularly ridiculous.

Like a Greek chorus, they all joined in. 'Yes, whose?'

'It was Patience Allardyce's suggestion,' Renfrew asserted blandly above the hubbub, conveniently forgetting his own participation and deciding as he did so that if anybody was to be thrown to the wolves it would not be himself if he could help it.

'I thought you and she agreed on that course of action together!' The speaker was Clarissa Bowen who was not prepared to let him get away with this.

Renfrew glared at her and then collected himself and replied in a neutral tone, 'Well, yes and no. Mrs Allardyce exceeded her brief, I fear. She was, shall we say, over-zealous.'

'Over-zealous? OVER-ZEALOUS!' Making no concessions to a philosophical attitude, Heinrich Muller was indignant and shouting and waving the magazine. 'It's a hatchet job. I was not amused! Mrs *Muller* was not amused!'

No. Listening to it, Clarissa dared say she wasn't. A risible picture of Mrs Muller as Queen Victoria, dumpy and dour in black bombazine rose before her inner eye. Of course we all look absolute absurd, thought Clarissa, including myself. She wondered whether to remind them all that she had tried to head off this particular disaster and the majority, including Muller and Larch, had been too vain to let her, and decided not to bother. It would have been hard to make herself heard. All were baying for blood. The scene she was witnessing was more reminiscent of the Colosseum in Roman times than a gathering of today's Christians.

'Where is Mrs Allardyce, anyway?'

'And Compton! It was one of the Causton newspapers! Where's he?'

'Yes, Compton! What's Compton got to say for himself?'

In desperation, Renfrew held up both arms and made a flapping motion to try to reduce the noise level and at the same time calm the meeting down. He partially succeeded and could just be heard to say above the noise, 'As of the day before yesterday, Mrs Allardyce has resigned!'

There was instant silence.

'*Why* has Patience Allardyce resigned?' asked John Hardcastle the doctor and Mark Ashworth the lawyer, as one and plainly mystified. Clarissa Bowen who knew the answer because Patience had told her, watched Renfrew narrowly to see what he would say. In the event, this turned out to be very little and very unilluminating.

'Mrs Allardyce had a problem to do with her personal life and deemed it better that she step down. The decision was entirely her own and in the circumstances perfectly appropriate.'

Put like that Patience's 'problem' could have been anything from being caught with her hand in the till to murder. In the interests of fairness, Clarissa decided to speak up. She did not raise her voice and it was with interest that Renfrew noted that the clear, well-modulated tones of a lady immediately commanded attention.

'Just in case some of you should get the wrong impression, Patience has done nothing wrong. Patience has stepped down, as Cedric puts it' (here she caught and held his eye) 'because her son was caught smoking cannabis. It was in the newspapers. Nothing more sinister than that.'

Jonathan Larch chipped in, 'On the contrary I think it is sinister. What kind of a mother can Mrs Allardyce have been to allow such a thing?'

Thinking: What a smug, self-satisfied prig, Clarissa rounded on him. 'Of *course* she didn't! It all happened at boarding school and as a result he was asked to leave.'

'Oh, *boarding* school! No wonder!' Larch was scathing. 'I consider that a dereliction of her duty! Why wasn't Mrs Allardyce bringing up her children herself I should like to know!'

Clarissa decided to give up on it. The man was a pill.

His professional attitude caught by the first part of this acrimonious exchange and picking up on it, 'There is a school of thought,' said Dr Hardcastle, whose private practice was in Chelsea, 'that a little cannabis is not necessarily a bad thing in these stressful times.'

Renfrew stared at the last speaker. Could he have heard right? Better to press on and not get sidetracked into even more contentious issues.

'Let us not digress,' said Cedric severely. 'Miles Compton is not here today because he is too ill . . .'

'I'd be too ill to attend as well if I'd made a gaff like that,' asserted a voice from the back. 'It was one of Causton's newspapers!' Renfrew looked to see whose it was. Mark Ashford, the lawyer, making trouble.

'I think, ladies and gentlemen, that what's done is done,' announced Renfrew, making in Clarissa's view the first sensible remark since they all arrived, 'and we must all look away from it and move on. We must not be deflected from our higher purpose by the slings and arrows of the media. Now, let us discuss what happens next!'

Hillary Causton came back from another business trip. Although, while abroad, he had read various airmail editions of his newspapers, for reasons of weight the *Clarion* colour magazine had not been included and so he arrived back in England with no knowledge of the perfidious Oates feature. As was now his habit, he took Patience out for one of their chaste dinners shortly, he hoped, to turn into the more carnal variety as soon as they were virtuously wed.

Tonight she seemed preoccupied. Never very vivacious but always graciously attentive to whatever it was he had to say (which was more than one could ever have said for Drusilla), on this occasion she seemed remote, even displeased. It could not have been anything he had done since they had not seen each other for the duration of his trip and all had been fine between them the day he departed. Causton wondered if she had changed her mind about their pact. There was only one way to find out. Taking her hand, he proposed that, regardless of the date they had already set, they get married as soon as possible. The response was both gratifying and immediate.

'I should like that very much,' said Patience.

He kissed her white plump fingers whose nails were painted a well-bred muted pink.

'Darling Patience, quite apart from the ring of your choice, of course, I should like to give you something else on the occasion of our marriage, another piece of jewellery, maybe. A brooch? Earrings? A necklace?' And then, mindful of how scathing

230

Drusilla had been in the face of what she considered to be a lack of generosity, 'A brooch, earrings *and* a necklace perhaps. Whatever you want, you shall have it.'

Her reply astonished him.

'I should like the head of Radley Oates,' replied the committed Christian, his wife-to-be. 'I don't mind if it is on a spike or on a platter, but that is what I would like.'

The sheer ferocity of what was, by any standards, an unusual request brought Drusilla to mind. Noting his stupefaction, Patience said, 'You haven't seen it, then?'

'No. I don't know. Seen what?'

'The Saturday colour magazine. They probably don't include it in the airmail issue.' She opened a capacious leather handbag and fished one out, folded in two. 'Turn to page 18!'

Causton did so. The first thing he saw was the mug shot of Radley Oates. The second was the headline. Heart sinking, he read on. When he had finished, he said, 'Patience, I had no idea they were doing this. What on earth was Compton thinking about to allow it?' As he spoke the words he remembered the panicky telephone call he had taken while trying to write his speech and his brusque dismissal of Miles's suggestion that the publicity should be reined back until the report was published. Now he saw the point of the request. Certainly, since Compton himself featured largely in a piece in which all the participants were portrayed as ridiculous or eccentric or both, it was not something his Chief Operating Officer would have wanted to see in print. Causton did not tell his bride-to-be any of this lest it should rebound on him. What he did say was, 'You shall have the head, if not in the physical sense certainly in the metaphorical. I'll fire Oates tomorrow.'

23

Patience rang Dorian and told her sister of her impending marriage. Dorian, who had heard of Hillary Causton of course, but who had never met him, was impressed. She opened her mouth to say, 'He's very right wing, isn't he?' and then closed it again for so was Patience. Instead she said, 'What do the children think about it? I assume they've met him?'

'Yes,' answered her sister. 'Hillary took us all out to dinner.'

'And?'

'He and Cordelia got on like a house on fire but Christian was less forthcoming.'

Patience frowned as she said this. Christian's sulky behaviour had verged on rudeness. It was possible, no, probable that this was because through the good offices of one of Hillary's contacts she and Hugh had been able to enrol their son in a strict boarding school miles from anywhere where the distractions were few and where, no doubt because of this, the work ethic flourished. Christian, it appeared, was not grateful for this intervention on his behalf. But I am, thought Patience, and so was Hugh. Try as she might she could not imagine herself and Christian and Hillary all trying to live together. And maybe the same went for Hillary, who had moved heaven and earth to settle the What To Do With Christian question.

Dorian's voice enquiring how Hugh felt about her engagement brought her to herself.

'Hugh's very happy for me. Very happy.'

I'll bet he is, Dorian thought, listening to this, well aware that her brother-in-law had agonised guiltily over his defection and that, now a Happy Ending was imminent, he would be let off this particular hook.

'Are you going to invite him and Flora to the wedding?'

'It will be a small wedding. Hillary does not want a large party,' said Patience without exactly answering the question. 'It has not yet been decided who will be asked and who will not.'

Good heavens! Is she saying that Robert and I aren't going to be invited?

Dorian decided to get off the tricky subject of the minuscule guest list.

'You'll get married in church, presumably though.'

'Oh yes,' said Patience, 'at St Cuthbert's. The Reverend Cedric Renfrew doesn't know it yet but he's going to conduct the service!'

There was an unmistakable satisfaction about the way this was said, a flintiness even, which was intriguing and indicated to Dorian that some sort of vendetta was in progress.

In fact, Patience's next port of call when she had finished talking to Dorian was the vicar. When she arrived he had apparently been working in his study. By now it was August. In spite of the heat of the day he was clad in the usual black from head to toe and still had his jacket on. Patience had never seen him without it. Perhaps he went to bed dressed like that. The very thought of it made her blush slightly as she remembered Cedric pouncing on her in her own house.

An air of exultation enveloped him when he opened the door and discovered her on his doorstep.

'Ah, my dear Patience! What can I do for you?'

'Ask me in to begin with.' Patience was brisk, preferring not to bandy words on a doorstep, be it his or anybody else's. When they finally achieved the privacy of his dismal den, she said, 'I have something to tell you.'

An apology for certain. Plus, possibly, a belated acceptance of his generous offer of marriage. Or maybe she was going to plead to be reinstated on the Commission. At this particular moment in time, Renfrew would not have been averse to such a negotiation, needing as he did a scapegoat for the Oates Fiasco. Complacently he waited.

'I have decided that I will marry again,' said Patience.

Renfrew preened. All the same he would not make it easy for her. Patience Allardyce must be made aware that he, Cedric, was in charge and not a man to be treated lightly. In the fullness of time, theirs would be a triumphant union. With a woman like this one on his arm a bishopric could eventually be his. The issue of the louche, drug-taking adolescent that was her unsatis-

233

factory son, so important when it came to levering her spitefully off the Commission, faded into insignificance. It became the Devil's blip, a minor aberration to be overlooked. For one must, of course, be charitable about such lapses. He appeared so sunk in thought that Patience was forced into asking him whether he was still listening. When he assured her that he was, she said, 'Hillary Causton has asked me to be his wife and I have accepted!'

The silence which followed this announcement was profound. Disappointment and chagrin were profound too.

'Hillary, that is Hillary and I,' Patience continued, 'would like you to conduct the wedding service.'

Not like to *ask* you to conduct the wedding service, Renfrew noticed. It was a three line whip. He was *expected* to do it. And since Hillary Causton was both rich and influential would *have* to do it. All the same he was determined not to make it easy for them.

'Of course! I shall be delighted to.'

They both knew he would not.

'But that will depend to a degree on the date you have chosen.'

'To a *degree*,' said Patience, 'but *only* to a degree, we are prepared to arrange the date around your availability.' She was, it seemed, determined to rub his nose in it. 'Hillary was most insistent that only you should officiate and it is my fervent wish as well.' Yes, you bet it was. Baffled and furious, Renfrew said, 'You are both divorced and may have to settle for a registry office wedding and a blessing.'

'Hillary would not like that.' Patience felt no need to amplify this statement.

They eyed one another. It was Cedric whose gaze dropped first.

'No doubt something can be arranged.'

'No doubt it can!'

She got up to go.

Unable to resist it, he said, 'I, that is we, the Commission were all very disappointed by the conduct of your protégé the journalist Radley Oates.'

'*Our* protégé and so was I. But you do not have to worry about

Mr Oates, I have dealt with *him*,' said the powerful one. It was hard to escape the inference that she would deal with Cedric too if he got in her way.

When, with overwhelming relief, he had closed the door behind her, Renfrew was left staring at the sermon he had been writing when she arrived and which, in the light of the way in which he had just been treated, no longer seemed appropriate. Instead with his tormentor, Patience Allardyce shortly to be Patience Causton, in mind, he chose as his starting point from the Gospel according to St Matthew: *Whosoever shall exalt himself shall be abased; and he that shall humble himself shall be exalted,* which, in an ideal world, seemed to sum up the way forward perfectly.

Hillary Causton rang Drusilla and paid her the courtesy of telling her that he was getting married again.

'Who to?' asked Drusilla.

'Patience Allardyce, whom you briefly met.'

'Oh yes! I remember.' There seemed no point in mouthing dreary, anodyne platitudes of the congratulatory variety and Drusilla was not given to these anyway. 'Mrs Perfect with the po face and chin like a dredger,' said Drusilla. 'You're making a big mistake there, darling. That's a ball breaker if ever I saw one!'

'Not like you, of course!' Hillary did not see why he should be expected to put up with this.

Drusilla decided to brazen it out.

'Not a bit like me. I was the perfect wife for you and you know it. But, and more importantly, *why* are you getting married?'

Why?

In an odd sort of way it was a hard one to answer. Hillary did not feel like exposing himself to his first wife's derision by saying *because I'm in love* and in the end settled for, 'Because I need a wife.'

'Well, of course you always were a great romantic,' was the ambivalent reply to this. 'Besides which you don't need a wife. You've got me. I'm your wife and I'd like to come back to you. I think we should give it another go.'

Hillary shuddered. 'Drusilla you are *not* my wife. We are divorced! Please do not run around London society saying that we are still married. And anyway,' (trying to edge away from it), 'what's the matter with Davenport? The last time we talked about him you said he was God's gift to women and very generous.'

'Charlie's no fun any more,' complained Drusilla. Listening to this and remembering pleasurable but exacting nights with his ex-wife, at the end of which he had been fit for nothing, it was Causton's view that Davenport was probably worn out. '. . . and he *works* all the time. So boring!'

'He probably has to work all the time in order to keep you in the style to which I made you accustomed,' observed Hillary drily, 'and since, quite apart from that, he and I are about to be engaged in a takeover battle for the same newspaper which, by the way, *I'm* going to win, if he wants to be in there with a chance he can't afford to let up.'

'I might have known you were in there somewhere.' Drusilla was tart. Then, with a sudden surprising change of tack, her voice languorously low and voluptuously husky, 'Darling, why don't you come over here? Charlie's in Paris for the day . . .' There was a shushing noise as of silk sheets and, although it was midday, it occurred to Causton that she might still be in bed. '. . . oh, please . . . do say yes! It would be just like old times . . . let's have one last valedictory fuck before she locks you up for good . . .'

Hillary, who felt he had been celibate for longer than anybody had any right to expect, found her siren song surprisingly hard to resist. The cadences of Drusilla's seductive bedroom voice conjured up images of his compact, curvaceous ex-wife at her most wanton.

Just once more.

Nobody need ever know.

The sound of his secretary buzzing through to inform him that his next meeting was about to begin broke the spell. With an effort, Hillary collected himself.

'It's out of the question, Drusilla,' said Hillary sounding stern and feeling regretful.

'Oh, very well!' She was suddenly businesslike again. 'So, since you're apparently hell-bent on this ill-advised union, when do I get my invitation?'

Startled by this outrageous assumption, Hillary was terse. 'You don't! This wedding is a private affair so don't try to gate-crash it because if you do, I'll have you thrown out. Now I have to go. Goodbye, Drusilla.'

'Goodbye, Hillary darling.'

Don't try to gatecrash it.

In the silence that followed Drusilla, who was naked, got off the bed and walked across the bedroom. She stood for a few moments thoughtfully looking at Leda and the Swan. Leda was naked too but also, unlike Drusilla, despairingly modest. The great bird reared before her. Its sharp beak was rapacious and cruel.

'Where is *my* swan, *my* Zeus?' Drusilla spoke aloud. Answer came there none. Maybe, after all, Charlie was. On the whole she did not believe it. Predictably, her preferred choice was the unavailable Hillary. Still mulling it over, she went into the next room and began to run herself a bath.

The summer, which had been mainly a good one, had a brief breakdown in late August before settling down to an Indian autumn. The leaves turned early and brilliantly and behind their massed flares of orange and crimson and yellow the sky was darkly blue. In spite of the temperature, which was still high, the air seemed thinner and clearer with the fresh invigorating tang which heralded the last months of the year.

'It's perfect weather for a wedding,' remarked Dorian to Robert.

'It is, isn't it!' He kissed her. 'Do you remember our wedding?'

'I do. You kissed me, just like this, in the taxi as we left. You said you would never stop loving me.' She sent him an elliptical smile.

'And despite the way it sometimes must have looked, I never did. I adore you. You know that.' He could have added that these days he was constantly afraid of losing her again. They never talked about the period they had spent apart and when Robert allowed himself to think about it he was forced to con-front the fact that during that time someone else had shared her bed and that that person might still be somewhere within her orbit, waiting for it all to go wrong again. In short, waiting for Dorian.

'Max Pointing was our good angel in all of this,' observed Dorian. 'We ought to ask him and . . . What's his lover called?'

'Nigel.'

'We ought to ask him and Nigel to dinner.'

'Yes we should and when I've finished the second draft of Alexander Pope, we will.'

It was in fact a dinner that was never destined to happen. Two weeks after this conversation took place, Max Pointing was found dead in bed where he had lain undiscovered for two days. He had been murdered. The beautiful youth, Nigel, was nowhere to be seen and despite appeals to come forward in order to be 'eliminated from the investigation' remained invisible until the police finally picked him up using a stolen credit card. A child of the age of media, like Christian Allardyce, Nigel decided to cash in while he had the chance and before being actually charged with the killing gave copious newspaper interviews. This, and the fact that Max Pointing had been a society antique dealer, provoked a feeding frenzy in the tabloids. Sullen and dangerous, with the classical good looks of a modern Antinous, Nigel's photograph stared out of the newspapers where it was shortly to be joined by that of Jonathan Larch, complete with wispy ponytail. *I WAS SEDUCED BY MY SOCIAL WORKER SAYS YOUTH HELPING POLICE WITH THEIR ENQUIRIES* ran the headlines and so it was that another member of the Commission was forced to tender his resignation.

A sorrowing Dorian adopted Rastas, feeling that it was the least she could do.

Drag his feet as much Renfrew might, the wedding of Patience Allardyce and Hillary Causton was all set to proceed as and when they wanted it to. At the end of the day it did not, however, look like being the small affair they had originally had in mind. The ceremony was scheduled to take place in early September and Patience threw herself into the preparations with gusto. Despite no longer being a member of the Commission, or maybe because of it, she was asked to fulfil a certain number of speaking engagements and was sounded out for another appearance on the God slot. All in all things were looking good and as she busied herself selling her house prior to moving into Hillary's Patience was light of heart. Sourly, Renfrew watched this frenetic activity from one remove but could be only as obstructive as he dared to be.

Another who would have liked to obstruct was Drusilla. Daily she scoured the newspapers for an announcement of his forthcoming wedding and found none. Briefed by Hillary, mutual friends closed ranks and refused to be interrogated on the matter. Then, on the social grapevine she learned that Radley Oates had been fired. Here at last was a chink in the Causton armour, a disaffected ex-employee with a line into the social circuit.

Drusilla rang him up. After she announced herself, Oates, who was working out his notice, warily held the telephone receiver at arm's length as though he feared it might explode.

'Are you still there?' enquired Drusilla, perturbed by the sudden lull.

'Yes I am,' said Radley hastily and then answering a different question, 'but not for very much longer I'm afraid.'

'So I gather,' observed Drusilla and then, 'I need some information.'

If anything this came as a relief. At least she wasn't about to compound all his other problems by suing him, not at this particular moment in time, anyway.

'What sort of information?' Radley was cautious.

'I want to know the time and venue of my husband's wedding.'

'What's in it for me?' About to join the dole queue, he could see no point in doing anything for nothing.

'Revenge!' answered Drusilla. 'Most important, Radley, and I dare say we can work out some token financial remuneration as well. So what about it?'

Reflecting that he had never expected to find himself and Drusilla Causton on the same side ever, 'I'm on!' said Radley. 'When do you need to know by?'

'As soon as you can! I want to give Hillary a surprise!'

A surprise? Radley was glad he was not Hillary.

Thinking of Peter, Radley said, 'I could probably find out today, if I really put myself out.'

'Excellent!'

'It is, let's say, a mission of some delicacy though. The fee would have to be commensurate with that!' He named a sum.

Drusilla halved it.

Radley halved the difference and added it back on.

Drusilla halved the half.

'Fine,' said Drusilla and then, without waiting to find out, 'I'm glad we are in agreement. Perhaps you would like to ring me when you have the information and then we could arrange to meet and exchange the one for the other.' She gave him Charlie Davenport's home telephone number. '*A tout à l'heure!*' said Drusilla and hung up.

Radley, who had nothing much else to do, decided to get straight on with it. Peter was not in the office which had once been Radley's own. Nor was Jeannie who had left the company. Watching Peter metamorphose into Radley Oates mark two had been a dispiriting experience for Jeannie. As time went by and confidence grew, instead of Radley it was Peter who disappeared off for three-hour lunches and returned claret-coloured with the staggers. The day he arrived back from one of these and attempted to put a hand on her thigh was the day Jeannie decided that she had had enough of being chased around her own desk by lecherous social diarists and quit. In her place sat Myra. Myra was a large, muscular girl with attitude. Nobody attempted to put a hand on Myra's thigh. However, as far as Radley was concerned, Myra had one over-riding advantage which was that she was a recent recruit and therefore did not know who he was.

'Hello,' said Radley on entering the office. 'You're new, aren't you?'

'Yes,' said Myra.

'Actually it's Peter I wanted to see.'

'Peter's not here,' said Myra unnecessarily.

They both looked at his empty chair.

'No,' said Radley, 'I can see that.'

'He's still at lunch. He won't be back until at least four o'clock if I know anything about it!' Loyalty appeared to be a foreign concept as far as Myra was concerned.

'Ah . . .' Radley appeared disconcerted. 'It's just that Hillary Causton has asked me to check that Peter has the correct time and place of his wedding and a photographer lined up and you know the Old Man. He wants it all done yesterday!'

Reluctantly Myra put down her novel and got up. She went over to Peter's untidy desk and stood looking at it inconclusively.

'I think some instruction came in a few days ago about it.'

'I'll look for it for you, shall I?' offered Radley, 'Since I know what I'm looking for.'

'Suit yourself,' said Myra with a shrug. She returned to her own desk and deeming it unwise to resume reading her book immediately, began to turn over a pile of what looked like filing in a lackadaisical manner. 'Oh, no, here it is! Eleven-thirty on Friday September 6th at St Cuthbert's and afterwards at Claridge's.'

'That's right,' said Radley. 'Thanks, Myra. No need to say anything to Peter since you and I have sorted it out.' And then, never intending to do anything about it, 'We must have a drink sometime.'

He went.

24

'*Dearly beloved*,' intoned the Reverend Cedric Renfrew through gritted teeth, '*we are gathered together here in the sight of God, and in the face of this congregation, to join together this Man and this Woman in holy Matrimony*.'

He paused to glower at the assembled guests before pressing on.

'Goodness, what a terrifying cleric,' murmured Dorian to Robert.

'Yes, a real death's head at the feast,' agree Robert *sotto voce*. 'There must be jollier ones around.'

On it went.

'*Which holy estate Christ adorned . . . commended of Saint Paul . . . not by any to be enterprised, nor taken in hand, unadvisedly or wantonly . . . carnal lusts and appetites . . .*' (another piercing, admonitory look at those gathered together at this point) '*. . . Procreation of children . . . fear and nurture of the Lord . . .*'

Ah, here it came!

It was too much to hope for, of course, but nevertheless Renfrew sent a mental supplication to the Almighty.

'*If any man can shew any just cause, why they may not lawfully be joined together, let him now speak, or else hereafter for ever hold his peace*.'

Still hoping against hope, he gave the pause the slowest possible count of five and, giving up on it, was just opening his mouth to resume when for once a prayer was answered.

'Yes, *I* can!' shouted a woman's voice.

There was deathly silence. Aghast, all, with the exception of Renfrew who was facing the back of the church anyway, turned around. Amid silence, high heels clacking on the stone flags and very much enjoying being the centre of attention, Drusilla moved up the nave of the church until she was standing beside the bride and groom. She was vibrant in brilliant Christian Lacroix scarlet with a small, matching sequined hat. Upstaging the bride, who was tasteful but unelectrifying in navy-blue silk Jaeger, was a particular pleasure.

Renfrew, who had prayed for exactly this to happen, was at a loss as to what to do next now it actually had. This particular invitation, though proffered many times, had not been answered before. He had never to his knowledge encountered the woman in front of him, for during the entire course of her married life Drusilla had not once accompanied Hillary to church. What he did register was her aura of steely determination and the way she radiated aggression. Here was a termagant. Not for the first time it occurred to Cedric to wonder what on earth had happened to what used to be regarded as the gentler sex. These days he seemed to meet nothing but female terrorists.

'Well? Aren't you going to ask me what I'm doing here? You've asked me to speak up, I've done it, the next move has to come from you!' Drusilla did not trouble to lower her voice. The acoustics in St Cuthbert's were surprisingly good and, like a laser, it penetrated to the back rows of pews.

Cedric jumped.

(Looking away from the fascinating scene being enacted in front of them, Dorian briefly turned to Robert and raised her eyebrows. 'She's got the vicar on the run, no doubt about it,' said Dorian.)

'Well, what *are* you doing here?' Even to himself Cedric sounded feeble.

'Self-evidently, Renfrew, this woman is disrupting my wedding!' Hillary, who was beginning to understand why certain people are driven to murder their spouses, spoke for the first time in a furious whisper. 'Get rid of her!' He felt as though he might be about to combust. I simply can't believe this is happening to me, thought Hillary. It has to be a bad dream.

'Yes, but who is she?' asked Renfrew.

('Yes, *who* is she?' said Robert to Dorian.)

'The first Mrs Hillary Causton!' The speaker this time was Patience who, after the initial shock of Drusilla's interruption, was beginning to rally.

('Loose social cannon about town,' supplemented Dorian for the benefit of her husband.)

'The *only* Mrs Hillary Causton!' said Drusilla smartly.

'The *ex* Mrs Hillary Causton!' was Hillary's contribution in a subdued shout. 'We are *divorced*, Drusilla!'

'That's a technicality as far as I'm concerned,' said Drusilla. 'I don't believe in divorce and,' turning on Renfrew, 'as a Man of God, neither should you!' Remembering her adultery, in the face of such brazen effrontery Hillary was speechless. Patience was not.

Refusing to get into debate, 'Are you going to leave of your own free will,' enquired Patience, 'or do we have to get the police to eject you?'

'I have made my protest on behalf of abandoned wives everywhere and, having done so, should be grateful to be allowed to leave with dignity!' reproved Drusilla, managing to sound like the epitome of wronged womanhood. 'But before I do I think a photograph is in order, don't you? One for *Hello!* magazine, chronicler of perfect marriages, perhaps!' As she spoke, she signalled and a troup of photographers raced up the nave. Flash-bulbs exploded all around them. '*Bonne chance!*' said Drusilla and left.

In the wake of her departure a mesmerised congregation all began to talk at once.

Shell-shocked, Renfrew said to Causton, 'What do you want to do now?'

'Get married, of course,' snapped Patience whose view it was that Cedric's conduct of the proceedings to date had been less than distinguished. 'It's what we're here for!'

Hillary stared at his bride in admiration. 'Absolutely!' Then to the vicar, 'Do you have the keys to the church?'

Dumbly, Renfrew nodded and then collected himself enough to mumble, 'They're in the vestry.'

'Right, go and get them. Lock the doors and let's get on with it, shall we? No more interruptions. And just to make sure the whole thing is legal, I think we should start again from the beginning!'

Recommencing and reiterating the words: *Dearly beloved, we are gathered together here* . . . though without any of the brio of the first time around, it was Renfrew's heartfelt view that, since the results were so unpredictable, he would never again ask God for a favour.

This time they got through the ceremony without incident.

In spite of an inauspicious start, the marriage of Hillary Causton and Patience Allardyce settled down remarkably quickly, some might have said too quickly. For whatever spark there had been to begin with did not ignite but became almost immediate a cosy glow. Sex with the second Mrs Causton was a decorous experience during the course of which she never gave the slightest hint as to whether she was enjoying herself or not and Hillary could not have provided the answer to this either. But if there were no sexual fireworks, there were no social fireworks either and as a consequence life was a great deal more restful.

Unlike Drusilla, Patience was interested in Hillary's newspapers and what went into them and suggested that she herself might like to contribute the odd article. Courtesy of her social position as the wife of a press baron, Patience's evolution into a media personality was now firmly underway. Mainly because of her entrenched right-wing views (one of which was that Britain was for the British) and sternly moralistic stance, her liberally educated children in particular found this very hard to come to terms with.

'You have to understand, Cordelia, that Mum's a fascist,' said Christian casually one day when they were talking about it.

'Oh, I think that's pitching it a bit high,' said Cordelia, who did not want to entertain the idea. 'Mum's insensitive but she's not sinister. I mean I know some of her views are old-fashioned . . .'

'Old-fashioned! Well, that's one way of putting it.' Christian laughed. 'Hillary Causton's to the right of Genghis Khan and Mum's to the right of both of them. I just wish she'd stay out of print.'

'So do I.' This was heartfelt. For once Cordelia was totally at one with her brother. 'I've tried to explain to her all about the multi-racial society but she just doesn't seem able to grasp it.'

'Doesn't *want* to grasp it,' observed her brother darkly, 'and Hillary's just as bad. Have you *heard* him on the subject of the Welfare State?' Since it looked as though Christian himself might end up on the dole unless, *mirabile dictu*, he succeeded in passing his exams, this was currently a subject in which he took more than a passing interest. 'He's a hanger and flogger too. It's my view Causton's a sadist. Look at this place he's got me into. No women, cross country runs, cold showers, it's more like Wormwood Scrubs than a school.'

'Mmm,' said Cordelia, taking a non-committal stance since she considered that Christian had gone a long way towards landing himself with the establishment he was currently at. 'I prefer Hillary to the vicar, though, don't you?'

'Only just!'

Part 3

'It wouldn't do any good,' Robert finished his second cup

25

'She's getting worse!' exclaimed Dorian, who was reading one of her sister's articles. 'Some of this stuff is positively inflammatory. I wonder whether I shouldn't ring Patience up. Have lunch with her.'

'It wouldn't do any good!' Robert finished his second cup of breakfast coffee and stood up with a view to going to his desk. 'She hasn't changed. It's just that now she has a quality national daily as a platform for her views.'

'Perhaps it's Hillary I should be having lunch with.'

'That wouldn't get you anywhere either. He agrees with her. Those newspapers have always promulgated the view that wogs begin at Calais. The union between your sister and Causton was truly a meeting of minds!'

Dorian looked at her watch. 'Good God, is that the time? I'd better get my skates on.'

Once out in the street she joined the rest of the herd all moving in the direction of the underground and then the City.

It was now ten months after the Causton wedding. Robert was in the process of checking the proofs of the Alexander Pope biography concerning which the publisher was cautiously optimistic. Alas biographies were not, on the whole, great moneyspinners yet there had even been a suggestion that he might like to tackle another one on a subject of his choice. In the interests of marital harmony Robert had not passed this piece of information on to Dorian as yet but was dicing with the idea of Jonathan Swift.

Hillary and Patience appeared to have settled down into married life and on a regular basis gave what were generally agreed to be staid, though worthy, dinner parties. Hillary himself was aware that where these were concerned there was an element missing and that this had extended itself to other areas of his married life as well. On the other hand peace had broken out all around him and after the war that had constituted his first marriage this was not to be under-estimated. In this life, it seemed, one could not have everything.

Hugh Allardyce, on the other hand, reckoned that at a comparatively late stage in his life he did have everything. He and Flora produced a daughter ('I think it's obscene at Dad's age,' said Christian on first receiving the news), who was sensibly christened Mary, Hugh being anxious to get away from the more exotic variety of christian name favoured by his first wife.

Radley Oates was not so content. The notice period expired and no job materialised, and indeed where would it have materialised from? The satisfaction derived from seeing Causton's flash-bulbed appearance on the front pages together with a stony-faced Patience Allardyce, a triumphant Drusilla Causton and a mesmerised vicar was evanescent. It had probably been evanescent for Drusilla as well. Paying the bills, some of which, such as the vintner's, were long overdue from balmier days, became a problem. These days he was not simply putting them off out of habit as he had in the past, stating as he did so that paying bills on time was bourgeois, but because there was, quite literally, nothing to pay them with. At this point Radley recognised that he was going to have to think of something just in order to survive materially. It was while he was idly leafing through his notes for the Charlie Davenport hagiography one idle afternoon that Radley saw a way out of his current difficulties. The solution was staring him in the face but, if he employed it, would mean that certain journalistic boats would be well and truly burnt. Given this fact, for the present discretion was probably the better part of valour. Maybe after all something legitimate would turn up.

Unaware that he was the subject of a Radley Oates debate, Charlie Davenport got on with life as best he could. One day he longed for Drusilla to move out, the next he did not. Ambivalence predominated. Maybe he really longed for the good old days when she was still Hillary Causton's wife and therefore her presence was fleeting. Then he could not get enough of her. Now he got altogether too much. Like many others, in order to take his mind off his domestic arrangements, Charlie threw himself into work but still at the end of the day had to go home to where Drusilla, voraciously ready for anything, awaited him. Of course the way to have done it would have been to tell her that he no longer wanted her in his flat, but he was aware that it would not have stopped there. Drusilla was a barbarian who could probably have taught the Goths *and* the Visigoths a thing or two. Charlie knew, because she had told him (with relish) all about the material rape and pillage that had been the upshot of her last confrontation with Hillary, and surmised that whereas his rival had got his Claude back, though only after a great deal of hassle, he was probably still haggling with the insurance company over the fragments of the Meissen collection never mind the vandalised oil painting of himself. And I *don't* want that to happen to me, thought Charlie. More in order to take his mind off his unsatisfactory domestic situation than anything else, but also to prove to himself that he could still do it, he began to plot a supremely audacious business move. Since this concerned her ex-husband he told Drusilla nothing about it.

All these scenarios began to unwind against the backdrop of yet another tropical summer. A brassy sun poured its molten heat on London day after day keeping temperatures in the high eighties. There was a hosepipe ban. In the city gardens wilted, the iron-hard parched earth cracked and houses subsided. To begin with such weather was celebrated and there was conjecture that, because of global warming or some other such phenomenon, drizzly, mild water-colour summers of the usual English variety were at an end. But as hot day was succeeded by even hotter day interrupted only by airless, sticky nights, irritability escalated, tempers began to shorten and in certain areas of the capital where deprivation and unemployment were rife, racial tensions ran high, finally igniting in an orgy of burning, looting and rioting.

In the light of all the street violence and yet another tactless article in one of the Causton newspapers, Dorian decided that, even if it was a complete waste of time, she would take her sister out to lunch. They arranged to eat at a fashionable Italian restaurant, where Dorian had booked a table in the garden. Sitting waiting for Patience to arrive it occurred to her that maybe it might have been better for them to have met in a less fashionable venue, nearer to the scene of the disturbances. Here in this well-heeled tranquil setting it was hard to believe that elsewhere police with riot shields were being stoned and cars overturned and set on fire, and that the whole thing was being partly fuelled by well-meaning but crass articles written by her sister.

As she watched Patience walk towards the table, Dorian observed that all the old sureness, temporarily in abeyance after the confidence-shattering defection of Hugh, was back. No doubt leading the sheltered life of the wife of a millionaire helped, the benefits accruing from this being neatly encapsulated by the fact that Patience had arrived without a hair out of place in a chauffeur-driven car, while Dorian had struggled to the restaurant on the overcrowded, airless tube.

'How's the Commission getting on?' she asked as they ordered their food.

'According to Clarissa Bowen the report is being written as we speak. There was a lot of dissension and in-fighting after the Oates article, you know . . .'

Yes, I'll bet there was, thought Dorian as she listened to this.

'. . . and without my presence it fell to Cedric Renfrew, never the most tactful of people . . .'

Not like Patience herself, of course!

'. . . to sooth ruffled feathers. Ultimately, however, he seems to have succeeded. And then, of course, there was that awful, sordid business of the homosexual murder . . .'

'Max Pointing was a neighbour of mine. Nothing sordid about Max, he was a lovely man who didn't deserve what happened to him. We took in Rastas, his cat!'

With distaste, Patience said, 'Really? Was that wise?' The way this was uttered seemed to indicate that she feared Rastas probably shared the sexual proclivities of his previous owner. 'It's my view that homosexuality should be a criminal offence. Of course, as a result of the publicity Jonathan Larch, the social worker, was forced to resign . . .'

'That's right. He was fingered by Max's lover. But was the accusation ever proven?'

'I have no idea!' Patience was dismissive. '. . . But regardless of all of that, I have to say I never liked Mr Larch. There was an awful censoriousness about his attitude . . .'

Quite! Dorian laughed silently into her saltimbocca.

'. . . He was one of those who wanted me to step down as a result of Christian's behaviour, you know!' Patience clearly still felt very indignant about this and it had to be said it did not sound as though there had been too much charity coursing around the Commission. 'Another was Cedric himself. Cedric could be bossy and interfering . . .'

Yes?

'. . . and had no sense of humour whatever . . .'

No?

'. . . which made him very heavy going . . .'

Absolutely! This conversation really was a little classic of its kind, Dorian recognised, Patience's sorrowful dissection of the others' shortcomings forming the perfect blue-print of her own. Deciding to get off the subject of the Commission for the moment and on to what she really wanted to talk about, Dorian put down her knife and fork. How to bring it up was the question. At length she said, 'I've been reading your pieces in the *Clarion*.'

'Oh, and what did you think? Hillary says I'm a natural, that they're really very good.'

It would, of course, be more than Hillary's marital life was worth to say anything else, reflected Dorian. Aloud, 'Yes, they're very good,' she reassured, though *pedestrian* was in fact the first word which came to mind. 'But I wasn't thinking so much of the style as the content.'

'Really?' Patience looked puzzled and not altogether pleased. 'They are all on topical matters and matters, moreover, which I believe need addressing.'

'Yes, but some,' (and one in particular), 'are currently very sensitive!'

'That, Dorian,' said Patience as to a bear of very small brain, 'is *why* they need addressing. Take all these riots for example. What's happening is an absolute disgrace and someone has to speak up and say so.'

'Yes, all right! Of course, there's criminal behaviour and that's a significant part of it, but there's also a deeper malaise. A lot of it's exacerbated by unemployment and poverty going hand in hand with educational shortfall and *that's* what needs to be *seen* to be sympathetically addressed if we are to head off more of the same.'

'Are we to let off muggers and looters? Are we to succumb to mob rule? Are we?' Patience sounded as though *she* might be about to succumb to an attack of histrionics. Listening to her it was possible to discern another unhelpful article taking shape, this time emanating from what had been supposed to be a helpful reflective lunch. Thank heavens that it had not, after all, taken place close to the heat of the action.

'No, of course we aren't!'

'So you think we should prosecute wrong-doers? Or better still, deport them!'

Dorian, who felt like shaking her sister, decided to have one more go at it.

'Patience, you can't deport people who are second or maybe third generation British! They have passports just like you and I. Obviously I'm not saying that criminal acts should go unpunished . . .'

Patience decided that she had had enough of liberal thought. In high dudgeon she stood up. 'I can't listen to any more of this. Please don't move, Dorian. I shall settle the bill on my way out.' She went. Or, rather, thought Dorian, watching her sister's huffed back retreating, stalked off. It brought to mind their uneasy childhood relationship during the course of which they had barely communicated because the two of them had nothing in common. And we still don't have anything in common, decided Dorian. In fact, I'm going to give up on it. Estrangement suits us better than sham sisterly closeness. If Patience was not my sister and I met her socially, I wouldn't give her the time of day. I've got more to say to Rastas than I do to Patience. At least Rastas listens. She felt suddenly furious and in an odd sort of way purged by a combination of her own anger and the decision she had just taken. Dorian glanced at her watch. It was ten minutes since The Departure and hopefully by now the coast was clear. She rose and made her way through the garden to the main restaurant. Patience was just leaving. The bill must have taken longer than usual to sort out or maybe she had been telling them how to draw it up and how to run their restaurant more efficiently while she was at it. Dorian paused behind the effective combination of a large palm and a bentwood coat stand. Without noticing her, Patience passed through the door and out into the King's Road. She signalled. Hillary's limousine driven by Hillary's chauffeur who must have been lurking drew to a smooth halt. Queenly, she waited for the door to be opened and, when it had been, vanished inside. Dorian was reminded of the way certain exotic flowers open up sticky velvet petals and suck their prey inside before swiftly and comprehensively shutting again. It occurred to her that this might be the last time she and Patience met as sisters rather than distant acquaintances.

In her turn, Dorian left the restaurant and set off along the King's Road towards Sloane Square station. The yellow afternoon heat hit her like a blast from a furnace. It enveloped and enervated. As she walked her primary emotion was one of bafflement. Patience was her own flesh and blood. As such, the foreign-ness of her own sister was unnerving and inexplicable. It was, nevertheless, a fact which no longer could be ignored.

Charlie Davenport and Drusilla Causton sat opposite one another in the dining room of his flat, or rather their flat as he supposed it was these days. In front of each was a plate of smoked salmon and a glass of Chablis. Although displeased by the fact that they were eating at home rather than at an expensive restaurant, Drusilla ate with gusto. The two of them had just returned from the Royal Opera House where they had seen *Samson et Dalila*, an opera which had appealed greatly to Drusilla in terms of musical seduction technique, emasculation of the luckless Samson and the final spectacular iconoclastic crash of the temple. For all the same reasons it did not appeal to Charlie. These days he felt more and more as though his own hair had been cut off. Like Samson he felt himself to be in the grip of a female Philistine. He picked at his food. Silence lay between them like a dead hand.

As he toyed with his food, Charlie thought back on the last year. In particular he thought of the way in which Drusilla had rampaged through Causton's wedding. The newspapers had been full of it, his own included. Well, after all, news was news.

Business was business. Her capacity for unpredictable destruction was alerting though. It could be said of Drusilla that she ticked like a time bomb. 'Why did you do it?' he had asked her afterwards. 'Why? You knew at the end of the day you weren't going to achieve anything.'

Her reply had been illuminating on one level and only served to underline what he now already knew, namely that there was neither rhyme nor reason to her. 'I don't really know,' mused Drusilla. 'I just felt I had to. I had the whole congregation in thrall. And you should have seen their faces! Well, you did, of course, in your own newspaper. It was worth it just for that!' Mayhem, it seemed, was her preferred element.

The subject of his thoughts finished wolfing down her food and then looked down the length of the table at Charlie.

'What's it like to be such electrifying company?' said Drusilla

Charlie recognised this combative remark as the beginning of a ritual dance, namely the opening salvo of a swapping of insults followed by some aggressive love making.

'Drop it, Drusilla,' said Charlie, 'I'm not in the mood.'

'Oh, but I am!' She stood up and moved along the side of the mahogany table. As she came she removed emerald earrings and emerald necklace which she dropped upon the floor. At this point she stopped and undid the bow which secured the thin strap of her short silver dress, thereby exposing one breast, and then the other bow so that the dress slithered to the floor, where it joined the emeralds. This interesting striptease took place in silence and with panache. Wearing only sheer silver tights and silver high-heeled shoes she came towards him.

And went too far.

'If you're not man enough to make love to me,' said Drusilla, 'I'll make love to you.'

The contemptuous words *not man enough* ignited something which had been lying dormant for years. The extent of his own murderous rage took Charlie by surprise. He slapped his lover hard. Caught off balance but not entirely averse to the rough turn events had taken, Drusilla flailed and fell backwards, knocking over Premier Cru Chablis as she did so and found herself pinned to the dining table with her head in the remains of Charlie's uneaten smoked salmon. Which would have been just about all right except that he seemed to have lost control totally and appeared intent on choking her to death. Speechless for once, with agonised eyes fixed on his face and ringed hands feebly trying to prise his fingers off her neck, Drusilla felt consciousness begin to slip. It was the sharp, scrunching sensation of something being ground underfoot that caused Charlie to momentarily stop and brought him to a realisation of what he was doing. Later Drusilla was to discover that the pulverised remains of her emerald necklace had probably saved her life. Without a word he released her and rushed from the room.

Retching, Drusilla slid on to the floor where she fainted and lay, like a sated Bacchante, in a mess of food, shattered crockery and spilt wine.

The following morning, having spent the night in his own spare bedroom while Drusilla and Leda and the Swan luxuriated in the master bedroom, shame caused Charlie to avoid the dining room, scene of last night's carnage. Drusilla it seemed was also unkeen on revisiting it and the two of them met in the kitchen over cups of black coffee. It was obvious to Charlie that asking her to leave would have to wait until her dark blue neck changed colour again. The bruise was surprisingly uniform in shape with two deeper shadows at the front, his thumb marks presumably, and looked like one of her own chokers. Probably, if push came to shove, the black pearls would camouflage it fairly satisfactorily. Meeting someone over breakfast whom you had attacked the night before was an odd experience, Charlie discovered, and not one he felt like lingering over. Nor, apparently, did Drusilla for as soon as her slice of brown toast and marmalade, eaten in uncharacteristic dignified silence, was finished she went, taking the remains of her coffee with her.

Charlie decided to drive himself to the office that morning. He felt that he needed time to think. Impulsively, halfway there he stopped the car on the Embankment and got out. It was still only seven-thirty and the London streets were comparatively empty. He leant on the stone balustrade beside an ornamental dolphin and breathed deeply. Below him wound the Thames, pewter-coloured, majestic and slow. The blue air was warm but at the same time crystalline and would be until the opaque shimmer that comes with extreme heat began to rise from the city pavements.

'I wish I'd never set eyes on Drusilla Causton,' stated Charlie aloud and with feeling, causing a tramp sitting on a seat behind him swigging from a bottle of meths to give him a funny look. Maybe, thought Charlie, when he got back to his flat later that evening he would find her gone. On the whole though he did not think so. Gone to make a complaint to the police more likely. These days he quite often thought of Dorian Ormond. The sight of her lying palely vulnerable in the hospital bed with her hair spread over the pillow had affected Charlie, and the image of her face with its subtle beauty and strange, feline eyes subsequently haunted him. He wondered if she was still married. There had been no other bedside visitor while he was there except for the willowy girl in the purple dress who had passed him on his way in and whom Dorian had told him was her niece, Cordelia. As his relationship with Drusilla deteriorated, it had more than once occurred to Charlie that perhaps he might ask Dorian Ormond out to lunch. So far he had not done so. All the same it remained an enticing possibility.

26

No job materialised for Radley Oates. Debts mounted and creditors became more and more vociferous until writs finally began to collect on his hall floor. Radley did not need to open these to know what they were so did not bother. This did not alter the fact that something had to be done before eviction became his lot. Accordingly he rang Charlie Davenport's secretary and made an appointment to see him. Then he extracted certain sheets plus sources from the fat file which contained the hagiography notes and went off to the local library where he photocopied them. This being done, he replaced the originals and locked all his research away in a filing cabinet and hid the key.

Charlie was surprised when his secretary told him about the Oates telephone call.

'I wonder what he wants?' Charlie asked himself aloud.

'He didn't say but he was quite insistent. If you want me to I can always ring him back and cancel.'

'No, don't do that.' Charlie was suddenly curious. 'But just book him in for half an hour.'

When she had left the room, he went back to what he had been working on, namely the feasibility of taking over the Causton empire.

Sitting in his own remarkably similar tycoon's lair, Hillary Causton buzzed through to *his* secretary.

'Get me Miles Compton, would you please,' requested Hillary, 'and tell him I'd like to see him in my office straight away.'

When Miles arrived, in expansive mood, Causton said, 'Sit down, sit down!' and followed this up with, 'I've had a good idea!'

Compton blenched. The last good idea had been the Commission, a martyrdom which was still going on though, thank heaven, in a much more muted way after the public humiliation of its unfortunate start.

259

'Nothing to do with the Commission this time,' said his Chairman, who was apparently able to read his thoughts. 'I want a top secret feasibility study organised on the possibility of a takeover of Charlie Davenport's empire. Breakup value, the lot!' Well aware that the words *feasibility study* did not actually mean that, but rather, loosely translated, *an endorsement of what I've decided I'm going to do*, Compton did not make the same mistake as the last time and openly marvelled.

'What an audacious plan,' oiled Miles. 'Brilliant! Absolutely brilliant! What a coup it will be. I'm sure it will work!'

'That's for you to ascertain,' observed Hillary, not sounding particularly grateful for such fulsome enthusiasm this time around, before going on to warn, 'These operations are extremely expensive to mount and even more expensive if they fail, so make sure you get it right!'

Recognising another Morton's Fork when it was presented to him, Compton unhappily wondered what it must be like to work for somebody reasonable who was not constantly springing these awful surprises and wanting everything done yesterday. Living under the constant threat of having his head chopped off should Hillary get it wrong was not very relaxing either.

'I'll set things in motion straight away, shall I?'

'Yes, do that. And while you're at it, I'd like some up-to-date figures showing where my television company's at. Oh, and a résumé concerning the current state of play with the Commission. That's something my wife wants.'

The Commission. He might have known he was not going to get away scot free on that count, thought Miles sourly. Why couldn't Patience Causton organise her own résumé with Renfrew? Working for Hillary was enough of a cross without working for his overbearing wife as well, which Compton considered above and beyond the call of duty.

It was more than his corporate life was worth to make a fuss.

'I'll see to it immediately,' promised Miles.

'What can I do for you, Radley?' enquired Charlie Davenport.

'It's not so much what you can do for me as what I can do for *you*!' answered Radley, reflecting as he uttered the words that maybe *to* you was a better way of putting it.

'What do you mean?'

'Well as you may or may not know, I've been fired!'

'Yes, I think I did hear something about it,' said Charlie. '*Why* were you fired?'

Radley was succinct. 'I upset the second Mrs Hillary Causton, who is a tartar!'

Not like the first Mrs Causton, of course, was Charlie's mental response to this. *What is it about Hillary and these women?* Making a resolution to stay well away from Causton's second shot at matrimony, he said aloud, 'So you need a job.'

It was exactly what Radley needed and had given up all hope of getting. Perhaps there would be no cause to employ draconian measures in order to stay afloat after all.

'Yes, I do.'

Optimism was dashed when Charlie, who did not want to take Oates back on board at any price, said, 'I'd like to help of course, but as things stand at the moment there isn't a slot for you. The timing's all wrong.'

So he was going to have to play hard-ball after all. Radley's right hand grasped the file. Reaching across the desk, he handed it to Davenport.

'Perhaps you'd like to read this.'

Charlie ran his eye down the first page. Expressionless, he laid the file down and rang through to his secretary. 'Put my next appointment on hold for a further fifteen minutes, would you?' In silence he went back to his reading. When he had finished, he said, 'It was a youthful indiscretion. Nothing more.'

'Maybe,' said Radley, 'but not one you'd want bruited about, nevertheless. Think of the ammo it would give Causton. And you say *youthful indiscretion* but we both know that that wasn't the only instance. My source is impeccable.'

Yes, Charlie dared say it was. Why was it that a certain sort of friendship so often went hand in glove with treachery?

'But it's not just that,' Radley continued smoothly. 'In the pursuit of research one turns over all sorts of stones . . .'

'What is it that you want?'

The answer was, of course, obvious on one level. All the same, Charlie thought he might as well ask. There might after

261

all be a less sinister option than the one he was entertaining at the moment. It transpired there was not.

'I want a regular income,' said Radley simply.

'Well, that's one way of describing blackmail.' Charlie was dry. He supposed the only alternative to a blood-sucking private financial arrangement was to take Oates back on to the staff. On the whole, although with this arrangement he would be getting something in return for his money, Davenport felt that his problems would be compounded by taking such a course, for Oates might take it upon himself to interfere on all sorts of levels and who would be able to stop him? At last he said, 'I need some time to think about this. As I don't have to tell you there's more than one way to skin a cat.'

'I don't care how you do it, so long as I get my money,' was Radley's reply to this. 'But don't take too long deciding, will you?'

There was a discreet knock at the door.

'Ah, that will be my secretary telling me my next meeting is about to come onstream,' said Charlie, sounding a great deal calmer than he felt. He pushed the file back to Radley. They both stood up.

'You can keep it, it will help concentrate the mind,' said Radley. 'I've got the originals.'

'Yes, of course you have!' There was just the faintest flicker of contempt in the way this was said. Radley held out his hand. Charlie did not take it.

'I'll be in touch,' said Radley.

'Yes, I'm sure you will,' said Charlie.

Over breakfast one morning (staff-terrorising business breakfasts at the Savoy were now a thing of the past), Patience said to Hillary, 'Darling, I think we should move house.'

Astonished, he put down the business section of the newspaper he was reading. It was the last thing he wanted to hear.

'Whatever for? We're very comfortable in this one.'

'Yes,' Patience persisted, 'but it's where you lived with . . .' She was reluctant to utter the name. '. . . with your first wife. I should like to get away from all of that.'

This struck a chord for so, thought Hillary, would he, though getting away from Drusilla was easier said than done as he had found out to his cost. On the other hand, no matter how well-heeled you were, moving house caused maximum disruption. He said so and was made aware by the tilt of his second wife's jaw that she was not happy with his answer. Looking around, he was forced to concede that there was still a great deal of his first wife's taste in evidence and though, on the whole, this had been excellent, now it had been drawn to his attention he could quite see Patience's point. So much of Drusilla was still about that he almost wouldn't have been surprised to see her walk through the door prior to sitting down and joining them both for breakfast.

'Wouldn't you rather just redecorate this place from top to bottom? Expense no object? So much easier!'

'No,' said Patience, who wished to rid herself and him as well of a malign presence. 'No, I definitely wouldn't. It's the memories apart from anything else. I think we owe it to our marriage to start afresh somewhere else.'

Put like that it was hard to resist. It was true to say that the ghost of past bad behaviour (Drusilla's) did linger on, mainly for Hillary in the shape of small pieces of his fractured Meissen which were still turning up in unlikely places, such as the top of pelmets, probably due to the force with which the whole precious collection had been hurled in the first place.

Watching her husband waver, Patience pressed home her advantage. 'I'll organise it all. You won't have to lift a finger, my love, and I promise we won't move out until the new house is almost ready.'

Hillary, who had a heavy day ahead of him and would rather have been focusing on business affairs of state than unnecessary domestic issues, against his better judgement allowed himself to be persuaded.

The door bell rang.

'Ah, that's the car.' Anxious to get away, he kissed her. 'All right, sweetheart, if that's what will make you happy, go ahead and do it,' said Hillary.

27

Robert Ormond finished correcting the proofs of Alexander Pope. The sense of release was wonderful. Pope is out there on his own now, was Robert's attitude. There was nothing more he as biographer could do except hope his book succeeded. Certainly both publisher and agent seemed optimistic. A lot would depend on how hard it was marketed and how much publicity they managed to garner.

'What I need,' said Robert to Dorian, 'is a stroke of luck.'

He got it.

Prompted by a combination of Cordelia and Patience, whose disapproval of her sister did not apparently extend to either her husband or his literary endeavours, one of Causton's newspapers bought the right to serialise extracts from the book. Robert took Dorian out to dinner to celebrate.

'If that doesn't give it a kick start, nothing will,' said Robert. He raised his glass. Responding, Dorian raised hers.

'I never thought to hear myself say it, but here's to the success of Alexander Pope!'

They both drank. Robert wondered if this was the moment to tell her that the publisher had suggested that he write another biography and it was at this point that Dorian pre-empted him by saying, 'Where do you think you'll go next?'

'You won't want to hear this but, to be frank, I'd like to do another biography, subject to be decided,' Robert said. 'However, after all we've been through together, it's not a decision I could possibly take without consulting you and if you don't want me to do it, I won't.'

It was the right sentiment to express and at the same time it put Dorian in a verbal armlock. Like Miles Compton she recognised Morton's Fork. Because, thought Dorian, if I say: *Fine, go ahead*, and the pattern set by the writing of Alexander Pope is a repeating one this marriage we've tried so hard to float will capsize. And if I say: *Please don't. It would be disaster. Which is more important to you? Another biography or our marriage?* Robert might say he wouldn't do it, but the resentment and the undermining sense of an opportunity missed at my insistence, would never go away. And at that point the marriage would probably slowly capsize anyway. She took a decision.

'Fine! Go ahead!' said Dorian.

Robert's face lit up.

'Really?'

She nodded.

'Oh, darling, thank you! It won't be like the last time, I promise, and I won't even consider it without a decent advance. Now I know I can bring off a biography like this everything will be different.'

Dorian certainly hoped so. The nagging doubt still remained, however. It was entirely likely, she recognised, that despite good intentions to the contrary, he would be unable to produce anything without a protracted agony accompanied by the appropriate *Sturm und Drang.* And I couldn't bear to go through that again, thought Dorian. In the event she did not voice any of these misgivings. There seemed to be no point and maybe, at the end of the day, he was right and it would be all plain sailing.

'Have you had any ideas as to whom you might tackle next?'

'Well, I have, as a matter of fact,' answered Robert. 'I wondered about Jonathan Swift.'

Dear God, more of the same. Another waspish wit. Dorian's heart sank.

'What do you think?'

Takeover was in the air. Mutually unaware of the fact, Causton and Davenport stalked each other. One had a sex life which was adequate but lacklustre coupled with a tranquil day-to-day existence, the other a sex life which was, if anything, over fulfilled and went hand in hand with daily domestic war. Without recognising it in exactly those terms, because egos needed massaging each took a private decision to make up the domestic shortfall by preparing for combat in the City.

Charlie was not entirely surprised and not pleased either by Drusilla's very practical view of the fact that he had come close to strangling her. Perhaps such attacks had been commonplace in her life to date. Given the way she operated this could be viewed as only too likely. Whatever the reason, the hopes he had briefly nurtured that she would move out as a result of his behaviour were dashed. They both watched the purple circle round her white neck, evidence of his assault, diminish and finally fade away altogether, she through the medium of her dressing table mirror and he across whichever room they happened to inhabit together. When the bruising had finally disappeared, though not until, Drusilla invited Charlie back into her bed again and he accepted. After all, reasoned Charlie to himself, I might as well get something out of all of this and there was no doubt that on that level he did.

It was also true to say that the question of What To Do With Drusilla had receded somewhat in the face of the rather more pressing What To Do With Radley Oates. In order to avoid a great deal of scandalous publicity it looked as though he was going to have to pay what Oates elegantly referred to as his retainer. And Charlie was under no illusions that it would stop there, for when did blackmail ever? All in all he felt himself to be embattled and work, always a favourite pastime for a successful tycoon, became his escape and his solace.

While all this Davenport soul-searching was going on, Radley Oates was quite content to bide his time for a while at least. It had also occurred to him that while he had what he referred to himself as 'the goods' on Davenport he also had, as a result of copious notes made for the Causton hagiography, the goods on Hillary. All stones had been turned over there too in the interests of research and had yielded a significant amount of nefarious information. It was interesting, though no doubt to be expected, that on the business front these transgressions were remarkably similar to those of Davenport since neither had ever scrupled to cut corners and such corners were mostly the same. But then, thought Radley, with himself in mind as well, who ever made a mint by sticking to the letter of the law? Answer: no one.

On balance he decided to keep Hillary and Hillary's indiscretions on file for the time being as a sleeper. To try and exhort money from both at the same time could well prove a greedy mistake and although Radley was not averse to being greedy, this, he told himself, looked like being his only source of income and, as such, he did not want to blow it.

The very presence of Patience Causton in his parish, never mind his church, continued to torment Cedric Renfrew. As the wife of one of the richest, if not the richest, of his flock, she now had considerable clout and no longer took any notice of his opinion at all. Nor did she seem particularly grateful to him for the fact that she was now a media personality, none of which, Cedric felt, would have happened if he had not proposed her for the God slot debate in the first place. Another inconvenience was that these days Patience was much too grand to do his typing, likewise sort out the parish newsletter and, having got used to having secretarial support for this sort of thing, he was reluctant to do without it. One of the elderly groupies volunteered to help him out and it was when he received the first fruits of this kind offer that he realised how very efficient Patience had been. The batch of correspondence which lay before him looked as though it had been pounded out on a fifty-year-old antique and no doubt had been. Errors proliferated and the ribbon had been used so often, probably in the interests of economy, that the image it was designed to produce was hardly there at all. Where full stops should have occurred there were little round holes due to the fact that the typist had been forced to strike the relevant key with great force in order to get it to register anything at all. Renfrew stared discontentedly at the heap on his desk. There was nothing else for it. He would just have to soldier on like this. It was either that or go back to tapping everything out himself on two fingers. Maybe church funds could run to a new ribbon, although at that point the mistakes would be very black and very glaring.

He received the news that the Caustons were looking for a new house with mixed feelings. On the one hand he would have been glad to see the back of Patience and what he perceived as on-going humiliation, but on the other hand if they moved too far away someone else's collection plate would overflow with Hillary's largesse. As usual the woman was a confounded nuisance.

Bad temper caused the sermons, always pointed, to become

even more trenchant until finally Hillary felt bound to remonstrate.

'Look, Renfrew, unless you want the congregation to stop coming, you'll have to be rather more encouraging,' warned Hillary. 'Fire and brimstone's fine but not all the time. You'll have to give them some hope of entering the Kingdom of Heaven at the end of the day, otherwise why should they bother sitting in draughty St Cuthbert's every Sunday?'

Without very good grace Renfrew complied with this suggestion. Once this useful outlet for aggression was blocked off, bile built up. His mood was not enhanced by the fact that the report on The Morals of the Nation was finally published and received with resounding indifference. It called to mind (possibly) the Wildean theory that any publicity was better than no publicity. Patience Causton, who could have given the whole thing a platform or even just the odd puff during the course of one of her frequent interviews, did nothing at all. In the end, since she appeared to be unaware of their need for support, Renfrew felt himself forced to say something.

'My dear Patience, do you think it would be possible for you to suggest that the work of the Commission might be featured and discussed during the course of one of the Sunday television debates?' ventured Cedric, trying to sound pleasant as he said it. After the *débâcle* of the last little lot, he drew the line at suggesting any more newspaper publicity.

Patience considered him in silence for a few minutes before deigning to reply. In the end, she said, 'I'm amazed you should think any small contribution I might be in a position to make would be helpful. I should hate to embarrass you in any way.'

This not very oblique reference to her ousting from the Commission gave him pause for thought.

'I should have thought you too forgiving and too good a Christian to harbour a grudge over being asked to step down. After all, I only did what seemed to me to be right at the time.' He ended grandiloquently, 'It was all for the Greater Good.'

Hah! was Patience's mental response to this. Aloud: 'I *am* forgiving and *have* forgiven,' stated Patience with a beatific smile. 'But I have *not* forgotten. I was wounded, Cedric. Deeply wounded! For, you see, *I* had not done anything wrong and still you cast me out.'

Put like that the prospect of getting anything out of her seemed bleak indeed. Forgiving, as Renfrew knew full well, was the easy part. Forgetting was another matter entirely and one she did not appear to be about to address. Furthermore, regardless of what she had to say on the matter, it was his view that she was either not being totally honest or deluding herself and had not, contrary to what she had just said, addressed forgiving either. It looked as though if he wanted her co-operation he would have to grovel.

'On reflection,' said Cedric, 'I think I was wrong.' Every word was an effort. 'In the circumstances I should not have asked you to stand down.' A pause and then very gruffly, 'I apologise.' Even to himself he did not sound sincere.

'Thank you,' said Patience, 'I accept your apology,' then, rather more ambiguously, 'in the spirit in which it is offered. Good heavens, is that the time? I must go. I am due at the BBC to record an interview for *Woman's Hour*.'

She went, taking his apology with her. There was no promise of anything in return.

Left choking on a large slice of humble pie, it occurred to Cedric that he must have upset the Almighty very deeply in order to merit treatment like this.

28

The street violence, which appeared to have died down for a while, suddenly flared up again. After a particularly tactless appearance on *Any Questions* during the course of which her firmly voiced opinions were of the All Blacks Should Go Home variety, Patience began to receive hate mail.

'I don't understand it,' she complained to Hillary. 'It's a free country isn't it? I should have a perfect right to express my point of view without being vilified like this.'

'Yes, but this may not be the time to do it,' said Hillary, who was also receiving the odd sackload of threatening letters due to the uncompromising right-wing stance taken by his newspapers with regard to the disturbances. Finally, one night when Patience was at home on her own, a large stone was hurled through one of the downstairs windows. It was followed by a brick. The following night, while they were both at a reception, more windows were broken. By now she had found another house which was currently being done up.

'In spite of the ensuing disruption, I think we should move there as soon as possible,' decreed Hillary, sighing to himself as he faced the prospect.

Dorian, who had no quarrel with either of her sister's children, invited Cordelia and Christian to tea. Christian brought to this civilised English occasion secret knowledge, namely that he had failed his A-levels and not only failed them but failed them with distinction. Even Cordelia, who by now was enjoying a gap year prior to university, did not know this and nor did his mother, though it would not be long before she did, since no doubt the school would inform her. The results had come through only the day before. Because he had done as little as he could get away with in the run-up to the examinations, Christian had not been surprised by his dire results and although he assured himself at regular intervals that he did not give a stuff, the prospect of the parental alarm and despondency which would be unleashed when the news became public was not something he looked forward to. There would be lectures and uncomprehending cries of *Why, darling, why?* Most of all Christian did not relish confronting his stepfather whom he secretly found daunting. Dad was all right. Dad would simply look pained, would *be* pained, but a combination of Mum and Hillary in pursuit of the highest standards, not just for themselves but for him as well and berating him for not achieving them, promised to be a real bummer.

As they travelled together to Kensington, Cordelia noticed his preoccupation but since she knew her brother to be moody, did not comment on it. The other thing she noticed when they were both finally sitting down in front of plates of scones and strawberry jam and cream was that there was a feeling of tension in the air between Dorian and Robert and that, in common with Christian, he did not say very much either. By the side of the knee-hole desk a large wicker waste-paper basket overflowed with screwed up A4 sheets, always a bad sign.

Cordelia wondered what Robert's next project was, for presumably, judging by the debris, there was a next project though, hopefully, it would not cause as much trouble as Alexander Pope. Surely *nobody* could cause as much trouble as Alexander Pope. She opened her mouth to enquire and was anticipated by Dorian.

'Jonathan Swift is the answer to your question,' said Dorian. The tone was neutral but to Cordelia's acute ear there was an undertone of resignation.

And to Robert's, apparently.

'There's no need to say it like that!'

'Like what?' asked Dorian.

'Like you did!' snapped Robert.

There was an embarrassed silence. Dorian bit her lip. She stared out of the window. Then, rallying, 'Would anyone like some more tea?'

'Oh, yes please!' Cordelia held out her cup. Suddenly remembering and anxious to change the subject, she turned to Christian. 'Have your results come out yet? I seem to recall getting mine about now.'

'Yes they have.'

All looked at him enquiringly. Christian decided to let them sweat it out and said no more.

Finally, 'And?' They waited expectantly.

'And nothing,' said Christian. He paused for maximum effect.

'*Well?*'

'I flunked the lot! But it really doesn't matter.'

'What do you mean it really doesn't matter?' Dorian was sharp.

Christian gave her a sidelong glance. His aunt suddenly sounded like his mother.

'Because I've decided to become a male fashion model and you don't need A-levels for that.' He was triumphant.

Dorian's first thought on hearing this was: My sister will be fit to be tied when he passes on this little lot. Aloud she said, 'What makes you think you can do it?'

For the first time Christian looked uncertain. 'There's nothing to it. Anyone can do it. If they have the looks, that is.' Clearly modesty was not going to hold him back.

The other three looked him up and down and decided that he probably did have the looks. Even the weak mouth might be an asset with some of the rather more louche get-ups.

'But isn't there a lot of competition for that sort of job?' ventured Cordelia, adding doubtfully, 'And it must have a limited lifespan. What are you going to do *after* you've been a model?'

Christian who, typically, had not thought this one through, flushed. 'If you can't be positive, why don't you stuff off, Cordelia.'

'I have to say that talking about what you're going to do after you've become a model assumes someone is going to employ you in that role in the first place.' Dorian was acid.

Speaking for the first time since this particular debate began, Robert said, 'I'm on Christian's side. The trouble with the women in this family is that they don't support their men when they want to break away from the norm and do something adventurous.'

Heart in mouth, Cordelia stole a glance at her aunt. Dorian's lips were pressed together and she looked as though she might be counting to ten. Finally, she said in an even voice which did not disguise her fury, 'I couldn't care less if my nephew wants to become a *lion tamer*, never mind a model. What I am trying to get across is that where precarious professions are involved it's as well to have a second string to the bow.' She looked as though she might be about to add something else and then apparently thought better of it and took a sip of her Lapsang Souchong instead. Unused to hostilities breaking out in the course of the genteel interval that was afternoon tea, Cordelia was at a loss as to how to stop them. It was obvious that the acrimonious exchanges she was witnessing were merely a symptom of a much deeper divide. Not for the first time it occurred to her to wonder whether the marriage between Robert and Dorian was going to survive. If it did not, what then? Cordelia suddenly became aware that she found her uncle very attractive and that this attraction probably stemmed from the night she had spent in his bed though not in his arms. Then, despite the fact that he and Dorian had been currently separated, Robert had seemed unattainable. Now she was not so sure. Just thinking about it caused Cordelia, who was still a virgin, to blush. She shook her hair over her face and bent her head over her plate hoping nobody would notice.

Nobody did. Anxious to get off the vexed subject of his academic shortfall and since neither his uncle nor his aunt seemed to be about to say anything, Christian said, 'Aunt Dorian, how often do you speak to Mum these days?'

Reluctant to say, 'Never,' Dorian was wary and finally came up with, 'Not regularly. From time to time,' and then, as if she didn't know, 'Why?'

'Well I just wondered if you'd put a word in for me,' wheedled Christian. 'Just because I've failed my exams I don't want to be sent back to Colditz.'

'How old are you?'

'You know I'm eighteen.' Christian was surprised.

'Quite and always banging on about how you aren't a child any more and wanting to be treated like an adult. Am I right?'

Christian, who did not like the way this conversation was going, was forced to agree.

'OK, so do you want to know what I think, Christian?' said Dorian. 'I think it's time you took responsibility for your own actions and it must be said that if you had put your back into your work and crawled through your exams there wouldn't be any prospect of you being sent back to school. But if you really feel you can't fight your own corner, why don't you ask Robert to intercede for you? He seems to think the course you're taking is the right one!'

Noting the fact that her uncle looked appalled in the face of this Parthian shot, Cordelia said hastily, 'Talking about talking to Mummy, I was going to ask you if you could possibly have a word with her about what she says in her articles and interviews . . .'

Never mind about *Any Questions*! thought Dorian, who had heard it and cringed. With something of a sigh, she said, 'Cordelia, I have. And got absolutely nowhere. I don't agree with her stance either though I do agree with her perfect right to take it if she must. But I have to tell you that I have absolutely no influence over what she says and does whatever. Firstly why don't you bring the subject up yourself . . .'

'I already have and I got nowhere too.'

'. . . and secondly, failing that, why don't you have a quiet word with your stepfather?'

'No point. He agrees with her,' said Christian.

Robert abruptly got up and walked out. Cordelia followed Dorian's troubled gaze watching him go. It was odd, mused Cordelia, how in this particular marriage the eighteenth-century dead had the power to wreak so much havoc. It was as though, while he was writing, Pope and Swift et alii were more real to Robert than Dorian was and, rather like an actor immersing himself in a role, he became them and lost sight of himself. Whatever it was, there was no doubt that Aunt Dorian seemed very fed up.

They all soldiered on with tea which by now had become a minefield. Suddenly, surprisingly after his black-browed, seething exit, Robert re-entered the room, sat down and ate a scone as though nothing had happened. Paradoxically, if anything this peaceful reappearance heightened the tension rather than reduced it. It was to be presumed such uneven behaviour was currently the norm. Whatever the truth of the matter Dorian was clearly unimpressed by her husband's rematerialisation and neither by look nor word acknowledged it. It seemed to Cordelia, that having watched her own parents' marriage fall apart, here was, though for different reasons, another one that was not working. This did not, in her view, induce much confidence in the marital state especially since she had now admitted to herself that she was attracted, maybe even in love with, Robert Ormond herself. The possible complications engendered by this piece of self-knowledge seemed endless. For the first time Cordelia felt a pang of envy where her brother was concerned. At the end of the day Christian, like Narcissus, was only in love with himself, a state of affairs that had to be simpler than the scenario she was currently contemplating.

Patience and Hillary did move to the new, unfinished house and as he had gloomily predicted it *was* chaotic. Builders swarmed all over it, ripping up floorboards, putting the same floorboards back again, installing bathrooms wrongly, re-installing bathrooms rightly, renovating the kitchen and generally upgrading everything. There were times when even Patience wondered if the disruption was all worth it. Hillary certainly thought it was not but at least he escaped the worst during the day by going to the haven that was his office. The phrase *It's always darkest just before dawn* might have been coined for just this sort of project. Almost between one day and the next there was suddenly light on the horizon, just. It was at this point that a newly installed leaking radiator in the room above brought down the ceiling in what was to be Hillary's study. Picking his way through large chunks of sodden plaster and the heaps of filthy Victorian rubble which had come down with it, Causton decided enough was enough. Given the mess they were living in at the moment, the time had come for a necessary and, more to the point, comfortable business trip. He said as much to Patience.

'We'll go together, my love, you need to get out of this for a while as much as I do,' said Hillary, and was astounded when his wife refused.

'How can I possibly go leaving all this behind?' was her reaction.

'Well, of course you can! Everything of value is still in storage. What can go wrong?'

A lot! was Patience's unspoken answer to this optimistic question. *If they can bring a ceiling down while we're living here what couldn't they do if we weren't?*

'I'll employ an architect to oversee the builders,' offered Hillary, conscious of his wife's unease.

'But once the rewiring is finished and the alarm's installed, the decorating begins,' objected Patience, 'and I simply *must* be here to direct that.'

For the life of him Hillary could not see why but, faced with her obduracy, was forced to give up on it. In the end, reluctantly, he went by himself, but not before he had given her a small loaded hand gun and shown her how to use it.

('Do you know how to use one of these? No? It's easy, darling. Like a water pistol. You just point it and fire.)

29

The shooting of Hillary Causton shocked friends and enemies alike. Ironically, because the accident happened around three o'clock in the morning, the newspapers, including his own, missed what even the victim of it would have designated a brilliant scoop and the first the general public heard about it was on the early morning radio news. There was no other information, just the fact: Press baron Hillary Causton shot.

The reactions of those who knew him best were all different.

'Good God!' Momentarily forgetting their differences, the Ormonds, who had been trying to resolve some of these for most of the previous night, stared at one another in disbelief. In the face of such shocking and calamitous news, old animosities faded into irrelevancy. Dorian, who in spite of the coolness between herself and her sister (which it was quite possible Patience had not even noticed), was one of the few who had been given the new telephone number, immediately dialled it. Out of order. She began to pull on some clothes.

'I'd better get over there,' Dorian said. 'If Patience rings here, tell her I'm on my way.' The isolating sound of the front door slamming behind her reminded Robert with a jolt of her last leaving after which she had not returned for over a year, and he suddenly saw with great clarity that in the light of his recent behaviour he could be in danger of losing her all over again and that if he did so, this time she would not come back.

In another part of London, in the same neck of the woods as the Causton mansion, Cedric Renfrew who was in the process of making a mug of cocoa also heard the newsflash. Hardly able to believe his ears, he stood transfixed, a cadaverous figure in an Edwardian night shirt below whose hem thin veinous legs gleamed blue-white through the black hair which covered them. He waited for further details. There was none. He considered the prospect of a world without Hillary. There was certainly the possibility of a bequest to St Cuthbert's in the Causton will.

Hillary had more than once hinted that such might be the case. Moreover, Renfrew's eyes narrowed, Patience was now a widow and a very rich one at that. Thoughtfully he sipped his drink.

For once Charlie Davenport was alone, Drusilla having taken herself off to a health farm. A habitual early riser, he savoured his first solitary morning since her unexpected arrival. Even the flat and all the inanimate objects in it seemed to breathe out for the first time in months. There was an unaccustomed lull, a sensation of dust settling. In relaxed fashion, eating a bowl of corn-flakes, Charlie wandered about what was once again, albeit only temporarily, his own domain. As he entered the bedroom, the clock radio switched itself on. 6.30 a.m. The *Today* programme. Only half concentrating, he found himself listening to the Hillary Causton news flash.

What?

With shaking hands Charlie put down the cereal and stood immobile, waiting for further information. There was no more, just the announcement. For the moment that was it. He switched the radio off. Pulling himself together he rang the news desk of one of his own newspapers and found that so far they knew no more than he did.

The extent of his own grief surprised and shocked him. Charlie wept. He mourned as for the passing of a loved one and in an odd sort of way that was exactly what Hillary had been and he, Charlie, had not recognised the fact until now. The person he had been in love with all along was Hillary himself and not Drusilla at all. Drusilla was merely a cypher. It seemed incomprehensible that he had not realised this fact before, even in the light of the Radley Oates visit. Charlie had thought he had long since put behind him what he had euphemistically and, as it turned out, optimistically, referred to as youthful indiscretions. Now he knew that he had not. And now that Hillary was dead he saw clearly that there was no longer any point in Drusilla as surrogate, a Hillary at one remove as it were.

Dislodging his lover, who was due back that same day, might not prove as easy as taking the decision to do it, Charlie recognised. Mindful of the push-you pull-me over the Claude Lorrain, he stood in front of his beloved Leda and the Swan. Now he knew how Drusilla was capable of operating, the question was not *whether* she would cut it in half in the event of a schism between them but *how* she would do it. Time was of the essence. He made two telephone calls straightaway. This being done, he exhumed some large suitcases from a cupboard. His face still wet with tears, though not for her, he began to pack Drusilla's clothes, shoes, jewellery and ultimately the mink coat into them.

Dorian drew up outside the Causton house. Today was September 1st and some of the trees had already changed. Despite the promise of another fine day there was a sadness, seediness even about the garden and what curtains there were were drawn giving the grand façade of the villa a sightless look. Two police cars were parked outside and a small group of journalists and photographers were gathered round the gate. *Faute de mieux* they all snapped Dorian as she ran through their ranks and up the front steps, where stood a policeman.

'Press?' said the constable. 'I'm afraid you'll have to . . .'

'Yes, in a manner of speaking,' replied Dorian, 'but not the sort you have in mind. I am Mrs Causton's sister.'

'Ah!' He stood aside to let her pass. 'You'd better come in, Mrs . . .?'

'Ormond,' said Dorian. Once in the hall she looked around. The house appeared on the inside at any rate as if it was well on the way to being finished. There was, however, not a builder in sight, presumably because they had been told not to come this morning. There was also no sign of Patience.

Questioningly Dorian looked at the officer.

'Is my sister here?'

'Mrs Causton's at the station making a statement.'

'Making a statement?' Dorian was puzzled and at the same time apprehensive. Why on earth would they want a statement from Patience? 'What do you mean? Are you able to tell me exactly what happened?'

He led the way from the hall into the drawing room which had lofty ceilings with fine cornices and tall, narrow windows. There was one sofa facing an ornate cream marble fireplace and a walnut desk with brass swan neck handles stood against the far wall. Otherwise it was empty.

'Perhaps you'd like to sit down, Mrs Ormond. Briefly, it looks as though Mrs Causton shot her husband by mistake, believing him to be a prowler.'

Dorian stared at him. *Patience had shot Hillary? Oh no! No, no, no! There must be some mistake.*

The sun struck through the cloud and, diffused by some sort of gauzy fabric which Patience must have pinned over the windows for privacy, irradiated the room and turned its lofty interior into a golden cube of light. It was hard to see this house as the scene of such a tragedy.

'Apparently,' resumed the policeman, 'Mr Causton returned early from a business trip abroad but was unable to tell her so because, probably courtesy of the builders, someone had accidentally cut through the telephone cable. We can only assume that because it was three in the morning he let himself in quietly because he didn't want to wake her. She heard a noise, got up to investigate and the rest is history.'

'But how did she contact the police if the telephone line was dead?'

'Mrs Causton had the presence of mind to use her husband's mobile phone.'

'And how did she come to have a gun? So as far as I'm aware my sister doesn't own one and doesn't know how to shoot. And why didn't she press the panic button?'

'There was no panic button. The alarm system was being installed later this week. She says the gun belonged to Mr Causton. He was worried about her being on her own and left it with her so that if necessary she could defend herself. She said she had been receiving a lot of threatening letters lately.'

'Yes. I believe they moved here because they thought it would be safer.' Dorian knew about it because Cordelia had told her. She felt shocked and shaky. It was ironic, reflected Dorian that everybody, with the exception of the fool who had severed the telephone cable, appeared to have acted for the best and the upshot had been a fatal accident.

She stood up. 'If you tell me where it is, I'll drive to the station.'

Thinking what a very attractive woman Mrs Ormond was, he escorted her down the steps, through the gate and past the press whose numbers had increased considerably just while he and she had been talking. Sympathetically he watched her unlock her car, reiterating as she did so the words *no comment* in response to shouted questions, as the reporters gathered around. When she had finally driven away, he resumed his vigil at the front door.

Wordlessly the two sisters embraced. Patience had the drawn, shell-shocked look which had been in evidence after Hugh walked out.

'I don't understand it,' wept Patience. 'I simply don't understand it! I've lived my life by the very highest principles and always, *always*, tried to do my best for the community, for *everybody*, and first Hugh left me and now, *now*, I've shot my own husband.' Still holding Patience, Dorian stared over her sister's shoulder. It was hard to escape the feeling that her sister was more worried about her high standards and their shortfall in terms of results than Hillary. Though Hillary, it had to be said, was beyond all that now.

'What happens now? Have the police finished with you?' asked Dorian. She wondered what to do with Patience since it was obvious that her sister could not go back to her own house, certainly for the time being. There was no spare bedroom in her own flat and anyway Dorian could not imagine Patience and Robert co-existing in a civilised manner for any time at all. All the same, what alternative was there?

She made the offer.

To her overwhelming relief it was declined.

'I have already arranged to go and stay with Clarissa Bowen,' said Patience, suddenly disconcertingly very practical. '*Clarissa* is a tower of strength.'

The unfortunate emphasis made Dorian feel that she herself was not, had in fact in some way been found wanting. Better rise above it.

'Besides, it will be much more convenient!'

Much more convenient? For what? Well, no matter.

'I'll drive you,' said Dorian. 'You won't want to go back to the house for the moment. It's being staked out by the tabloid press.'

'Thank you, Dorian, but there is no need. It is all arranged.

The chauffeur will do that.' Patience stood up. Ice maiden. Of course she always had been hotter on principle than humanity but still Dorian found her composure in the face of what by any standards was a personal catastrophe, unnerving. There was a knock at the door and a policewoman entered the room.

'Your car is here, Mrs Causton.'

'Thank you.' Patience turned back to her sister. 'Dorian, I can't thank you enough for your support and concern.' The right words but devoid in an odd sort of way of the right sentiment. Hollow. They embraced once more and Patience left. After a short interval, Dorian left as well.

Incarcerated in the health farm, Drusilla neither watched television nor listened to the radio but took the opportunity instead to plough through a large tome in the shape of a recent biography of Benjamin Britten. Because of this she missed the news of Hillary's accident. Now it was the end of her stay. Fighting fit and ready for anything, she was preparing to take her leave. Self-absorbed as ever, it did, however, occur to her as odd that Charlie had not rung her during her stay. On the other hand she had not needed him so what did it matter? Well, she would see him tonight and he could explain himself then.

In the event she arrived at the flat just before lunchtime. She tipped the taxi driver, who had lifted the bags as far as the front door for her and then put her key in the lock.

It would not turn.

Perhaps it was bent. Drusilla pulled the mortice out again and held it up. It appeared to have nothing whatever the matter with it. She tried again. Still no luck. As she did so her eye caught sight of a small white envelope propped against the bottom of the door. Intrigued she picked this up and discovered that it was addressed to herself. On the unlikely off chance that Charlie had not gone to his office today, she banged the door knocker very loudly before settling down to read the letter.

The letter said,

My dear Drusilla,
    As a direct result of today's tragedy . . . (Drusilla frowned. Tragedy? What tragedy? What on earth was he talking

about?) . . . *I have decided to end our affair.* This was a Nasty Surprise. She read on. *Nothing you can do or say will make me change my mind. I have packed up all your belongings and had them sent to the Savoy where I have booked you into a suite for a month, at my expense, naturally.* (I should think so too.) *When you have finally found yourself somewhere else to live, I should be grateful for the return of my suitcases . . .* (Vuitton. Drusilla's eyes narrowed. Some hope! He could whistle for those) . . . *meanwhile, what more can I say?* wondered Charlie who seemed at a loss as to how to round off a letter which by any standards could not be described as run of the mill. Eventually with the help of Cole Porter, he irritatingly concluded . . . *It was great fun/but it was just one/of those things!*

    Yours ever,

    Charlie

    PS I hope we can remain friends.

'Well we *can't*!' said Drusilla aloud. 'Fuck you, Charlie.' She screwed up his letter into a tiny ball and posted it through the letter box. Then, leaving her bags where they were, she went in search of the porter.

'I should like you to bring my luggage down to the hall for me, Frank, and then order me a taxi.' Noting her high colour he reluctantly prepared to do her bidding and, reflecting that he did not like Mrs Causton or her highfalutin' attitude towards those like himself whom she clearly considered serfs, Frank said, 'Where shall I say it's to?'

'The Savoy,' snapped Drusilla, very queenly.

As instructed, he got on with it and, as he did so, wondered what had upset *her* for plainly something had.

Radley Oates, who had arrived late to collect his monthly cash stipend which was normally left in a brown envelope with the same porter, nearly ran into Drusilla as she was finally leaving. Even from where he was, he could see that she had a face like thunder. Luckily, she did not see him. The black cab disappeared off down the road.

Radley sauntered into the entrance hall and found Frank, who was making a cup of tea in his cubby hole and seemed very out of sorts. Frank, who did not like Mr Oates and his attitude any more than he liked Mrs Causton, shovelled three sugars into his cup and said with a certain amount of satisfaction, 'Nothing here for you today, I'm afraid.'

Mr Oates's disappointment was gratifying to behold.

'Are you *sure*?'

'Sure as I can be!' Frank dunked a biscuit in his tea and opened up a copy of the *Sun* at the sports page.

Unsure what to do next, Radley hesitated.

'Maybe Mr Davenport forgot,' helpfully suggested the porter.

'He's never forgotten before,' said Radley, willing Frank to get up and go and have another look.

'There's a first time for everything,' observed Frank, master of the cliché. 'Why don't you ring him?'

Radley considered this suggestion and rejected it. A telephone call would give Davenport the opportunity to get his secretary to fob him off. Since an immediate injection of cash was a high priority, better simply to go to the office.

'You have a visitor, Mr Davenport,' said Charlie's secretary, buzzing through.

Charlie froze.

'It's not Mrs Causton, is it?'

'No, it's . . .' Here there was a brief questioning exchange, '. . . Mr Oates.'

'Show him in.' Charlie stood up and resumed pacing up and down his office which he had been restlessly doing ever since he arrived. There had been no further news concerning Hillary's shooting, which probably meant that the PR firm responsible for burnishing the Causton image had swung into action. Charlie wondered what the circumstances could have been to warrant so much secrecy.

Radley entered. By now Charlie was standing with his back to the window. He did not proffer his hand.

'Would you like some coffee or tea?' enquired his secretary.

'There will be no need for that,' answered Charlie. 'Mr Oates will not be staying long.'

No, just long enough to pick up a brown envelope full of money, thought Radley, both nettled and alerted by the tone of this last remark. He waited. There was a prolonged, some might have said, loaded silence and then Charlie said, 'I take it you've heard the news.'

There was a tremor in his voice.

Radley blinked. The news? In fact he had not because he had overslept and consequently left the flat in a hurry. So far as he could remember there had been nothing particularly momentous in his daily paper. He looked questioningly at Davenport.

'No. At least I don't think so. What news are you talking about?'

'Hillary Causton's been shot dead!'

'Good God!' Of all the things he might have said, this was the last Radley expected to hear. Since the two had been sworn enemies, he was surprised that Charlie seemed so affected.

Rallying, he said, '*Why?* And who *by*, for Christ's sake?'

Charlie spread his hands helplessly. 'I've no idea.'

'How come it isn't in this morning's newspapers?'

'Apparently it took place in the small hours and therefore missed both the first and second editions. No doubt the evenings will have a field day. If they can find anything out that is. There seems to be a blanket of silence over the details.' Then, pulling himself together with a visible effort, 'Anyway, what can I do for you?'

Radley stared at Davenport. Now the other man had moved away from the window where the light was behind him, he saw clearly that Davenport was in shock. What he could not work out, was *why*. In the world that Radley inhabited the removal of a rival was a reason for celebration.

'I'm here for my monetary blood transfusion,' Radley replied euphemistically. 'You forgot to leave my envelope with Frank.'

'No, I didn't forget,' was the unnerving, sombre reply to this.

'*No?*'

'No. No more envelopes!' stated Charlie.

'What! Are you saying you don't care if I . . .'

'That's exactly what I'm saying,' said Charlie. 'It no longer matters to me what happens. Publish and be damned as far as I'm concerned. Now that Hillary has gone there is very little point to my life any more.' His grief was palpable.

285

The man sounds like a jilted lover, thought Radley, digesting this. And then the penny suddenly dropped. In a manner of speaking, that was exactly what he was. Jilted by death. The truth of the matter had been staring them all in the face, Charlie included, and nobody had recognised it. Not even Drusilla whose sophistication in sexual matters was famous. Though not those involving the heart. As far as Drusilla was concerned, the heart simply got in the way. Maybe in an odd sort of way that was why she had not seen it.

It seemed to Radley that there was no point in staying. Davenport had got to his feet and was standing, staring out of the window in a distracted despairing way.

'All bids are off,' Charlie suddenly said aloud to nobody in particular.

Bids? With no idea what he meant, but certain that whatever it was it did not pertain to himself, Radley quietly let himself out.

It was while travelling home on the tube, which was more and more his mode of transport these days, that Radley saw the solution to his problems. Like Paul on the road to Damascus he wondered how he could have been so blind. Back in his flat he opened the drawers of the one filing cabinet he had room for. Both were stuffed with dogeared files all containing a jumble of research on Davenport. With no secretarial help to sort him out (Oh, for the return of Jeannie whom he had not properly appreciated at the time!), the whole exercise was in chaos. Relegated to the back of the top drawer was a comparatively slim file which contained what Radley described to himself as The Goods on Hillary. Just by dint of his interesting life and untimely demise, especially the way it had happened, Hillary Causton was now a hot biographical publishing property with maximum in-built publicity. But best of all, one could not libel the dead. This was a book which could be written with no holds barred. Staring into the middle distance, Radley fantasised. The best seller lists beckoned, closely followed by the television rights, in short an on-going gravy train and a lot more lucrative than milking Charlie Davenport for what he was worth every month. Fame and fortune would be his.

Better get organised.

With the exception of anything which overlapped the Hillary Causton story, Radley began to feed the Davenport information into a small shredder which among other things, a typewriter included, had conveniently followed him home the day he had left the paper for good. When he had finished he put the debris into a large black plastic bag and dropped it into the rubbish shute.

The same day in another part of London, Cedric Renfrew chewed the end of his pen. Even Cedric, hotly pursuing his duty as a Servant of the Lord and convinced that right was on his side, realised that this letter was a delicate one to write. All the same it must be written. It was imperative, especially with a sagging church roof, a fact that had only lately come to light, that the Causton money together with the Causton widow should be kept within this parish. Now that Patience was once more attainable, his ire against her evaporated and he saw her previous rejection of his suit as maidenly reticence rather than dismissal. It was all there to play for and this time he would not make the mistake of dallying to the point where other events and other ambitions overtook his own.

In the end.

My dear Patience, wrote Cedric,
   I was shocked beyond measure to learn of your husband's untimely death early this morning. It is a sad loss to you and a sad loss to this parish. In the wake of this tragedy I should like you to know that I am here for you in your hour of need.

Cedric put down his pen. The question was how to get across *and not just in this your hour of need but for ever and not just in a professional capacity either.* It was proving a harder letter to write than he had anticipated. After some thought he continued:

   As you know, we have had our differences in the past, but these are as nothing compared with what has happened. God moves in mysterious ways and maybe this was destined to heal the rift between us and bring us closer together once more.

287

He was aware that this did not sound quite right. On the other hand it was as near as he dared get at this stage to letting her know that he still entertained hopes of a marital liaison between the two of them. Resuming, he wrote:

> *Of course at this moment in time you are bereft, a comparatively young widow, but remember in the depths of your grief, dear Patience, that life must go on. Hillary himself would not wish you to wear weeds for ever.*

It was probably time to bring the letter to an end. A few minutes' deliberation suggested an apposite biblical quote might be the best way. With the unreliable Radley Oates in mind and more importantly the fortune hunters who would no doubt gather around, he penned: *BUT!*

> '*Beware of the scribes, which love to go in long clothing, and love salutations in the marketplaces, And the chief seats in the synagogues, and the uppermost rooms at feasts: Which devour widows' houses, and for a pretence make long prayers.*'
> Lastly, with a triumphant flourish, he put *Yours, Cedric.*

It was not until he had sealed up the envelope that it occurred to Cedric that he did not know where to send his letter for he had no idea where Patience was. Finally he decided to telephone Clarissa Bowen. *She* would know.

She did.

'As from tonight, Patience will be staying with me,' said Clarissa. 'A letter, you say? Is it important?' On receiving an affirmative reply, she said, 'Well, maybe the chauffeur could collect it later on when he goes to the house to pick up some things for Patience.'

Cordelia and Robert were sitting together in the flat when Robert heard what he had been waiting for. Cordelia had been weeping. Dorian's closing of the front door had a muted defeated quality about it. Watching him turn eagerly expectant towards the direction of the hall, Cordelia knew without a shadow of doubt that, despite their differences, these two were locked together by something which transcended these and that, because of this, she herself never would have Robert. She lowered her eyes. It was probably better to know it now, before she made an irredeemable fool of herself. As Dorian entered, she rose.

'Oh, Cordelia, don't go,' said her aunt, noting her disconsolate face.

'I have to. I'm meeting Christian for lunch in Chelsea.'

'How is he bearing up?'

'Oh, all right, I think,' said loyal Cordelia, unwilling to disclose that Christian's first reaction on hearing the news had been to conjecture whether he himself would be a beneficiary when the will was read. 'You know Christian. He doesn't show his feelings much.'

That's probably because he doesn't have any, mused Robert, uncharitably.

When Cordelia had gone, he took Dorian by the hand.

'Come and sit down,' said Robert. 'I want to talk to you. But first did you see Patience? What happened?'

'In a manner of speaking yes I did,' replied Dorian, 'but I never really felt that she and I connected. Same old story, really.'

'She must be devastated.' For once Robert was prepared to give his difficult sister-in-law the benefit of the doubt.

'Yes, but she seemed more upset that it was *she* who shot Hillary than that Hillary had been shot in the first place. I asked her to come and stay with us . . .'

Robert put his head in his hands.

'. . . but, you'll be sorry to hear, she refused.'

Robert took his head out of his hands.

'Look, let's stop talking about Patience and focus on us.'

'I don't know what to say that hasn't been said already. And unless something changes as a result, no amount of focusing will make the slightest difference anyway.'

'I'm aware of that,' answered Robert, 'and the truth of the matter is that the awful finality of Hillary's death has shown me what is really important to me. I don't want to lose you and I don't want to stop writing either. Ergo, I, Robert Ormond, have got to get a grip, ditch the prima donna act and grow up.'

Dorian stared at him. Without make-up she looked young and vulnerable again, more like the girl he had married.

'I love you,' said Robert. As statements go it was short and very much to the point. There seemed no point in embellishing it. It said everything as it stood.

'I know!' replied Dorian. Her light, citrine-coloured eyes glittered with unshed tears. She ran a hand through her hair. 'I know. I love you too but it may not be enough.' Her lack of conviction wounded him and at the same time filled him with the determination to prove her wrong. He took her hands. For once helpfully, and possibly for the last time before Swift took over, Pope intervened.

If to her share some female errors fall,
Look on her face, and you'll forget 'em all.

Tenderness overtook Robert. 'We'll see, but let's go on trying anyway, darling, shall we? *Please?*'

He leant forward and kissed her. Dorian closed her eyes and let him. She felt suddenly very, very tired. Since it was beginning to seem that Robert was her fate, better to give up fighting it perhaps and take this marriage for what it had to offer. The powerful physical chemistry which had always existed between the two of them was a good start but only that. What lay beyond it was down to the two of them and as things stood was anybody's guess. Shelve it. Concentrate on the present for now and let tomorrow take care of itself. With gathering passion and a sense of the inevitable, she kissed her husband back.

30

Watched by Clarissa, Patience slit open the envelope containing Renfrew's letter. She read it in silence and then, with raised eyebrows, passed it over.

'Good gracious,' ejaculated Clarissa, running her eye over it, 'not only has he comprehensively got the wrong end of the stick, but he's practically proposing! How very inappropriate. Moreover the cautionary biblical quote fits Cedric to a tee although I don't suppose that's what he had in mind. What are you going to do?'

Patience was brisk. 'For the moment nothing,' adding more ominously, 'I intend to deal with Cedric later.'

The telephone rang. Clarissa answered it.

'Yes, she's here.' She handed the receiver to Patience. 'It's for you.'

'Patience Causton speaking,' said Patience and then, after listening intently for a few minutes, her face lit up. 'That's wonderful news! I'll come straightaway!'

In between getting out of the car and walking up the steps and through the imposing front door of a large country house, Patience noticed for the first time that the garden smelt of autumn. Despite the sun the air was crisp and sweet. Ahead of the rest, one majestic tree burned flame red and another dark orange. With the exception of the beds adjacent to the house, where chrysanthemums and asters bloomed yellow and purple, vermilion and cerise, the surrounding grounds were mainly laid to lawn which was interspersed with spreading august horse chestnut, copper beech and yew. In the distance flat as a pane of glass a small round ornamental lake reflected the sun.

Like one in a dream Patience walked along a long wide corridor for the second time that day. At regular intervals amber sunshine poured through open windows laying broad blocks of brightness across the midnight blue pile of the carpet. Her destination was the last room on the right. Stepping from light to dark and dark to light again, she finally reached it. After a moment's hesitation, she turned the brass beehive knob, opened the door and stepped across the threshold. Trembling, she moved across the room.

The figure lying on the bed neither moved nor spoke but only looked at her.

The iron self-control on display since the accident evaporated. Tears began to flow. 'Oh, Hillary,' said Patience, 'I'm so terribly sorry. Can you ever forgive me?'

31

When the news broke, because his PR advisers had successfully kept the secret from the other evenings until after the early edition, Hillary Causton was his own evening newspaper's scoop. *PRESS BARON SURVIVES SHOOTING* ran the headline. *'Reports of my death greatly exaggerated!' says tycoon.* In certain quarters, reactions to this were mixed. Charlie Davenport did not know whether to laugh or cry. Drusilla had gone. Hillary was back. The status quo was re-established, though, gallingly, in the course of this happening the Causton evening paper had comprehensively trumped his own. But worst of all, thought Charlie, *I told Radley Oates to get stuffed.* Publish and be damned, I said, and if I'd known then what I know now I wouldn't have done it!

For different reasons, having shredded the evidence, Radley was equally aghast. Dreams of bestseller stardom evaporated. There would be no point in a Causton biography. He, Radley, would be sued out of existence if he attempted such a thing. It looked like a life of penury.

Kneeling down to pray for enlightenment, the Reverend Cedric Renfrew was also in turmoil and seriously considering whether to give up on the Church as a career. Misunderstandings had proliferated and wires had crossed to the point where it did not seem to Cedric that he and his Maker were on the same wavelength at all. Moreover he did not relish the reaction of Hillary Causton when Patience showed him the letter he had written her, as she surely would. Perhaps now was the time for a visit to his bishop. Time to bow out gracefully while he still had the chance, though this raised the question of what to do next. It would have to be something where his very special gifts would be appreciated. Politics, perhaps?

In her suite at The Savoy, Drusilla Causton's reaction to the press reports was predictable. 'Good God, she only winged him!' observed Drusilla, casting her eyes to heaven and pre-

293

suming whatever the papers might have to say on the matter there had been some sort of marital upheaval of the sort with which she was all too familiar. 'Hillary has married a woman who can't even shoot straight!' Well, that was his funeral. Almost had been. Feeling suddenly very hungry, she seized the telephone and rang room service.

'For dinner,' instructed Drusilla, with Charlie's bill in mind, 'I should like caviare, Lobster Thermidor and a bottle of Dom Pérignon.' This being done she opened up the new well-reviewed biography of Alexander Pope by someone she had never heard of called Robert Ormond which had just slipped into the hardback non-fiction bestseller list and prepared to read until the meal should arrive. *Ormond.* Drusilla frowned. In actual fact the name did ring a bell. Hadn't the name of one of Charlie's reporters who had been careless enough to get herself run over been Ormond? Dismissing it and proceeding to flick through the pages before getting down to the book in earnest her eye was caught by a particularly apposite quote.

Chaste to her husband, frank to all beside,

A teeming mistress, but a barren bride, Pope had percipiently penned.

Much diverted, 'That's *me*!' said Drusilla, never one to shy away from self-knowledge, even self-knowledge of the uncomfortable kind. 'That's definitely *me*! And *that's* the key to what happens next. The only way I can operate how I want to in this life is with Hillary as my spare wheel. I want Hillary back and I'm going to have him!' It should not be as difficult to achieve as it might have been either, since presumably her ex-husband was none too pleased at having been shot. Patience had definitely put up a black there.

On impulse she got up and went and rummaged through one of Charlie's leather suitcases, finally succeeding in exhuming a silver-framed photograph of her ex-husband which she stood up on the table in front of her. Unsmiling, authoritative, every inch the successful businessman and blissfully unaware of what was coming next, his image looked back at her.

In the absence of the champagne which had not yet arrived, she raised an imaginary glass.

'To us, Hillary!' said Drusilla. 'To us!'

OTHER TITLES AVAILABLE